Advance Praise for *Ba*

"For those of us who came of age in
Anthony Polito's novel is like being teleported back to high school. Filled with pop culture references that will have you saying, 'I remember that!,' this is a love letter to a time when happiness was a pair of Calvin Klein jeans, and every heartbreak could be fixed by listening to your Bonnie Tyler or REO Speedwagon albums. Most important, though, it is a portrait of a friendship between two boys struggling to find themselves without losing each other."

—Michael Thomas Ford, author of *Last Summer*

"With the Motor City running on empty in Reagan's America, Frank Anthony Polito's characters dance their mystery dance of teenage longing as if Motown never left for California. Sexy, funny, and wiser than it wants to be, *Band Fags!* pulses with a ragged beauty and bounces to its beat. I give it a 98.6."

—Thorn Kief Hillsbery, author of *What We Do Is Secret*

"More than just a novel, *Band Fags!* is a virtual time machine that transports you smack dab into the cheesy heart of the '80s. It's like a queer *Wonder Years* as it follows Brad's and Jack's memorable journey through high school hell. Screamingly funny, surprisingly charming and, ultimately, truly moving, it's a fresh take on the importance of friendship during the worst/best years of your life."

—Brian Sloan, author of *A Really Nice Prom Mess* and *Tale of Two Summers*

"A consistently hilarious story of the best-friendship we all seem to have had, set in a time we can never seem to forget—the totally awesome '80s—*Band Fags!* never misses a beat in its affectionate, moment-by-moment chronicling of the complicated journey we take from cradle to closet to what lies beyond."

—Matthew Rettenmund, author of *Boy Culture*

"*Band Fags!* is like the gay teen flick John Hughes never got around to making. Let's face it, there's a Band Fag in all of us and Frank Anthony Polito has his on speed dial. This book is a sweet, funny, deeply felt valentine to the wonder/horror of coming of age in the 1980s. You might just pee your parachute pants."

—Dennis Hensley, author of *Misadventures in the (213)* and *Screening Party*

"These Band Fags march to their own quirky beat in a timeless tale delightfully syncopated against an '80s soundtrack. This surprisingly tender story of best friends locked in a tug-of-war of self-discovering is booby-trapped with Polito's pitch-perfect wisecracks and hilarious observations."

—Steven Sorrentino, author of *Luncheonette*

"This former 1980s band fag declares *Band Fags!* totally wicked awesome. With pitch-perfect dialog, and high stepping charm, Polito hilariously shows how not all hearts beat to the rhythm of the same drum major."

—Josh Kilmer-Purcell, author of *I Am Not Myself These Days*

"Frank Anthony Polito's *Band Fags!* plays like an eighties after school special; it feels like dropping right back into the oh-so-important questions of who sits where in the lunchroom, who "likes" who, and which friends might be "fags." Polito absolutely captures the voice of a not-ready-to-be-gay-teenager in the eighties, and spins characters who face real problems, ridiculous concerns, and the meaning of friendship over the years."

—Alex MacLennan, author of *The Zookeeper*

BAND FAGS!

Frank Anthony Polito

KENSINGTON BOOKS
http://wwwkensingtonbooks.com

KENSINGTON BOOKS are published by

Kensington Publishing Corp.
850 Third Avenue
New York, NY 10022

All Kensington titles, imprints and distributed lines are available at special quantity discounts for bulk purchases for sales promotion, premiums, fund raising, educational or institutional use.

Special book excerpts or customized printings can also be created to fit specific needs. For details, write or phone the office of the Kensington Special Sales Manager: Kensington Publishing Corp., 850 Third Avenue, New York, NY 10022. Attn. Special Sales Department. Phone: 1-800-221-2647.

ISBN-13: 978-0-7582-2265-7
ISBN-10: 0-7582-2265-3

First Kensington Trade Paperback Printing: June 2008
10 9 8 7 6 5 4 3 2 1

Printed in the United States of America

To Grat Dalton,
my Best Friend since 7th grade.
In memory of his beautiful mother,
Linda Vickers-Dalton-Belfiori

Acknowledgments

First and foremost, I thank my editor, John Scognamiglio, for encouraging an actor-turned-playwright to flesh out a two-character world and for his guidance and friendship along the way. To everyone at Kensington for making me feel welcome, especially Joan Schulhafer, Maureen Cuddy, Adeola Saul, and Guy Chapman in publicity, all my friends in the "Bull Pen," Amanda Rouse, Mercedes Fernandez, Peter Senftleben, Megan Records, Amy Pyle, Jenny Klion, and Colleen Martin; Doug Mendini in sales; Kristine Noble for taking my cover design and making it totally awesome, and, of course, Laurie Parkin, and Steven and Walter Zacharius.

Thank you to my mom and dad, Dawne and Frank Polito, for their constant support throughout the years, and to my brother and (soon-to-be) sister-in-law, Shawn and Judy Polito, my sister and brother-in-law, Julie and Dennis Drew, my nephews, Ryan and Matthew, and my new little niece, Hannah—I love you all.

Thanks to Amanda Thousand, for tips on being Editor-in-Chief of *The Hazel Parker*, to my fellow Band Fags: Eva Rietz, Mike Rackov, and former HPHS Marching and Concert Bands director Mr. Paul Kline, for helping to jog my MSBOA Band Festival memory.

Special thanks to Brian Sloan for encouraging me to use the

title *Band Fags!*, to Rich Kiamco, and my fellow ex-Detroiters, Mark LeGault and Kenneth Walsh, for putting me in touch with the "Giver Goddess." And to Judy Tenuta herself, for allowing me to quote her hilariousness—and for the potted meat product, way back when.

Last but not least, I thank my partner, Craig Bentley, for taking care of me for these oh-so-many years and for finally being The One. To him, I owe my every success—past, present, and future.

Contents

—7th GRADE—

1982–1983

We Got The Beat

"See the kids just getting out of school
They can't wait to hang out and be cool . . ."

—The Go-Go's

"Friends hold you back."

This is what she tells me. Like it's the key to unlocking the Secrets of the Universe. Like they're some Magical Words of Wisdom I can't possibly afford to ignore. Like she's that crazy little psychic woman from *Poltergeist* telling Carole Anne to "Go into the light."

Normally, Jessica Clark Putnam is the nicest teacher in the whole wide world. The kind that allows you to hang out in her office after school eating popcorn. The kind that takes you to Downtown Detroit to see the Symphony, along with every other kid in Band at Webb Jr. High School. The kind that talks to you like you're a Real Adult . . . And not a 12-going-on-13-year-old.

She's one of the prettiest teachers, too. With short brown hair, curled back on the sides, kinda poufy on top—a slight wisp of gray at the temples. She's also got a nice smile. Full of straight white teeth. But at this very moment, the look on her face makes her totally unrecognizable.

"After everything I've done to get you that scholarship?" Mrs. Putnam asks in utter disappointment. "You realize what a wonderful opportunity this is, don't you? You'd be a fool to pass it up."

I can't even believe this is the same woman who stands before us every morning in 2nd hour Varsity Band, flailing her arms about in 4/4 time, head nodding in rhythm, pounding the beat into our brains from high atop her podium. Like she's God.

I proceed to explain how totally grateful I am for the "wonderful opportunity" and all. But I really don't wanna spend two whole weeks at a stupid Summer Band camp all by myself.

"What about Bradley?" she reminds me. By whom she's referring to VB trombone player and my new Best Friend, Brad Dayton.

As outstanding 1st chair musicians, Brad and I have been awarded partial scholarships to attend the prestigious Blue Lake Fine Arts Camp. The only problem is . . . BLFAC costs like $300 for a two-week session. And Brad hasn't explained to Mrs. Putnam how his parents recently got divorced and his Deadbeat Dad is refusing to pay child support for him and his three sisters. Which means no money for Brad to spend two weeks at an exclusive Summer Band camp.

Which is what I tell Jessica Clark Putnam. But she's not having it . . . Not one little bit.

"Just because Bradley Dayton can't go to Blue Lake," she informs me, "doesn't mean it should stop you from going by yourself."

The other problem is . . . I live in the Detroit suburb of Hazel Park. Better known as Hazeltucky to the folks who don't live there. And Blue Lake Fine Arts Camp is located in Muskegon—all the way on the *other* side of the state. And two weeks is a long time for a 12-going-on-13-year-old to spend away from home. Especially one who's never done it before.

Which is when Jessica Clark Putnam tells me, "Friends hold you back."

She proceeds to explain how when she was a kid growing up in Rochester, NY, all she ever wanted was to be a Professional Flautist. For those of you not in the know, this means "flute player." Which explains why she left home at the tender age of 18 after receiving a full scholarship to the University of Michigan. Never once looking back or contemplating for one moment the family or friends she left behind.

I have no idea what else to say. If there's one thing I can't stand, it's disappointing a teacher . . . So I say nothing.

Ever so sweetly, Mrs. Putnam responds to my silence. "You *do* want to go, don't you?"

I nod my head. What kid in his right mind wouldn't? After all, this is a "wonderful opportunity."

How I ever got myself into this mess, I have no idea . . .

I've gotta admit, being picked as 1st chair when 7th grade started back in the Fall came as a surprise to me. Out of the nine other trumpet players, I never expected to be The Best. Though I did practice my butt off for an entire week till I got every last note of my sixteen bars right. Let's just say . . . If my Dad had to listen to "Irish Folk Dance" one more time, he was gonna kill me!

One of the hardest things I've had to get used to about being in junior high is . . . being *forced* to stay for Lunch every day. Back in elementary school at Longfellow, I used to go home on account of we lived right around the block. But at Webb, if you look around the cafeteria, it's like, *all* the boys sit together and *all* the girls sit together. At totally separate tables. Even the guys and girls that are going together don't sit with each other during Lunch. Sure, you see them walking down the hallways together all the time—arms around each other's waists, hands in back pockets. But when it comes to eating lunch, they won't be caught dead at the same table! Which I think is totally stupid. I mean, I'm a guy and I'm *supposed* to like girls. Which is why I don't pay attention to those dumb rules. I sit with whomever I want.

In fact, sitting with a group of girls during Lunch is how I met my Best Friend . . .

One afternoon in early September, I was sitting in the cafeteria with Ava Reese, Varsity Band 1st chair clarinet, Carrie Johnson, VB 2nd chair clarinet, and Katy Griffin, VB 2nd chair trombone. Even though she's super skinny, Ava's always on a diet and hardly ever eats anything. Which is why she was busy going around the table with her Sign-In Book, asking everybody the questions and marking down our answers with her trusty #2 pencil.

"Calvin's or Jordache?"

"Calvin's," answered Ava's new Best Friend, Carrie. Though she barely opened her mouth since she *just* the day before got her braces tightened and they were killing her.

"Calvin's," agreed Katy, as if there was no other choice. Which was kinda weird, if you ask me. Not weird-weird, but . . . Katy's kind of a Tomboy and since I've known her, I've only ever seen her wearing Levi's or cords. In fact, when I saw her walk into the Band Room on the First Day of School, I totally thought she was a guy. Not that I'm saying I don't like her or anything, 'cause I totally do. Maybe it's her short feathered-back hair, I don't know. All I know is . . . Boy can she throw a football!

"Ladies and gentlemen . . ." An adult male voice cut in over the cafeteria loudspeaker. Followed by the obnoxious sound of banging on the microphone. "Is this thing on?"

Lucky Mr. Grant . . . He gets the honor of babysitting us every day during Lunch. His main job is to read Today's Announcements so we know things like when yearbook pictures are being taken. Or to remind us how important it is to sign up for fluoride treatments. Stuff like that. Though the girls I'm friends with would probably listen to Gorgeous George talk about *anything.*

Personally, I don't get what's so great about him. I mean, he's got this totally cheesy mustache! Though I guess his hair's kinda cool. Sandy brownish-blond, feathered-back on the sides, kinda spiked on top. He's also got nice eyes. Bright blue. And a nice smile, I suppose. I guess he's *kinda* attractive. Not that I judge other guys, 'cause I don't.

"We interrupt this program," Mr. Grant said, "to bring you another episode of . . . *Dear Bobby.*" He sounded more like a cheesy radio announcer than a junior high Social Studies teacher. Every day for the past week and a half, Mr. Grant had been reading us a letter he confiscated from one of our fellow 7th graders. He always started off with a recap from yesterday's installment. Which was what Gorgeous George was about to do at that very moment . . .

"When we last left *Dear Bobby,*" he began, "Shelly had invited Bobby to meet her at the Roosevelt playground after school . . ."

A chorus of hoots and hollers erupted from the Jock table at the far end of the cafeteria. Sitting among the group was the Star of the Show, himself. Though from the shade of red his face was turning, Bobby Russell was clearly *not* enjoying being the Center of Attention.

I don't think I've mentioned . . . Bobby's also in Varsity Band. 2nd chair trumpet. Which means he sits right next to me. Which always seemed kinda odd that he could be like, Mr. Popular *and* be in Band. But somehow Bobby pulls it off.

" 'Maybe we can make out on the curly slide,' " Mr. Grant read next. " 'You're a really good kisser, you know that?' "

And the crowd went wild!

With that, Bobby's blond head whipped around. He got up

from his seat and sprinted across the cafeteria to a table over by the windows full of Cheerleaders. Sitting among the group burying her head in shame was his costar, Shelly Findlay. Who happens to be VB 1st chair flute, aka flautist. It was hard to hear what Bobby yelled at Shelly over the clang of silverware against molded plastic plates. But reading his lips I could make out something like, "You better get that f-ing letter back!" Though Bobby didn't say "f-ing letter." He said the real word!

"Will Bobby make out with Shelly on the Roosevelt playground curly slide?" Mr. Grant continued, concluding today's installment. "Tune in tomorrow—same time, same channel—for another exciting episode of . . . *Dear Bobby.*"

And with that, we returned to our regularly scheduled program . . .

"Calvin's or Jordache?" Ava looked at me, twirling a lock of her curly brown hair.

I took a swig of my low-fat chocolate milk, unsticking the PB of my PB & J on white bread from the roof of my mouth. I was *just* about to answer when I heard the plop of a puke-colored plastic tray on the table.

"Fuck those! I like *Sergio Valente*'s better 'cause they make your ass look hot!" At which point, Bradley Dayton popped a freshly-dipped-in-ketchup tater tot into his mouth and squeezed in beside Carrie, directly across from where I sat. I noticed he'd chosen the hamburger over the grilled cheese option.

"Sergio's aren't one of the choices," Ava told Brad, kinda snotty.

"Yeah," echoed Katy, like she was Ava's own Personal Bodyguard.

"Who cares?" Brad retaliated. "Write it in . . . Number 4."

"Whatever," Ava said. Then she wrote Brad's answer down and turned the page. "John Cougar or Rick Springfield?"

"Rick Springfield," Brad chimed in. "Definitely."

"I wasn't asking you," Ava snapped back.

"Yeah," echoed Katy.

"Number 4 . . . Write it in."

I noticed the words Eat Shit and Die! scrawled in red on a white quarter-sized button pinned to Brad's pink Braggin' Dragon polo shirt—worn with the collar up. Which is when I got a good look at him for the very first time . . . Reddish-brown hair, feathered back on the sides, with freckles on his cheeks and nose. Now that I think about it, he kinda reminds me of Ron Howard. Ron "Opie" Howard. Not Richie Cunningham.

Brad must have noticed my staring because he looked across the table at me and was all like, "Who the Hell are you?" Totally deadpan.

I was like, "I'm Jack." Even though my real name's John, everybody calls me Jack or Jackie.

"Jack who?"

"Paterno . . . Varsity Band 1st chair trumpet."

To which Brad replied, "Oh." Then he laughed.

"Smurfs or Garfield?" Ava continued, turning the page.

And that's pretty much the entire story . . . *How I Met My Best Friend.* By John R. Paterno.

Though it wasn't till almost an entire month later that I even spoke to him again . . .

After weeks and weeks of hot pursuit—love letter after love letter, phone call after phone call—Lynn Kelly and I finally started going together. Like my Mom always says, "Good things come to those who wait."

In case I haven't mentioned it . . . Lynn Kelly is the girl I've liked since the day I got to Webb Junior High. First of all, she's totally pretty. With shoulder-length blond hair, curled back on the sides, and a nice smile. Secondly, she's very "developed," if you know what I mean.

As 7th graders, we don't get to pick our schedules. They assign our classes to us and it just happened to work out that Lynn and I had the *exact* same schedule that semester . . .

1st hour: Science w/Mr. Davidson.
2nd hour: Varsity Band w/Mrs. Putnam.
3rd hour: Reading Lab w/Miss Blundell.
4th hour: Health w/Mrs. Strong.
5th hour: Math w/Mr. Nichols.
6th & 7th hour: Enriched English & Social Studies w/Ms. Lemieux.

Which was kinda weird, if you think about it. Not weird-weird, but . . . Even if we could've chosen, Lynn went to elementary school at Lee O. Clark so we never even met each other till we got to Webb. It's like we were meant to be together and now we were.

One day in late October, I was over Lynn's house . . .

Like most of my friends, her parents are divorced. So she lives with her Mom over on Orchard, behind the hill in Martin Road Park. Which pretty much serves no purpose other than during the Winter when it's covered with snow and it's an awesome place to go sledding. Lynn's Mom was still at work so we were lying together on her couch, watching MTV. Which was kinda awkward because Lynn is like, 5'7" and I'm only 4'11".

"Now what?" Lynn asked. Men at Work's "Who Can It Be Now?" video had just ended.

"Now what, what?" I replied.

To which she rolled her hazel eyes at me. "We've been going together for two whole days, Jackie . . . Aren't you ever gonna kiss me?"

So I did . . . For all of about five seconds.

"That's not a kiss," she informed me. "Don't you know how to French?"

Of course, I knew *how* . . . I'd just never done it before.

"Close your eyes," Lynn instructed. Then she proceeded to stick her tongue halfway down my throat!

After waiting all that time, I honestly didn't see what the big deal was about kissing. It certainly was nothing like I expected. In fact, it was kinda gross and slimy.

"Not bad," Lynn said. "You'll get better with practice."

But what I want to know is . . . How was I supposed to do that? When a couple days later during Ms. Lemieux's 6th hour Enriched English, Lynn passed me the following note . . .

Jack,

You know I think you're a real sweet guy. But I don't think this is going to work out. I hope we can we still be friends.

Lynn

I tried acting like it didn't matter. Even though it totally did! I mean, how was I gonna get through the rest of the semester when Lynn Kelly and I had every single class together?

When I got home from school that day, my Mom asked if I was ready for dinner . . .

"I'm not hungry," I told her, trying to make it clear just how p.o.'d I was without actually saying so.

"Jackie!" she called out from the kitchen where she was stirring a simmering pot of mostaccoli. "What's wrong?"

"Everything," I replied. Then I stormed into my bedroom. Though I had to cut through my 8-year-old sister's room first on account of mine's an addition on the back of our house. Jodi was playing on the floor, her hair up in pigtails looking so darn cute I could kick her! Instead, I practically stepped on her and her stupid Strawberry Shortcake dolls as I passed.

"Mom . . . Jackie kicked me!" she hollered.

"You're such a Total Liar!" I shouted back.

"I know you are but what am I?"

I flung open the flimsy accordion-fold door separating our bedrooms to find my 4-year-old brother passed out on the bottom bunk, thumb stuck in his mouth. I thrust the door closed behind me, hating the fact that I had to share a room with Billy even more than I usually did.

I climbed the ladder to my bed, not caring if I woke up my stupid little brother. Who's really not stupid at all. I love him and my sister, both. I was just p.o.'d at that moment. I stared at the white drop-ceiling no more than four feet above me. For the first time, I took note of the textured pattern in each tile. Kinda like a bunch of white rainbows intertwining with one another. All of a sudden, my eyes started to burn. So I rolled over, facing the knotty pine paneled wall.

And I cried . . . And cried . . . Like a little baby, I know.

For some reason, I couldn't get Lionel Richie and Diana Ross singing "Endless Love" out of my mind. Which made me cry even more! Ever since I first heard that stupid song, all I wanted to do was find somebody to love. Who would love me back . . . For real.

Like in the movies and on TV.

Later that same night, I was going through the Sign-In Book I made a couple days before. Even though most guys at school would only sign them—not make them—I didn't care. I knew there had to be somebody I could call. Somebody I could talk to. Somebody who might understand the pain and heartbreak I was going through and actually give a crap.

Then I came to the page titled PHONE NUMBER . . .

"398-5836" with the number 4 scrawled beneath it was the first one. I figured, what the heck? I'll give Mr. Sergio Valentes a call . . . Why not?

"Dayton residence." A woman answered in a slight Southern accent.

"Is Brad there?" I said, polite as could be in case she was his Mom.

"Who's calling, please?"

"This is Jack Paterno . . . From school."

"Just a moment . . ." Then I heard, superloud, *"Br-a-a-dley . . . Telephone!"* Then to me the woman said, "He'll be right with you." Much more subdued.

I made myself comfortable on the green shag carpet in the hallway between our living room and kitchen. The extra-long olive green telephone cord wound its way around the doorway as I laid on my back with my feet propped up against the wall.

After a moment I heard, "Hello?"

"Hi, Brad," I said.

"Who is this?"

"It's Jack."

"Jack who?"

"Paterno . . . Varsity Band 1st chair trumpet."

To which Brad replied, "Oh." Followed by, "What do *you* want?"

Good question. Why was I calling this guy I barely knew, expecting him to care about my problems? What was I even gonna say?

And then it *poured* out of me . . . *How Lynn Kelly Broke My Heart into a Million Pieces.* By John R. Paterno.

"Dah-dah, dah-dah," said Brad, interrupting me halfway through. From his tone, I took it to mean, "Yeah, yeah." As in, "Get on with it, already."

So I repeated, "Dah-dah, dah-dah." Then I quickly finished my sob story.

"I didn't even know you were going with Lynn Kelly," he informed me. "You know Max thinks she's hot, don't you?" By whom he meant Max Wilson. This guy in our class that Brad's been friends with since like 4th grade.

Actually, Max's Mom and my Dad work together at Farmer Jack's up on 9 Mile and John R. So I kinda already knew Max, myself, before the school year started and we met up again in Mr. Davidson's 1st hour Science.

"So what do you think I should do?" I asked Brad, hoping for some sympathetic advice.

"Get over it."

Easy for him to say . . . Brad didn't just spend the last two months of his life totally devoted to somebody, only to get dumped by her—in a note! How would I ever get over this?

Six months later, I was *still* in love with Lynn Kelly . . . So was Max.

Don't get me wrong, he's not a bad-looking guy. Tall and thin with blue eyes and brownish-blond hair. But he's got so much of it. I'm telling you, Max Wilson has just about the smallest forehead I've ever seen! Plus he's got a Tin Grin. And his complexion isn't exactly the clearest. So why in the world would Lynn Kelly ever be interested in him? Not that he's not a cool guy or anything, 'cause he totally is.

In April, when my parents took their yearly vacation to Las Vega$ with my Aunt Mary and Uncle Jim, I got to stay over Max's house. Which was totally awesome! I never spent the night anywhere on a School Night, let alone an entire *week*.

After school on Friday, Max met me and Brad in the Band Room. The minute Lynn Kelly materialized with her saxophone in tow, he started whining like a Total Baby. "Come on, you guys . . . Let's get the fuck outta here!"

"Buh-bye, Lynn!" Brad called out, making sure to draw her attention towards Max as he slipped out the side parking lot door ahead of us.

"See you on Monday!" I chimed in, giving a wave. Even

though she broke my heart into a bijillion pieces, I've managed to stay friends with Lynn. Besides, Brad and I could never resist watching Max squirm.

The three of us walked over to some Party Store on Hilton where we waited for Max's Dad to pick us up when he got off work. In case I didn't mention it . . . Max's parents are divorced. This happened to be the weekend Max had to go to his Dad's house. Which meant I was going, too. And for some reason, Max invited Brad to tag along, don't ask me why!

Even though we'd been in school together for the past eight months, I still wasn't sure how I felt about Brad Dayton. Sometimes I thought he was kinda weird. Not weird-weird, but . . . How do I explain it? The way he acts. Like, he's always hanging around with the girls. Giggling and laughing. And there's something about his voice. The way he talks. He kinda sounds like that guy from *Too Close for Comfort*. Not Ted Knight. The neighbor, Monroe.

Okay, I'll let you in on a little secret . . . There's this rumor going around school that Brad Dayton's a Total Fag. I don't know how it got started. All I know is . . . it did. Of course, there are always kids who pick on other kids just for the fun of it. They like to say mean things, whether they're true or not. Back at Longfellow, there was this girl named Tuesday Gunderson. People used to pick on her all the time. The minute our teacher walked out of the room they'd be all like, "Whoever talks loves Tuesday Gunderson!" Just because Poor Tuesday had a funny name and wasn't the prettiest girl in the world.

But I never did.

I mean, I'm not stupid enough to believe *everything* I hear. Why should I think Brad Dayton's a Total Fag? Just because he's always hanging around with the girls? Giggling and laughing. And because of the way his voice sounds? Like the faggy next-door neighbor from *Too Close for Comfort*.

Besides, I hang around with girls. And I'm not a Total Fag . . . Am I?

I spent the next hour kicking Max's butt in Ms. Pac-Man. Even though I'm *much* better at regular Pac-Man—my high score back in 6th grade was 188,910—I'm almost just as good at Ms.

"Would you hurry up and die, already?" Max groaned. "My Dad's gonna be here any minute . . . I want a turn!" He furiously chomped a piece of watermelon Bubblicious. Something I had a feeling his orthodontist would *not* approve of.

I've gotta admit, Max is pretty good at video games. But Brad has no hand-eye coordination whatsoever. After like five seconds, he always gets killed. Then he starts pouting like a Total Baby.

"Today!" Brad loomed over the tabletop, totally obstructing my view of Pac-land.

"Thanks a lot!" I cringed as Poor Ms. Pac met her demise after bumping into brown goblin Sue. Not to be confused with Clyde, her husband's look-alike nemesis.

"You're welcome," Brad sarcastically smirked. "Can we go now?"

Around 4:45 PM, Max's Dad showed up to drive us over to his house in Roseville. Near 11 Mile and Gratiot. Which is pronounced "Gra-shit," in case you had no idea—because why would you unless you happen to hail from Motown?

After all of half an hour, we became *totally* bored out of our minds . . .

"This is lame!" Brad sighed. "Let's do something."

"Like what?" Max wanted to know.

"Yeah," I said. "Like what?"

"I don't know . . . *Something.*"

I turned to Max. "What else is there to do?" After all, we were at *his* Dad's house.

"Travis has got porn!" he announced, his acne-prone face

lighting up. Poor Max . . . His complexion looked especially bad that day. Like a proverbial pizza. Lucky for me, I don't have that problem. I get a couple pimples a year tops, thank God!

We headed down the hall past the front room. Though it always sounds more like "French Room" whenever Max says it. We spied his Dad sitting on the beat-up faded green couch in his blue mechanic's coveralls, his name—Travis—stitched in red across the left side of his chest. Beer in hand, he was watching *The Dukes of Hazzard.* Which used to totally be my favorite show back in like 5th grade. But ever since they brought on those two new guys to replace Bo and Luke, I can't stand it.

"Your Dad must like beer," Brad whispered, counting the seven or eight empty Goebel cans cluttering up the coffee table.

"Duh!" Max replied. Then we sneaked into Travis' bedroom.

As my Mom would say, "It looked like a cyclone hit it." Talk about a Total Pigsty! Dirty laundry everywhere. On the floor, on top of the dresser, covering the unmade bed. Which Brad immediately plopped down on. The gurgle of water sloshed around inside the mattress beneath him.

"Careful!" Max warned. "That's a waterbed."

"Dah-dah, dah-dah," said Brad kicking back, hands behind his head against the zebra-striped pillow.

"So where's the porn?" I asked. Though I wondered, *Do I really wanna see it?* My Uncle Roy's got a ton of porno mags at his house. One time, I saw a copy of *Penthouse* sitting on the back of his toilet. Of course, I *had* to take a peek. Being that I'd never seen one before.

To be honest, I wasn't that impressed. I mean, what's the big deal about a bunch of naked girls? I think they'd all be so much prettier with their clothes on. Especially the ones with the humongous areolas covering their entire boobs. (Gross!)

Max opened his Dad's top dresser drawer, a pile of black socks and white underwear spewing forth. He was all like, "Check this out." Sure enough, from beneath the rubble he removed a real-live nudie magazine. Though it was one I'd never heard of before.

"What is it?" Brad asked

"What do you think it is, Asshole?" Max snapped. "Don't tell me you've never heard of O-U-I before?" Which is exactly how he said it. "O-U-I." Spelling it out.

"I think you mean *oui,*" I corrected. Not that I've ever taken French. But I know O-U-I is pronounced "wee," meaning "yes," *en français.*

Max was all like, "Whatever." You'd think he would know a simple French word like "*oui.*" After all, he was in Ms. Lemieux's 6th & 7th hour Enriched English & Social Studies with the Smart Kids.

"This is boring," Brad decided after we flipped through the magazine for a while. Page after page of naked girls.

To which Max was all like, "What do you mean 'boring'? This chick is hot." He turned to the centerfold—a glossy color photo of a pretty dark-haired girl wearing pink lemonade lipstick. With one hand on her boob, her tongue flickered forward. Like she was trying to lick her own nipple. (Gross!)

"Don't tell me *you* wouldn't fuck her," Max challenged.

Like I've said, pictures of naked girls I can take or leave . . . So I said nothing. Neither did Brad.

Then Max added, "She totally looks like that girl from Culture Club, doesn't she?"

Brad turned to me, eyebrows raised. Then back to Max and he said coolly, "What girl from Culture Club?"

"You know . . . The lead singer."

As much as I hated breaking the news to him, I said, "Um, Max . . . the lead singer of Culture Club's name is *Boy* George . . ."

At which point, Brad joined me in perfect unison. ". . . 'cause he's a boy!"

Which is when it finally happened. In our mutual belittling of Max Wilson, Brad Dayton and I formed a bond. We had at last become Friends.

The next night, the three of us sat in the French Room watching *Saturday Night Live* on Channel 4 . . .

"We interrupt this program for a Special News Bulletin . . ."

"What the fuck?!" Max groaned. He threw a pillow at the TV. We all expected President Reagan or somebody else stupid to come on at any minute.

Till the announcer continued with, "Buckwheat has been shot." And Eddie Murphy appeared on-screen dressed as our favorite character. Next to Mr. "Can you say 'Skumbucket?'" Robinson, that is.

We also watched this totally dumb movie on Cinemax called *H.O.T.S.* Which *supposedly* stands for "Help Out The Seals." But really it's all about these big boobed sorority girls having wet T-shirt contests and playing strip touch football. Stuff like that. Of course, Max totally loved it. Brad on the other hand was all like, "Whatever." Me, I could take it or leave it.

Once the movie ended, we laid around in bed in the dark, talking about which girls at school we liked and what we'd do with them if we ever got the chance. Actually, Max was the only one lying in bed. Brad and I had the pleasure of sleeping in sleeping bags down on the shag carpet.

"I'm still in love with Lynn Kelly," I sighed, pressing my pelvis against the floor.

"So am I," echoed Max, most likely doing the exact same thing against his mattress.

To which Brad—lying flat on his back—said, "I don't think I like *anybody*."

"What about Carrie Johnson?" I pried. A couple months before, I'd witnessed him sticking his tongue down her throat on the dance floor at the Fun Night.

"I don't know . . ." Brad sighed. Then he rolled over and went to sleep.

A few days later, we were back at Max's Mom's house on University in Ferndale . . .

I should probably explain something. Even though I live in Hazel Park, the dividing line for the HP school district cuts off at Hilton Road. Right in the middle of Ferndale. Which is the next city over from Hazeltucky and where Webb Junior High is technically located. So about half of the kids going to school with me live over there.

"They've been *totally* playing this video to death!" I groaned.

We were sitting in the French Room watching MTV when Michael Jackson's "Beat It" came on. Which I'd seen like a bijillion times already.

Max was all like, "Who cares? Martha Quinn is hot!" Totally drooling.

Brad was all like, "Whatever." Then he got up from the blue faux-velvet love seat and headed towards the kitchen.

"Where the Hell you going?" Max called out.

"To call the Party Line," Brad informed us, walking away.

In case you don't know—because why would you?—the Party Line is this phone number you call where you can talk to all these different people. Mostly guys. But sometimes girls. I don't know how it works *exactly*. All I know is . . . you dial an exchange, like 542 or 543 or 545, followed by 9998. Usually you get a busy signal. But sometimes if you're lucky and you keep trying long enough, it'll connect.

"Hello?" As per usual, a guy answered. An *older* guy. Like 18 or 19. Most of the time, they're looking for sex. Sometimes they just wanna talk. But the fun part is . . . most of the time they think we're *girls*. Because our voices haven't changed yet, probably. "What's your name?"

"Tiffany," Brad replied, as per usual doing the talking. "What's yours?"

"Chuck," the guy answered, trying to act all cool.

"Wanna fuck, Chuck?" asked Tiffany.

"How old are you?"

"16."

"Sweet," Chuck said, laughing at his own joke. "I'm 25."

To which Brad was all like, "Perfect . . . I *love* older guys."

Meanwhile, Max and I had our ears up to the phone, trying desperately to hear what Chuck was saying and not pee our pants. We were totally cracking up!

"What're you wearing?" Chuck asked next.

"Just my bra and panties," Brad lied, suppressing a giggle himself.

"Hot . . . You're totally giving me a hard-on, you know that?"

"Wish I could suck it," said Tiffany the Total Slut.

At which point, Max's Mom appeared through the back door, home from a hard day's work at Farmer Jack's . . .

"What are you boys up to?" She plopped a brown paper bag of groceries down on the kitchen table.

"Nothing," Max said lickety-split. Then he grabbed the phone out of Brad's hand and returned it to the cradle on the wall. "What's for dinner?"

"I'm thinking about ordering a pizza from Randazzo's," Max's Mom informed us. Which is the best pizza in all of Hazeltucky. "How's that sound?" She kinda reminds me of Annette Funicello. Skippy peanut butter Annette. Not M-I-C-K-E-Y.

In between wolfing down several slices of pepperoni, Brad and I struck up a conversation with Max's sister, Maggie. She's a Senior at Hillbilly High and kinda reminds me of that actress from *Fast Times at Ridgemont High,* Phoebe Cates.

Maggie proceeded to tell us all about how much she hates

this Freshman girl we know from Webb, Kylee Belestergaard. Something about her being a Ho-Bag and giving Maggie's ex-boyfriend a blowjob in the Hillbilly High parking lot after the Friday night Varsity Football game. I guess Max didn't appreciate it when Brad and I followed Maggie into her bedroom after dinner. Because pretty soon he was standing outside her door, screaming his head off.

"Mom! Tell Maggie to leave my friends alone."

"Mom!" Phoebe Cates screamed back. "Tell Max to get off my case."

"Ma-a-a-x," Annette Funicello said calmly from the French Room where she sat watching Joan Collins and Linda Evans duke it out on *Dynasty.*

"Why do you have to be such a pain in the ass?" Max retorted.

"Your friends are the ones talking to me," Phoebe Cates informed him. Which was true. Brad and I couldn't help it we thought Max's sister was totally cool. Then she added, "I can't help it if they think I'm cooler than you."

We glanced over at Max. His face was *totally* turning red. He looked like he was gonna cry at any minute. "Fuck off!" he shouted. Causing my and Brad's jaws to drop to the floor.

"What did you say, young man?" Annette Funicello was now up on her feet and in the hall intercepting Max and his sister as they were about to get into a knockdown-drag-out fight. Which was totally hilarious. Max's Mom can't be more than 5' tall and both her kids are *at least* 5'5".

"Max?" she said. This time using her "mean" voice. "Tell your sister you're sorry . . . *Now.*"

Brad and I stared down at the pink and baby blue afghan folded across the end of Maggie's bed. Which is where we'd been sitting the entire time. I wanted to make myself disappear. Only there was nowhere to go. Maybe staying over Max's house while my parents were in Las Vega$ wasn't such a good idea after all!

Suddenly, Max shouted, "I'm sorry for telling my stupid sister to fuck off!"

"What did you say?" Annette Funicello asked for the second time in less than five minutes.

"I'm sorry for telling my stupid sister to fuck off!" Max repeated. This time through tears. As if saying it once wasn't already enough.

To which Max's Mom had no idea *what* to say. So instead, she cracked up laughing. So did Max. Even Brad and I started laughing, too. Though Maggie didn't find it funny. She just rolled her eyes and stood there, hands on her hips, in what we had recently learned during Ms. Lemieux's 6th hour Enriched English is called "akimbo."

"Now go to your room," Annette Funicello said, serious as all get-out.

"But—" Max tried to protest.

"I mean it . . . You're grounded."

"What about Jackie?" Max knew I was staying for at least two more days.

"I don't care if Jackie's here or not," Max's Mom informed him. "He and Brad can play together without you for all I care."

Which is exactly what we did . . . By the end of my weeklong visit, Brad and I had officially become Best Friends. Which was just about the time our teacher, Jessica Clark Putnam, called us into her office after 2nd hour Varsity Band and closed the door behind us . . .

I remember it was her birthday that day—May 7th. Somebody said she was turning 30. But I couldn't believe it. She didn't look *that* old. Our Band Aide, Freddy Edwards, brought in a cake his Mom baked especially for the occasion. Freddy's a 9th grade sax player in 1st hour Symphonic. Which is the top band at Webb. And of course, *all* the girls think he's a Total Babe.

Personally, I don't get what's so hot about him. So he's got pretty blue eyes and a nice smile and good hair . . . Big deal! And so what if he wears cool clothes and he's on the wrestling team. So he's got a nice body. Not that I judge other guys, 'cause I don't.

"Have either of you ever heard about Blue Lake Fine Arts Camp?" Mrs. Putnam asked us.

Brad and I looked at each other, having no idea what she was talking about. But from the expression of pure delight on her face, it must have been someplace special.

"Nestled in the beautiful Manistee National Forest in Michigan's western lower peninsula, Blue Lake Fine Arts Camp is a Summer Music Camp with Dance, Theater, and Art programs for talented young people who come from all parts of the United States and all walks of life." At least according to the brochure JCP gave us. Which Brad and I both read *at least* a hundred times.

Which brings me full circle to . . . "Friends hold you back."

Jessica Clark Putnam smiles, a twinkle in her chestnut-brown eyes as she and I continue standing alone together in the instrument storage room. "Tell you what . . . If Bradley's *somehow* able to come up with the money, then will you go?"

"Of course." But how the heck is that gonna happen? Brad's family is so broke, he can barely afford to pay attention!

Sure enough, a week later Mrs. Putnam receives an anonymous donation for $150 for Bradley Dayton. Thus enabling him and me to spend the two longest weeks of our lives at Blue Lake Fine Arts Camp.

Along with all the other Band Fags!

WEBB LEGEND

—1983—

Jack,
to my Best Friend. Hope you have better luck with the girls next year. Ha ha.
Your friend, Brad
"88"

Jack,
To a really sweet, funny, nice, cute, witty, smart guy I had almost every class with this year. Thanks for all the good times. Hope we can make some new memories next year!
—Love ya,
Lynn Kelly

Jack,
a sweet and nice guy I met this year in Varsity Band. I hope we know each other for a long time. Good luck in 8th grade.
Love, Katy

To Jack,
A really great friend I like even more than bresil sprouts. Even though you got me grounded that time you stayed at my house! Hope we stay good friends. See you later.
Max

To Jack,
A guy that I met in Varsity Band. Your a cute and sweet guy and you better stay that way!
Ava Reese.
P.S. Sorry for teasing you about Lynn Kelly all year.

Jackie,
You are a multi-talented student whom I thoroughly enjoy! Keep up your conscientious efforts. You can do anything you put your mind to!
Ms. Lemieux

—LISTS—

SPORT	EVENT	WINNER
Football	Super Bowl	Washington Redskins
Baseball	World Series	St. Louis Cardinals
Basketball	NBA Title	L.A. Lakers
Hockey	Stanley Cup	N.Y. Islanders
Tennis	Wimbledon	Jimmy Connors
Soccer	World Cup	Italy
Tennis	Wimbledon	Martina Navratilova

DEATHS
Grace Kelly
John Belushi
Tennessee Williams
Natalie Wood
Henry Fonda

PRICES	
Album	$8.98
45 record	$1.99
Designer Jeans	$40.00
Concert Tickets	$12.00
School Lunch	$1.10

Paul Lynde	Dance Ticket	$2.00
Ingrid Bergman	Unleaded Gas	$1.15
Leonid Brezhnev	Movie Ticket	$4.00
Blair Moody Jr.	Big Mac	$1.25
William Holden	Yearbook	$8.00

—FRESHMAN—

1984–1985

Johnny, Are You Queer?

"Johnny, what's the deal, boy?
Is your love for real, boy?"

—Josie Cotton

September 1984.

A year and four months have passed since Brad and I went to Blue Lake Fine Arts Camp as piddly little 7th-going-on-8th graders. I can't even believe it's our third and *final* year at Webb Junior High. As Freshmen, we're gonna Rule the School!

In case you're wondering what we're still doing in junior high, I should probably explain . . . In the "Friendly City" of Hazel-tucky, you don't go to high school till your Sophomore year. Which is totally lame, I know. But apparently back in like 1967, the only junior high around was Howard Beecher. And once there got to be too many kids living in the Hazel Park school district to fit in one school, they built another junior high and divided the Freshman class into two.

Depending on where you lived, you either went to Beecher—with all the Burn-Outs—or to the much cooler *new* junior high, Webb, named after some guy, Wilfred D. Which is where my

Mom went. Up till 9th grade when she got pregnant with me, got married, and dropped out.

Okay, I know what you're thinking . . . *Your Mom got pregnant with you when she was 14 years old? How the heck does that happen in this day and age?* But that was like, 1969, "The Summer of Love." And to be perfectly honest, I don't wanna think about *how* it happened. (Gross!)

There's this picture of my parents taken on their wedding day. Standing in front of my grandparents' house in the January snow. My Mom looks so tiny and scared. But my Dad's got his arm around her, holding on like he's never gonna let go. And to this day, he hasn't. I've gotta admit, I'm proud of them. Most people thought it would never work. A 17-year-old boy marrying a 14-year-old girl. But fourteen and a half years later, they're still together.

In a way, I think my being born was a good thing. My mother always says all she ever wanted was to fall in love, get married, and raise a family. Which is what she did. Maybe a little sooner than she expected, but . . . How many people can say they've done *exactly* what they wanted to do with their lives?

Though thinking about it now, it's hard to believe. I mean, *I'm* 14. And I'm still a kid. I've got a bijillion things I wanna do with my life. And dropping out of school, getting married, and having a baby is not one of them. Back in 6th grade, they showed us that After School Special, *Schoolboy Father*, and it totally freaked me out!

One time, my Dad told me this funny story . . . Senior year, he gets caught smoking in the boys' bathroom at Hillbilly High. This Hall Monitor walks in and she's all like, "Young man . . . Do you want me to call your parents?"

And my Dad's like, "No . . . But you can call my *wife!*"

So this afternoon before 7th hour, we're standing at Brad's locker . . .

He's got Algebra Man. Who just after Lunch today finished teaching my class trinomials. Under his real identity—Mr. Bond—he's also the Cross-Country coach. He's also totally crazy! About once a week, he comes into class dressed up as Algebra Man. Complete with mask, cape, the whole shebang, he teaches us in character for the entire hour! What makes it even crazier is . . . After Algebra Man leaves, Mr. Bond will come back into class and he's all like, "How come *I'm* never around when Algebra Man pays a visit?"

Lucky me . . . I've got Gorgeous George for Civics. Other than from reading Today's Announcements to us on a daily basis during Lunch, I didn't really know him at all till this year. He used to be Brad's Swimming coach back in 7th grade and Brad says he was always pretty cool.

"Can I come over after school and watch *Days?*" Brad asks me. By which he means *Days of our Lives.* "I don't think I've seen it since before school started . . . What's up?"

Even though I know the bell's gonna ring any minute, I can't resist giving Brad the lowdown. "Oh, my God . . . It's getting sooo good!"

"Tell me!"

"Well," I say, "you know Stefano, right?" By whom I'm referring to Salem's resident Evil Villain, Stefano DiMera. "It turns out he's still alive after all."

To which Brad exclaims, "Shut the fuck up!"

"*And,*" I continue, "he's going after the prisms." By which I'm referring to the three different colored pieces of glass that will magically cure Stefano of his inoperable brain tumor once he finds and puts them all together. Thus allowing him to take over the world.

Now you're probably thinking . . . *Soap operas are for middle-aged housewives and teenaged* girls. *Not 14-year-old boys.* Which they totally are. But I can't help it if I'm addicted and so is Brad.

"It must be nice having your own TV and VCR right in your bedroom," he says enviously. Then he throws in, "Too bad it's a Beta." Just so I won't think he's jealous of me. Even though I know he totally is.

"Shut up!" I say. I can't help it if my parents won $500 on their last trip to Las Vega$. So my Dad decided to buy a brand new TV and VCR for our living room and give me the hand-me-downs.

"You better call your Mom and make sure it's okay if I come over," Brad decides.

"She's not gonna care," I tell him. "My Mom totally likes you."

"I don't know, Jack . . . Remember the time me and Max spent the night at your house back in 7th grade and your Mom totally kicked us out in the morning?"

"She did *not* kick you out!" I remind Brad for the bijillionth time.

"Yes, she did," he insists. "I'll never forget it." At which point, he does his best impression of my Mom, all loud. " 'Jackie! Tell those boys to get the fuck out . . . *Now*.' "

To which I've gotta protest. "My mother would *never* say the F-word," I defend. Because she wouldn't.

"Like mother, like son," Brad replies, deadpan.

Though I don't exactly hear him over the *zhit-zhit* sound of my pant legs rubbing together as we make our way to class. All I wanted last year was a pair of parachute pants to go with my white sleeveless T-shirt with the orange sun and the Chinese writing on it. Now that my Mom *finally* broke down and bought me a pair, they've gone out of style!

The middle hallway is abuzz with in-between-class activity. A group of Webb Warrior Cheerleaders pass by us wearing green and gold W sweaters, led by Symphonic Band 1st chair flautist

Shelly Findlay. Who is no longer going with Bobby Russell, in case you're wondering. I decided that Shelly kinda reminds me of the lead singer of the German one-hit wonder band, Nena. Remember the ones who sang "99 Luftballoons"? I totally loved that song and practically begged Mrs. Putnam to let us play it for the Memorial Day parade last year. But she had none of it!

I look over my shoulder just in time to catch Shelly's eye. "What's up, Fox?" she says, raising her thumb, forefinger, *and* pinky to give a little semicircular wave.

"Hi, Shelly," I say, forcing a smile. Then I see her turn to her Cheerleader Friends and start cackling her little brunette head off.

I realize Shelly *could* be laughing about something some cute boy somewhere said to her sometime. Or maybe she could be laughing at me and my so-last-year parachute pants! I don't know. All I know is . . . I feel totally self-conscious right now.

"I'll meet you at the locker at 3 o'clock," Brad informs me. Which is when I notice for the first time how suddenly empty the hallway has become. Which is when I go deaf as the 7th hour bell begins to chime.

Brad covers his ears. "Have fun with Mr. Grant," he teases. Then he disappears into Algebra Land. Where Mr. Bond is nowhere to be seen, pending the imminent arrival of the Man of a Thousand Equations.

I sprint down the hall and into Gorgeous George's room, crossing the threshold just in the nick of time. Everybody knows if you're late for Grant's class, he makes you stay half an hour after school for Detention—just you and him. Which is about the *last* thing I would ever wanna do!

I've gotta say, Brad's been acting kinda weird, lately. Not weird-weird, but . . . Ever since he found out I've got Mr. Grant for Civics this year, he's always making comments about him in one way or another. Maybe he's mad 'cause he's got Mrs. McKenzie, who's *at least* 60 years old. And Mr. Grant's only like half her age.

"Nice of you to join us, Mr. Paterno."

The whole classroom bursts out laughing. Though I really don't give a care. They're all just jealous because I'm a straight-A student and have been since 7th grade. And with only two more semesters to go, I'm on my way to winning the Student of the Year Award. Right now, it's between me and Ava Reese, Symphonic Band 1st chair clarinet. Though I found out she got a B+ in Biology last semester. So as long as I don't get anything less than an A this year, the award is as good as mine!

"Okay, People . . . Time for Current Events." Mr. Grant takes up the long metal rod-thingie from the ledge on the chalkboard. Reaching up with it, he pulls down the projection screen from above. Of course, he has to turn around to do this—giving the entire class a shot of his butt. Not that I'm looking or anything, 'cause I'm not. But you can't miss it, his pants are sooo tight!

"You want me to get the lights, Mr. Grant?" Carrie Johnson volunteers, making me gag. That girl would eat dog food if Gorgeous George told her to, I swear!

"That would be lovely," he replies, flashing his pearly whites.

Not that I'm staring at him or anything . . .

After class, Brad walks with me over to my house. My family lives on Shevlin. Which is four blocks south of 10 Mile. In case you don't know—again, why would you?—Hazel Park borders the city of Detroit on its south side at 8 Mile and extends north up to 10 Mile. Why all the roads running north/south around here are called "something Mile," I don't know! All I know is . . . they start at like 6 Mile, and go all the way up to 30-something Mile. And in Hazeltucky, the closer you live to 8 Mile the less well-off you tend to be. Not that my family is "well-off" by any means—my Dad's the Produce Manager of a Supermarket. Though I've got pretty much everything a kid could ask for.

Like my own 10-speed and Atari 5200. Not to mention my own personal color TV *and* VCR right in my bedroom. Which is where Brad and I are right now, just finishing up today's episode of *Days of our Lives* . . .

"Now what?" he asks as the "sands through the hourglass" theme finally fades.

"Wanna see my Kristian Alfonso scrapbook?"

Brad gives me a look. Like he's smelling a fart or something. "Who the Hell's Kristin Alfonso?"

"Kris-*tian* Alfonso," I correct. "How can you not know who she is?"

"Um . . . Because I don't," he replies, sprawling out on my brother's bottom bunk bed.

"She plays Hope on *Days of our Lives,*" I inform him. "Duh!"

Hope Williams-Welch, to be exact. The daughter of Doug Williams and Addie Horton, who unfortunately got hit by a car and died shortly after Hope was born 18 years ago. Which was totally fine for Doug, considering he was in love with Addie's daughter, Julie, at the time he knocked Addie up in a drunken stupor.

The thing is . . . Hope's totally in love with this guy named Bo Brady. He's like a Total Rebel. With long dark hair and a beard. He also rides a motorcycle. He kinda reminds me of this country singer my Mom likes, Eddie Rabbit. I guess you could say he's attractive. Not that I judge other guys, 'cause I don't.

But for some reason, Hope's married to this other guy, Larry Welch. Who's the Salem D.A. and, like, a Total Crook. He's also totally in cahoots with Stefano DiMera, the Evil Villain everybody thinks is dead. But Bo & Hope are onto Stefano. They totally suspect he's still alive and trying to get control of the prisms so he can take over the world. Which he totally is.

The actress who plays Hope is named Kristian Alfonso. K-R-I-S-T-I-A-N. She's totally beautiful. With long, dark, curly hair, she's also got a tiny little birthmark under her lower lip just above her chin. She kinda reminds me of Brooke Shields from *The Blue Lagoon*. I found out in *Soap Opera Digest* that she just started on *Days of our Lives* about a year ago. Which makes me so mad I didn't tune in sooner because I'm totally in love with her!

I even joined her official Fan Club. For the modest fee of $12/year, I received: (a) a color 8" x 10" glossy photo, autographed in purple ink by Kristian Alfonso herself, (b) a T-shirt with a gorgeous black-and-white Kristian Alfonso on the front, (c) an "I ♥ Kristian Alfonso" bumper sticker, (d) a button/badge featuring the exact same photo as the autographed one, only in black-and-white, and (e) an official Kristian Alfonso Fan Club membership card—#1307.

This past Summer, I actually thought about starting my own Kristian Alfonso Fan Club when I first started watching *Days*. Kinda like Marcia Brady did for Davy Jones that one time. I'd be lying if I didn't admit that I secretly hoped one day Kristian Alfonso would show up at my front door and go to the Prom with me.

Too bad I was sadly informed of the existence of the "official" Kristian Alfonso Fan Club when I soon thereafter wrote to her in c/o *Days of our Lives*, asking permission to start my own. So I joined just a couple weeks ago, on August 24th.

Which brings me back to the Kristian Alfonso scrapbook . . .

"Sure," Brad says. "Let's see it."

I reach for the 3" brown photo album sitting on my desk. I've been cutting out articles about KA from *SOD* and pasting them inside. I've even got a bunch of pictures of her taped up next to my bed. This way, she's the last one I see before I fall asleep at night. My goal is to fill up the entire wall.

"Isn't she beautiful?" I can't help but beam with pride for the new Love of my Life.

"Totally," Brad agrees. Though he flips through the scrapbook in a matter of seconds. Then he tosses it aside like yesterday's *Detroit News.* "Okay . . . Now what?"

"Wanna listen to some records?" I reach for the brown faux-leather case where I keep my collection. Back in 5th grade, my Aunt Sonia bought me a $5 gift certificate for Harmony House. With it, I purchased such 45 RPM hits as "Centerfold" by J. Geils, "My Kinda Lover" by Billy Squier, "Keep on Lovin' You" by REO Speedwagon, and my favorite, "Don't Stop Believin'" by Journey. Though to this day I still haven't figured out where South Detroit is! I also really don't listen to that kinda music anymore. I've since been adding to my collection with more New Wave-kinda bands. Like Culture Club, Eurythmics, Thompson Twins, etc.

"Lemme see what you got." Brad grabs hold of the record box and begins pulling them out. One by one he tosses them aside, apparently not finding any to his liking.

"Careful with those!" I tell him. "You're so destructive sometimes."

To which Brad rolls his eyes. "I am not!" Then he exclaims, "Oh, my God . . . I *totally* love this one!" He hands me the record and I look at the label . . . "Johnny, Are You Queer?" by Josie Cotton. "Put it on," Brad orders. *"Today!"*

As much as I hate to, I do as my Best Friend tells me. Though this song is definitely *not* one of my favorites, don't ask me why!

Maybe it's because I can't stand the way Josie Cotton sings it. All nasal and whiny and annoying. Or maybe it's because the song reminds me of the very first Fun Night way back in 7th grade when I first met Lynn Kelly, the Love of my Life, and thought we had a Future. Or maybe it's because my real name happens to be John . . . Though nobody ever calls me "Johnny."

It also doesn't help when it gets to the "Johnny, are you queer?" part and Brad turns to me, singing along.

"Stop!" I demand that very instant.

The thing is . . . I'd never even heard the word "queer" or "fag" till two years ago. Before that, I was always the Most Popular Boy at Longfellow School. I *always* had girlfriends. Well, not "girlfriends." But friends who were *girls.* Then I got to Webb and all of a sudden people think I'm a fag, don't ask me why!

Maybe it's because I used to sit with a bunch of girls during Lunch every day back in 7th grade—one of them being Lynn Kelly, the Love of my Life. Or maybe it's because one time during Ms. Lemieux's Enriched English & Social Studies, I finished my class work early so I wrote out the entire lyrics to that "Valley Girl" song by Moon Unit Zappa on the board. Or maybe it's because I was at Lynn Kelly's house one Saturday afternoon and she invited a bunch of her friends over and word got around I was the only boy hanging out in a group of girls . . .

Though shouldn't that make me a Total Stud and not a Total Fag? I don't know. All I know is . . . *I* know I'm not.

Who cares what anybody else thinks?

She Bop

"We-hell- I see them every night in tight blue jeans
In the pages of a blue boy magazine . . ."

—Cyndi Lauper

"You wanna see it or what?"

Like Max Wilson and Lynn Kelly, Brad also lives in Ferndale. Which means technically he's not a Hazeltuckian. Like me. At this moment, his Mom's over visiting his Grandma with his two little sisters, Nina and Brittany. While his older sister, Janelle, is at the movies with her boyfriend, Ted. Which means nobody else is home at his house so we can pretty much do whatever we want.

Unfortunately, there's not a whole lot to do on the corner of Wanda and Webster at *Dayton's Depot*. Which is what the wooden sign Brad made in 7th grade Woodshop says that his Deadbeat Dad hung above the front door. First of all, their TV is black-and-white and they haven't got Cable. Forget about Atari or a VCR! I once offered to bring mine over. But when Brad asked his Mom if it was okay, I heard her say something about me being "arrogant." So I decided to forget the whole thing.

"What?" I reply in answer to Brad's question. Not like *What? I didn't hear you.* But like *What do you wanna know if I wanna see?*

"You *know* what," he says, giving me a look. Which he has every right to do.

I know *exactly* what Brad's asking me if I wanna see . . . It's the whole reason why I'm sitting here on his bedroom floor, futzing with a piece of fuzz or lint or something on the tannish-gray carpet.

"Where'd you find it, anyways?" I stall, looking around Brad's bedroom. Which is just off the kitchen at the back of the house. Even though it's a lot smaller than mine, at least he's got his own room. But he's got only the one single bed. Which is why I hardly ever spend the night over here 'cause *I'm* the one who gets stuck sleeping on the floor.

"Upstairs," he tells me. By which he means in his sister Janelle's bedroom. "I totally freaked out when I saw it."

"Where'd Janelle get it from?" I can't even believe she's in possession of such a horrendous thing.

"Her Best Friend, Lydia Cardoza, gave it to her for her Sweet Sixteen." Now Brad's the one futzing with a piece of fuzz or lint or something on his bedspread where he sits. "I thought it would be fun for us to look at it together . . . You know what I mean?"

My answer to that question would have to be "N-O."

"I always kinda wondered what they were like," Brad confesses. "Haven't you?"

I guess *maybe* I have . . . But still I worry. "Won't your sister know it's missing?"

"It's not like we're gonna keep it . . . Besides, Janelle's gonna be at the movies with Ted for at *least* another hour."

In case you have no idea what the heck we're talking about . . . Let me backtrack a little to this morning before 1st hour.

So there I was, digging through Brad's locker. Which is always a Total Mess. But I finally managed to locate my Band folder beneath a pile of his dirty Gym clothes. (Gross!)

You're probably wondering why all my books and folders are in Brad's locker when I have a perfectly good one of my own—#685. The answer is . . . He's been sharing it with me since the beginning of last year. Which is when I had the pleasure of meeting Craig Gershrowski. Better known as Fuck Face.

To make a *very* long story short . . . Fuck Face is an 8th grader who came to Webb last year. Apparently he went to elementary school with Lynn Kelly at Lee O. Clark and he's got a Total Crush on her. Which is why he got all mad when I called her one day after school while he was over trying to put the moves on her.

Apparently, word had gotten around that everybody at school thinks Brad and I are *both* Total Fags. Just because we're in Band. And we like to dance at Fun Nights. And we both have a lot of friends who are girls. Like Lynn Kelly. Who I was still totally in love with at the time. Which is what I told Fuck Face. Though why I thought I owed him any explanation, I have no idea. Well, when Fuck Face found that out, he decided to spend the good part of my second year in junior high amusing himself by calling me names.

Like Sissy Boy . . . And Queer Bait . . . Or my personal favorite, Faggot Ass Faggot.

What Craig Gershrowski didn't seem to get was . . . I liked Lynn Kelly. The way a boy is *supposed* to like a girl. So how could I possibly be a Faggot Ass Faggot?

After a month of having to look at his braces-wearing pizza-face in between classes—not to mention dealing with his off-color comments—Brad kindly offered to let me store my stuff in his locker.

Which is where I found myself standing as he finally rounded the corner this morning, totally out of breath.

"Oh, my God . . . You'll never guess what happened last night!"

"What?" I replied. Again, not like, *What? I didn't hear you.* But like, *What happened?* Brad sounded so serious, I was thinking maybe somebody died or something.

He practically shoved me aside to hang up his green and gold Warrior Marching Band windbreaker, panting. "So I'm upstairs in Big Boobs' room . . ." By whom he means his older sister, Janelle.

To which I said, "Dah-dah, dah-dah." Though I was totally tempted to reprimand him. I knew *exactly* what Brad was upstairs doing in Big Boobs' room . . . Smoking! Which he knows I do *not* condone one little bit.

"Dah-dah, dah-dah," he echoed, getting on with it. "So I'm sitting there in Janelle's room . . ." He gathered his thoughts along with his Band folder. "When I look over on her nightstand and I see it . . ." Then he trailed off.

"See what?"

Brad looked around the crowded hallway. Then he turned back to me and whispered, "A copy of *Playgirl!*" This he said as if it was the most horrifying thing in the whole wide world.

"So . . . ?" I said, totally out loud in my regular voice. I mean, what's the big deal, anyways? I've seen plenty of naked guys in the locker room at school. Not that I'm *looking* or anything.

"So . . ." Brad said, like he was totally about to wet himself. "Guess who was on the cover?"

"I don't know," I grumbled. Because I honestly had no idea. Maybe that guy from *Footloose*? He's pretty popular these days.

"Go on, Jack!" Brad prompted. "Take a wild guess."

"Would you just *tell* me, already?" I said, not wanting to guess wrong and look like a Total Fool. Then I slammed his locker door shut emphatically.

"*Somebody's* awfully cranky this morning," Brad said as we moved down the middle hallway en route to the Band Room.

"*Somebody* was up late last night," I complained.

"Doing what?" he asked, full of wink-wink/nudge-nudge innuendo.

"Catching up on *Days of our Lives* . . . I've been so busy practicing this week, I haven't had a chance to watch a single episode." Mrs. Putnam passed out a ton of new sheet music for our Christmas Concert in December. Which is still like two months away. But it'll be here before we know it.

"Busy practicing what?" Brad raised an eyebrow, giving me a look.

"My instrument."

"Which one?" he asked. "Skin flute?" By which he meant beating-off. Which he knows full well I *don't* do!

"Are you gonna tell me who you're talking about or what?" Now I was totally fed up. It's bad enough I've still got Craig Gershrowski hassling me. The other day, he pushed me into the girls' locker room. Right when Ava Reese and Carrie Johnson were in there changing for Gym. I didn't need my Best Friend giving me a hard time!

"Take it easy, you Big Baby," Brad teased. "I'll tell you." Then he added, "You're not gonna believe it," ever so dramatically.

"Probably not," I said, rounding the corner past the Guidance Counseling Office. I sneaked a peek through the glass doors looking for Audrey. By whom I mean my new friend, Audrey Wojczek, 1st hour Office Aide.

Sure enough, I spied a mass of long flaming hair behind the counter. Even though I know the School Secretary frowns upon it, I knocked on the glass. Audrey looked up from her filing, caught my eye, and waved for me to stop in. I gave Mickey Mouse a tap upon my wrist as I was about to be late for class. At which point, Audrey rubbed the inside corner of her eye. With her middle finger! It's a lucky thing I knew she was only kidding around. Otherwise, I'd probably have taken offense. Instead, I waved good-bye and continued down the hallway with Brad . . . Who'd been yakking a mile a minute this entire time.

"Isn't that incredible?"

"Isn't what incredible?" I asked, missing the whole point of the story.

"Forget it," Brad snapped, totally annoyed. "I hate it when you do that." Then he charged down the hallway ahead of me.

"Br-a-a-d . . ." I called after him. "I thought you were gonna tell me who's on the cover of your sister's *Playgirl!*"

Which got his attention and 'round he spun. "Would you shut your big fat trap?" he hissed. "How would you like it if I told the whole school about your parents' Sex Drawer?" By which he meant the bottom drawer of my Mom's dresser, where this past Summer, we somehow found this dirty paperback called *Pretty Penny* when Brad was over spending the night. Which was all about this slutty teenager named—what else?—Penny, and her sexual misadventures.

I could tell Brad totally wanted me to beg. Which is why I said, "I'll be your Best Friend." Even though he knows I already am. Which is why he finally gave in and told me what was up . . .

"None other than JEH." By whom he meant Jon-Erik Hexum. "I almost died when I saw it was him . . . Can you believe it?"

In case you don't know—because he's not *that* famous—Jon-Erik Hexum is an actor. You might remember him from a TV show called *Voyagers!* In which he played this Time Traveler named Phineas Bogg. But maybe not. The show only ran for like one season. I used to watch it with my Dad on Sunday nights at 7:00 PM back when I was in 7th grade.

The reason Brad seemed so amazed by all of this was . . . Just the other night we were talking on the phone and he started telling me all about this made-for-TV movie called *Making of a Male Model.* Starring Joan Collins and JEH.

In the movie, Joan Collins plays Kay Dillon, a successful modeling agency owner in search of a new Hunk to represent. Enter Jon-Erik Hexum as Tyler Burnett, a corn-fed farm boy who Kay transforms into the hottest male model of all time. According to Brad, it's "sooo good!"

"I just read he's on some new TV series," I say, remembering I saw something somewhere about JEH making a comeback. "With Jennifer O'Neill, I think."

"Never heard of her," snarled Brad. "What's the show called?"

"*Cover Up,*" I answered. "It's all about this detective guy who goes under cover as a male model."

"That's gotta be him!" he declared, totally psyched.

Which explains why nine hours later, we're on our way up the stairs leading to Big Boobs Janelle's bedroom. In search of a copy of *Playgirl* magazine . . . "Entertainment for Women."

The funny thing about Janelle and her boobs is . . . whenever we're in Brad's room and we hear her coming down the stairs, she's always like, "Ouch! Ouch! Ouch!" With every step. Holding on to her breasts in pain. Brad says one of these days, she's gonna give herself a couple of black eyes!

He picks up the magazine from the nightstand. Right where he said it would be. I catch a glimpse of the blue cover with yellow letters . . . *"COVER UP" STAR* JON-ERIK HEXUM: TV'S SEXIEST BODY BARES HIS MIND. I can't even believe Brad's sister left it lying out in the open like that. Their Mom is *very* religious. Somehow, I don't think she'd approve of her 16-year-old daughter looking at *Playgirl.* Or her 14-year-old son and his Best Friend, for that matter!

"Here," says Brad, handing it to me.

I take note of the tan suit jacket and blue open-collared shirt

JEH is wearing on the cover. Which perfectly matches his bright blue eyes. "Let's go back to your room," I whisper. Not that anybody else is home to hear me. But there's something about being up in Janelle's bedroom that totally creeps me out.

Maybe it's because it's her Personal Private Space and we have no right to be nosing around in it. Or maybe it's because her room is kinda like an attic, with the kinda ceiling that's slanted on both sides because of the roof. Or maybe it's because on the slanted ceiling itself, Janelle's hung up a bunch of posters of half-naked Chippendales dancers.

Maybe it's just me. But I feel kinda weird looking at them. Not weird-weird, but . . . like I've already said, I don't judge other guys. But some of them are so good-looking, it totally makes me wanna puke! They've all got these totally muscular, totally perfect bodies. I swear they must work out at least five hours per day.

I have no idea why we're doing this. But here we are again, back in Brad's room . . .

"Open it," he says, encouraging me. "Go on . . ."

We're sitting side by side on his bed with the November 1984 issue of *Playgirl* resting between our laps, listening to Cyndi Lauper singing her latest on 96.3 WHYT. I begin turning the pages, passing by columns titled *Intimacy File—Whose Fantasy is it Anyway?*, *Health—Organic Groceries: Super Health or Super Hype?*, and *Arts and Entertainment—Michael Jackson: Sweet and Sexy, He's Pop's Greatest Thriller.* The only thing I don't see are any naked guys.

"Keep going," Brad tells me when I question this.

I turn another page, only to find a Sex Quiz. Followed by an article on "Sexual Variety." Followed by a full-page ad for English Leather Musk cologne, in which a good-looking, cheesy-mustached guy with a totally hairy chest to match, wears *nothing* but a Santa Claus hat and a smile.

"'He Knows If You've Been Good,'" I read. "'So Be Good for Goodness Sake.'" *Oh, brother!*

"Oh, my God . . . Look at him!" Brad gasps.

Of course, I can't help but notice the guy's got a totally big dick.

"Do you think *we'll* look like that when we grow up?" he asks me. "He's pretty cute, right?"

To which I reply, "I don't judge other guys," 'cause I don't. Though I admit, "I wouldn't mind *looking* like him."

"Well," Brad begins, "if you were a *girl*, would you think he's cute?"

Which is a fair question to ask, I suppose. "If I was a *girl*?" I say. "I guess I might . . . Would you?"

"Probably," he answers. "I mean, if I was a girl." Then he flips the page and *totally* starts freaking out. "Oh, my God . . . That guy's got a hard-on!"

"Gross!" I say, turning my entire head away from the page. "I can't even believe they can show that kinda stuff."

"I know . . . It's *totally* disgusting," Brad agrees. But when I reach out to turn the page, he places his hand on the magazine to stop me. Then he practically shouts in my ear, "Wait . . . Lemme see that again!"

So I turn the page back . . . And we stare at it . . . For just a few minutes more.

Page after page, we continue flipping through. Naked guy after naked guy after naked guy. Finally, we come to *Playgirl*'s Man for November. A blond-haired, blue-eyed Hunk with a small patch of hair sprouting in the center of his chest sports a blue unbuttoned denim shirt with the sleeves rolled up. His name's Jeffrey Erickson. But neither of us has ever seen or heard of him before.

"What would you think of him," Brad asks, "if you were a girl, I mean?"

"If I was a girl?" I say. "I'd think he was okay, I guess."

"Just okay?" he asks, suddenly skeptical of my taste in men.

"I think I'd think the other one is cuter," I confess. By whom I mean the guy on the page before last. The one with the dark hair, dark eyes, and *smooth* chest.

"You would?" says Brad, making a face. "I'd think my guy is *much* cuter than yours."

After another ten minutes or so I have to ask, "So what about JEH?" I mean, he's the reason we're even looking at this trash in the first place! "Isn't he in here somewhere?"

"Duh!" Brad says. Like I'm a Total Idiot. "He wouldn't be on the cover if he wasn't, would he?" He takes hold of the magazine, flips to page 30, and exclaims, "Tah dah!" Like he's David Copperfield making the Statue of Liberty vanish on TV. Then he presents the magazine to me again. This time with a flourish.

I'm totally unimpressed.

Sure, there's a picture of Jon-Erik Hexum all oiled up, one bulging bicep behind his head, shirt off. On the opposite page he wears a black tuxedo, *cigarette* in hand—don't even tell me he smokes! But in no way is he *naked*.

"That's it?"

"What do you mean?" replies Brad. Again, like I'm a Total Idiot.

I skim through the four-page article all about how JEH is the "male answer to Christie Brinkley" and how he turned down roles on *The Dukes of Hazzard* and *CHiPs* before ever doing *Voyagers!* Both of which I had no idea about. Another interesting fact I learn is . . . He went to Michigan State University. Which is where I've been thinking about applying to college after I graduate from Hillbilly High. Which isn't till June 1988, and seems like a bijillion years from now!

There are also pictures of JEH from *Cover Up*, wearing army fatigues and holding a machine gun. And another with Joan

Collins in *Making of a Male Model.* But again, in no way is he naked in *any* of them!

"I thought the whole point of *Playgirl* is naked guys," I reiterate.

"All the *other* guys are naked," Brad affirms.

"Yeah . . . But who cares about them? They're Total Nobodies."

To which Brad informs me, "My sister Janelle says they *never* show full frontal of the celebrities . . . It's bad for their careers."

To which I reply, "That is sooo lame . . . They could at least show his butt!" Then I toss the magazine aside. "What a Total Rip-off!"

After all of about five seconds, Brad gets up from the bed. "Be right back."

"Where are you going?" I inquire.

"To the bathroom." He starts out of the room. Then he crosses back to where *Playgirl* has landed in the corner. "I might be a while," he tells me, picking the trashy magazine up off the floor. "I better take something with me to read."

And away he goes!

Bless You Boys

"Bless You Boys
This is the year . . ."

—Curtis Gadson, Saturday Night Music Machine winner

It appears that Christmas has come early to the Motor City.

For the first time in 16 years—on October 14, 1984—Detroiters can finally say, "We're #1!" At least when it comes to Major League Baseball.

"Jackie, get in here!" my Dad calls out from our living room. He and my Mom have gathered in front of the TV with my Aunt Sonia and Uncle Mark, cheering the Home Team on to V-I-C-T-O-R-Y. "The Tigers just won the World Series!"

A chorus of hoots and hollers erupts from the Peanut Gallery. Outside, a dozen car horns blare blissfully. Followed by my Aunt Sonia's enthusiastic words, "Bless—You—Boys!"

I only hope she doesn't start singing that stupid song! Ever since the Tigers found themselves on a winning streak this season, it's been *all* over the radio. From WHYT to WRIF, you can't escape it.

Just then our telephone rings . . .

"Hello?" I answer.

"Put your clothes on . . . *Now.*" I instantly recognize Brad's bellow. "I mean it, Jack . . . Get dressed," he orders. "We'll be over in fifteen minutes to pick you up."

"Where are we going?" I ask.

"Cruising Woodward." By which Brad means Woodward Avenue. The main thoroughfare from the city of Detroit leading out to the suburbs. Also known as M-1.

"But I'm watching TV with my brother," I inform him. We had just sat down to watch the conclusion of the NBC epic miniseries *V: The Final Battle*. Starring Marc Singer and Faye Grant. Who just so happens to be a graduate of Lake Shore High School in St. Clair Shores, another suburb of Detroit.

"Who cares? They're throwing a *huge* parade for the Tigers and my Mom's taking us."

"Downtown?" I question, knowing Detroit's reputation as the "Murder Capital of the World."

"Don't be such a Pussy," Brad teases. Which is the first time I've ever heard him use the P-word in all the time I've known him.

"Who's all going?" I ask. Not that it matters. It still isn't safe.

"Me, my Mom, and my sisters."

"What about Max?"

"Fuck Max," says Brad. "He's too busy hanging out with Dickhead." By whom he means Tom Fulton, this Jock who used to be one of Max's Best Friends back in elementary school at Webster. Ever since he started wearing contacts and got a decent haircut, Tom's been a Total Jerk to me and Brad both.

I remember one time back in 7th grade, me and Max and Brad were over Tom's house hanging out one Saturday afternoon. We had a Total Blast, playing Atari and calling the Party

Line and stuff. We even got Tom to pretend his name was Tammy and talk to one of the guys. And boy was he good at it . . . He came up with some totally wild things to say, which I won't even repeat. Too bad when we got back to school on Monday, I tried talking to him during Ms. Lemieux's 6th & 7th hour Enriched English & Social Studies, and he totally blew me off!

I can't even believe Tom's going with Marie Sperling now. She used to be all Little Miss Innocent, back in 7th grade. I swear, you could tell her a joke in 1st hour and she wouldn't start laughing till 5th. Even though she's always been a Total Sweetheart, none of the Popular Guys wanted anything to do with her. Then last Summer, puberty kicked in and BAM!

Now that I think of it . . . Marie kinda reminds me of Kristian Alfonso. Whom I'm still totally in love with. She's gotta be the most beautiful girl I've ever seen in my entire life. Every night before I go to bed, I pray that one day I'll find a girlfriend who's as beautiful as Kristian Alfonso. If only that could happen, I know I'd be set. Then I could prove to all those Jock Jerks out there—like Fuck Face Craig Gershrowski—that I'm not . . . *You know.*

With regards to the Tigers' Parade, I start to tell Brad, "I don't know . . ."

It's not that I don't care about the World Series, don't get me wrong. Even though I'm not technically a Sports Fan, I have a fond affinity for the Detroit Tigers. Back in 4th grade, my Dad used to take me to Tiger Stadium all the time. I'd sit there in the bleachers with my program on my lap, memorizing all the players' names *and* their numbers: #1—Lou Whitaker, #3—Alan Trammell, #4—Aurelio Rodriguez, who was always my Aunt Sonia's favorite 'cause he wore patent leather shoes. Not to mention #8—Ron LeFlore, #10—Rusty Staub, #13—Lance Parrish, #19—Dave Rozema, #33—Steve Kemp.

But partying with a bunch of strangers in Downtown Detroit of all places is the last thing I wanna be doing . . .

"Come on!" Brad practically begs. "The Tigers haven't won the World Series since like 1965."

"1968," I correct, only knowing this fact because my Dad's been stressing it this entire season.

"It could be the Year 2000 before they ever make it to the World Series again," he tells me. "And by that time, we'll be too old to even care."

"Okay . . ." God forbid I should miss out. Which is why I have no other choice but to give in and agree to go along.

"Awesome!" Brad cheers. "We'll be right over." Then he throws in, "We gotta pick Bobby up first." By whom he could only mean Bobby Russell. As in *Dear Bobby* . . . from the letter Mr. Grant read aloud to us in the cafeteria at the beginning of 7th grade.

In case I haven't mentioned it . . . Bobby happens to live just four blocks away from me on the other side of John R, over on Moorhouse. Across I-75 from where he went to elementary school at Roosevelt with Symphonic Band 2nd chair clarinet Carrie Johnson. Though I couldn't figure out why he'd be coming along with us. I mean, he's been in Band with me and Brad for the past two years. But it's not like either of us is friends with him.

Which is why I have to ask, "Why's Bobby Russell coming?"

To which Brad replies, "I don't know . . . What's the big deal?"

"No big deal." Though Brad knows how much I can't stand Bobby Russell. I mean, he sits right next to me in Band. But whenever I see him outside of class, he acts like he doesn't even know who I am. Probably because every time he's challenged me for 1st chair, he's always lost.

But because I'm the bigger person I say, "Hey, Bobby," as I crawl into the backseat of Brad's Mom's tan little K-Car fifteen minutes later . . .

“ ’s up, Jackie?” says Bobby, chomping a huge wad of grape Bubble Yum, barely looking at me. He’s too preoccupied acting ever so cool in his sea green hospital scrubs, left arm draped over the back of the front seat where he sits with Janelle—and her boobs—on his lap.

“Where’s Ted?” I ask nobody in particular. Just to remind Bobby of the presence of Ted Baniszewski in Janelle Dayton’s life.

“Work,” Janelle answers matter-of-factly.

Like her brother, Janelle Dayton’s got reddish-brown hair. Though hers is a lot bigger and curlier. According to Brad, she’s got way more freckles than he does. But she wears so much makeup, you can hardly tell. Don’t get me wrong, she is kinda hot. Though maybe it’s just her boobs.

We drive west on 8 Mile towards Woodward listening to Ernie “The Voice of the Tigers” Harwell recapping tonight’s World Series victory: “After a disappointing loss in San Diego on Wednesday night, the Tigers were back in Motown where they defeated the Padres in games three and four at Tiger Stadium.

“Hopes ran high for the Home Team tonight as right fielder, Kirk Gibson, dropped two bombs into the upper decks in the 1st and 8th innings, in addition to stealing home in the 5th on a shallow fly ball to right field.

“Catcher Lance Parrish also sent one bouncing into the bleachers and relievers Aurelio Lopez and Willie Hernandez held the Padres at bay for the 8–4 victory. Manager Sparky Anderson has become the first skipper to guide two separate franchises to World Series victories after winning with the National League’s Cincinnati Reds in both ’75 and ’76. Congratulations also go out to series MVP, shortstop Alan Trammell.”

“Hey J,” I hear Bobby say to Janelle, “wha’s up with Ted and the job?”

“He said, ‘No problem,’ ” Janelle replies.

To which Bobby says, "Cool."

"What job?" I ask, being nosy.

"Ted's getting me and Bobby jobs at Country Boy's," Brad announces. Which is this Total Dive diner on the corner of 9 Mile and Vassar. Though in all the years I've lived in Hazeltucky, I don't think I've ever once set foot inside.

So I ask, "What kinda jobs?"

"Busboys . . . $2.92 an hour to start, plus tips."

Then I say, "How come you didn't ask me if I wanted a job?" Not because I want or need one. But because this is the first I've heard about it and I wanna know why my Best Friend is keeping secrets from me.

"Please!" Brad groans. "I can just see you working as a busboy, Jack."

Even though he's right—I could *never* do such menial labor—I tell him, "You still could've asked."

The drive down Woodward ends up more of a traffic jam than an actual "parade." In fact, the ones doing all the parading are us fans. Not a Detroit Tiger is anywhere in sight. But what I fear might turn into a re-creation of the '67 Cass Corridor Riots amounts to a huge par-tay in the streets.

I can't even explain how totally cool it is to see so many people celebrating together. Black, white, Caldean, you name it . . . All thanks to the "Roar of '84!"

Of course, Brad's Mom—Laura Victor-Dayton-Victor, having gone back to using her maiden name since divorcing Brad's Deadbeat Dad—is a nervous wreck the entire time she's behind the wheel. Hands at 10 and 2. Staring straight ahead.

"Br-a-a-d," she drawls in her Alabama accent. "You boys be careful, you hear me?" To which she's referring to the fact that Brad and Bobby are now totally hanging out the passenger window. Meanwhile, I'm crammed in the backseat with little sisters Nina and Brittany.

We're just about in the heart of Motown at this point. Down on Woodward near I-75. All four lanes are *jammed* with people. Shouting, cheering, rejoicing. It's hard to even tell there's a road ahead of us to drive on, it's so packed.

An older black man clad in the official Kirk Gibson #23 pinstriped jersey shouts, "We did it!" As if his sitting at home watching on TV had anything to do with the Tigers' victory. Then he High-Fives both Bobby and Brad before launching them into a chant of "Bless—You—Boys!"

I only hope they don't start singing that stupid song!

To our right, I see a glow of red. Which must be the Fox Theatre marquis. On the left, searchlights from the parking lot crisscross the cloudy sky. Woodward Avenue is a Sea of People and our tan little K-Car is Moses, parting it.

I've gotta admit, despite all the excitement surrounding me, I'm a little p.o.'d. Brad's barely talked to me this entire time. From the minute I got in the car back at my house, he and Bobby have been like proverbial peas in a pod . . . What's up with that?

Personally, I don't see what's so hot about Bobby Russell: #1—he's got braces; #2—he's got bleached blond hair, spiked on top, à la Billy Idol. Which wouldn't be so bad except for #3—he's also got a totally stupid six-inch dyed black tail hanging down from the back.

I mean, maybe he *used* to be kinda cute when he was younger. I saw a yearbook picture Carrie Johnson had of him from back when they went to Roosevelt together and he didn't look so bad. But that was before he broke out with acne. And started smoking!

"Now what?" Laura says to nobody in particular.

Looks like we've come to the end of the line. Woodward and Elizabeth. Next to a totally cool old-fashioned diner, complete with neon sign, called the Elwood Bar & Grill.

"Why can't we take Jefferson back?" Brad asks.

"That's what I was *planning* to do," his Mom replies, totally frustrated. "They won't let us through." Ahead, we can see the cops blocking off the rest of the avenue.

"Fucking pigs!" Bobby Russell shouts out his window at the Men in Blue.

I see Laura give him a look. Though she doesn't say anything. I've got a feeling she doesn't care for Bobby Russell either.

"What are we gonna do, Mom?" Brad asks.

"I don't know, Bradley!" she snaps. The tension in the car is starting to rival that of the throng outside.

"How are we gonna get home, Mommy?" Brittany cries out.

"Mommy, I'm scared!" Nina chimes in.

"Please sit and be quiet . . . Everybody!"

Poor Laura . . . All of a sudden the whistle from a traffic cop is blown, totally freaking her out. We can see the officer giving us the "Turn Your Vehicle Around" hand signal. Which means we have no other choice but to head back up Woodward, through the traffic jam towards Ferndale/Hazel Park.

At which point, Laura sticks her head out the window. "Officer?" she says demurely, all the while trying to maintain control of the steering wheel *and* keep the screaming kids in her car under control. "Can you pretty please help us?"

Now here's the thing about Laura Dayton . . . The woman is a Total Looker! I can't even tell you how many guys at school have commented on how hot she is.

One time, I went shopping at Oakland Mall with her and Brad and we ran into this guy from school, Rob Berger. Who's actually pretty cool, for a Jock. The next day in Mr. Davidson's 4th hour Biology, Rob was all like, "Who was the Total Babe you and Brad Dayton were at the Mall with yesterday?"

And I was like, "Um . . . She's his *Mom.*"

"Get the fuck out!" Rob Berger said. Like he couldn't even believe it.

Which is why all Laura has to do now is bat her eyes at Mr. Traffic Cop and she'll have us out of here in a jiffy . . .

"I need to get my children and their friends home to bed," she explains when he leans in the window. Trying to get a closer look at the Hot Momma, I'm sure. "It's a School Night, you know?"

To which Mr. Traffic Cop replies, "Of course, Ma'am." With a wink and a smile. Then he throws in, "Would you mind my asking where the children's father is this evening?"

"I have no idea," Laura smiles. "We're no longer married."

Ding-ding-ding!

Mr. Traffic Cop pulls back the blue and white "Do Not Cross" barrier, allowing divorcée Laura Victor-Dayton-Victor, her four children, and their two friends to pass in her tan little K-Car.

"He sure was handsome," Brad's Mom sighs. In the rearview mirror, I see her smiling to herself, knowing she's still got "It."

"Didn't he look just like Ponch from *CHiPs?*" adds Brad.

I take a peek out the back window, deciding the cop wasn't *that* great. I mean, I used to be a big *CHiPs* fan back in like 3rd grade, and he was no Erik Estrada! In fact, my Best Friend at the time, Joey Palladino, and I used to watch the show every Saturday night and talk about it on Monday in Mrs. Fox's class. We were always arguing over who was cooler, Ponch or John. I always picked Ponch, of course.

Too bad Joey's family moved away the Summer after 6th grade 'cause his parents didn't want him going to school in Hazeltucky anymore. Now he lives in Clarkston—way out past 30 Mile—and I've only seen him a couple times since he left. At first, we kept in touch all the time, running up our parents' phone bills talking once or twice a week. But after we both got to junior high and made new friends, we pretty much stopped. Which is a Total Bummer because up till Brad came along, Joey was like my Best Friend ever.

"That cop totally wanted you," Bobby says to Laura, trying to smooth-talk her.

To which she gives him another look. I've got a feeling Laura really doesn't care for Bobby Russell at all. And I don't blame her . . . He's a Total Loser!

So how come he doesn't wanna be *my* friend?

Holding Out For A Hero

"Where have all the good men gone?
And where are all the gods?"

—Bonnie Tyler

"Oh, my God . . . Did you see the News?"

Four days later, I'm home in my bedroom talking to Brad on my brand new telephone. Which is just an extension, but still . . . Finally, I've got some privacy!

"I did," I say in Total Shock. "I can't even believe it."

We both just got the official word from Channel 7's Bill Bonds . . . "TV star Jon-Erik Hexum has died."

Apparently, JEH got bored while on the set of *Cover Up*. So between takes, he started fooling around, putting a .44 Magnum prop gun up to his head. "Let's see if I've got one for me," he joked. Which became his Famous Last Words as he pulled the trigger.

The impact from the blank fractured his skull, sending a quarter-inch thick fragment into his brain. After being rushed to a nearby hospital where he underwent emergency surgery, he slipped into a coma. With his mother's permission, Jon-Erik was flown to

Las Vega$ today—October 18, 1984—where he was taken off life support and died peacefully. His organs are being donated at his request. He was three weeks shy of his 27th birthday.

"I can't even imagine living for only twelve more years," Brad sighs, holding back tears.

"I know . . . I've got a bijillion things I wanna do with my life still."

We observe a Moment of Silence. Then Brad says, "You know . . . I been thinking . . ." Then he trails off.

"About?"

"About how JEH died."

Knowing we both already know all about it, I say, " 'member? It was an accident."

"Yeah . . . But maybe it wasn't," Brad speculates. "Maybe he did it on *purpose.*"

Which is the dumbest thing I've ever heard. "What reason could JEH possibly have for wanting to kill himself?"

"Well," says Brad hesitantly. "Maybe he was a Big Fag and he couldn't take it anymore . . . You know what I mean?"

"No . . ."

"Think about it, Jack," he advises me. "I mean, here he was, this totally gorgeous guy . . . Rich and famous . . . And he doesn't have a *girlfriend?*"

"What about Emma Samms from *Dynasty?*" I point out. "They were together a lot."

"I know . . ." Brad replies, hesitating again. "But maybe that was just a cover up . . . You know what I mean?" Then he gasps at the realization he's come to. "Just like the name of the TV show JEH was on when he died!"

To which I'm like, "I never thought about it that way."

And Brad's like, "Maybe that's why he did it." Totally hypothesizing. "Maybe he couldn't keep it a secret anymore . . . Maybe it was eating away at him inside . . . And instead of dealing with it, he decided to kill himself and make it *look* like an accident."

"Yeah . . ." I start to say. "But do you really think JEH could have been . . . ?" Now I have to hesitate a moment. Brad and I *hate* to use that word. By which I mean the G-word, don't ask me why!

Maybe it's because of the way it looks when you write it out. With the downward tail of the "g" and the downward tail of the "y" and the teeny-tiny "a" stuck there all alone in the middle. Or maybe it's because Brad and I both know it's not a Nice Word and neither of our Moms would approve of us using it. Or maybe it's because we've both had it directed at us more times over the past two years than we care to remember.

So instead, I use our favorite euphemism . . . *"Like that?"*

"It's possible," Brad answers. "You know what I mean?"

So I think about it . . . JEH was this totally rugged and masculine guy. How could he possibly be *like that*?

"Please!" Brad snorts when I question his thinking. "Haven't you ever seen the Village People? My sister Janelle says they're *all* Big Fags and look at them."

I can't even believe that mustached guy I saw on Dick Clark's *Rockin' New Year's Eve* back in like 1979-going-into-1980 with the hard hat and tool belt is G-A-Y. Which is exactly what I tell Brad next.

"Yep," he confirms. "Total Fag."

To which I have nothing left to say.

"You know what else I been thinking?" says Brad again. "Maybe I could come over and we can hold a séance on Devil's Night."

In case you don't know . . . This is October 30th in Detroit. When people go out soaping car windows and TP-ing houses before burning them down. All in the name of good Night-Before-Halloween fun.

"That way," Brad continues, "we can communicate with JEH and ask him the *real* reason he did it." By which he means shot himself in the head.

"Do you even know *how* to do a séance?" I have to ask.

"Sure," he informs me. Like it's no big deal. "I saw Ginger do one on *Gilligan's Island* before . . . All you need are some candles and some photos . . ." Both of which he promises to bring along with him. "And then you just do a chant."

I can just imagine Brad burning my parents' house down. Still, I guess I *would* like to know. Especially if it's because JEH was *like that*. Not that I'd care or anything, 'cause I wouldn't.

Which explains why I've let Brad talk me into coming over my house twelve days later, to conduct his so-called séance . . .

Though he's late.

He was *supposed* to meet me in front of Hardee's up on John R across from Farmer Jack's at 8:30 PM. Which is where we always meet each other, halfway between both our houses. But looking at my watch now, it's almost 8:40 PM.

Ten minutes later he pulls up on his 24" lime green Schwinn 10-speed, a look of terror on his face. "You afraid Jason's gonna get you or something?" I ask. "Or maybe Michael Meyers?" Considering tomorrow's Halloween, it seems more fitting.

"Shut up, Mr. Still-Sleeps-With-a-Night-Light-On!" Brad retaliates. Like a Total Baby. Then he whines, "I totally got egged on my way over here." He shows me the yellow splatter on the back of his green and gold Warrior Marching Band windbreaker.

"You're the one who wanted to leave your house on Devil's Night," I remind him.

"Today!" Brad indicates for me to hop on the back of the hand-me-down he recently got from his sister Janelle's boyfriend, Ted. The frame's a bit rusty and the brakes kinda squeak. The tires are also a little wobbly. But at least Brad's got a way to get to his job at Country Boy's and to my house whenever he wants.

I climb on back of the torn leather seat, taking care not to get egg yolk all over my navy blue hooded sweatshirt I got at Blue Lake Fine Arts Camp the Summer before last. Suddenly Brad snaps, "Watch it!" Totally scaring the crap out of me.

"What the Hell is your problem?" I wonder.

"You wanna get stabbed?" He shows me the Ginsu steak knife he's got tucked into his back jeans pocket. Which I can't even believe he's actually wearing in public.

About a week ago, Brad had a little accident while doing his laundry. After spilling an entire cup of Clorox on the left knee of his new black jeans, instead of pitching them in the trash or giving them to Goodwill or the Salvation Army like any normal person would, he decided to get creative. By dipping the *entire* left pant leg in a bucket of bleach, thus turning them white! Then when he came waltzing into Old Lady McKenzie's Civics class the next day feeling all fashionable, she took one look down her nose at him and groaned, "What is *that?*"

Which is what I ask Brad now, with regards to the Ginsu . . . Though I can only imagine why he's brought it along.

"For Protection."

"Oh, Brad . . . You are sooo dramatic," I sigh. Then I grab hold of his waist for dear life and we begin pedaling down the block.

Back at my house . . .

We start the so-called séance by placing the cut out non-naked photos of JEH—compliments of Big Boobs Janelle and *Teen Beat* magazine—around a makeshift shrine of candles we've set up on the floor in front of my TV. Then we put a very special record on my turntable . . . Bonnie Tyler's "Holding out for a Hero." Which happens to be the theme song from the JEH/ Jennifer O'Neill *Cover Up* TV show, in case you're not aware.

"God, he was a Total Babe!" Brad gushes. Like a Total Girl. "Wasn't he, Jack?"

Looking at all the photos spread out on display in front of me, there's no denying that Jon-Erik Hexum was an attractive man. With his dark curly hair, chiseled jaw, and sculpted muscular body . . . But I say nothing.

"If you were a *girl*, would you think he was a babe?" asks Brad.

"If I was a *girl?*" I reply. "Sure, I would."

I watch as Brad pulls out a purple Bic lighter from his denim duffle bag—the one he made himself in Mrs. Wood's 7th grade Sewing. One by one, he begins lighting the candles. Making the room even more ooky-spooky as they reflect off my TV screen.

"God, I loved his voice!" Brad gushes again. "It was so deep and sexy."

Watching the candle flames flicker in the darkness, I say nothing.

"I wish *my* voice sounded like that."

Again, I say nothing.

"I still can't believe he shot himself," Brad sighs. "I mean, what was he *thinking* putting a gun up to his head? What a waste!" Then he reaches into his duffle bag once more. This time, he removes a raggedy pink bath towel.

"What are you doing?" I ask, having no idea what Brad's got planned next.

He stands up, bends over at the waist, wraps the towel around his head. The *exact* same way my Mom does after she washes her hair in the kitchen sink in the morning. Then he stands upright, flings his head back, and announces, "Okay . . . I'm ready." But he's quick to add, "Are you *sure* your parents went to bed?" For the bijillionth time.

"Their bedroom door was shut," I answer. For the bijillionth time.

"Maybe they're just having sex?"

"I doubt it." I know for a fact that can't be the case. "My

parents only have sex on Saturdays," I tell Brad. Like clockwork. Which is something I don't even wanna think about. (Gross!)

"Did you put your ear up to the door?"

I give Brad a look—head tilted, forehead crinkled, nostrils flared. "Are we gonna do this, or what?"

"Okay, okay," he snarls. "Jeez!" He sits back down beside me. Then he says, "Gimme your hand."

To which I immediately respond, "I don't wanna hold your hand!"

Brad gives me the exact same look I just gave him. "It's how you gotta do it," he says, informing me of the strict rules to performing a séance. "We gotta channel all our energy into making JEH appear to us." He reaches his hand out. I reluctantly take it, noting how rough and callous-y it feels. In all the time I've known Brad Dayton, I don't think I've ever held his hand. I also notice the yellowish stain on his right middle finger . . . from all the nicotine in his cigarettes!

But I say nothing about his filthy, filthy habit.

"Now close your eyes," he instructs, all mysterious-like, "and concentrate."

I sit quietly in the ensuing silence, doing my best to think Happy JEH Thoughts . . . Till I hear what can only be described as the sound of a dying cow.

"Ohm . . . Ohm . . ."

I peek open my right eye, only to find Brad—eyes closed/pink towel around his head looking like a Total Dweeb—*chanting*. Like a Buddhist monk. Or whoever it is that chants.

"J . . . E . . . H," he says, drawing out each individual letter in his best Ginger-Grant-from-*Gilligan's-Island* voice. "Can you hear me?"

Nothing happens . . .

"Hello?"

"This is never gonna work," I tell him adamantly. "Why are

we even doing this? Why should we care about resurrecting the spirit of some dead actor-guy, anyways?"

Totally calm, Brad does his best to explain his reasoning to me—still as Tina Louise. "JEH won't show himself," he coos, "if he thinks you don't believe." Then he continues with the "ohms" while I continue to sit, eyes closed. "Jon-Erik Hexum," Brad says, this time employing the full moniker. "If you're out there, give us a sign."

Nothing happens . . .

"Knock three times to let us know you're there," he continues.

Nothing happens . . .

Brad assures him, "There's nothing to be afraid of." Then he adds, "We want to help you . . . We want to know the truth. Why did you leave us? Were you afraid? Afraid of who you really were? Afraid of what you were feeling deep down inside of you?"

"Gimme a break!" I mutter.

"You can trust us, Jon-Erik," Brad promises. "We won't tell *anybody* your secret."

Suddenly from out of the darkness . . . There comes a knock!

"Holy shit!" Brad jumps a mile. "Did you hear that?" Then he looks around the room for some kinda Presence looming in the dark. "Hell-ooo! Is anybody there?"

Another knock . . . Then another . . . And another.

"Jon-Erik Hexum, is that—?" Brad stops. Which is when he catches me knocking on the side of my put-it-together-yourself Sauder faux-wood laminated TV stand. *"Ja-a-ack!"* Then he pushes me—hard.

"Ow!" I practically holler, holding my shoulder in pain. "That hurt."

"I can't believe you did that," he scolds. "You totally had me freaked out . . . I thought it was really him."

"I'm sorry," I apologize. "I couldn't help it." But it's not like I didn't tell Brad what a dumb idea I thought it was from the get-go. And to twist the proverbial knife *and* pour salt on the proverbial open wound, I add, "This is sooo stupid!"

"No, it's not!" he vehemently declares.

"Yes, it is!"

"Well it's your fault if it doesn't work," Brad insists, placing the blame right where it belongs. It *is* totally my fault because I *don't* think it's gonna work. And I tell him so.

He hisses at me, "Nonbeliever!" Then he shuts his eyes and starts in again with the chanting. "Ohm . . . Ohm . . ."

Because I can't possibly sit here for a minute longer—along with the fact that it's getting late *and* it's a School Night—I come up with a quick way to get myself out of this . . .

"Oh, no!" I cry, in my best "Now *I'm* getting freaked out" voice. Then I jump up and pull the string on the overhead ceiling fan/lamp, flooding the room with light. "I just thought of something."

"What?" says Brad, eyes still closed. Remaining in what he calls "character."

"What if this really works?" I wonder. "Then what are we gonna do?"

"Um . . ." he replies. "That's the point, isn't it?"

"Yeah . . . But what if something happens to us?"

Which is the moment when Brad loses it. He flings my hand away, opens his eyes, staring right at me. "What the fuck are you talking about, Jack? What if *what* happens to us?"

Okay, don't laugh at me . . . But I've actually been worrying about this ever since Brad proposed the whole JEH séance idea. I mean, if JEH really was G-A-Y . . . What if he was like a Total Pervert or something? Here we are, a couple of young and reasonably attractive boys. Who knows what he could try to make us do when/if he appeared to us?

Of course, Brad—being the sicko he is—wants to know *exactly* what I'm blabbering on about.

"Well," I begin, "have you ever seen that movie *The Entity?*"

"I don't think so . . ." Being that his family can't afford Cable, how could he?

"It's all about this woman who's raped by this Evil Spirit," I explain. *"Over and over again."*

"Sounds kinda hot . . . Maybe we should rent it sometime!"

"I'm being serious," I whine. "Nobody believes her when she tells them about it and there's nothing she can do to stop it from happening."

"So . . . ?"

"So . . . What if JEH tries to do something like that to us?"

Brad hesitates a moment. I can see he's thinking over what I've just said, carefully weighing our options. "You mean something sexual?" he ponders.

"You know what they say about guys who are *like that,*" I remind him.

"I never thought of that," Brad admits. "But it's a risk I'm willing to take." And with that, he rises to his feet, pulling the string on the overhead ceiling fan/lamp, plunging the room back into darkness. "Ohm . . . Ohm . . ." he continues.

For like the next hour!

Okay, I bet you're wondering what happens . . . Does the spirit of Jon-Erik Hexum ever appear to us? And if so, does he take advantage of the pair of helpless 14-year-old boys who want nothing more than to unlock the truth behind his mysterious demise? Does he?!

What do *you* think?

Do They Know It's Christmas?

"There's a world outside your window
And it's a world of dread and fear . . ."

—Band Aid

"Where to next?"

I can't even believe Brad's asking me this question . . . With only twelve Shopping Days left till Xmas, here we are running around Universal Mall like Chickens with our Heads Cut Off. Does he not realize *he's* the one who needs to shop and should have planned out exactly where we're going?

Every Christmas back when I was a kid, my Mom would take me to see Santa Claus at Universal Mall on 12 Mile and Dequindre. Which is pronounced "Dee-qwin-der," in case you can't figure it out. Not the *real* Santa Claus, mind you. But one of his very convincingly disguised Helpers. After giving Santa's Helper my "What I Want for Christmas" spiel, I'd go for a ride on the carousel in front of his Village before my Mom would treat me to a frozen Coke and giant soft pretzel—hold the mustard.

Of course, back then it was called Universal *City.* I'll never forget the humongous mosaic on the building's façade depicting Saturn and her rings, smack-dab in the middle of the Universe. I could stare at it for hours!

So far Brad and I have been to Kresge's, Crowley's, and Montgomery Ward's. On top of spending forty-five minutes in Spencer's looking at Chippendales greeting cards, don't ask me why!

"I'm getting my Mom a book," Brad decides. Then he heads off, weaving through the crowd of other Xmas Shoppers towards where he *thinks* the bookstore is located.

B. Dalton's is a Total Nightmare once we find it. Full of rummaged-through display tables and scattered books everywhere! Though a stack of 1985 Garfield calendars remains perfectly intact on their shelf. But maybe it's because Garfield is sooo 1982.

"Any idea where they keep the Danielle Steel?" Brad asks. Like I'd know.

"You're getting your Mom a Sex Book for Christmas?" I question. I can't even imagine Brad's Southern Baptist Church-going Mom *looking* at a trashy romance novel, let alone reading one.

"Hell no . . . You think my Mom would even *look* at that trash, let alone read it?" he responds, reading my mind.

"Then who's it for?" I wonder. Though I'm pretty sure I can figure it out for myself.

"Duh!" he answers. Then he makes his way to the back of the store.

I follow Brad into the stacks marked "Adult Contemporary Romance." I can't even believe some of the titles: *Leftover Love . . . A Ruling Passion . . . Dark Remembrance.* And the covers! Half-naked guys with long flowing hair. Totally hairless, totally *muscular* bodies.

"Check this out," Brad says, handing me some piece of trash he's just found on the shelf.

"'They wanted to love . . . in a world that worshipped only pleasure.'" I read the words printed on the cover. "Gordon Merrick . . . *Now Let's Talk About Music.*"

A dark-haired, well-tanned, shirtless man wearing light blue swim trunks rests poolside, a chilled bottle of champagne on ice in a silver bucket beside him. On the man's right shoulder rests a diamond pinky-ringed hand . . . Belonging to that of another *man!*

I shove the book back in Brad's direction, hoping nobody's seen me touching it. "Gross!"

He echoes my sentiments with, "I know!" Then he reads me a passage, all about some guy named Ned totally coming onto another *guy* named Gerry.

To which I reply, "That's disgusting."

"Wait . . . It gets better." With dramatic flair, Brad continues to the part where Ned drops down to his knees . . . and gives Gerry a blowjob.

"Gross!" I gasp, looking around to make sure nobody's paying attention to us. Which nobody is—thank God!

"Pretty trashy, isn't it?" Brad smiles before adding, "Let's buy it!"

I can't even tell you how shocked and totally appalled I am at this moment. Which explains why I blurt out, "No fucking way!" Which is probably the first time I've ever used the F-word in my life.

"Jack!" Brad gasps in mock-horror. "Your Mom is gonna wash your mouth out with soap when I tell her what you just said." Then he laughs.

"I mean it," I tell him, putting my foot down. "We are not walking up to the register with that thing and buying it!"

"Watch me," says Brad. Then he walks *right* up to the register and hands the trashy book to a middle-aged librarianesque-looking lady working behind the counter. "Good afternoon, Ma'am," he says politely.

Without blinking an eye she tells him, "$3.95, Dear."

At which point, Brad turns to me. "I need to bum a dollar, Jack."

To which I hesitate . . . Before reaching into my JC Penney Plain Pockets and pulling out a $1 bill.

"Merry Christmas," Librarian Lady says once our transaction is complete.

"Merry Christmas to you," Brad replies, all sweet and innocent. Then to me he says, "Let's get the fuck outta here!"

Five days later, we're back at my house . . .

"Oh, my God . . . I had another one!"

"When?" I ask. Though I'm wondering if I really need to know.

"This morning," Brad informs me. "Right before I got up."

"I hate you!" I hiss. Because I *still* haven't had one. Then I ask, "What's it feel like?" Because I have no idea and I'm dying to know.

"Good, I guess," he tells me. Like it's no big deal. "Sometimes, I don't even know I'm having one till I wake up and I'm all wet and sticky."

In case you haven't figured it out, we're talking about Nocturnal Emissions. Being a young boy, this is one of the first things they prepare you for in 6th grade Sex Ed. "Whether you like it or not, one day, you *will* have a Wet Dream." Though I suspect my body didn't get the memo because at the ripe old age of 14-going-on-15, I've yet to experience the pleasure.

Meanwhile, Brad's been having them *every* morning for like the past year and a half. It's getting to the point where all he has to do is close his eyes and BAM! Or should I say, "Squirt?"

"This sucks!" I declare. "I'm *never* gonna have one."

"Maybe if you didn't beat off so much . . ."

To which I give Brad a look. Does he really think I do that? I mean, all the guys at school *say* they don't . . . But can you honestly believe them?

I ask, "Do you remember what you dreamed about this time?" Only because he's my Best Friend and we tell each other everything.

Which is why I'm surprised when Brad answers, "I don't know . . . I think *somebody* was giving me a blowjob. But I'm not sure exactly who it was." Then he totally changes the subject. "Pass me the glitter."

Yes, you did hear correctly. Yes, Brad did say, "Pass me the glitter." As in that sparkly colored stuff used for writing your name on the top of your Christmas stocking. Or for decorating homemade Christmas wreaths. Which is exactly what we're doing at the moment. Making Christmas wreaths and decorating them.

The question you're probably asking yourself now is . . . *Why the Hell are you guys making Christmas wreaths?* To which the answer would be . . . Spring Break '85.

Shortly after Brad started working at Country Boy's, he got it into his head that we should go to Florida on Spring Break. My Grandpa Freeman lives down in Winter Haven from January till May and he says we can stay with him, no problem. The only thing is . . . not only do we need to save enough for the plane tickets, we also need spending money for when we're down there. And $2.92/hour busing tables is not gonna cut it! Not even with tips. Which explains why we're making Christmas wreaths out of cardboard, tissue paper, and glue. With a dash of glitter.

"First you take your tissue paper and cut it into squares . . ."

A long time ago in like 1965, when my Mom was a kid, she used to make Christmas wreaths with *her* Mom and sell them door-to-door. Or wherever she could get people to feel sorry for her and buy them. Which is why Brad and I spent the entire

Saturday after Thanksgiving sitting around our kitchen table learning the Finer-Art-of-Christmas-Wreath-Making . . .

"Next," my Mom continued, "fold the square in half, longways." Which she did, demonstrating as she went along on a 4" x 6" piece of white tissue paper. "With your pinking shears," she explained, "make four or five cuts along the fold." This she demonstrated to perfection, taking up a pair of yellow-handled scissors with funky jagged teeth. "Then fold your square back the other way." At which point, she used her nose to assist in turning the square/rectangle inside out, revealing five or six puffy loops where she had made the cuts.

At which point, Brad said, "I'm confused."

At which point, I concurred. "Me, too."

"Why'd you smell the tissue paper like that?" he asked, referring to that weird thing my Mom did with holding it up to her nose.

"I don't know," she admitted. "It's just the way I've always done it ever since I was little."

For a moment, I watched my Mom travel back in time. Long before little 14-year-old Dianne Freeman ever got It on with 17-year-old John Paterno in the back of his '67 Mustang at the Galaxy Drive-In, resulting in my not-so-Immaculate Conception.

Yes, you did hear correctly . . . Yes, my father's name is also John. And like me, everybody calls him Jack. Though I'm not technically a "Junior" on account of we have different middle names. He's John William and I'm John Robert. Which does indeed make my parents "Jack and Dianne." Like the John Cougar song. Though for some reason, my Grandma Freeman decided to spell my Mom's name with an extra N, don't ask me why!

For a moment, she's no longer 29-year-old Dianne Paterno, sitting with her 14-year-old son and his Best Friend since 7th grade in their modest three bedroom home in Hazeltucky, MI. She's a 10-year-old girl again, making Christmas wreaths with her own Mom across town in Ferndale. Too bad my Grandma Freeman died when I was 7 and my Mom was only 22. I can't imagine losing my Mom *ever,* let alone at such a young age. Right then, I felt like giving her the biggest hug and telling her how much I love her. But since Brad was sitting there at the table next to me, I decided I'd better not.

Now with only seven Shopping Days left till Christmas, here Brad and I sit on my bedroom floor making homemade Christmas wreaths. Like a couple of Total Losers . . .

"Can I ask you a question?" Brad says to me as I fold over my bijillionth white tissue paper square the way my Mom expertly taught us. "Who on *Days of our Lives* do you think is cuter? Pete or Bo?" By which he means Pete Jannings or Bo Brady.

Why Brad's developed this fascination with cute guys over the past couple months—and is always asking me if I'd think they were cute or not if I were a girl—is totally beyond me. I'm beginning to think he's testing me or something. Trying to see if what certain people at school, like Craig Gershrowski, say about me is true or not. How many times do I have to tell him, I don't judge other guys?

Though I probably would think Pete Jannings is cuter. If I were a *girl,* he'd totally be my type . . . Dark hair, dark eyes, and a totally smooth and perfect body. Not to mention his washboard abs, muscular arms, and beefy chest that pushes together in the middle kinda like cleavage.

Which is why I tell Brad, "I guess I'd think Pete's cuter . . . If I was a girl." Though being a guy myself, I can't stand him!

"You're kidding?" says Brad, making a face. "I'd definitely think Bo is cuter than Pete."

"You would?" I can't help but call his criteria for judging men into question. "I don't think I'd like kissing a guy with a beard."

"I would!" he exclaims, eyes lighting up.

"Bo's got a hairy chest," I remind him.

"I know!"

"You like that?"

"Well . . . My sister Janelle says hairy chests are sexy," he informs me.

"Really? They kinda gross me out." I hope to God I don't have a hairy chest when I grow up.

Brad adds, "Jon-Erik Hexum had a hairy chest . . . You know what I mean?"

Which is true . . . JEH was totally hairy, and it totally worked for him!

"I guess maybe I'd think they *both* were kinda cute," I say. "If I was a girl."

"Me, too."

Suddenly, I remember something I forgot to tell him . . . "My Mom got us a booth at the Longfellow holiday craft show this weekend." For a mere $5, Brad and I get an entire folding table to ourselves where we can display and sell our wares to the General Public.

"Ooh, that'll be fun," he teases, trying to unstick white tissue paper from his thumb and index finger. "You, me, and a bunch of old ladies!"

Even though Brad's probably right, I remind him it was *his* idea to spend Spring Break in Florida . . . Not mine!

"Do you think we'll ever sell enough of these damn Christmas wreaths to get the money?" he asks me.

"I hope so," I reply, "'cause if we don't, we'll have to start saving our lunch money."

"Then I'm fucked," says Brad. "I'm on the Free Lunch plan since my Dad left."

Which I totally forgot. "Sorry . . ."

"Don't be sorry," he tells me. "Be happy your parents are still married after all these years."

I sprinkle a dash of glitter on my finally-finished Christmas wreath, not wanting to address the fact that Brad now comes from a Broken Home. Meanwhile, Life is still Fine and Dandy here at the Paternos with Jack and Dianne.

I attempt to liven up the conversation by saying, "I can't wait to go to Disney World on Spring Break." Even though I've already been *twice,* I can't help but get excited thinking about watching Brad totally freak out on Space Mountain.

He gives me a look. "We are *not* going to Disney World on Spring Break . . . We are *way* too old for that."

"What are we gonna do instead?" I wonder.

"All I wanna do is lay on the beach and get a great tan," he replies. "And get laid!"

I try my best to conceal my laughter. "Like there's even a chance."

Brad gives me another look. "It could happen . . . We're in 9th grade, aren't we?"

"So . . . ?"

"So . . . People have sex when they're in 9th grade," he insists.

"No, they don't." What person in their right mind would risk having S-E-X at such a young age?

"Your *Mom* was in 9th grade when she got pregnant with you!" Brad reminds me. In case I forgot. "Dianne was the exact same age we are now and she was totally having sex."

"Yeah . . . But she's a *girl.*"

"So . . . ?"

"So . . . Girls mature faster than boys." Which is another thing they've been cramming down our throats since 6th grade Sex Ed.

"Whatever," says Brad, blowing me off. "Bobby says it's gonna happen . . . Soon."

Which is fine for somebody like Bobby Russell to say. He's

got a different girlfriend every week. But I don't. And neither does Brad . . . Which is what I remind him.

"Duh! When you're on Spring Break, it doesn't matter," he quips. "There are *tons* of people on the beach and *everybody* is hot and it just *happens.*"

"But we're staying with my Grandpa Guff," I tell Brad, hating to burst his bubble. "And he doesn't live anywhere *near* Daytona." Which is where all the Hazeltucky Hillbillies go on their wild Spring Break adventures. "I just don't see us having much opportunity to get laid . . . Sorry."

Now Brad looks totally disappointed. But come on! Does he really think we're gonna go from being Total Band Fags to Spring Break Studs? Then he says, "You're my Best Friend, aren't you?" Getting all serious.

"What are you talking about?" I'm dreading Brad's gonna say something mushy and embarrass me. "You know I am."

"And we'll always be Best Friends, won't we?" He avoids my gaze. "No matter what?"

"Of course," I affirm. "How could we not?"

At which point, Brad looks at me, sticking out his right pinky. Like he expects me to link mine with his or something. "You have to promise, Jack."

So I do . . . I link my pinky with Brad's and I promise.

"Good." He breathes a sigh of relief. "'Cause whoever gets laid first has to tell the other one everything about it . . . And I mean, *every* detail. Who, where, when. What it *feels* like . . . Okay?"

"Okay . . ." Why am I not crazy about this agreement?

Having eased his troubled mind, Brad goes back to the wreath he's been working on for what must be like the last hour . . .

"How's this?" he asks, finally. Then he holds up the most pathetic looking thing I've ever seen. I'm not even kidding when I say this . . . It makes the tree on *A Charlie Brown Christmas* look like the one in Rockefeller Center in New York City.

"Um . . . You might wanna fluff it up a bit," I begin my criticism. "And go a little easier on the glitter next time."

At which point, Brad throws down his pathetic excuse for a Christmas wreath, scattering loose white tissue paper squares everywhere. Then he reaches for his duffle bag. Which can only mean one thing . . .

"I need a cigarette!"

Sooner Or Later

"They tell me not to worry
Don't be in a hurry . . ."

—Rex Smith

"Pretend I'm the Mommy and you're the Daddy . . ."

Every day back in Kindergarten, Audrey Wojczek would *force* me to play House with her during Free Time. Off to work she (Mrs. Jackie Kennedy) would send me, a peck planted firmly upon my John F. cheek. Even though I kept reminding her my middle name is Robert, not Fitzgerald!

I can't even tell you how mortified I was when I found my picture in the lower right-hand corner of our Kindergarten class photo—right next to "Audrey Ostrich." Which is what I used to call her. Though never to her face. Like my Mom always says, "If you can't say something nice . . ." Not that Audrey looked like an ostrich or anything. She was just so much bigger than me—and to this day she still is! Not that I'm saying she's *fat* or anything, 'cause she's not. But she is a bigger girl. Like 5'6" or so and I'm only 5'2" with my Nike hi-tops on.

I also can't even tell you how relieved I was when I returned to 1st grade the following September, only to learn Audrey's family had moved to Minnesota. For the next two years she would reside in Duluth before returning to Hazeltucky and attending Catholic School at St. Mary Magdalen's. So close and yet far enough away for me to never see her again . . . That is, till she came over to Webb this year and we met up in Mr. Davidson's 4th hour Biology.

In case you don't remember—because how can you keep track of so many different people, places, and things?—Audrey Wojczek is my friend who works in the Guidance Counseling Office during 1st hour. The one with the long red hair down to her "childbearing hips," as she likes to call them.

I'm over her house on Woodward Heights. Which is technically 9½ Mile. But nobody ever calls it that. Not to be confused with Woodward Avenue, aka M-1 . . .

"Happy Fucking New Year!" Audrey shouts for the whole wide world to hear—or at least all of Hazeltucky.

We've abandoned Times Square on TV in favor of a Paterno Family tradition . . . Banging pots and pans outside on the front porch. As kids, I never understood *why* we did this or where the tradition had come from. But every December 31st since I can remember, this is what my sister and brother and I always did, don't ask me why!

"You look like Cousin Itt," I tell Audrey. Minus the bowler hat and glasses, of course.

She's got her long red hair draped over the front of her shoulders covering her bare arms down to her waist. Though it's obviously not keeping her warm by the way her teeth chatter like crazy. "Bite me!" Audrey snaps. Then she says, "Fuck this shit . . . I'm getting the Hell back inside." For a girl with a Catholic School upbringing, Audrey Wojczek's got quite the mouth on her.

The distinct smell of what can only be described as "Audrey's House" hits me the minute I follow her through the door. A cross between mothballs and kitty litter, maybe? Not that I'm saying it's a *bad* smell or anything, 'cause it's not.

"Now what do we do?" she asks, still shivering.

I look at my watch . . . 12:08 AM. "It's kinda late, isn't it?" I say.

To which Audrey gives me her "Don't Even" look. Which consists of turning her head slightly to one side, furrowing her brow, and pursing her lips. I can't *exactly* describe how she looks when she does it. But trust me, she looks mean.

"Boo hoo," she fake cries. "You gonna turn into a pumpkin, Paterno?" Which is what she calls me after she's given me her "Don't Even" look. "It's not like it's a School Night."

I give my folks a quick call, to ask if I can stay out a little longer. Normally, I have to be home by Midnight. But since it's a holiday and we're on Christmas Break and all, I figure they're not gonna care.

"Let me talk to Mom," I tell my little brother when he picks up the phone.

"She's in bed," he informs me. "So is Dad."

Did my parents not get the memo that it's New Year's Eve or what? Ever since my Mom realized she's turning the Big 3-0 this year, I swear she's started acting like an Old Lady. Unless they're having S-E-X. Which they can't be . . . It's a Monday night!

"Where are you?" Billy asks me.

"Over Audrey's," I answer, as if it's any of his business.

Then my smart-aleck little brother says, "Is Audrey your girlfriend?"

To which I reply, "Go to bed." Then I hang up the phone.

I return to find Audrey sitting on her couch, buried beneath a patchwork quilt that her little Polish Grandma must've made a bijillion years ago. "I'll share my blanket with you," she offers.

To which I decline, choosing to sit in the comfy armchair next to the fireplace—*way* over in the corner of the room. There's definitely something weird going on with Audrey. Not weird-weird, but . . . With her Mom out for the evening, it's the first time we've been alone together in her house. Or anywhere, now that I think of it.

On a small end table, I notice the framed photo of a rather good looking guy wearing a maroon and gray Hazel Park Vikings football uniform—#63. Down on one knee, he holds the ball under his arm, a look of stern seriousness on his square-jawed face.

"How's your brother?" I ask. Though I've never personally met Mike Wojczek, there's something about this picture that makes me want to.

"He just got an apartment with a friend of his," Audrey tells me. "Some guy named Rob."

Apparently, Mike graduated from Hillbilly High back in like 1980. According to Audrey, he works at some bar down in Detroit. He kinda reminds me of that guy from *All the Right Moves*, Tom Cruise. Except his mess of hair is red—not brown.

"Where's the apartment?" I ask.

"Royal Oak." Which is another suburb where my Grandpa and Grandma Paterno live. Over by Woodward Avenue and 10 Mile.

"How come your brother never comes over to visit?"

"He was just here Christmas Day," Audrey replies. "Jeez! You writing a book?

"No . . ." I was just making conversation.

"Wanna build a fire?" she suggests now. "We can watch a movie or something."

Not that I really want to. But still I reply, "What's on Cable?"

Audrey flings me the *TV Book*. Which is the Detroit *Free Press* version of *TV Guide*. I can't even believe it's already 1985. Even though it's printed in black-and-white right before my very own blue eyes.

That's when I see it . . . 12:30 AM . . . Channel 50.

It's love at first sight for Jessie Walters when she spots heartthrob Michael Skye singing with his band at the local shopping mall.

In case you aren't familiar, there's this After School Special-type movie called *Sooner or Later,* about this 13-year-old girl, Jessie, who falls in love with this 17-year-old guy, Michael. But she totally has to lie to him about her age otherwise he'd never go out with her. I won't ruin the plot. But let's just say . . . There's a scene where Jessie eats an entire chocolate cake! I don't know how I first heard about it. All I know is . . . It stars Rex Smith and Denise Miller. Who you might remember as Archie Bunker's niece on *Archie Bunker's Place*. Not Stephie, as played by Danielle Brisebois. Archie Bunker's other niece, Billie.

Okay, I know what you're thinking . . . *Sounds like a Girl's Movie,* Sooner or Later, *starring Rex Smith.* But what can I say? I've been dying to see it ever since it first aired on TV, back in like, 1979.

I'll never forget that night . . .

There I was, counting down the hours till I would sit my 8-year-old self down in front of our 24" Panasonic color-console television to witness the Network Television Premiere of *Sooner or Later*. There was only one problem . . . That exact same night, my Aunt Sonia decided to throw a Tupperware party. Which meant my Mom would be gone the entire evening. Which meant I had to stay home with my Dad . . . Which I hated!

Not that I hate my Dad or anything, 'cause I don't. But to tell the truth, back then he kinda scared me. Not scared-scared, but . . . In 1979, my Dad was all of 27 years old. He was also a Total Hippie. Not a hippie-hippie, but . . . He had shoulder-length dark hair, a mustache, and he smoked! Actually, people used to think my Dad kinda looked like Tony Orlando. Who was *kinda* good-looking, I suppose. But to tell the truth, he reminded me more of that crazy guy who killed all those people, Charles Manson.

The other problem was . . . Not only was 1979 back before the invention of the VCR, it was also back before the Paternos owned more than one TV set. Which meant if I wanted to watch *Sooner or Later*—which I did—I was gonna have to sit and watch it with my Charles-Manson-look-alike Dad.

But this was only the beginning of the Disastrous End . . .

An hour before Showtime, what happened? Our doorbell rang. Slowly, I opened the front door. Staring down at me was a handsome older man—full head of dark hair, nice smile, big teeth. He kinda reminded me of Lyle Waggoner from *Wonder Woman*, if you remember him.

"Is your Daddy home, Little Girl?" His baritone voice reverberated through my tiny little body.

"Um . . ." I replied. Though I didn't bother telling him, "I'm not a Little Girl, I'm a Little Boy." Because not only was I slightly embarrassed by his remark, I was actually used to it from past experience. Like the time I went with my Grandpa and Grandma Paterno to a spaghetti dinner at their American Legion hall. I was 5 or 6 at the time and this very nice elderly woman manning the cash register at the end of the buffet line looked down at me, all smiles.

"What's your name, Little Girl?"

But did I bother telling her, "I'm not a Little Girl, I'm a Little Boy?" No . . . Instead, I replied in my 5 or 6-year-old girl-sounding voice, "Jackie."

"Is Jackie short for Jacqueline?" Cash Register Lady asked.

To which my Grandma chimed in, "No . . . It's short for *Jack*."

Cash Register Lady gasped in horror, "No!" Then to me she said, "You're too pretty to be a *boy.*"

Back in 1979, my Dad called out from the bathroom where he'd been busy trimming his Tony Orlando/Charles Manson mustache, "Jackie . . . Who is it?"

"Paterno!" Big Teeth Man called back. "Stop whacking off and get your ass out here." He let out a laugh before realizing he shouldn't say things like "whacking off" in front of a Little Girl. Even though being only 8 years old, I had no idea what "whacking off" meant. Not to mention we've already established, I wasn't a Little Girl.

It turned out Lyle Waggoner was my Dad's Boss. For some reason, I got the distinct impression my Dad wasn't too excited to see the guy in his house when he rounded the corner of our living room, pulling on his black sleeveless T-shirt.

"How come you didn't tell me what a pretty daughter you've got?" Lyle Waggoner asked my Dad.

"Jackie . . . Go play in your room," my Dad told me. Though he didn't look at me when he said this.

"But—" I started to say.

"You heard me," my Dad finished.

So I went to my room. Where I played with my Lite Brite, followed by a couple rounds of Perfection. With some *Brady Bunch Goes Love Boat* thrown in, starring the Fisher-Price Little People.

Pretty soon it was 7:50 PM . . .

How long had I been waiting for this moment? How long had I been dreaming of the day I'd finally get to witness Rex Smith singing "You Take My Breath Away"? But Lyle Waggoner looked like he was nowhere *near* being ready to get a move on. Especially since he just cracked open another Michelob Light, "For the Winner."

So what did I do? Even though I knew my Dad wouldn't appreciate it . . . I started crying.

"Hey, there," Lyle Waggoner cooed, after he noticed me blabbering away around the corner in the hallway. "What's the matter, Darlin'?"

Again, not looking at me, my Dad said, "Would you knock it off?" Though he was kinda half-laughing/half-sounding angry. Probably because he was totally embarrassed that his Big-Teethed Boss was sitting in his living room on his couch thinking his Little Boy was his Little Girl!

"But I wanna watch *Sooner or Later,*" I sobbed. Which came out sounding more like, "Wah Wah wahwah wah *Wahwah wah Wahwah.*"

"What's that?" Lyle Waggoner slurred, reaching a big calloused hand out to me. "Come over here an' tell me what's wrong."

TV Book in hand, I crept into the room. I showed Mr. Big Teeth the "Of Special Interest . . ." page, knowing I at least had *his* Booze Breath sympathy.

"Who's this?" Lyle Waggoner took a look at the tiny black-and-white photo of Rex Smith sporting his Farrah Fawcett hairdo and smiled. "Looks like somebody's got a little crush." Then he took another swig of his beer. "You wanna watch a movie?" he asked. "G' right ahead, Sweetheart . . . 's your house." At which point, he gave my Garanimaled bottom a gentle pat.

I moved to change the channel when my Dad stopped me. "I told you to go play in your room." Using his "mean" voice. Which is something he hardly ever did and it totally took me by surprise.

"But I wanna watch *Sooner—*" *or Later,* I was about to say. Till I was cut off.

"We're not watching that Faggot Movie!" my Dad announced. Again, half-laughing/half-sounding angry. Being only 8 years old, this was the first time in my life I'd ever heard the word "faggot," so I had no idea what it meant. Though from the tone in my Dad's voice, I got the impression it wasn't a *good* thing.

So what did I do? I didn't watch *Sooner or Later* . . . That's for sure!

Instead, I returned to my room where I passed out on my bed after exhausting myself from a serious cry. The good news is . . . Later that night, after Lyle Waggoner *finally* decided to drag his drunken self home, my Dad sneaked into my room. Without saying a word, he sat down beside me on my bed. I pretended not to notice when he wiped my tear-stained cheeks with his own calloused hand before softly making a confession. It turned out, the only reason my Dad wanted me to leave the room so bad was because he didn't want me being subjected to his Boozer of a Boss. Who he said he couldn't stand!

Then my Dad made me a promise. "Next time your movie is on," he said, "we'll watch it together . . . Just you and me, okay?" Even though we never actually did, I've gotta give the man credit for trying.

Back on New Year's Eve, 1985 . . .

I suggest to Audrey we watch *Sooner or Later* on the Late-Late Show. To which she vehemently objects. "Hell no! I can't stand that movie."

Which crushes me like a ton of bricks. "What's wrong with it?"

"I saw it when I was in like 3rd grade, and it totally sucked!" Audrey snarls. Then she adds, "The book sucked even more."

"There's a book?" I ask. How am I totally not privy to this fact?

"You've never seen it?" she asks, surprised. "It's got the chick on the cover with the locket around her neck." By whom she must mean Denise Miller as Jessie Walters. Which is exactly the same as the album. Which my Mom bought for me on 8-track.

Back in like 1980, after I missed seeing the movie on *Sooner or Later* Night.

"Can I borrow it sometime?" I practically beg. At this point, I don't care what Audrey might think about my wanting to read a Girl's Book.

But she answers, "I don't got it anymore." Totally bursting my bubble. "Sister Mary Hitler caught me reading it and the Bitch took it away."

So what do I do? I fake a great big yawn . . . "Excuse me!"

"Too bad we're not at your house," says Audrey, ignoring my stretching to give added emphasis to how tired I've all of a sudden become. "We could watch *Somewhere in Time* on your VCR."

In case you haven't seen it, I won't ruin the plot. But *Somewhere in Time* is this totally romantic movie from like 1980, about this guy—played by Superman, aka Christopher Reeve—who travels back in time after seeing this picture of a woman—played by Jane Seymour, who I loved in *Dallas Cowboy Cheerleaders*—hanging on the wall in The Grand Hotel. Which is located Up North on Mackinac Island, and is pronounced "Mackinaw," by the way.

When Audrey and I found out it's the favorite movie of both of us, we made a pact that someday we'd go to Mackinac Island together and stay in The Grand Hotel. That is, whenever one of us gets our driver's license and a car. We also plan to find the special trees along the lake where Richard Collier and Elise McKenna, aka Christopher Reeve and Jane Seymour, meet for the first time.

"I think I'm gonna call it a night," I firmly decide.

"Party Pooper . . . It's New Year's Eve, for chris'sakes!" Audrey chides.

"Sorry . . ." I grab my jacket from the hook near the door.

"I'll walk you halfway," she offers, donning her long wool

coat. Which means Audrey Wojczek has made up her mind and there's no point in telling her she doesn't have to bother. "Ladies first," she tells me. Then she gestures for me to go ahead of her.

"Ha-ha," I say. "You're so funny I forgot to laugh."

For the second time in less than half an hour, I head out into the cold dark night. We start down the deserted block towards my house, taking the long route on Woodward Heights rather than cutting through St. Mary's Field. Which totally creeps me out—especially at night. When we come to Battelle, I'm about to make a right and continue down to Shevlin. Which saying it right now sounds totally stupid to me . . . What's a Shevlin, anyways?

"Thanks for walking me halfway," I tell Audrey. Though I can barely hear myself over the Def Leppard blaring from the White Cutlass that's just stopped at the red light on the corner.

That's when I hear, "Hey, Faggot!" And I see Fuck Face Craig Gershrowski hanging his head out the back window, totally wasted. "Wanna suck my dick?"

Of course, I ignore him. I don't know who he's with or who's driving the car. All I know is . . . Once the light turns green, they're gone in a squeal of burning Goodyears.

"Fuck you!" Audrey shouts after them, hot breath clouding the cold air. Then she turns to me, fire in her eyes matching her fire-red hair. "When are you gonna grow some balls and stand up to that kid? He's an 8th grader, for chris'sakes!"

"I know . . ."

"You want me to kick his ass for you?" she offers. "You know I will."

"No, thanks." Even though I'd pay money to see that happen. For now, I'll just continue to avoid conflict rather than deal with it. Which is one thing I've gotten good at.

Like if somebody cuts in front of me in the Lunch Line, I'll act like I don't even notice it. Especially if it's some Jock Jerk.

Or if somebody accidentally-on-purpose bumps into me in the hallway between classes, I'll keep on walking like I don't even notice it. Especially if it's some Jock Jerk. Or if somebody happens to be parading around naked in the locker room after Gym, I'll continue changing my clothes like I don't even notice it. Especially if it's some Jock Jerk.

"There's gotta be a way for you to get back at that Fuck Face," Audrey muses.

"Let me know when you figure it out," I reply.

To which she sighs, "Oh, Jackie . . . What am I gonna do with you?"

To which I say nothing.

On the off chance that Brad's right and Audrey *does* have a crush on me, I'd hate to lead her on. I mean, it's not that I don't like her. I just don't like her-like her. In that way.

I'm about to start off when Audrey stops me. "Where's my hug?"

Suddenly, I'm engulfed in a sea of Suave strawberries. I have no other choice but to return her embrace. Though not *too* enthusiastically. Again, no leading the Poor Girl on.

"I'm so glad we're friends," she says softly in my ear.

Again, I say nothing.

Audrey kisses me on the cheek. Like she used to back in Kindergarten during Free Time. "Call me tomorrow," she orders. "Make it sooner than later."

Which reminds me . . .

With thoughts of Rex Smith and Denise Miller, I free myself from Audrey's embrace. Then I sprint down the block, arriving home *just* in time to turn on WKBD-TV, stick a blank VHS tape in the old VCR, and hit REC.

The sound of applause fills my ears as Michael Skye takes to the Shopping Mall stage before the cheering crowd of late-'70s teenagers. And who do I see sporting a shoulder-length crimped hairdo complete with topknot, singing backup and playing tambourine? None other than Fran from *The Great Space Coaster* . . . I had no idea she was really an actor!

So what if the song Rex Smith is singing sounds kind of cheesy? So what if he's poured himself into these totally tight Jordache jeans with these ridiculous looking suspenders? So what if his white T-shirt sparkles with silver glitter, the words *The Skye Band* printed in funky late-'70s style script? It's really him . . . After all these years!

"Good things come to those who wait."

Holiday Road

"I found out long ago
It's a long way down the holiday road . . ."

—Lindsey Buckingham

March 18, 1985

Dear Claude,

Oh, my God . . . You're not gonna believe what happened on Friday after school. I almost diiieed!

So I'm walking thru Green Acres Park behind the Rec. Center with Bobby Russell and who do we see? Little Richie Tyler. You know, the faggy little 7th grader who plays flute in Prep Band and carries his books like a girl? Anyways . . .

So me and Bobby are smoking a cig and all of a sudden he's like, "So . . . Did you fuck her or did you just eat her out?" Totally joking around but faggy little Richie doesn't know that. He's like, "You guys are gross!" And Bobby's like, "Nobody's talking to you, you little faggot!"

And Richie's like, "I'm not a fag! I'm not a fag!" In his whiney little fag voice.

Then he tries to get past us but Bobby blocks his way. He's like, "Where's your flute?" But Richie totally ignores us and starts running across the playground over by Roosevelt. So Bobby and me start chasing him thru the snow, over the I-75 catwalk and thru the parking lot at Calvary Baptist.

All of a sudden, Richie hits an icy patch and totally wipes out. So there he is, on the ground, crying like a Total Baby. And get this . . . Bobby says, "I got a flute right here you can practice on." Then he grabs his dick.

So I'm like, "Let's go, Bobby." And he's like, "Hold on a sec." Then to Richie he says, "Listen here, you little fag . . . Next time I see you, you better keep your mouth shut. Or I'm gonna shove something in it to keep it shut for you." Can you believe it?

Okay, gotta go . . . Write me!

Rusty

In case you haven't figured it out . . . I'm Claude and Brad's Rusty. Taken from our new favorite movie, *National Lampoon's Vacation*. Even though it's from like 1983, neither of us ever saw it till it came on Cable this year. We totally love Imogene Coca as Aunt Edna and know all of her lines by heart. In fact, we've gotten to the point where all we do is watch her scenes and fast-forward through the rest of the movie. That's how much we love her.

"Claude" is what Aunt Edna calls Chevy Chase's character, Clark. And Rusty is the name of Chevy Chase's son, as played by a pre-*Sixteen Candles* Anthony Michael Hall. This is how Brad and I have started addressing each other when writing letters back and forth. Just in case Mr. Grant should happen to get his hands on one of them and read it aloud over the cafeteria loudspeaker during Lunch.

That same day, we're hanging out in my bedroom after school, *supposedly* practicing our duet for the upcoming Spring Concert next month. But after about half an hour, we totally get side-tracked . . .

"Then what did you do?" I ask, dying to know what else happened with Brad and Bobby and faggy little Richie Tyler.

"Nothing . . . I went over Bobby's house and we hung out for a while."

Being the Worry Wart that I am, I stop to consider. "What are you gonna do if Richie tells somebody?"

Brad exclaims, "I'll totally kick his ass if he does!" Then he asks, "Somebody, who?"

"I don't know . . . What if he tells Mrs. Putnam?"

"I doubt he'll say anything," Brad confidently decides. "I know *I* wouldn't say a word if something like that happened to me."

"I don't know why you even hang out with Bobby Russell," I tell him, after a moment. "He thinks he's sooo hot and that everybody else does, too."

"No, he doesn't," Brad scoffs, sounding just like his Mom. Our big joke lately is . . . Whenever he tells Laura something's wrong—like he's dying or sick or something—she's all like, "No, you're not." Like she totally doesn't believe him.

"Yes, he does," I insist, knowing for a fact that practically every day in 4th hour Biology, I have to listen to Bobby Russell going on and on and on about what a big dick he's got and how he can get a blowjob anytime he wants one. Which is what I tell Brad at this very moment.

To which he responds, "From who?"

The question is more like . . . Who *can't* Bobby Russell get a blowjob from? At least according to Bobby. "But you know what they say?" I say. "Guys who like to talk are the ones with nothing to talk about."

"Oh, he does!" Brad reports.

Though how he's privy to such information, I have no idea. Which is why I say, "How would you know?"

"Oh, you know . . . Me and Bobby used to be on Swimming together and sometimes we'd take showers after practice and I'd see it."

"You would?" I ask. Though I don't know why I'm surprised. Like I've said, I've seen plenty of naked guys in the locker room at school. What's the big deal?

"It looked pretty big to me."

"Figures," I say, totally disgusted.

"Well," Brad says hesitantly. "I hate to change the subject, but . . . There's something I should probably tell you . . . And I don't think you're gonna like it."

After all the planning and the endless Christmas wreath making, I can't even believe Brad has the nerve to stand here in *my* bedroom and tell me he's not going to Florida on Spring Break with me. In the two and a half years I've known him, I don't think we've ever had a fight—at least not a serious one. But something tells me this could be a first.

"I'm sorry," he apologizes. "I can't help it if my Dad's a Total Deadbeat and my Mom can't afford to pay for my plane ticket by herself." By which he might as well add, "The way *your* parents are paying for yours."

"But my Dad's already bought them," I say. By which I mean the plane tickets to Orlando. Where my Grandpa Freeman will pick us up and take us to stay at his trailer park in nearby Winter Haven. My Dad bought my ticket and Brad's and his parents are supposed to pay him back. That's the deal we worked out. And Brad knows it. "What about your Country Boy's money?" I ask. "What about all your tips?"

"I been giving every penny I make to my Mom since before Christmas," he informs me.

Poor Laura Victor-Dayton-Victor . . . Back in mid-December—after failing to pay the gas bill for the *third* time—they finally cut off the heat at *Dayton's Depot.*

What I don't think I've mentioned is . . . Back in like the 1950s, Brad's house used to be a store. So it's huge! The living room used to be the main part so it's like, 30' x 50' or something ridiculous like that. With these totally high ceilings. Like 20' high. And these two matching chandeliers hanging down. Not fancy chandeliers. But I totally wanna swing on them!

What's really cool is . . . During the Summer that Brad and I were at BLFAC, *The Daily Tribune* ran an article all about how Brad's Deadbeat Dad converted this old store into a house. That is, before he walked out on Brad and his Mom and his sisters, thus earning him his nickname. Now every once in a while people stop by wanting to see the inside. Especially the ones who'd been there when it was still a store . . . "Back in the day."

You can probably imagine just how much gas is required to keep a place like that warm. And how expen$ive the bill must be. Which his why Brad, Janelle, Little Nina, and Little Brittany had to go without any presents this past Christmas. Other than the ones donated by the Central Freewill Baptist Church in Royal Oak. And why Poor Brad spent practically the entire Winter staying the night over my house. Which was fun and all, but . . . I still felt sorry for him.

"So . . . You're just not gonna go on Spring Break?" I ask Brad, getting back to the subject.

"I don't see how I can," he replies. "Unless maybe I start selling my bod on 8 Mile." Then he gets all Blair Warner from

Facts of Life with another one of his so-called Brilliant Ideas. "Hey, that's not a bad idea! How much do you think I can get?"

I choose to ignore Brad's attempt at being funny. "This is serious," I remind him. "We've been planning this for months."

"I know . . . I suck," he apologizes. "But there's nothing I can do."

"What the fuck?!" I explode. Might as well throw in, "I can't even believe this shit!" I swear I'm not usually a violent person. But if Brad Dayton wasn't my Best Friend since 7th grade, I think I'd punch him right in the face.

"Jack—"

"This is a Total Crock," I tell him. "And you know it."

"Jack—"

I catch a glimpse of my reflection in the floor-length mirror hanging on the wall next to my closet. I can't even believe how red I'm turning. I look like Violet Beauregarde in *Willy Wonka & The Chocolate Factory* when she turns into a blueberry . . . Only red. "I've been busting my ass for the last five months to make this happen," I practically shout. "Now you're gonna bail on me?"

"*Jack,*" says Brad, on the verge of using his "mean" voice. "Would you shut the fuck up for two seconds and listen to me?"

Even though there are a bijillion more things I could say right now, I bite my tongue.

"I'm happy your parents can afford to send you to Florida to see your Grandpa on Spring Break," Brad calmly continues. "And buy you your own VCR and TV and stuff," he conveniently adds. "But some of us aren't so lucky to get whatever we want. So you're just gonna have to get over it."

I know it's not Brad's fault his Dad's a Deadbeat and his Mom barely makes a dime working at Detroit Osteopathic Hospital doing God only knows what. So I simply say, "I'm sorry . . . I'm a Total Jerk."

To which Brad replies, "It's okay . . . You're not that much of a jerk." Then he laughs.

This still doesn't solve my problem as to what I'm gonna do about Spring Break '85. As much as I love and miss my Grandpa Freeman, I just can't see spending an entire week in Florida alone with him at his trailer park. And I can't even imagine him going to Disney World and riding on Space Mountain at the ripe old age of 65!

Which is why I decide, "I guess I won't be going, either."

"Don't let my being poorer than dirt stop you," says Brad.

"You're my Best Friend," I tell him. "I won't have any fun without you."

"Thanks . . ." Brad starts packing up his trombone. Which I guess means we're calling it quits on practicing for the night. "I better go," he informs me. "I told Bobby I'd stop by . . . Since I was in the neighborhood and all."

Even though I'm always saying how much I can't stand the guy, suddenly I'm like, "We can invite Bobby over here if you want," don't ask me why! It's not like I really *hate* him or anything. Besides, he's sat next to me in Band for the past *three* years. Just because he's never made an effort to be friends with me doesn't mean I shouldn't try with him.

"Um . . . That's okay," Brad responds to my suggestion.

"Why not?"

"Um . . . I think Bobby wants me to come over there."

"Okay . . . I'll go with you."

"Um . . . I think his parents are gone."

"So . . . ?"

"So . . . I think Bobby wants to smoke pot."

"Again?" I say, knowing for a fact that Brad smoked pot with Bobby just this past weekend.

"I really don't want to."

"Then why do you keep doing it?" I ask, applying the pressure.

"I don't know . . ."

" 'member what happened on Saturday night?" I remind him. One o'clock in the AM Brad calls my house—totally freaking out—thinking he's having a heart attack. Thank God he didn't wake up my parents, ringing my phone off the wall . . . I would have totally gotten in trouble!

"I really don't like it," he confesses. "It totally makes me paranoid and I always end up doing things I don't wanna do."

"Like what?"

"I don't know . . ."

I can tell Brad's avoiding my question by the way he's chewing on what's left of his French fry fingernails. But being that he's my Best Friend, I let him off the hook. Though now I'm wondering if maybe there's more to the Bobby Russell/Richie Tyler story than he's told me.

"I probably won't do it anymore with him after tonight," Brad vows.

"Do what?" I ask, raising an eyebrow à la Kristian Alfonso from *Days of our Lives* whenever Hope suspects someone is up to no good.

"Smoke pot," he tells me. "Duh! What'd you think?"

Which makes it my turn to tell him, "You know you don't have to do anything you don't wanna do."

Brad replies, "I know . . ." And with that, he's out the door!

I can't even believe my Best Friend since 7th grade is totally blowing me off. Now what am I gonna do? Then I remember the copy of *Now Let's Talk About Music* . . .

I find Gerry and Ned safe and sound beneath my bottom dresser drawer where I've hidden them for safekeeping. I figure nobody's gonna think to remove the *entire* drawer, should they decide to go snooping around in my Personal Private things. With my brother off playing in our neighbor's backyard, I've finally got some much needed privacy. Might as well do a little reading . . .

I crawl up into my top bunk, lie down, and locate my place on page 186 . . . Gerry the Brit is chaise-lounging poolside on the *Homo Boat.* Boyfriend André snoozes beside him. Enter Hank the American, a deluxe French edition of *Madame Bovary* in his hand. Gerry the Whore's all like, "My! What a good bod—I mean, book you've got there." To which Hank the Hustler's all like, "Thanks . . . Wanna fuck?"

And they're off!

I'm paraphrasing, of course. But the gist is . . . Gerry's got this insatiable appetite for S-E-X with M-E-N. And to top it all off, he's hung like a horse. Back in the day, he used to be a kept boy for some older man. But now, Gerry's a full-fledged adult and on the prowl aboard some "Fags Only" cruise ship. Getting It on whenever and with whomever he likes.

On to page 188 . . . Gerry's found the lube. Totally hot and bothered, he begs Hank to give him the you-know-what up the you-know-where. Even if it means cheating on Poor André. The minute they're done, Gerry decides he wants Hank to fuck André, next . . . While he watches? (Gross!)

I toss the stupid book aside, wondering why I'm even reading it in the first place. I might as well watch *Days of our Lives.* Bo & Hope are trying to track down this psycho killer, The Dragon, who's running around Europe killing off members of the Royal Family. Along with Shane Donovan—this James Bond-like detective who works for some FBI-like group called the ISA—who's also got the hots for Bo's sister, Kimberly. The only thing is . . . Shane is about to find out his dead wife, Emma, has come back from the grave. Even though she was presumably murdered years ago by The Dragon himself. At which point, it'll most likely be *The End of Shane & Kimberly*, who's going blind due to some rare visual disorder she's developed, God only knows how!

Now that I think of it . . . I *do* have today's episode on tape. So it's not like I have to watch it right this minute. And since I've already started reading *The Adventures of Ned & Gerry*, I might as well finish it.

Page 191 . . . André discovers Gerry naked in the bathroom of their cruise-ship cabin with Hank the Hustler. But is he upset at finding his Lover in the arms of another man? No . . . He joins in on the action!

After reading a few pages, I notice something odd . . . The sweatpants I'm wearing must be getting a little small. Because they're feeling awfully tight in the crotch all of a sudden. Maybe I'd better take them off and make myself more comfortable?

Which is exactly what I do . . .

That's better!

Dancing In The Dark

"You can't start a fire
You can't start a fire without a spark . . ."

—Bruce Springsteen

"Today!"

As I dig through Brad's locker looking for my Band folder and Algebra book, I inform Mr. Impatient, "We gotta wait for Audrey."

"What for?"

"She's walking home with us."

"What for?"

"Because she lives over by me," I explain. Even though I know he already knows this.

"No," Brad replies. "Because she likes you."

I roll my eyes. "She does not," I declare. Even though I know he's already made up his mind so it makes no difference what I say.

As she rounds the corner, I immediately notice Audrey's got this weird look on her face. Not weird-weird, but . . . It's kinda like what my Mom would call "The Cat that ate the Canary."

So I'm like, "What's up?"

And Brad's like, "You look constipated . . . Want some Correctol?" Then he laughs.

Knowing I should never attempt to hang out with Audrey and Brad at the same time, I do my best to keep the peace. Which is why I change the subject. Immediately.

"What do you got there, Aud?" I ask her. She's been holding a folded piece of pink *While You Were Out* message-pad paper in her hand. Which I assume has something to do with her look of excitement/constipation.

"Oh, nothing . . ." Audrey holds it up. Then she unfolds the memo, slowly and deliberately, before reading us the Confidential contents contained therein: "29-36-09."

"Sounds like your measurements," Brad cracks. Even though he knows that Audrey's got a thing about thinking she's fat.

"Very funny," she replies. "How's that hair of yours holding up?" By which she's referring to the fact that our Health teacher, Mrs. Strong, recently taught us that a majority of men with red hair—like Brad—eventually lose it once they become adults. Which has got him all freaked out considering his Deadbeat Dad went bald by the time he was 30. Which for Brad is only a little over fifteen years away.

We move down the hallway towards the building's side exit. "Sounds like your locker combination," I say, working my way in between my two Best Pals, getting us back on subject.

"Not *my* locker com," Audrey announces as we burst through the double doors onto a warm 70° day out on Woodward Heights.

"So who's com is it?" asks Brad once we reach the concrete sidewalk directly opposite the humongous radio tower across the street belonging to WOMC. Why they call it "Detroit's Big O" when the station is located in Ferndale, I have no idea.

"None other than Fuck Face Craig Gershrowski's."

It seems that while filing away some files in the Guidance Counseling Office during 1st hour, Audrey unexpectedly came upon the Personal Record belonging to my Arch Nemesis. In which she learned: (a) Fuck Face's middle name is Francis, (b) he was held back in 2nd grade, and (c) the combination to his locker, #686!

Fast-forward to the following Thursday, May 23rd . . .

Around 7:00 PM my Dad drops me off in the side parking lot at school where I'm about to meet my date, 8th grader Tracy Cardoza. You might remember that her older sister, Lydia, is Brad's sister Janelle's Best Friend and the one who gave her the JEH *Playgirl* for her Sweet Sixteen.

"Over here, Jackie!" Tracy calls out from where she sits on one of the little wooden benches in the graveled courtyard outside the commons by the Guidance Counseling Office.

"You look awesome," I tell her after making my approach. Then I present Tracy with the white and pink-tipped carnation corsage my Mom helped me pick out at The Daisy Petal up on John R.

"Thank you!" she exclaims. Like she wasn't expecting to be given a carnation at the traditional end-of-the-year Carnation Dance or something. Which is kinda like the Freshman Prom. Except anybody at Webb can go. Including the piddly little 7th graders.

Tracy extends her wrist as I slip the corsage onto it. Happily, I discover it goes well with her dress. Which totally reminds me of the one worn by her favorite singer—and fellow Detroiter—Madonna, on the cover of her latest album, *Like a Virgin*. Complete with long white gloves and matching scarves worn in her teased blond bob.

I've gotta say, Tracy Cardoza has come a long way this year. When I first met her back in September, she was totally quiet and kinda shy. I wouldn't call her mousy. But let's just say . . . Compared to the way she looks now she was like a totally different person. Tracy and I have 6th hour Creative Academics together with Mrs. Babbage. Who everybody's taken to calling Cabbage Patch. Not that she isn't nice or anything, 'cause she totally is. But the thing that sucks about having Mrs. Babbage for both 6th hour Creative Academics and 3rd hour English is . . . I was *supposed* to have Ms. Lemieux. Same teacher I had for 7th grade Enriched English & Social Studies. I can't even tell you how disappointed I was when I entered the classroom on the First Day of School to find we had a brand new teacher.

What's even more odd is . . . When Brad and I asked Jessica Clark Putnam if she knew what happened to Ms. Lemieux all she said was, "Good riddance to bad rubbish." Which kinda surprised us. So we asked her what she meant by her remark and JCP just rolled her eyes, mumbling something about Ms. Lemieux being "an incompetent buffoon." Which has since gone on to earn a place right up there with "Friends hold you back."

Personally, I think Mrs. Putnam was always jealous of Ms. Lemieux, whose first name just so happens to be Cinnamon, believe it or not. For a 35-year-old *divorcée,* all the guys in our class thought Cin—as Brad and I liked to call her—was totally hot. With her curly brown mane of hair and curvaceous figure, Ms. Lemieux always came to school looking her best. Which is what her last name means in French, you know? "The Best." I'm telling you, she could have easily been a model back in the '70s, that's how awesome she looked. And she was totally cool on top of everything else.

Sometimes Cin would take me and Brad out to lunch with her. The minute we got in the car she'd be all like, "Do you mind if I smoke?" As she was lighting up. Of course, I totally *did.* Though I never said anything. I mean, who am I to tell a teacher she should stop killing herself?

"Where's Brad and What's-Her-Name?" Once we're finished with all the corsage formalities, Tracy asks me this.

"You mean Ginny?" I reply, referring to Brad's date.

In case I haven't mentioned . . . Ginny is this girl Brad met two Summers ago at Blue Lake Fine Arts Camp. As far as I know, he hadn't talked to her since. Then a couple weeks ago, he called her up, invited her to the Carnation Dance and surprisingly, she said yes.

I can't blame him for wanting to be seen with someone who's not from Hazeltucky. Or even Ferndale. I'm sure all the Jock Jerks will be dying to know who Ginny is. From what I remember, she's *very* cute. Plus she lives in Clarkston. Which is the same fancy suburb out past 30 Mile where Joey Palladino—my Best Friend from Longfellow—and his family moved after 6th grade . . . I've gotta remember to ask Ginny if she knows him.

"Hey, you guys!"

I look over my shoulder to see Brad and Ginny making their entrance. He's all decked out in his Sunday Best. Blue blazer, matching tie, and tan dress pants while Ginny's got on a very frilly pink gown. Like something you'd wear to a wedding. Compared to Tracy's Madonna dress, it's like Night and Day.

"Don't you look sharp?" I tell my Best Friend. Though I'm actually kinda pissed he's wearing a jacket *and* tie and didn't bother to tell me. I thought we were going casual-nice here. Now I look like a Total Slob wearing a pair of gray pleated dress pants I borrowed from Brad, along with my favorite gray and white pinstriped button-down dress shirt I got on sale at Merry-Go-Round. Though I've actually gotten a lot of compliments on it. Even from Mr. Grant.

"Cool shirt," he told me the first time I wore it to his class a few months ago. "Too bad you're not my size . . . I'd have to borrow it." Then I swear he gave me a wink!

The Dance is a Total Blast. Tracy and I have an awesome time, dancing almost every slow song together. Except for when

Carrie Johnson corners me, wanting her *Days of our Lives* update. Turns out she loves Peter Reckell—the guy who plays Bo—just as much as I love Kristian Alfonso, and May 23, 1985 is not only the day of the traditional end-of-the-year Carnation Dance. It's also the long awaited wedding of Bo Brady and Hope Williams.

Actually, Carrie's been a *Days* fan longer than I have. She started watching with her Mom back in 5th grade. Back in the days of the Salem Strangler or Salem Slasher. Whichever serial killer was running around terrorizing the women of Salem at the time. Once Carrie found out I had a VCR at my house and taped *Days* every day, she made it my responsibility to fill her in on what's been happening.

"What did Hope's dress look like?" she half-whispers in my ear, as we spin round and round to "All I Need" by *General Hospital*'s very own Jack Wagner, speaking of Soaps.

"I hate to say it," I tell Carrie, "but I wasn't that impressed." Even though I read in *Soap Opera Digest* that the dress cost $20,000. I think what I didn't like most about it was the veil. Which was more like this poufy headpiece-thingie, totally covering all of Hope's hair. And everybody who knows Kristian Alfonso knows what beautiful long dark *flowing* hair she's got. I don't know why anybody would ever decide she should cover it up.

"What about the actual ceremony?" Carrie asks. I can totally tell she regrets not skipping school to stay home and watch today. But Webb Junior High policy says if you're absent from school on the day of a dance, you can't go. And I know Carrie wouldn't miss seeing Mr. Grant all decked out in his suit and tie wearing his *really* tight dress pants . . . Which he totally is!

I proceed to tell Carrie all about Bo & Hope's wedding. How it took place at this humongous cathedral in London, where Bo & Hope and Shane & Kimberly had all been looking for The

Dragon. Where—just as I predicted—Shane found his presumably dead wife, Emma, alive and well. Of course, she has no memory whatsoever of the time she spent missing! It was definitely a *Days of our Lives* not to be missed. Which is what I tell Carrie Johnson. Even though I know she already knows it.

When the song ends, I thank Carrie for the dance and she thanks me for the update. Then I join Tracy who's been waiting for me over on the sidelines near where all the Wallflowers always sit. I told her she should feel free to dance with somebody else while I was dancing with Carrie. But Tracy said she'd rather not. I think she really likes me.

"Audrey's looking for you," Tracy informs me as I return.

I look up at the silver-framed regulation School Clock on the wall . . . 8:30 PM. Time for *Operation Revenge of the Band Fags!*

"What did she say?" I ask.

"She told me to tell you to get your ass in gear," which is Total Audrey, "and for you and Brad to meet her you-know-where to do you-know-what."

Which is all part of *Operation Revenge of the Band Fags!*

I spot Brad and Ginny out on the dance floor, about to break into the next fast dance. Which is why I motion for him to come over to where I'm standing with Tracy and the Wallflowers.

"What the fuck?" Brad scowls as he and Ginny join us. "You know how much I love Wang!" By which he means Wang Chung, as the DJ starts spinning "Dance Hall Days."

"It's time . . ." I tell him. Though I'm not sure I'm gonna be able to go through with *Operation Revenge of the Band Fags!* Even though I realize this is probably my last opportunity.

"Let's kick it!" says Brad, sounding all JEH from his *Cover Up* days.

"Would somebody please tell me what's going on?" Ginny asks, totally confused.

Tracy replies, "Don't ask . . ."

"Jack and I got some business to take care of," Brad explains to his date.

"What kind of business?" Ginny asks, half-laughing/half-sounding concerned.

"Let's just say Jack's got a score to settle," Brad answers, "and I'm gonna help him."

Which is when Tracy chimes in, "I'm telling you, Ginny . . . You don't even wanna know."

If you're anything like Brad's date, you're probably wondering what the Hell is going on . . .

Not only is May 23, 1985 the biggest night of the year on account of it being the traditional end-of-the-year Carnation Dance. It's also *Operation Revenge of the Band Fags!* Which might explain why Brad and I are scurrying down the empty front hallway, instead of "Dancing in the Dark" with the rest of our Freshman class. Which happens to be this year's theme, as thought up by Freshman Cheerleading Captain Shelly Findlay, herself.

We stop at our locker momentarily to pick up our supplies. "Hurry up," I tell Brad. "Audrey's gonna be pissed we're taking so long!"

"Would you shut up about Ostrich, already?" Brad hisses. "You are such a goddamn Worry Wart!"

Why I ever bothered to tell him I used to call Audrey "Ostrich" back in Kindergarten, I don't know. All I know is . . . One of these days Brad's gonna slip and say it right to her face. And then I'll be totally busted!

He pops the locker open, pulls his duffle bag from atop a pile of papers and books and Gym shoes and dirty shorts and other general crap he's accumulated over the past three years. "Perfect!" Then in his best Faye Dunaway as Joan Crawford in *Mommie Dearest* he says, "Let's go."

So let's see . . . We've got Craig Gershrowski's locker combination. We've got a duffle bag full of supplies. Now we're on our way to meet Audrey Wojczek at Fuck Face's locker . . . You're probably *still* wondering what exactly it is we're gonna do.

The sound of wooden-heeled dress shoes against gray-tiled floor rings in my ears like the rhythm of the metronome Mrs. Putnam uses to keep time during 1st hour Symphonic Band. I've gotta admit, there's something I enjoy about the empty hallways of Webb Junior High when they're all dark and quiet like this. It's much more peaceful than when they're filled with a bunch of obnoxious screaming 12–14-year-olds!

"What the Hell is taking you guys so goddamn long?"

"We had to stop and get the supplies," I tell Audrey, who's been waiting impatiently for us at locker #686. She actually looks kind of pretty in pink frills with dyed matching flats. Too bad she came Stag.

"Did you get everything?" Brad holds open his duffle bag for Audrey to inspect its contents. "This'll show that Fuck Face Fucker," she snarls. Then she gets to work, spinning the dial on Craig's locker. "Nobody messes with my Best Friend and gets away with it."

Brad and I stand guard. Just in case Craig Gershrowski feels it necessary to drop by during the middle of the Dance. Though he's probably too busy sucking face with the piddly little 7th grader he conned into coming with him. (Gross!)

"Who the fuck does he think he is, anyways?" Audrey mutters. "Did you get a load of what he's wearing?" By which she's referring to the black tuxedo with red cummerbund and matching bow tie Fuck Face's Mommy rented for him in honor of tonight's Special Occasion. "This is a fucking junior high dance . . . Not a goddamn high school Prom."

All of a sudden, I realize how weird it feels to be standing next to my old locker #685. Not weird-weird, but . . . There was a time back in 7th grade when I'd walk down this hallway and

I'd stop in this exact same spot every single day. I distinctly remember the picture I hung on the inside of my locker door . . . Teri Copley from *We Got It Made,* wearing this white long T-shirt/mini-dress, belted at the waist, with little fringe-like cuts on the sleeves. Pre-*Flashdance,* but almost the exact same kinda style. Of course, this was back before Kristian Alfonso ever came into my life! Now it's like locker #685 never even belonged to me. Like I totally abandoned it when that Fuck Face Fucker Craig Gershrowski descended upon Webb Junior High . . . Which I totally did.

I hear the POP of a locker door opening and turn to see Audrey just about wetting herself. "Yeah, Baby!" she exclaims.

"Hell, yes!" Brad cheers.

"Hurry up," I implore, looking down the hallway for any signs of Intelligent Life or Carnation Dance Chaperones like Gorgeous George Grant or Jessica Clark Putnam.

"Eggs," Audrey says to Brad, totally sounding like a TV doctor asking for a scalpel during surgery.

"Eggs," Brad repeats, playing the part of the dutiful nurse/assistant. He pulls from his duffle bag a yellow carton of Grade A Jumbos and hands them to Dr. Audrey. She crouches down in front of Fuck Face's locker, preparing to do the deed.

I can't bear to look at what happens next . . . I hear the sound of shell against metal locker. Followed by the PLOP of eggs being cracked into a pair of Adidas hi-top tennis shoes.

"Shit!" Audrey curses.

"What?" I ask, still not looking.

"I just got yolk on my brand new shoes." And to show just how pissed off she really is, Audrey tosses a couple extra eggs into Fuck Face's locker at random.

Meanwhile, Brad's busying himself down on the floor, looping together pieces of Scotch tape and affixing them to the back of several naked-man pictures we cut out from *Playgirl.* Compliments of Big Boobs Janelle. The plan is to cover the inside of Fuck Face's locker door. Then come tomorrow morning when he opens it, he'll get a nice little surprise to the tune of a bunch of raging hard-ons!

He also won't find any books. Because we're taking them—all! Then next week, when Brad and I are on our way to Bob-lo Island for our traditional end-of-the-year Band trip, we're throwing them off the Bob-lo Boat into the Detroit River. I only wish I were standing at locker #685 tomorrow morning to see the look on Fuck Face Craig Gershrowski's fucking face.

This'll teach him to fuck with the Band Fags!

Hot For Teacher

"I think of all the education that I missed
But then my homework was never quite like this . . ."

—Van Halen

Talk about the End of an Era!

I can't even believe it's Memorial Day—the last time me and Brad will ever march through the streets of Hazeltucky as Webb Warriors. It seems like only yesterday we were piddly little 7th graders learning how to high step and mark time (march) and pinwheel around the parking lot, all the while keeping an instrument held up to your face.

Of course, it totally rained on our parade. Like it does every year. But that didn't keep us from moving in time, five across, down the middle of John R. Starting at 8 Mile, we continued on for a mile and a half, turning left on Woodward Heights near St. Mary Magdalen's. Then down another half mile and over to the Rec. Center on the other side of I-75 near Green Acres Park, where we put on one final show for the judges in the grandstand. Which is really just a set of wooden bleachers some custodians from one of the elementary schools set up.

But it's no wonder we got straight I's this past Winter at the Michigan School Band and Orchestra Association Festival—better known as MSBOA. You should've heard us rocking out to Sousa's "Stars and Stripes Forever" and "Freedom" by Wham! I've gotta admit, I used to think the lead singer was a Total Fag back when I first saw the "Wake Me Up Before You Go-Go" video on MTV. But ever since "Careless Whisper" came out, I kinda like them.

Though it's not like it was our last time ever marching in a parade. Once we get to Hillbilly High in the Fall, we'll be playing at the Varsity Football Home games on Friday nights. Not to mention in all the parades from Hamtramck to Holland . . . Looks like Brad and I are doomed to be Band Fags for another three more years.

After the parade, I *thought* maybe I'd spend the afternoon hanging out with Brad. But when I asked him what he was doing, he informed me that since Bobby Russell's house was just on the other side of the freeway, he was gonna go over there. So I went back to my house—by myself.

The next morning before 1st hour . . .

"What are you doing after school?" Brad asks me. Like he doesn't even realize how pissed I was when he abandoned me post-parade.

"After school today?" I barely look at him, thinking maybe he'll get the hint.

"No . . . After school *yesterday.*"

As per usual, we're gathering our things in between classes from his locker. Which is still a Total Mess, despite the constant reminders we keep getting from Faculty and Administration that we need to start clearing them out. Only eight more days left of school till Finals. Then another week after that, Summer Vacation officially begins.

"I should *probably* study for my Civics exam," I decide. Partly because it's true and partly because I'm beginning to think Brad doesn't appreciate what a Good Friend I've been these past almost-three years.

"When's the test?" he asks.

"June 12th."

"You've still got like over two whole weeks," he replies, doing the math.

"Yeah . . . But Grant's really sticking it to us with the Branches-of-Government-this and Electoral-College-that," I tell him. "How am I ever gonna memorize everything?"

"Sounds like Total Bullshit to me," Brad replies.

But how would he know? Seeing that he's got Old Lady McKenzie. She's been giving the exact same tests year after year after year so everybody's got all the answers from some cheat sheet that's been in circulation since Michigan's own Gerald Ford was President. Brad obviously doesn't realize how hard Grant's test is gonna be . . . Or how much I've got riding on it.

"If I don't get an A," I remind him, "I'll fuck up my 4.0 and then I won't get the Student of the Year Award."

"Oh, no!" Brad exclaims, not even bothering to comment on the fact that the F-word is becoming a consistent part of my vocabulary lately. "What're you gonna do, Jack?"

"What *can* I do?" I catch a glimpse of myself in the tiny mirror hanging on the inside of Brad's locker door. Boy, do I look desperate! Not to mention, like Hell.

I reach into my back pocket, remove my red-handled vent-brush, and run it through my recently trimmed hair. Tracy Cardoza's older sister, Lydia, goes to Cosmetology School at Jardon and she cut it for me over the weekend. The good thing is . . .

she charged me only $5. Which is a lot less than I'd pay at BoRics or Fantastic Sam's. Though I can't even believe how wavy my hair has gotten in the last year or so. Back when I was a kid, I had totally straight, totally white blond hair. Now it's like I hit puberty and *all* my hair has become dark and curly!

"You should totally talk to Mr. Grant about this," Brad advises me, referring to the fact that I'm totally gonna fail my Civics final unless a Miracle occurs.

"What am I supposed to say?" I can't help but notice the stress-induced zit erupting from the center of my chin. *Great!* I slam the locker door and begin down the hallway.

Brad follows close behind. "You could always say something like, 'Please don't fail me, Mr. Grant,'" à la his new favorite actress, Marilyn Monroe. "'I'll do *anything* to get an A in your class.'"

I scoff, "Yeah, right!" Like I'd really say something that stupid.

"I bet Grant could think of a way for you to get one," Brad speculates, raising a brow.

To which I say, "Would you shut up?"

To which he doesn't. "You know what people say . . ."

I'm like, "Mr. Grant is not *like that.*"

And he's like, "I don't know . . . Everybody thinks he's a Total Fag."

I'm about to say, *People say that about* us . . . But I can't bring myself to even think it, let alone say it out loud. The last thing I'm gonna do is give the Assholes we go to school with the satisfaction. The last thing I'm gonna do is start doubting myself—doubting my Best Friend. If Brad was a Total Fag, I know he would tell me. And I'd do the same. But I know he's not and I know he knows I'm not either. So what's the point in bringing it up?

Instead I say, "People say that about *a lot* of people and it doesn't mean they're . . . *Like that.*" I sneak a peek at my reflection in the Guidance Counseling Office windows, confirming what I know is true . . . The person I see looking back is totally Normal. He's just like everybody else in this totally stupid school.

Brad replies, "Oh, I know . . ." But as we mosey on our way, he continues with his hypothesis. "I'll never forget when Mr. Grant was my Swimming coach back in 7th grade . . . He'd always come into the locker room when me and Bobby Russell were in there and walk around in a towel." Then he throws in, "Sometimes he'd even take a shower . . . Right in front of us."

Why do grown-up men always feel the need to show off in front of little boys? I remember one Summer when I was like 9 or 10 years old, I went to Open Swim up at Hillbilly High with my Best Friend at the time, Joey Palladino. Whenever we'd be in the locker room changing, this older Lifeguard Guy would come in and do the exact same thing. Which was how I first learned about the existence of pubic hair, by the way. (Gross!)

"Does Mr. Grant have a nice body?" I find myself wondering aloud. It looks like he might through his clothes and all. He's got this one white short-sleeved polo shirt and his arms look pretty big when he wears it. So does his chest.

"He's got a *great* bod!" Brad informs me. Followed by, "He's got a big dick, too."

"How would you know?" I ask, picking my jaw up from the floor.

"Duh! I saw it when he was taking a shower."

I pull Brad aside, across from Principal Messinger's Office, next to the trophy display cases in the front commons. "Did Mr. Grant ever catch you looking at him?" I ask. "I know I'd be a little weirded out if I was a 30-year-old man and some little 12-year-old boy was watching me take a shower."

"I wasn't exactly *watching* him," he explains. "He was just in the shower and so was I . . . And there it was, plain as day." By which he means Mr. Grant's Private Parts.

I don't know what else to say . . . So I say nothing. That's when I notice the blue jeans I'm wearing must be getting a little small—just like my sweatpants. Because they're feeling awfully tight in the crotch all of a sudden.

Which is when Brad volunteers, "I could totally talk to Mr. Grant for you."

As much as I appreciate his concern, I'm like, "What would *you* say that I can't?"

And he's like, "I don't know . . ." Dreaming up something clever. "I could always say something like, 'Listen, Mr. Grant . . . My Best Friend, Jack Paterno . . . You know, the really cute guy in your 7th hour Civics class? He *really* needs to get an A on his Final.' "

Something tells me I'm not gonna like where this is going . . .

" 'In fact,' " Brad impishly continues, " 'he's sooo desperate, he's even willing to give you a blowjob for it.' "

Okay . . . I did *not* just hear Brad say what I thought he said, did I? Is he actually suggesting what I think he's suggesting?

"I'm not giving Mr. Grant a blowjob!" I protest emphatically. Out of fear of being overheard, I lower my tone to a hushed whisper. "I don't even know the first thing about blowjobs . . . Giving *or* getting."

"What's there to know?" asks Brad, full-voiced and matter-of-fact. "You just open up your mouth and suck!" Then he informs me, "If you don't wanna do it, I will."

Okay . . . Again, I did *not* just hear Brad say what I thought he said, did I? Is he actually suggesting what I think he's suggesting?

"You're my Best Friend since 7th grade," he replies when I ask him. "I'd do *anything* to help you out."

"But come on . . . Would you really do something *like that?*"

I can understand if Brad were to help me cheat in some way. Steal a copy of the test or something. But to have S-E-X . . . With a 30-year-old *guy*? Just for the sake of my being named Student of the Year . . . It seems like he'd be going a bit too far.

"I think it would be fun," Brad confides. "Seducing a teacher . . . Talk about scan-ju-lous!" By which he means "scandalous." But ever since he saw some old Lana Turner movie with her on trial for murder, that's how he pronounces the word, don't ask me why! Then he adds, "It's not like Mr. Grant's a Total Dog or anything!"

Brad's right. They don't call him "Gorgeous George" for nothing. Still, I don't know . . .

"Why would Grant be interested in getting a blowjob from me?" I ask. "Of all people."

"Come on, Jack!" he cries. "You're young . . . You're cute . . . Grant's a Big Fag." Then he adds, "He's not gonna turn down a free blowjob . . . Would you?" Followed by, "If you were a Big Fag, I mean?"

Brad's right. What guy in his right mind would? Still, I can just imagine . . . Principal Messinger stops by after school to talk with Mr. Grant, only to find him sitting on his desk—trousers around his ankles—with the potential Student of the Year down on his knees in front of him!

"You should think about it," he says when I express my concern. "If you don't get an A in Grant's class, Ava Reese is gonna get *your* Student of the Year Award." He points to the wooden plaque prominently displayed on the top shelf of one of the cabinets.

In the mirrored panel behind it, the desire in my eyes reflects back at me. I imagine how my name—JOHN R. PATERNO—would look engraved on the gold metal plate marked "1985." As much as I don't want to admit it, Brad's right. Even though Ava's my friend and I served as her Campaign Manager when she ran against Tom Fulton for Student Council Mayor, I'd hate to see her steal what's rightfully mine . . . What I've been busting my ass for these past three years.

Which is why I say, "I've come this far . . . I'd hate to blow it now."

To which Brad replies, "Then maybe you should blow Mr. Grant, instead!"

I can't even believe I seriously consider it—for all of about five seconds. I mean, how bad could it possibly be? I'm sure a lot of people have done a lot of worse things to get what they want in life. Why shouldn't I? Still, there's got to be a way for a boy to get an A in his Civics class other than pimping himself out to his *male* teacher. Which is what I tell Brad.

"You sure?" he asks, "I can totally stand outside Grant's room and be your lookout."

"Thanks . . . But I don't think that'll be necessary." Even though I totally wanna win that award, knowing it's my one big chance to show all those Jock Jerks at Webb Junior High that I'm a Somebody . . . And not just some stupid Band Fag!

As we turn down the hallway leading to the Band Room, Brad reaches into his back pocket and pulls out a piece of folded up paper. "Oh, my God . . . I totally forgot about this."

"What is it?" I ask on Auto Pilot.

"I got this ad out of some trashy magazine I found," he answers, handing it to me. "You can buy these porno tapes through the mail real cheap."

I unfold the crinkled piece of paper. Sure enough, that's the headline . . . *REAL PORN, REAL CHEAP!* In bright bold letters across the top. And in smaller print, *VHS or Beta.*

"I thought it might be fun to order a couple," Brad continues as I take in the other pertinent info. "We can watch 'em sometime when I'm over spending the night."

Which is where I draw the line! "Why do we always have to do these crazy things at *my* house?"

" 'cause you're the one with your own TV and VCR right in your bedroom," he reminds me.

"Absolutely not!" I declare, shaking my head spastically.

"But I've never seen a porno before," Brad half-whispers/half-whines. "Have you?"

My answer to that question would have to be "N-O." Still I say, "But *Man, Woman, and Horse*? Come on!" If you think the title is disgusting, you should see the accompanying photo. I won't even attempt to describe it.

"What about *Boy and Goat*?" he asks hopefully. "That one sounds pretty interesting to me."

"Gross!" I exclaim, cringing at the thought. "Since when are you into bestiality?"

"I'm not!" Brad rips the magazine ad from my hands, refolds it, shoves it back into his pocket. "I just gotta find *some* outlet for my horniness."

"Well, you're not watching your disgusting mail-order porno tapes on *my* VCR!" I inform him. End of subject.

To which Brad says nothing. Then he laughs.

"What?" I ask. Don't even tell me there's more to the story.

"Um . . . It's too late, Jack."

Which is exactly what I feared. *"Br-a-a-d . . ."*

"I already ordered them," he confesses, giggling. "They'll be here in four to six weeks . . . Keep your eyes peeled."

My jaw drops. "You sent them to *my* house?" I'm about to say, *I can't even believe you did that* . . . Except that I can. Instead I say, "I thought I warned you . . ."

By which I'm referring to the time last Summer when my Dad opened up our phone bill, only to discover a bunch of unknown long-distance toll calls on it. Which he accused *me* of making! Of course, I had no idea what the Hell he was talking about. So my Dad called up Ma Bell and was politely informed the number belonged to an "Adult Services Line." Which led me to conclude that only Brad could be behind something so "scan-jul-ous." And sure enough, when I told him how much trouble I'd gotten in, he admitted he had found the number in the back of the JEH *Playgirl* and called it when he was over spending the night after I had gone to sleep!

"Don't let your Mom find them," Brad advises, referring back to the porno tapes. Then he heads into the Band Room, leaving me outside in the hallway, shaking my head in shame.

The good news is . . . After studying my ass off for like two weeks straight, I get nothing less than a solid A on my Civics final. Thus securing my perfect 4.0 GPA and ensuring my victory over Ava Reese as Student of the Year.

The very next day I get the following note from Tracy Cardoza . . .

June 13, 1985

Hi, Jackie—

So it finally happened . . . The moment we've all been waiting for. Fuck Face finally cracked! After days and days of Algebra Man reminding him to turn in his textbook before the end of the semester or he's gonna flunk him, the Fucker had a breakdown.

He started crying about how some "A-holes" broke into his locker at the Carnation Dance and stole his books and cracked eggs in his $50 gym shoes! And now all his Jock friends think he's a Total Fag since they saw a bunch of pictures of naked guys hanging on his locker door.

I almost felt sorry for him—not! Tell Brad and Audrey I said, "Good job!"

Love, Tracy Cardoza

PS—Congratulations on winning Student of the Year! Are we still going to Farrell's for ice cream on Friday night to celebrate?

With a smirk on my face, I refold Tracy's note. Then I place it in the small red metal lock-box sitting on my dresser where I store all my special letters for future safekeeping. Next to my digital alarm clock/radio with built-in cassette player I got for my last birthday. Which is coming up again, two weeks from today on June 27th.

I can't even believe I'm going to be 15 this year . . .

God, I'm getting old!

WEBB LEGEND

—1985—

Jackie,

To a real gentleman. Thanks for taking me to the Carnation Dance. Good luck at H.P.H.S. I'll see u there in a few years!

—Love, Tracy Cardoza

Jack,

What a guy!! What would I do without a friend like you! Don't ever forget Ms. Lemieux's class in 7th grade or JEH or zit face Gershrowski. Don't forget Varsity Band or Blue Lake. I know I won't. Don't ever forget Edna, Clark, Rusty, or Lana on Trial. Well that was the good times. Now it's time for hard work, fun, CARS, double dates, and then graduation. Thanks for being a great friend and brother, in that time of need when they did the worst—turned off your facilities. What would I do without you? Well thanks.

—Your friend 4-ever, Brad Dayton

Jackie,

We've been brought together again by fate. One day we will go to Mackinac Island. We'll have fun in High School next year.

—Love ya, Audrey (sorry so short!)

Jackie,

To a nice guy that I met in Varsity band a long time ago! It's been fun knowing you, even though you stole my Student of the Year Award (just kidding!) I hope you get over Lynn Kelly and go on with your life. You really make me sick when you are always chasing after her.

Call me sometime!

—Love ya, Ava

Class of "88"

K.I.T. 541-0838

Jackie,

Well what am I supposed to say? That your a nice + sweet guy? Give me a break! Just kidding! I am glad we are friends even though you drive me crazy. I hope I have you in a class next year so that you can tell me about 'DAYS.' Maybe we'll have a VCR by then. Well gotta go now. Have a nice life.

—Love, Carrie Johnson

P.S. I love Peter Reckell!

MOCK ELECTIONS

—1985—

MOST POPULAR

Tom Fulton
Shelly Findlay

BEST PERSONALITY

Brad Dayton
Shelly Findlay

PRETTIEST EYES

Bobby Russell
Ava Reese

MOST FORGETFUL

Brad Dayton
Marie Sperling

MOST MODEST

Max Wilson
Carrie Johnson

BEST ATHLETE

Rob Berger
Katy Griffin

BEST BOD

Bobby Russell
Lynn Kelly

CLASS CLOWN

Bobby Russell
Audrey Wojczek

BEST COUPLE

Tom Fulton and
Marie Sperling

MOST LIKELY TO SUCCEED

Jack Paterno
Ava Reese

—SOPHOMORE—

1985–1986

Obsession

"I will have you
Yes, I will have you . . ."

—Animotion

Talk about Destiny or Fate or *whatever* you wanna call it!

One of the benefits of being an official member of the official Kristian Alfonso Fan Club is . . . I'm privy to certain information before it's made Public to the rest of her non-Fan Club member fans—4x/year I receive a copy of the official Fan Club newsletter, *Kristian's Korner.* Inside, various updates can be found as to what Kristian Alfonso's been up to—apart from appearing as Hope on *Days of our Lives.* Like what she did on her Summer Vacation. Or how she attended a Benefit Concert put on by Gloria Loring, who plays Liz Chandler Curtis, and is the singer of the *Facts of Life* theme song, by the way.

You can probably imagine the excitement I felt after receiving my Summer 1985 issue, only to discover the really big news on page 3. Under the heading "Itinerary" was a list of dates where Kristian Alfonso would be making Personal Appearances. And at the bottom of the list, you'll never believe what it said . . .

"8/24/85—Food Town Expo at Lucas County Recreation Center, Toledo, OH."

In case you don't know, Toledo is only like an hour south from where I live in Hazeltucky. Straight down I-75. And don't you think it's pretty coincidental that the day I'm gonna finally meet the Love of my Life is exactly one year from when I first joined her official fan club?

Of course, there's no way my Dad would ever drive me all the way to Toledo, OH, just to see Kristian Alfonso. He won't even drive me over to Brad's house without complaining. So I immediately got on the phone, called my Aunt Sonia, and begged her to take me. Though there wasn't any doubt in my mind that she'd say yes.

The thing about Aunt Sonia is . . . In all these years, she and my Uncle Mark have never had any children. So they've always treated me and my sister and brother like we're their own.

Practically every Summer back when we were kids, they used to take us camping. One time, we spent two weeks traveling around Up North with them. We went to Hartwick Pines State Park in Grayling and Tahquamenon Falls in the Upper Peninsula. We even made it to Copper Harbor, which is the furthest point north you can go in the state of Michigan, in case you're not aware. Except for Isle Royale out in Lake Superior and *nobody* ever goes there. It's full of nothing but wolves and moose and stuff.

In preparation for the big day, I've done something extra special that will ensure my chance to actually meet Kristian Alfonso . . . Up Close and Personal.

One sweltering Sunday afternoon back in mid-July, I found a full-sized 8" x 10" black-and-white picture of KA in *Soap Opera Magazine*. Not to be confused with *Soap Opera Digest,* which is like half the size and not nearly as informative. I tore the picture out and, with a pencil and ruler, graphed it into ½" x 1" squares. Then on a sheet of white poster board my Mom picked up at Arbor's, I did the exact same thing, only larger. Like 2" x 3". Back in like 5th grade, we learned some mathematical formula in Art for making it specifically to what they call "scale." But I can't remember the exact equation so I just played it by ear.

Then basically all I did was . . . Focus on one square at a time, drawing exactly what I saw in each one in order to make an exact copy of the original—only larger. Like 22" x 28". Kinda like what Sonny Malone does in *Xanadu*, except he does it with album covers.

I'm not even kidding when I say that I spent the entire day of July 14, 1985 working on this project. Once it was finished, it looked pretty damn good. If I do say so myself.

Now here we are, six weeks later at the Lucas County Recreation Center in Toledo, OH . . .

I have no idea why my Aunt Sonia insisted on bringing my sister and brother along with me and Brad. But I didn't wanna complain for fear she'd tell me to forget the whole darn thing. Then what would I do? Like my Mom always says, "I'd be up Shit's Creek without a paddle!"

It turns out that Food Town is pretty much the Toledo equivalent of Farmer Jack's. At the Expo there are all these tables and booths set up by companies like Kellogg's and Betty Crocker and Kraft, giving away a ton of free samples. Like Shake 'n Bake and Hamburger Helper and Pop-Tarts. Which are all totally useless to me and totally *not* the reason I'm decked out in my official Kristian Alfonso Fan Club T-shirt worn beneath the vintage 1960s periwinkle blue cardigan sweater I found in my Uncle Roy's closet from back when he was a kid. On which I've pinned five different Kristian Alfonso buttons/badges I had specially made for the occasion at Buttons 'n Bows in Universal Mall.

So what if Brad thinks I look like a Total Dork and is totally embarrassed to be seen walking up and down the aisles with me? He's just jealous because he doesn't have his own Kristian Alfonso T-shirt on account of he couldn't afford the cost to join her Fan Club. He's just jealous because people are staring and pointing at *me* as I pass them by . . . Guess it's pretty obvious why I'm here, huh?

"Ladies and gentlemen," a radio announcer-like voice booms over our heads from the loudspeakers. "Food Town proudly welcomes, from *Days of our Lives,* Kristian Alfonso and Charles Shaughnessy . . . Better known as Hope Brady and Shane Donovan."

"Come on, Jack!" Brad grabs hold of my arm and begins pulling me through the crowd. A small stage has been erected in the far corner of the Lucas County Recreation Center. Around it, the hundred or so audience members who have gathered burst into applause. Though none can compare to the enthusiasm of one 15-year-old Jack Paterno who's traveled 70 miles—all the way from Hazeltucky, MI—just to be here on this Historic Day.

"Where the Hell is she?" Brad rests a hand on my shoulder, stretching up to the tips of his toes, neck craning. "Do you even see her?"

I'm about to tell him to get the Hell off me, when suddenly, she appears out of nowhere . . .

Flashbulbs pop from all directions as Kristian Alfonso takes to the stage. I wedge the Poster Board Portrait carefully between my knees, holding it in place while I lift my Kodak Disc camera to my eye and snap away. I also read in *Kristian's Korner* that KA loves teddy bears, so I've wrapped the Poster Board Portrait in special Care Bears paper I picked out at the Hallmark Store across from Farmer Jack's . . . God, I hope she likes it!

"Is that *her?*" asks Brad. From the sour face he's making, I can tell he's thinking exactly what I'm thinking. But he's the one who says it . . . "She looks different."

I've heard the camera adds ten pounds and that people always look taller on TV. And from the looks of Kristian Alfonso standing no more than a hundred feet away, she can't be more than 5'4", 110 pounds. But something about the Live and In Person version of her doesn't look quite right. By which I mean she doesn't look the way she does on television.

"What happened to her *hair?*" Brad wonders, wincing.

He's right . . . It's not long and flowing and all done up and perfectly styled the way it is on TV. Instead, she's got it pulled back in a plain old boring ponytail.

"And what the Hell is she *wearing?*"

I'll tell you . . . Pleated khaki pants that come down to just above her ankles, with an orange colored short-sleeved top with this paisley printed gold lamé vest over it. I'm not saying it looks bad, 'cause it doesn't. It's just not something I think Hope Williams-Brady would be caught dead wearing on *Days of our Lives.*

But I don't care. Because it's really her . . . And she's about to say something!

"Good afternoon," Kristian Alfonso speaks into a silver handheld microphone, the sound of her voice booming from a pair of large speakers set up on either side of the stage.

"Hello, Everyone!" her costar, Charles Shaughnessy, greets in his British accent. "It's certainly a pleasure for Kristian and I to be here this afternoon." Which he pronounces "ahf-tuh-nyoon," of course.

"Thank you so much for having us," Kristian Alfonso adds.

I can't even believe I'm breathing the exact same air that she is. My face is starting to hurt from my totally ear-to-ear permagrin, that's how totally geeked I am at this moment. The funny thing is . . . Even though I can *see* Kristian Alfonso addressing the sea of slightly overweight Ohio housewives surrounding her, I can't *hear* a word she's saying on account of the beating of my heart, totally drowning out everything around me.

Till I hear Charles Shaughnessy say the Magic Words . . . "Does anyone have any questions?"

A bijillion hands shoot up in the air.

"Raise your hand, Jack!" Brad shouts in my ear. He practically yanks my arm out of the socket, lifting it high above my head. Though I'm not particularly worried. I'm sure Kristian Alfonso's just gotta see me standing in the crowd what with the way I'm dressed and all. She's just gotta call on me. I'm her #1 Fan of All Time . . .

But she doesn't.

"Hi, Hope." A middle-aged woman with a nasally midwestern twang greets Kristian Alfonso after the microphone is passed her way. I don't even bother to listen to the totally stupid question she asks because I can't even believe she just called Kristian Alfonso "Hope." Doesn't the woman realize she's got a *real* name? K-R-I-S-T-I-A-N!

"My question is for Shane Donovan," the next Ohio Mom says. Again, failing to understand that these people are merely actors who play *characters* on TV.

With each question I wait in anxious anticipation for my turn. Though I'm beginning to fear it's never gonna arrive.

"You better do something," Brad impatiently advises. "Otherwise, you're never gonna get a chance."

God help me, I didn't just travel 70 miles to Bum Fuck Toledo *not* to seize my moment! I raise my hand higher, reaching up as far as I can towards the rafters. My back starts to spasm but I ignore it. The reward will be worth the pain.

"How you doin', Kristin?" Some guy who's gotta be like 30

years old just got hold of the mic. I can't even believe he just called Kristian Alfonso "Kristin." I bet he's never seen an episode of *Days of our Lives* in his life. Then he's like, "I just wanna tell you, you're beautiful . . . You got a boyfriend?"

To which Kristian Alfonso humbly replies, "Thank you." Kinda half-laughing/half-embarrassed. Then she throws in, "And yes, I do have a boyfriend . . . Sorry." Which I don't even think is true. Otherwise, I'm sure I would've read about it somewhere.

Seeing her Live and In Person, I get the sense that Kristian Alfonso feels a little uncomfortable in front of all these Total Strangers. All these people who think they know *everything* about her just because they see her every day on television. But I guess it's all part of her job. In fact, she probably wouldn't even have one if it weren't for the love of her fans . . . Like me and Brad.

"Kristian!" we both scream. Like a couple of Total Girls.

Brad helps me hoist the Poster Board Portrait high above our heads hoping to catch her attention. But she still doesn't see us. "We've gotta get closer," he tells me. As much as I can't stand confrontation and I know it's rude to push our way towards the front, I know Brad's right. This could be our one and only opportunity.

So we make a break for it . . .

"Excuse me," he says politely, navigating a path through the crowd. "Excuse me . . . Pardon me."

"Pardon me . . . Excuse me," I echo. We're like Bugs Bunny in that one where he's at the movies working his way across the entire row, totally annoying everybody in the theater.

Despite receiving a few dirty looks, I feel that most people are on our side and want us to succeed in our mission. Especially once they've seen me all decked out in my official Kristian Alfonso Fan Club T-shirt and loaded down with my Kristian Alfonso badges/buttons like some Total Stalker.

"We've only got time for a few more questions," I hear Charles Shaughnessy say at this point. "Anyone else have anything they'd like to ask either Kristian or myself?"

"OVER HERE!"

I have no idea where the loud and obnoxious voice comes from. But it cuts through the crowd, giving Kristian Alfonso no other choice than to look in its direction. We all watch as she taps Charles Shaughnessy on the arm and aims. Then she says, "Hello!"

I can't tell who she's talking to . . . Somebody in the crowd . . . Who is it?

Then I realize . . .

That somebody is ME!

I look down and discover *I'm* holding the silver audience microphone in my hot little hand. How I ended up with it, I have no idea. But I raise it to my mouth, preparing to speak.

"Hi, Kristian."

"Hi," she says, all smiles. Looking right at me!

"H-h-h-i . . ." I can't even believe how nervous I am at this moment. I can actually hear my voice trembling as it fills the air. God, I hate the sound of it! "Um . . ." I don't know what else to say . . . So I say nothing. I'm like Cindy Brady in that one where she goes on the Quiz Show and totally freezes up.

"We've got a present for you," Brad tells Kristian Alfonso, taking hold of the mic.

"You do?" she asks, as if she's surprised anybody would even *consider* bringing her a gift.

How could I forget the Poster Board Portrait wrapped in Care Bears paper?

"Show her," Brad orders, nudging me.

So I do . . . Still totally nervous, I hold it up where Kristian Alfonso can finally see it.

"Is that for me?" she beams. "Thank you!"

Since we can't get any closer, we pass my Poster Board Portrait through the crowd where it finally reaches Kristian Alfonso on stage. She takes one look at the wrapping paper and her face totally lights up.

"How cute!" she coos. "I love teddy bears."

And I'm like, "I know . . ." (Duh!)

"We read it in your Fan Club newsletter," adds Brad. Even though *I'm* the one who actually read it and told him.

Next we watch as Kristian Alfonso unwraps my present, as we anxiously await her reaction.

"Oh, my!" she gasps. "Did one of you draw this?"

Brad admits, "He did." As much as he wishes he could take credit. Then he points to me, his Trusty Sidekick.

"It's beautiful," Kristian Alfonso compliments.

All I can do is nod my head and mutter, "Thanks."

Then she holds the Poster Board Portrait up for the entire audience to admire. First the right side. Then the left. All around us, the buzz of voices from the crowd . . . "Look at that!" "Isn't that nice?" "Wow!"

Poised and ready I stand, eye to my camera. Kristian Alfonso looks directly into the lens and I snap a photo of her—the REAL Kristian Alfonso—holding the Poster Board Portrait that I, John R. Paterno, drew especially for her.

At which point, she says, "Tell me your names."

Which is when the slap of harsh reality hits me, smack dab in the face . . . Kristian Alfonso has no idea who the Hell I am! Even though I'm her #1 Fan of All Time and a member of her official Fan Club, I'm just another nameless face in the Food Town Expo Crowd.

"Jack Paterno," I reply, totally devastated.

"I'm Brad Dayton," says Brad, not sounding nearly as disappointed.

They say that everybody is entitled to their Fifteen Minutes of Fame. I wonder, is this mine? People continue to whisper and point as they pass me by. "There's the guy who drew the picture of Hope from *Days of our Lives.*" It's like I've stolen the show.

"Okay, now what?" my Aunt Sonia asks us after the crowd thins out. Have I mentioned yet that she kinda reminds me of Laverne from *Laverne & Shirley*? Though she hates it when I tell her that. "You guys wanna walk around some more?"

"Sure," answers Brad for all of us.

"Jackie?" My Aunt Sonia turns to me for confirmation.

"I don't care what we do." My mission is accomplished . . . I can die now.

We continue walking around the Food Town Expo, taking in the displays of Shake 'n Bake and Hamburger Helper and Pop-Tarts. But I don't notice anything going on around us. I'm stuck on Cloud Nine. Till we round a corner . . . and there she is again!

Kristian Alfonso, escorted by a burly looking Security Guard, walks among the crowd. Fans stop dead in their tracks. Heads turn, amazed at the fact that she's even more Up Close and Personal than she had been just a few moments ago up on stage.

Despite cries of "Hope!" and "Kristian!" and the pop of flashbulbs in her face, I can tell she's trying to avoid making eye contact with anybody. As much as I want to call out to her myself I realize how rude it would be to do so. Besides, I've already had my big moment, haven't I?

"Hey!"

I turn to see Kristian Alfonso heading right towards me. Totally in my direction. The next thing I realize is . . . She's standing by my side. I'm talking "Gee, Your Hair Smells Terrific" close. Even though Brad is right there beside me, Kristian Alfonso puts her arm around *my* shoulder and starts walking *me* through the crowd.

I can't even tell you how it feels to have everybody screaming at us and taking our picture. It's like everything moves in slow motion. Or maybe it's totally speeded up. I can't describe how surreal it feels. Between the stark overhead lights and the electric strikes of lighting coming from a bijillion cameras, I have no idea what's going on or where Kristian Alfonso is leading me.

But you can bet I'm following . . .

"How long did it take you to draw that picture?" she asks, talking directly into my ear.

"Um . . ." I can't even believe I'm totally speechless. "A few hours," I manage to answer after a couple of deep breaths. Even though it's the truth, I hope Kristian Alfonso doesn't think I'm bragging or anything, 'cause I'm not.

"You're kidding!" she replies. "You're a very talented artist."

And with that, she kisses me . . . On the cheek. But it still counts.

Just wait till the folks at Hillbilly High hear about this next week when we start school! Never in my wildest dreams did I imagine that I—John R. Paterno, from Hazeltucky, MI—would ever walk arm in arm with *Days of our Lives* star Kristian Alfonso . . .

I will never forget this day for as long as I live.

Blister In The Sun

"I'm high as a kite, I just might
Stop to check you out . . ."

—Violent Femmes

"Wanna smoke some pot?"

I told Brad what a stupid idea it was for us to walk from my house near 10 Mile all the way over to his house near 8 Mile. Especially when it's dark outside. But would he listen to me? No!

So here we are, walking down Wanda in Ferndale at 10:00 PM at night. We just passed by Max's Mom's house on the corner of University, the blue glow of the TV lighting up the French Room. Though I've got a feeling Max probably isn't home. Being that it's Saturday night and all. Ever since he started hanging out with Tom Fulton again, he's pretty much no longer friends with me. He probably even thinks I'm a Total Fag, now. Just like all those other Jock Jerks we go to school with. Which makes me kinda sad . . . I always thought Max was different. I thought he really liked me.

A block past Max's house we come to Wanda Park. Which is

totally dark and deserted at this hour. Except for a few Burn-Outs hanging around smoking. Though from the nauseatingly sweet smell wafting in our direction as we approach, my guess is . . . they're not plain old cigarettes.

"Come on!" Brad tells me. Like we can just join right in.

"No way!" I vehemently object. Yet I follow him as he crosses towards the dilapidated picnic table in the middle of the overgrown park. None of the kids sitting on top do I recognize. From school or anywhere else for that matter. Probably because I make it a point not to associate with *those* kinda people!

Suddenly, a dark blue Ford Escort comes whizzing around the corner from up ahead near the Faygo factory. Maybe it's black, I don't know. All I know is . . . it's doing at least 50 MPH in a 25 MPH zone. I expect the driver to slow down as she's obviously gotta see us standing in the middle of the street. Instead, the four-door picks up speed, coming right at us! I practically jump out of my skin and onto the narrow patch of grass between the sidewalk and the curb, totally hitting the deck as the scent of burning rubber fills my nostrils.

"Ya stupid Band Fags . . . Get the fuck outta the road!"

I look up to see Brad standing in the middle of Wanda, hands out in front of him. Like he can really stop the car from mowing him down with his Magic Super Powers. Which is when I hear the female passenger call out, "Hey, Sophomore . . . Wanna buy an elevator pass?" Which I know has gotta be a joke. Because there aren't any elevators in Hillbilly High.

Sure enough, I recognize the mass of curly brown hair leaning out the window as belonging to that of the HPHS Senior Class President, Alyssa Resnick. Not to mention, Flag Corps Co-Captain, member of Chorale, and recently elected Homecoming "Top 25." Which means by this time next week, I could be friends with the Homecoming Queen. Not bad for a piddly little Sophomore who started high school a little less than a month ago.

"Get in the car . . . Now!"

I breathe a sigh of relief to see the driver isn't some Varsity Football player. She's Junior Luanne Kowalski—known as "Lou" to her friends. Though when I first met her, I thought it was "Lu," L-U. But she soon informed me of her preferred spelling, L-O-U.

Brad and I met both these girls two weekends ago when the Viking Marching Band participated in the Frontier Days parade in this tiny little town called Charlotte, located on the other side of the state. Not quite as far as BLFAC in Muskegon. But pretty darned close when you're riding with a group of Band Fags on an official yellow School Bus for over two hours! Which is where we officially met Alyssa and Lu—I mean, Lou—after they sat down behind us and totally started talking about how much they love Monty Python and *Pee-wee's Big Adventure*. Both of which I've never seen.

Brad actually already knew Lou from Symphonic Band at Webb, back when we were in 8th grade and she was a Freshman. Being that they both play trombone, Brad and Lou were in the same section so they talked all the time. But I really never had anything to do with her. Which was totally fine by me.

"Haven't your mothers ever told you how dangerous it is walking the streets of Hazeltucky after dark?" Lou says, once Brad and I are out of harm's way and sitting side by side in the back seat of her car.

"*Somebody* wouldn't listen to me," I reply, shooting Brad a look.

The dark interior momentarily brightens as I hear a familiar SNAP that instantly reminds me of my Dad. I can see Lou's just pulled out a silver Zippo, and with its blue flame she lights the Marlboro Red dangling from her lower lip. Which surprises me. I never thought Luanne would be a smoker. Being that she's not at all the Burn-Out type. In fact, she's very Preppy. She never ever wears jeans. With her it's always slacks worn with paisley printed shirts and argyle sweaters with matching socks. And penny loafers complete with pennies in the slots. Which, according to *The Preppy Handbook,* is one of the true signs of being a Total Prep.

Brad takes Lou's lighting up as a signal for him to smoke too. "Where are you Ladies off to?" he asks, exhaling in my general direction—just to piss me off, I'm sure. I casually crack my window, breathing in the cool September air.

"Who you calling a Lady?" Lou says, looking up in her rearview mirror at us.

"You guys ever been to the Tombs?" Alyssa turns around in her seat. Which is when I realize who she kinda reminds me of . . . Molly Ringwald, from *Sixteen Candles.* Something about her mouth. The way the upper lip kinda curls when she smiles.

"I don't know," Brad answers. "What's the Tombs?"

Alyssa starts to giggle. "Oh, my God . . . You guys are Virgins?" By which I'm assuming she means we're Virgins when it comes to the Tombs. Even though I'm an actual *real* Virgin. But how would Alyssa know that?

"Initiation time," Lou sneers, totally sounding like one of those Frat Boys straight out of *Porky's* or some other stupid movie where bad things happen to good little Sophomores like me and Brad.

I've got a feeling I don't like the sound of where this whole night is heading . . .

Luanne makes a right at 9 Mile, barely slowing down as she takes the corner. Pedal to the floor, she cranks up the volume on the radio. I don't recognize the band we're listening to, but I like them. They sound kinda New Wave and yet pop-y. "Who is this?" I call out over the music.

"Violent Femmes," Alyssa answers. Obviously she's a fan because she's totally singing along with every word.

"Cool," I say. Even though I have no idea what the Hell a Violent Femme is.

Lou takes a right onto the service drive near Gas 'n Go. Then she makes a quick left onto the "Motor Vehicles Only" bridge over I-75. Followed by another quick left onto the opposite service drive near the Holiday Inn. Meanwhile in the backseat, Brad and I are being tossed around like I don't know what. Not that I'm complaining or anything. It's totally cool to be riding around in a car with your new High School Friends.

After we pass Farmer Jack's on the right, we hop on the freeway. Brad glances over at me, trying not to look *too* worried as Lou swerves in and out of traffic at 70 MPH. "Where are you taking us?" he calls out over the roar of the engine.

"To the Tombs," Alyssa answers, matching his volume.

"Where?" Brad asks again.

"Sit down and shut up!" Lou bellows. "You'll find out when we get there."

Apparently the Tombs is all the way out on Rochester Road. Which is where we get off I-75 at exit 67. Now we've gotta drive down the highway for another five miles or so.

"We're getting close," Alyssa says when a pair of Golden Arches on the corner of Avon Road whiz by.

"I could go for a bacon double cheeseburger," says Brad. "Can we stop?"

"I said, sit down and shut up!" Lou roars. Which is exactly what Brad does. One thing I forgot to mention about Luanne Kowalski is . . . Back when Brad and I were in junior high, we always kinda thought she might be *like that.* Which I'm beginning to think again now, simply based on the way she drives with one hand on the steering wheel, the other holding her cigarette. She kinda reminds me of the Marlboro Man. Something about the way she wraps her index finger around it, covering her face with the palm of her hand when she raises it to her lips. It's totally masculine!

Not to mention her language . . .

"Where's that *fucking* turnoff?" Lou asks herself after about another five miles. She slows the car down, peering out her window towards the left side of the road. "Here we go . . ."

I look out and see the black on white nondescript sign marked DRAHNER. Which is this totally dark, totally bumpy, and totally deserted road. Not a streetlight or another car to be seen anywhere.

"Look out!" Alyssa cries from out of nowhere.

"What?!" Brad gasps, jumping a mile.

"Did you see that?" she asks us.

"Where?" I say, closing my eyes, not really wanting to see whatever it is Alyssa *thinks* she might've seen.

"Up ahead," Alyssa answers. "A guy with an axe!"

Brad screams, "Holy shit!" Then he grabs on to me for dear life, as Alyssa and Lou both start laughing.

"You Sophomores are such pussies," chuckles Lou.

The road winds and turns and dips up and down. Gravel spits beneath our tires as Lou does her best to avoid the bijillion potholes. Which equal in number the stars I see looking up at the sky through the rear window . . . I'm totally freaking out.

To make matters worse, Alyssa says, "There it is . . ." Then she ducks down in her seat to get a better view out the front windshield.

"Oh, my fucking God . . ." says Brad, pressing his face up against his window on the driver's side. "We're not going in there, are we?"

I stick my head between the front seats trying to see whatever it is they're looking at. On the left side of the road is a graveyard. Inside the graveyard is a hill. And built into the side of that hill is . . . the Tomb.

"Hell yeah, we are!" Luanne informs us. "Just as soon as we find someplace to park."

Why Alyssa and Lou refer to it as "the Tombs" (plural) when apparently there's only one Tomb (singular), I don't know. All I know is . . . I'm totally scared shitless at this moment.

"I'm not going out there," I protest once we pull off the road and park Lou's car on the grass and everybody gets out except me. I can just imagine us getting totally stranded out here in BFE, with some psycho killer in a freaky mask stalking us! Like in *Friday the 13th* or *Halloween*.

"Don't be such a Sophomore," Alyssa tells me. "I'll protect you from the monks."

"What monks?" I have to ask, this being the first I've heard about any.

"The ones that live in the monastery."

"What monastery?"

Alyssa grins. "You'll find out." Then she opens my door and reaches out a hand. Which I reluctantly take. Even after I close the door quietly behind me so as not to wake up the neighbors, she doesn't let go.

"But it's cold," I whimper, already starting to freeze in my maroon and gray Viking Marching Band windbreaker.

"I'll keep you warm," Alyssa assures me, snuggling up close.

"Come on!" Lou orders from where she and Brad stand on the side of the dirt road puffing on yet another cigarette.

The four of us begin walking, Brad and Lou ahead of me and Alyssa. "You know that song we were listening to in the car?" she says softly. By which I'm guessing she means the one by the Violent Femmes. Which is all about getting just one kiss—and just one F-U-C-K. "I played it just for you."

If I didn't know better, I'd think the HPHS Senior Class

President, Flag Corps Co-Captain, member of Chorale, and recently elected Homecoming "Top 25" was flirting with me. But that can't possibly be the case. I mean, Alyssa Resnick is *very* Popular. And I'm a Stupid Sophomore!

So all I say is . . . "Oh, yeah . . . ?"

I'm happy to report that we never make it to the Tomb. Or even into the graveyard, for that matter. Apparently, one of the neighbors heard our car pulling up and felt it his duty to make sure those "pesky kids" didn't go causing any trouble. Guess we drove all that way for nothing. Talk about anticlimactic!

The next night I call Alyssa on the phone around 9:30 PM . . .

"I can't talk too long," she says since she's doing her laundry. On top of fighting with her Mom—again. I guess the short of it is . . . Alyssa's Mom got pissed at her for coming home late last night. So Alyssa threatened to leave home and go live with her older sister. Which apparently she's done before.

Even though we only talk for like twenty minutes, over the course of our conversation we find out we've got a few things in common . . . #1—Alyssa's not only seen the movie *Sooner or Later,* she's also read the book *and* the sequel, *Waiting Games.* Which I totally didn't even know existed.

#2—Though she says she likes *Bloom County* better, she also likes the comic strip *Arnold* by Kevin McCormick. Which is totally my new favorite since I first read it in the *Free Press* this past Summer. In case you don't know, *Arnold* is all about this big-nosed short kid named—you guessed it—Arnold, and his friend, Tommy, who is taller and kind of a Geek. They're both in like junior high, so they spend a lot of time in the cafeteria talking to Bertha the Lunch Lady.

One of my absolute favorites so far is from this past June 9th. Tommy's standing in the Lunch Line with his tray of meatloaf when all of a sudden we hear Arnold scream from out of the frame, "It moved!" Arnold then goes on to inform Bertha that throwing raw hamburger against the wall and yelling, "Die, Cow, Die!" isn't the way you tenderize meat. All the while, Tommy's got his usual wide-eyed blank expression on his face . . . Totally hilarious!

The next morning before 1st hour English with Mrs. Malloy, I find a card from Alyssa stuck inside my locker—#1427. Right outside the cafeteria near the Gym.

On the front of the tan speckled envelope, Alyssa's written To Mr. Jackson L. Tightwad. Even though I told her my real first name is John and my middle initial is R. I guess she got the "Tightwad" part from the fact that I told her my Dad's one and I take after him when it comes to spending money. Below that it says, From The Blinker. Complete with a doodle of closed eyes with lashes. Stemming from the fact that Alyssa totally blinked when they took her Homecoming "Top 25" picture.

On the front of the card is a cartoon hand pointing to a red box with the words "Scratch and Sniff." Upon opening it, the words "Very good! What other animals do you do?" appear. Followed by Alyssa's own addition, How about a cow? Ha, ha. Love, Alyssa. Stemming from the *Arnold* comic strip and "Die, Cow, Die!"

Inside the card, I find the following handwritten note on teddy bear stationery . . .

9/22/85
9:57 PM

Dear Jackson L. Tightwad, (What a bitch, I know!)

Why the Hell did I ever come back home? She's gonna be sorry if she starts anything with me and I leave again. Anyway, thanks for calling to say good night. It was really nice of you.

"Arnold" was pretty funny this week but "Bloom County" was funnier.

I don't think I ever answered your question about "Waiting Games." The book isn't mine. It belonged to a girl from my church. You probably wouldn't appreciate it as much as "Sooner or Later." It's all about how Jessie finally gets laid and thinks she's preggers but she doesn't know for sure. (Gee Alyssa, you sure know how to ruin a story!)

Sorry again about Saturday. You looked pretty pissed off most of the night. But Lou thought you guys were fun to hang out with. Especially Brad. What a crazy guy!

So can I ask you a question? It's kind of personal, so you don't have to answer but I've been thinking about it a lot. Why do you always look so down on yourself? I don't think you realize what a cool person you are. You said people often tease you about being sensitive and caring. Fuck them! They're the ones who suck, Jack. Not you. But let me tell you something. If you happen to fall madly in love with someone, don't tell them too much about you too soon. Not unless you know they feel the same way. Because I've got a feeling you're the kind of guy who gets hurt easily and I don't want that happening to you. Maybe that sounds crazy but I know how sensitive you are. We've got a lot more in common than you think!

Well darling, it's time for me to get going. See you later. Write back if you get a chance. Take care! Love, Alyssa (what a signature)

P.S. Tomorrow we find out who makes "Top 5." Blinkers are disqualified automatically!

P.P.S. What about lunch in the cafeteria? If so, wait by my locker (249).

As it turns out, Alyssa does not get elected to Homecoming "Top 5." However, Freddy Edwards does. Remember the Total Babe Band Aide from 2nd hour Varsity Band back in 7th grade? Believe it or not, after all these years of being Mr. Popular Wrestler, Freddy still plays sax in the Marching Band and Wind Ensemble. Unlike most of my friends who all dropped out once we got to Hillbilly High. Like Lynn Kelly and Shelly Findlay and Katy Griffin. Even Bobby Russell no longer sits next to me after doing so for three years on account of he thinks our teacher, Mr. Klan, is a Total Fag—just because he's over 35 and he's never been married.

It looks like all that's left of my Band Friends are Ava Reese, Carrie Johnson, and Brad, of course. Sometimes I think he and I are gonna be Band Fags forever . . .

God, I hope not!

You Spin Me Round

"All I know is that to me
You look like you're lots of fun . . ."

—Dead or Alive

What the Hell was I *thinking*?

How come whenever you take photos—on vacation, during the holidays, wherever—they never turn out the way you imagine they're going to at the time you're actually taking them?

It's like you remember things being one way while you're living the moment. Then three months later, once you've mustered up enough energy to take the film in for developing—on top of paying an exorbitant amount of money to Arbor's or Kmart's or wherever it is you took them—you get the photos back, only to find that the images depicting your vacation or holiday or whatever look *nothing* like how you imagined they would at the moment you imagined them.

Like this one of me taken Up North at my Grandpa's cottage this past August . . . Standing on the faded-wood planked dock down by the lake, I'm wearing my green and gold Warrior Marching Band windbreaker, white hi-top tennis shoes, and teal blue sweatpants. I distinctly remember posing for the camera, fishing pole in hand, a smile upon my face, thinking I looked perfectly fine. But examining the photo now in October, I can't even believe I'd go out in public like that!

I mean, granted it was a very windy day. But the pouf-ball of hair on my head makes me look like Richard Simmons! At least according to Brad. Not that he looked any better in his light blue Speedo, crammed inside the middle of this gigantic black rubber inner tube we found.

Boy is that a story . . .

After *much* begging and pleading, Brad's Mom said it was okay for him to spend ten whole days Up North with me and my family at my Grandpa Freeman's cottage in Gaylord. Which is just above your middle knuckle if you do the Michigan hand map thing. On one of our daily sunbathing trips to Otsego Lake, Brad and I came across this beat-up old tool shed off to one side of the dock.

"Something tells me we're not supposed to go trespassing in there," I told Brad as he was about to do just that.

"It's not like it's locked," he informed me with regards to the blue and silver Master lock attached to the plywood door. He deftly removed it, tossed it aside, and took a peek inside. "Well, well, well . . . What do we have here?"

Amid a clutter of regulation orange life jackets, old wooden row boat oars, and ratty aluminum lawn chairs, we discovered one gigantic black rubber inner tube. I'm telling you, this thing was huge! It had to be like three feet in diameter if not four. I'm betting it came from a semi tire or something, that's how big it was.

Which brings us to another one of Bradley Dayton's harebrained schemes . . .

For no other reason than he's totally crazy, Brad came up

with the idea that we should: (a) take the gigantic black rubber inner tube up the twenty or so maroon-painted steps that lead down to the faded-wood planked dock, (b) climb inside, and (c) roll ourselves down in it.

To which I replied, "No fucking way!"

"Come on!" Brad pleaded. "It'll be just like in the Mountain Dew commercial." Then he assured me, "We can totally test it out first."

Why I always let Brad talk me into these crazy things, I have no idea. But the next thing I knew, we were hauling the gigantic black rubber inner tube up the twenty or so maroon painted steps. Upon reaching the summit, we placed it on its side. Then we gave it a push . . .

Round and round she went. Down the steps, across the dock, into the lake. Smooth as silk.

"Who's first?" Brad asked once we retrieved the wet rubber from the cool lake.

"This was *your* idea," I reminded him. Enough said.

Back we went to the top of the hill, gigantic black rubber inner tube in tow. At the top, I helped Brad climb into the center.

"What are you doing?" he asked me as I took out my camera.

"Capturing the moment for Posterity's Sake," I replied. Then I snapped Brad's photo and prepared to give him the old heave-ho.

Wait!" I watched as he literally put his foot down to stop from rolling away. "You better go down to the bottom and be there to catch me . . . Just in case."

I scoffed before replying, "There is no way in Hell I'm gonna get knocked flat on my ass when that thing comes barreling down those steps at 100 MPH."

"Fine!" Brad exclaimed, wiggling his way out of the black rubber donut. "I'll go . . . When I get to the bottom, roll the tube down and I'll see if I can stop it."

So what do you think happened?

When the gigantic black rubber inner tube came barreling down the steps at 100 MPH, Brad totally got knocked flat on his ass. Needless to say, he did *not* climb back inside at any point after that, nor did he ever roll down the hill "just like in the Mountain Dew commercial."

Later that night, back at the cottage we all sat around with my Aunt Sonia and Uncle Mark, who came up to visit for the weekend, telling Ghost Stories. Which totally freaked both me and Brad out. So much so that at 3:00 AM, he woke me up *begging* me to hold his hand while he went to the bathroom.

"Can't you just wait till morning?" I pleaded, not wanting to open my eyes for fear of actually waking up.

"No," Brad whined. " 'member how I wasn't feeling too good so your Mom gave me that Correctol?"

"What about it?"

"Well," Brad continued. "The box said 'The Gentle Laxative' . . . So I took *three* just to be safe."

Needless to say, Brad spent a good portion of that night giving sacrifice to the Porcelain God in my Grandpa Guff's bathroom . . . And to this day, I haven't let him live it down!

Three months later, not a whole lot has been happening . . .

Tonight, I'm having a Halloween party. Which is the big excitement in my life at the moment. I figure since I have a bunch of new friends, it'll be fun for us to get together outside of school for a change. With the help of my Mom, I found this frumpy old housedress that belonged to my Grandma Freeman before she died. I put rollers in my hair and a hairnet on my head. Then I put on a pair of my Mom's panty hose rolled down to my ankles, along with her pink fuzzy bath slippers. Top it all off with a pair of black plastic framed glasses I found in my brother's toy box, and voilà! Instant Aunt Edna from *National Lampoon's Vacation*.

Brad's the first to show around 7:00 PM. He's got on this slinky purple dress, fake pearls around his neck, and tits down to his navel. On his head he's placed a curly gray wig and perched a pair of wire-framed glasses on the end of his freckled nose. "Just call me Whorey Dorey," he declares. Which is the name he's given to his Old Lady Prostitute.

"Don't tell me what you got in that thing," I say when he hikes up his dress, revealing a silver metal flask strapped to his thigh. "If my Mom finds out you brought booze to my party, she'll kill you!"

When Audrey arrives wearing an old pair of Mickey Mouse ears as her costume, Brad calls her "Lame . . ."

"Bite me!" Audrey snaps, in typical Audrey style.

"Who are *you* s'posed to be?" he asks Alyssa after she appears dressed in a long pink nightgown, her hair in pigtails, carrying a large plush Opus from the *Bloom County* doll.

"That's for me to know and you to find out, Sophomore!" she answers, in what I'm pretty sure is her Pee-wee Herman impersonation. Though I *still* haven't seen his *Big Adventure* yet. Personally, I think Alyssa looks kinda cute. Especially with the freckles she's eyebrow-penciled on her nose and cheeks.

I haven't quite figured out what's up between her and me. It's like we eat lunch together in the cafeteria all the time. And we talk on the phone almost every night before we go to bed. But it's not like we're officially going together or anything. Maybe it's because I haven't actually *asked* her? I don't know. All I know is . . . I do like Alyssa. And I'm pretty sure she likes me, too. Otherwise, why would she spend so much time hanging out with a Sophomore?

I've gotta say . . . Lou's costume comes as more of a surprise—not! The minute I hear "Falling in Love Again" as she descends the stairs into my parents' basement, I know right away what to expect. Though I have no idea where she got the Marlene Dietrich top hat and tails from. Maybe Randazzo's? Which is a tux rental place in Sterling Heights—not to be confused with Randazzo's Pizza in Hazel Park.

As my parties usually are, this one ends up being a Total Blast. At first I'm not sure how my new High School Friends are gonna react when I serve up Ritz crackers with Cheez Whiz and suggest we play Spin-the-Bottle. But it's what we've always ended up doing at my Boy/Girl parties in the past.

"Out of my way, Sophomore!"

Cheri Sheffield is the first to spin. Also a Senior at HPHS, she's been Alyssa's Best Friend since like 8th grade back at Beecher. Which is the *other* Hazeltucky junior high where all the Burn-Outs go. Though neither Cheri nor Alyssa are what I would call "Burn-Outs" so I guess there goes that theory. She kinda reminds me of Mallory from *Family Ties*. Only Cheri's blond beneath the long dark Witch's wig she's wearing, complete with green-painted face, long crooked nose, and wart right on the end. She's also a little on the heavier side. Not that Cheri's fat or anything, 'cause she's not. But like Audrey, she's a bigger girl. Like 5'8" maybe?

Even though she was good about dressing up for the party, I thought Cheri would totally object to playing such a baby game. But she totally grabs the Mountain Dew bottle from my hand and spins away. "What if I land on a girl?" Cheri wonders. And she does as it comes to a halt on her younger sister, Elizabeth, aka Betsy.

Also a Sophomore, Betsy and I met in Mrs. Carey's French 1 class this semester. She looks cute sitting across from me in her maroon and gray Hillbilly High JV Cheerleading uniform. She kinda reminds me of that girl from *Square Pegs*, Sarah Jessica Parker. Only much prettier. Though looking at her and Cheri sitting side by side, it's hard to tell they're even related. Considering Betsy's hair is brown and she's a lot thinner.

"I'll take your turn for you," Cheri's boyfriend, Erin Ahrens, jokes. A Junior tri-tom player in Marching Band, Erin is also 1st chair clarinet in Wind Ensemble. I've gotta admit, he looks totally cool in his homemade Vampire costume, complete with fake fangs. Though if you ask me, having a name like Erin Ahrens seems a little redundant, don't you think?

"You are not kissing my sister!" Cheri objects, turning crimson at the thought.

"I'll do it," offers Lou, sounding totally serious. Looking at her closely now, with her shoulder-length bobbed hair tucked up under that top hat making her nose seem even more prominent, I realize who Lou kinda reminds me of . . . That guy who played the Burn-Out in *The Breakfast Club*, Judd Nelson. Of course, I don't tell Luanne that. She'd probably kick my ass.

"You are not kissing my sister, either!" Cheri squeals. And with that, she gives Betsy a peck.

As luck would have it, Betsy's spin of the bottle lands directly on Yours Truly. Though being only time #1, all I get is a kiss on the cheek. "Our First Kiss," I joke, before she plants one on me.

"Watch it there," Alyssa threatens. Though I can't tell who she's talking to—me or Betsy. I wonder if maybe she's a little jealous?

I take my turn. Round and round she goes. Where she stops . . .

"Ooooooo," Brad howls, looking down at the bottle now pointing at him. "How 'bout it, Jack?" Then he laughs.

"I'm not kissing you!" I state emphatically.

"Cheater!" Alyssa hollers. Followed by a chorus of "Kiss! Kiss! Kiss!" from my overly enthusiastic guests.

"Fine!" I reply. "But it's only #1 so he's just getting the cheek."

"More than Alyssa's gotten," Lou says smugly. Which prompts another chorus of hoots and hollers from the Peanut Gallery.

Brad takes his turn, kisses Cheri.

Cheri spins, lands on Erin. For him it's like, "Been there, done that."

Erin follows suit, landing on Miss Wojczek, whose face totally matches her hair when he leans over to kiss her cheek. "I promise I von't bite," he tells Audrey, à la Count Dracula. Though he sounds more like The Count on *Sesame Street*, if you ask me.

To which Audrey comes back with, "What if I want you to?"

And the crowd goes wild!

The highlight of the evening ends up being when Brad's spin lands on Lou—3 times in a row—and they have to French. Right in front of everybody.

"Are you cool with this?" Brad asks Lou, his voice quavering a tad. " 'cause I don't want you to think I like you . . . You know what I mean?"

"No!" Lou roars. "What the fuck *do* you mean?"

"You know . . . It's not like I think of you as a sexual object or anything."

To which Lou responds, "Tell me something I don't already know." Then she grabs the back of Brad's head, opens her mouth, and crams her tongue down his throat in what's gotta be the most awkward situation I've ever seen Brad in.

Around 10:45 PM, the party breaks up on account of Cheri and Betsy have to be home by 11:00 PM. We all walk the Sheffield Girls out to the red Chevette parked across the street from my house. "Thanks for inviting us," says Cheri.

"It was fun," Betsy throws in. "See you on Monday in *le français*."

"Can you give me a ride home, Lou?" Brad asks, knowing

she lives over near Webb on Martin Road. Which is just down the block and on the other side of 9 Mile from Wanda.

"Let's stop by EB's on the way and grab some coffee," Lou suggests. By which she means the Elias Brothers' Big Boy restaurant. *Home of the Original Big Boy.* Which is basically like a Big Mac complete with a "special sauce" that's really just Thousand Island dressing. "Aly, you coming with?"

"I think I'll pass," Alyssa replies. "Kate's being a Total Bitch again." The one whom she's talking about is her Mom.

"We can give you a ride," Cheri tells Alyssa. "You're totally on our way." Cheri and Betsy live over in the fancy part of Hazeltucky called the Courts. Which is an area south of 9 Mile consisting of five semicircular blocks—kinda like the ones on *Knots Landing*—and some pretty nice two-story houses.

"I think I'm gonna walk home," Alyssa tells her friends. "It's not that far."

"You sure?" Lou says, nostrils starting to flare.

"I'll be fine . . . Maybe I can get the Sophomore here to walk with me." I assume she's talking about me. It's a good thing I've changed out of my Aunt Edna getup into my jeans, tennis shoes, and navy blue BLFAC hooded sweatshirt. Which I think I'm finally starting to outgrow, now that I'm up to 5'6". Which is pretty good considering I'm finally as tall as my Dad.

"Are you kidding?" Audrey says, piping up for the first time in a while. "Jack's not gonna walk you home . . . His little brother's braver than he is."

"Thanks a lot!" I tell my so-called friend.

"Looks like she burned you," Alyssa teases, making a connection with Audrey for the first time the entire night.

Which is why Audrey offers to walk with her. Being that her house is only three blocks down from where Alyssa lives off Woodward Heights on Harding.

"I'll go with you guys," I give in, not about to let myself look bad in front of my unofficial girlfriend.

Betsy yawns. *"Pardonnez-moi!"* Then she and Cheri climb into the Chevette and they're off!

Now that I think of it, Cheri and Betsy could've totally given Audrey a ride home. Being that they have to pass right by her house on the way to the Courts. I wonder if maybe they *don't* like her, the way Audrey's always worrying.

"Call me tomorrow," Brad tells me before climbing into Lou's car. I watch as she drives away in a squeal of tires and dry leaves . . . Without even saying good-bye!

"What's her problem?" I ask Alyssa, referring to the fact that Lou barely said a word to me the entire night except for when she was insulting me.

"Who knows?" Alyssa shrugs. "Lou's been OTR for like the past week."

"OTR?" I say, having no idea what the Hell she's talking about.

"Forget it," says Audrey. "You're a guy."

Down the block we go on Shevlin. Followed by a right on Vassar. Then down to the corner of Woodward Heights.

"Do I still get my hug?" Audrey asks sheepishly, hesitating to reach out in her usual take-charge manner.

"Of course." I know Alyssa's not gonna care if I hug one of my Best Friends good-bye. "Mmm . . . Suave Strawberries."

"Enjoy it while you can," Audrey whispers in my ear. Then she disappears inside.

"That girl's got it bad," Alyssa laughs as we continue on our way.

"Who?" I ask.

"Ostrich," Alyssa replies. "She totally wants you." Then she takes my hand and leads me into a darkened parking lot . . . Behind the Hazel Park Church of Christ!

"Where are you taking me?" I whimper. Not that I'm scared or anything, 'cause I'm not. But I'm a little nervous about what I think is coming next.

"Don't be scared . . . I'll protect you."

Alyssa pushes me—literally—up against the yellow and orange brick building. "Ow!" I can't help but cry, feeling a sharp pang against my back. "You're hurting people."

"You ain't seen nothing yet," she whispers in a way that can only be described as "seductively." Then she presses her warm body against mine.

In the seven weeks I've known Alyssa Resnick, I've never been this close to her. In fact, since the time I laid with Lynn Kelly on her couch watching MTV back in 7th grade, I don't think I've been this close to *any* girl.

"Somebody might see us," I fear, as per my usual Worry Wart self.

And with that, she kisses me . . . On the mouth. Tongue and all.

Unfortunately, nothing happens. By which I mean Down There. And I've gotta admit, it usually never does. At least not when it comes to girls.

The few times in my life that I've actually made out with a member of the Opposite Sex, not once have I gotten the slightest bit aroused. Not once have I felt like I could take things to the next step, i.e., having S-E-X. Not even a kiss on the cheek from Kristian Alfonso in Toledo, OH, got my motor going!

And yet . . . The slightest thought of Jon-Erik Hexum or Mr. Grant taking a shower at school or some Random Guy riding the escalator at Oakland Mall and it's like . . . I have no control!

As much as I hate to admit it, maybe there's something wrong with me . . .

Maybe I am *like that*?

SECRET

"I've got a secret and I can't explain
All the time I've waited for this day . . ."

—Orchestral Manoeuvers in the Dark

I think I've *always* known.

For as far back as I can remember, I've always felt this way. Even before I'd ever heard the F-A-G word, I knew I was different. Maybe it's because my Mom really wanted a daughter? Not that she isn't happy having a son. But the way she sees it, if I'd been born a girl, my life would be a lot easier. I could grow up, get married, and have a baby. Like she did. I could stay home and take care of the kids while my husband went to work. Like she did. Then one day, I could be the Proud Mother of an almost-16-year-old boy who thinks he might be . . . *Like that.*

It could also be the fact that the only other boy in my family before my brother Billy came along was my cousin, Jimmy, who's like five years older than me, so we barely ever played together. Instead, my childhood Best Friends were Jimmy's sisters, Rachael and Rhonda.

Growing up, it was always *Jackie & the Girls.* Which explains why I had no other choice but to play *The Brady Bunch* with them whenever our Moms would get together for a visit. But did I ever get to be Greg or Peter or Bobby? No! Because everybody knows Carol Brady has *three* daughters. And Rachael always got to be Marcia, 'cause she was the oldest. And Rhonda had to be Cindy, 'cause she was the youngest. Which left me delegated to the role of middle child, Jan, 'cause I was in the middle.

Of course, when we weren't playing *Brady Bunch* it was always *Charlie's Angels.* Though did I really have to be Kris Munroe? Why couldn't I be Bosley? Or Charlie, even? Because *nobody* wants to be Bosley and Charlie's just some voice in a stupid box! Besides, everybody knows Charlie has *three* angels. And Rachael always got to be Kelly 'cause she was the pretty one. And Rhonda had to be Sabrina 'cause she was the youngest. Which left me delegated to the role of Kris, 'cause I had blond hair and blue eyes . . . Just like Cheryl Ladd.

At least my pretend name was rather unisex so I could get away with it. Could you imagine if Farrah Fawcett had never left the show and my Dad heard Rachael and Rhonda running around shouting, "Cover me, *Jill!*" I don't think he would've been too pleased.

But to be honest, I didn't mind playing these girl games. Don't get me wrong, I also loved my red toy fire engine and my Matchbox cars—especially the little blue Mustang that looked exactly like my Dad's '67 fastback, with tiny little doors that opened and closed. And my GI Joe doll.

Yes, I had a doll. But it's not like it was a Barbie or anything. Though one time in like 1st grade, I asked Santa's Helper up at Universal City for a pair of Donny & Marie dolls. Complete with cardboard TV studio set and plastic 45 RPM record you could play on your portable Fisher-Price record player while you danced Donny & Marie about the stage in their purple and pink designer costumes . . . And lo and behold, I actually got them!

Like he did every year, my Uncle Roy came over on Christmas morning and helped me put together the little black plastic TV camera and we put all the stickers on all the pieces, right where they belonged. Then we put that plastic 45 RPM record on my portable Fisher-Price record player and put on our very own *Donny & Marie Show*. Of course, I was Marie. Not because I wanted to *be* Marie Osmond, 'cause I didn't. I mean, if I were Marie Osmond, I couldn't possibly have a crush on my own brother, now could I? (Gross!)

Okay, I'll let you in on a little secret . . . Back when I was the ripe old age of 6, I had a Total Crush on Donny Osmond!

Those toothy-grinned Mormons might have stolen the hearts of America when they first took to the airwaves on *The Andy Williams Show*. But it was the purple socks-wearing/"Puppy-Love"-singing Donny who stole mine in 1976. I remember watching the very first episode of *Donny & Marie* with my cousins Rachael and Rhonda, lying on beanbags in the rumpus room of my Aunt Mary and Uncle Jim's house. When the closing credits rolled and Donny & Marie completed their last lap around the ice, accompanied by their Rockette-like Ice Dancing Girls, I knew I had found my One True Love!

I distinctly remember making a Dear Diary with Rachael and Rhonda out of lined notebook paper, folded in half and stapled, after watching the episode of *The Brady Bunch* in which Marcia wrote of her undying love for Desi Arnaz Jr. Of course, the information contained within my Dear Diary was extremely Private and Confidential. Even my own favorite cousins knew nothing of the contents that lay within.

"Dear Diary," I wrote in my best little 1st grade cursive. "I love Donny." As in Osmond.

Then one afternoon, while Rachael and Rhonda and I listened to our favorite Supertramp *Breakfast in America* album, lying on their trundle bed in their purple and pink bedroom, we completely forgot to hide our Dear Diaries. You can imagine the horror I felt when my 11-year-old cousin, Jimmy, burst through the door, informing us he'd gotten his dirty little been-out-catching-frogs-down-by-the-pond hands on them.

"Nooo!"

Lucky for us, my Aunt Mary intervened after she heard Rachael and Rhonda and I screaming our heads off. But it didn't help any when she decided to play along with her son, threatening to take a peek at our secret Dear Diaries herself.

"Nooo!"

"What is your problem?" she asked when my cries became hysterical.

"I don't want you to read my Diary," I bawled. Which came out sounding more like, "Wah wah wah wah wah wah wah wah-wahwah."

"What kind of secrets could you possibly have at your age?" my Aunt Mary wondered. Which is a totally legit question, one would think. I know she wasn't trying to be mean. But it didn't make me happy to stand idly by and watch her as she was about to discover my Secret Crush . . . Which is why I reached out with my tiny little hands and tore the pages from her grasp.

"Nooo!"

With my yellow #2 pencil, I did my best to erase the words that would have most definitely been used against me in a Court of Law. My Aunt Mary retaliated by overpowering me, and with her much larger adult hands, pried the crumpled pages from my fingers . . . Which made me cry even harder.

"Would you knock it off, already?!" She looked at the page where I'd written the three little words I didn't want her to read. I knew she could still clearly make them out, their impression marring the page. Of course, I felt completely humiliated. What would my Mom say when my Aunt Mary told her? What would my *Dad* think?

"Why are you crying?" she asked me now. "I read what you wrote and there's nothing wrong with it," she assured me.

There isn't? Were my Feelings of Love perhaps Normal after all? Even though I felt them for another boy?

Aunt Mary looked me directly in the eye. Gently nodding her head, she made sure there was no mistake as to the meaning of what she was about to say next . . . "There's nothing wrong with loving your *Daddy*."

Almost ten years later, has anything changed? As hard as I try—as hard as I fight it—sometimes I still feel . . . *like that.* Not so much when it comes to Donny Osmond anymore. Though every once in a while I'll see an old picture of him circa 1976 and I get that same funny feeling inside. By which I mean Down There.

Which is the main reason I had no interest in letting Luanne's Mom read my cards at their New Year's Eve party last night . . .

Did I mention Lou's Mom is a Witch? Not witch-witch as in green face, pointy black hat, flying around on a broomstick on Halloween. But Witch as in she worships trees and tells fortunes and stuff like that. More like a Gypsy, I'd call her. Though not gypsy-gypsy as in mole on her cheek, scarf on her head, running around the village stealing children.

Like most of my friends' parents, Mrs. Kowalski is divorced. And because Lou's an only child, it's been just her and her Mom living alone together for a long time. So they're more like sisters than mother and daughter, the way they hang out together. Which might explain why Lou's Mom told her she could invite everybody over on New Year's Eve and offered to give us our Predictions for the Coming New Year.

As cool as I thought it would be spending the holiday evening with a bunch of my High School Friends, the last thing I needed was for Lou's Mom to expose all my Deep Dark Secrets in front of all the Band Fags.

"You wanna meet for dinner at Big Boy's first?" Brad suggested. Which has become our recent Hang Out of sorts. It's the only place that will allow us to sit and smoke and drink coffee for hours. By us, I mean Lou and Brad and Max—who apparently is no longer friends with Tom Fulton so he's started hanging out again, just like Old Times. Thank God Alyssa hasn't picked up The Habit. At least not the one involving nicotine. Proudly, I partake in neither. (Gross!)

Lou also invited Cheri and Betsy Sheffield to her party. But a last minute Michigan Blizzard popped up on Doppler 4 prompting Mrs. Sheffield to forbid her daughters from driving the mile across town for fear they might get killed. Talk about being paranoid! In all my years, I've never known anybody to get into an accident, let alone die from one.

So the so-called *soirée* ended up more like a Triple Date of me and Alyssa, Brad and Lou, and Max and Audrey . . .

We arrived at EB's around 9:30 PM. A blanket of white covered the deserted parking lot. Through the windows it looked totally dead inside. Sure enough, we had no problem getting our favorite table in the front corner near the kitchen.

"Can I get you something to drink?" Our waiter for the evening approached our table. He whipped out his trusty notepad from the back pocket of his black Dockers. I immediately recognized him as Kevin Ebersole, a Junior in Luanne's class at Hillbilly High.

"Coffee," ordered Lou, an air of superiority in that one word that seemed to say, "*I'm* the Customer, *you're* the Waiter . . . Don't you dare forget it."

"Coffee," said Brad politely. "Please."

"The same," added Audrey. I couldn't help but notice the way she stared down at her menu, totally avoiding Kevin's gaze.

"I'll have coffee," said Alyssa with a smile.

Max popped a wad of watermelon Bubblicious into his mouth. "Make it five."

"And for you?" Kevin turned to me, last but not least.

"A large Sprite with lemon," I answered.

Only to be teased by Alyssa. "He's always a problem."

"No problem at all," Kevin replied, his red and white checked bow tie choking him. "I'll be right back with your drinks."

After he'd headed towards the kitchen, Audrey looked up. "He's kinda cute, huh?" Her cheeks were a bit flushed, which I noticed right away.

"Not my type," Luanne grumbled. She thumbed through her menu looking at the selection of sandwiches. "Think I'll have a Slim Jim."

"I've always thought so," said Alyssa, getting back to the subject of Mr. Ebersole. Which, I must admit, surprised me a little. Not that Kevin doesn't seem like a nice guy. But I wouldn't call him "cute." He kinda reminds me of a Campbell's Soup Kid. All rosy-cheeked and red-faced and *M'm! M'm! Good!* Though he is kinda tall with dark wavy hair. And he's got a nice smile, I suppose.

A few minutes later, Kevin returned. With the utmost ease he balanced the six beverages on a single brown plastic tray. "Here we go . . ." I couldn't help but notice the way his top teeth rubbed against his bottom lip when he talked. Like a rabbit.

"My, aren't you efficient?" Alyssa teased when Kevin began distributing the hot mugs around the table. Or was she flirting? It was hard to tell. Not that I thought I had any reason to feel jealous. Unless that's how Alyssa *wanted* me to feel.

Kevin handed me my large Sprite. "Can I get anyone anything else?"

As much as I hated being difficult, he seemed to have forgotten the lemon I had *specifically* requested. See, what I like to do is . . . First I squeeze the lemon into the glass. Then I add a single packet of sugar, causing a volcanic eruption of bubbles and fizz. Which is totally cool and totally makes the Sprite taste better, don't ask me why!

"Can I get some lemon?" I asked, hoping not to be too much of a pain. So I added, "Please."

To which Alyssa said, "Guess I was wrong about your being efficient, Kevin."

Which made Kevin laugh nervously. "Sorry . . . I'll get it for you right away." Then he headed back towards the swinging double doors.

Just as he walked away, Lou called out, "Bring an ashtray, would you?" Like Kevin was her own Personal Slave or something. Then she pulled out her pack of cigarettes. As did both Brad and Max. I held back the urge to cough as a hazy cloud began billowing above our table.

"Can I bum one of those?" Audrey asked. She helped herself to one of Max's Marlboro Lights, holding it tight between her lips.

"Since when do you smoke?" I wanted to know, totally disgusted.

"Since when is it any of your business?" I was told, as Audrey lit up.

At that moment, Kevin Ebersole returned. Audrey immediately hid her Cancer Stick beneath the table, shooing away the evidence with her opposite hand. "Sorry about that," he apologized, placing a small ceramic dish filled with yellow citrus wedges in front of me.

"No problem," I assured him. Even though it was, I wasn't about to say so.

"Just don't let it happen again," teased Alyssa. "Or else."

Or else what? I couldn't believe she was blatantly flirting with another guy right in front of me! I knew for sure I'd have to do something about it once we got over to Lou's house later that night.

Around 11:00 PM we found ourselves sitting around the Kowalski living room . . .

Personally, I wanted to watch Dick Clark on TV. But nobody else seemed to appreciate the importance of a structured New Year's Eve countdown. Instead, we listened to some tape of a band I'd never heard before called Echo & the Bunnymen. Thank God Lou's Mom had a headache from drinking too much champagne and asked if she could take a rain check on the Tarot Card reading. Which was totally fine by me. Like I said, the last thing I wanted was to have all my Deep Dark Secrets exposed in front of all my friends.

"Party time!" Lou announced. She returned from the kitchen, a humongous green jug of Carlo Rossi white wine held high. I'm not even joking when I say . . . This thing was huge! Like the size of a gallon of milk, if not bigger.

"Crack that puppy open," Alyssa demanded enthusiastically. Despite being ultrareligious, I guess she doesn't have a problem with underage drinking.

Even though I knew my Mom would ***kill*** me if she found out, what was I supposed to do when the humongous jug o wine found its way into my hands? Not take a drink and embarrass myself in front of everybody? But who knew I'd end up so wasted so quickly? Don't get me wrong, I had a Total Blast . . . At least what I can remember.

The highlight of the evening came when Audrey lit a cigarette off the stove in Lou's kitchen and completely singed her bangs. Talk about a stink! I told her she always wears way too much hairspray. Besides, Audrey knows she shouldn't be smoking in the first place. Then Brad totally cracked us all up when he disappeared and we found him outside in Lou's front yard lying flat on his back in the snow making angels!

"I am sooo drunk!" he groaned, staring up at the twinkling stars.

"And you're gonna be sooo sick!" I informed him. Not that I'd ever had a hangover before. A gentle snow fluttered down and I felt the urge to catch the flakes on my tongue, à la Linus Van Pelt. After all, it was officially January so Sister Lucy should have no objection.

It felt good to be alive.

Though not so much so this morning . . .

"I am *never* drinking again!" Brad groans from the bottom bunk beneath me. "What time did we go to bed?"

"Late," I reply, half-asleep and not nearly ready to wake up. Truth be told, I don't remember what time we even got home. I was pretty darn wasted.

Brad says, "I still can't believe it's 1986 . . . We are getting sooo old!"

"Tell me about it . . ."

Then out of the blue he asks, "Are you gonna have a Sweet Sixteen party this year?"

To which I inform him, "Boys don't usually have Sweet Sixteen parties, Brad."

"Why not?"

"I don't know . . . They just don't."

"Well, that sucks! Why do girls get to do *all* the fun stuff?"

I choose to say nothing, hoping he'll get the hint I'm trying to go back to sleep . . . But he doesn't.

"They get to go out on dates and make the guys pay," Brad rambles. "And they never even have to work, unless they want to."

I start fake-snoring. But it still doesn't shut him up.

"They're especially lucky when it comes to having sex . . . I mean, it must be easier for a girl to get laid, 'cause guys are so horny *all* the time . . . I know I am! I think if I was a girl, I'd probably be a Big Whore. I'd have as much sex as I wanted to, with whatever guy I wanted to." Then he adds, "Sometimes I'm so horny, I don't know *what* I'm gonna do." Followed by, "I gotta find a girlfriend soon or I'm gonna explode!"

"What about Luanne?" I say, knowing that she and Brad spent a lot of the time hanging out in her kitchen at the party last night.

Which is when he informs me, "I don't think Lou thinks of me in that way, Jack."

Which is why I take the opportunity to say, "Maybe we were right about her all along?"

"Meaning?"

"Maybe she really is . . . You know."

"Is what?"

"Like that."

Brad replies, "You know I don't like to believe rumors."

"I'm just saying . . ." I'm not to trying to be a jerk. I just figure if anybody would know anything about Luanne it would have to be Brad. He spends the most time with her. Even more so than Alyssa does lately.

"Why would I know?" he asks me, sounding kinda defensive.

I can't even remember how many times I've called over Brad's house and had his Mom tell me, "He's out driving around with that Luanne Kowalski girl."

But I say, "Forget I said anything." Then I roll over and close my eyes.

After a moment, Brad says, "What's up with you and Alyssa, anyways? Are you guys officially going together now or what?"

"What makes you think that?" I ask. Even though it's true—Alyssa and I *are* officially going together—it's none of Brad's business.

"Because you guys spent over half the night making out in the bedroom!" he reminds me.

"So?" I reply. "I was drunk . . . Besides, Alyssa attacked me."

"You make it sound like you don't really like her," says Brad, giving me what's beginning to sound like the Third Degree.

"I do . . ."

"So what's the problem?"

"For one thing," I begin, "Alyssa's a Senior . . ."

"And do you know how many Sophomore guys would kill to be in your position?"

What I try to explain to Brad is . . . Despite being totally nice and very Popular, Alyssa Resnick is no Kristian Alfonso. Not that I'm not saying she's not pretty, 'cause she totally is. But she's a little on the bigger side. Like most of the girls I've known who've liked me. And for once in my life, I'd like to date a girl who's smaller than me. Is that so wrong?

"Alyssa was on the Homecoming 'Top 25' and everything," Brad reminds me, as if I don't already know this.

"But she's so religious," I say. "She's *always* listening to Amy Grant and Michael W. Smith . . . Sometimes just being around her makes me feel guilty."

"About what?"

"I don't know . . . I always feel guilty about *everything* I think or do."

"Well, what kind of things are you thinking or doing?" he asks, getting all *Murder, She Wrote* on me.

"Nothing!" I cry. "Forget I even said anything."

"It's not like you're a Big Fag," says Brad, pressing on. "Are you?"

Even though Alyssa and I are officially going together so I have *nothing* to worry about anymore, I don't wanna lie to my Best Friend.

Which is why I say, "You of all people should know the answer to that."

But the big question now is . . . What *is* the answer?

Oh, L'amour

"What's a boy in love
Supposed to do?"

—Erasure

Wanna know what I *hate* most about Valentine's Day?

Besides the fact that it's been totally fabricated by some guy at Hallmark in order to sell greeting cards and boxes of chocolate and flowers to totally stupid people all in the name of L-O-V-E, in all my 15-going-on-16 years of being alive, I've *never* had anybody to call "My Valentine." So why should 1986 be any different?

In case you're wondering what happened to Alyssa . . . We broke up. From what I've heard, she's dating that guy Kevin Ebersole now. Remember, the waiter from Big Boy's on New Year's Eve? To which I say, "Good for her." I hope she's happy.

Even though it lasted only like six weeks, we had some good times. Especially making out in the backseat of her car out at Quarton Lake in Birmingham. But it was pretty much inevitable. Considering I'm a Sophomore and Alyssa is graduating from

Hillbilly High come June 12th and heading off to Central Michigan University in the Fall.

On top of the fact that I'm now totally in love with somebody else . . .

"Attention, s'il vous plait!"

Nobody wanted to be sitting in French on the first day back to school after Christmas Vacation learning to conjugate "irregular" verbs. Except for straight-A students Betsy Sheffield and Jack Paterno. We were about the only ones paying Mrs. Carey any *attention*—as per usual. So she pretty much directed all her comments at us from where she stood in front of *la classe* before *le tâbleau.*

Don't get me wrong, Mrs. Carey's a very nice woman. But a lot of kids like to take advantage of her. And not because she's the only black teacher at Hillbilly High. It's more like she's kinda clueless. Like, somebody will walk in totally late for class and be all like, "I'm sorry Mrs. Carey." To which she'll reply, *"Bien, bien."* And she won't even mark them tardy or anything.

Brad's also got Mrs. Carey for French I. He told me this girl in his class, Stacy Gillespie, was sitting in the back of the classroom the other day using her hairspray and lighter to make a torch! But Stacy's a Punker, so what do you expect? With her short dark hair sticking straight up and off to one side, she looks like she got hit on the back of the head with a board

But I totally like Mrs. Carey. She's helping me translate my collection of *Arnold* comics into French, beginning with *"Il y a un poumon dans le potage!"* In which Arnold informs Bertha the Lunch Lady to turn in her hairnet after finding a lung in his soup.

"Je voudrais vous presenter un nouvel étudiant . . ."

The scent of pine filled the room as the door opened and the aforementioned new student entered. The tall, dark, and oh-so-cliché but handsome guy stood silently before our class, basking in Polo by Ralph Lauren. Believe it or not, he kinda reminded me of Donny Osmond circa 1976.

"Cool pea coat," Betsy leaned over to whisper in my ear.

At least 6' if not taller, he wore this navy blue pea coat over a pair of light blue Guess? jeans, cuffed at the bottom. Though upon closer inspection, I could see his pants weren't just rolled up the way we used to roll them back in 6th grade. This guy folded the legs over at the bottom *before* he cuffed them. So they were supertight around his totally bare ankles, drawing attention to his loafers—complete with shiny new copper Abe Lincolns in the slots. I could totally tell Betsy thought he was cute. As did most of the girls in our class, which had suddenly fallen silent. Even the Popular Guys were paying attention to their new competition.

"Bonjour . . . Comment ça va?" We all listened as the New Guy spoke, in quiet—yet totally perfect—French. *"Je suis heureux de faire votre connaîssance."*

To which Mrs. Carey said, "Tell everyone your name, Dear."

To which New Guy replied, *"Je m'appelle Joey Palladino."*

Of course, I was like, *No fucking way!*

After four years of living way out past 30 Mile in Bum Fuck Clarkston, Joey Palladino had returned to Hazeltucky . . . Not that I wasn't happy to see him, 'cause I totally was. I just never expected his parents would get divorced after almost sixteen years of marriage and that he and his Mom would move in with his Grandma over on Carlisle. Right next door to the house he lived in back when we were Best Friends at Longfellow.

"Bonjour, Joey!" Betsy said shyly when her turn for introductions came around. *"Je m'appelle Betsy Sheffield."*

"Bonjour, Betsy!" Joey replied, a smile on his face as Betsy's clearly the cutest girl in our class. Not to mention the Preppiest, with her Oxford shirt, plaid pants, and cordovan penny loafers.

I can't even believe how totally nervous I was as I got ready to speak next. As far as I could tell, Joey hadn't recognized me. I mean, it had been over three years since I saw him last at his Grandpa's funeral. I remember feeling awful seeing Joey sitting in the front row of the Ashley-Scott Funeral Home crying the entire time. I remember totally wishing I could reach out and put my arms around him and make everything all better . . . But I couldn't.

"*Bonjour, Joey,*" I say, taking my turn. "*Je m'appelle Jack Paterno.*"

I watched Joey's face closely as he made the realization that we already knew each other. Though I don't know if the look he gave me meant he was happy to see me or not. All I know is . . . At that moment, I was totally psyched!

I should probably point out that while we were indeed Best Friends back at Longfellow, Joey Palladino and I were also each other's worst competition. Beginning in 3rd grade when our parents signed us up for a league at Hazel Park Bowl, we would constantly keep an eye on each other's score. Most of the time mine was higher—not that it mattered since we were on the same team. And on Track and Field Day, we'd battle it out to see who could run faster or jump farther and/or higher. Which usually ended up being Joey. But being that we were both straight-A students, it wasn't as easy to compare us when it came to schoolwork. Though our classmates would often try, taking polls as to who was the smartest and/or waging their bets when it came time for the annual Spelling Bee.

"So how come you're still not in Band?" I asked Joey as we cut across St. Mary's Field on the way over to my house after school. Back in 6th grade, we both started playing trumpet together. If I remember correctly, Joey was pretty good. Though I was always better.

"I got sick and tired of being called a Band Fag," he told me.

Joey and I got to talking after French and I invited him over so we could have a chance to catch up. Though I didn't mention it to Brad when he asked if I wanted to go to the movies with him and Max on account of I didn't want him getting jealous. I didn't bother to invite him along either, 'cause he never met Joey before and I really wanted it to be just me and him . . . like Old Times.

Once we got to my house, I kicked my little brother out of our room. Then I dragged an old photo album from my closet that was filled with pictures my Mom took the last time Joey had been at our house before he moved away. Back before I started school at Webb Junior High or had ever heard the name Bradley Dayton. Which seemed kinda weird to think about. Not weird-weird, but . . . It's hard to remember what my life was ever like without Brad in it.

"Look what a dork you were!" Joey squealed, flipping through the photos.

To which I replied, "Look how fat *you* were!"

"I was not fat."

"And I wasn't a dork."

We plopped down on the floor, side by side, the photo album on our laps between us. Okay, so maybe I did look a little dorky back then with my over-the-ear feathered-back hair. And maybe Joey was indeed a little chubby. But judging by the looks of him now, you'd never guess he was once that same 12-year-old kid in the photos.

"Is it hot in here?" Joey asked. Then he took off his navy blue V-neck sweater.

When it got caught around his head, I reached over and gave him a hand. I couldn't help but notice the vein popping out from the center of Joey's bulging bicep and how totally chiseled his chest looked beneath his white V-neck undershirt.

"So I take it you've started lifting." By which I meant weights.

"A little," he admitted. "I got a bench set up in my Grandma's garage . . . You wanna come over sometime. I'll show you a thing or two." Then Joey grabbed hold of my puny little arm and held it a moment. "Not bad, Paterno."

If I didn't know better, I would've thought Joey Palladino was flirting with me. Not that I think Joe's *like that*, 'cause I know he's not. But even if he is, why should I care? He's still my friend.

At that moment, the telephone rang . . .

"You wanna get that?" Joey asked me.

"My Mom'll pick it up in the kitchen," I told him.

Sure enough, a moment later my Mom called out, "J-a-a-ckie . . . It's Alyssa!" Why she couldn't just take a message, I don't know. All I know is . . . I picked up the phone, totally annoyed.

"Hello?"

"I'm gonna kill her!" Alyssa groaned. "Kate is being a Total Bitch . . . Again!" She began rambling on about how much she can't stand her Mom and how she can't wait till June 13th when she turns 18 and can move out of the house and never have to see her ever again.

To which I totally wanted to reply, "Dah-dah, dah-dah."

"I need to get out of here for a while," she told me. "Can I come over?"

I answered, "Um . . . I'm kinda busy right now."

"I'll watch *Days of our Lives* with you . . . I don't care."

I informed Alyssa my friend Joey was over and we were in the middle of something.

"Since when do you have a friend named Joey?" she replied, kinda snotty.

I proceeded to explain the *History of Jack & Joey.* Not that it was any of Alyssa's business. I also explained that I'd already made plans and couldn't just send Joey home after he walked all the way over here with me in the freezing Michigan cold.

Which is when she said, "He sounds like a cool guy . . . I wanna meet him."

Again I said, "Um . . ."

And Alyssa said, "Um, what? You don't want me to meet your friend?"

I suggested, "Can't you go over Cheri's?" Which didn't go over too well.

"Forget it!" And with that, Alyssa hung up on me . . .

"What's up?" Joey asked after I returned the phone to its cradle.

"Nothing important," I told him. Then I said, "So when can I start lifting with you?"

"Soon as you want," he answered, flashing his toothy Donny Osmond grin.

And that's when it hit me. After all these years . . . I'm still in love with Joey Palladino!

Whenever he's not around, I can't stop thinking about him. When I wake up in the morning, all I do is wonder when I'm gonna see him next. Though it's usually not till Lunch when Joey meets me in the Junk Food Line where we both order a package of King Dons and a chocolate malt. Then we sit alone together at our favorite table by the windows, overlooking the courtyard where this past Fall we took our Marching Band photo out in front of the fountain.

I don't even care if Alyssa's stopped talking to me. So what if Brad and Lou get pissed off 'cause I don't wanna eat with them in the Band Room. All they ever wanna do is hang out in there with all the other Band Fags and I am sooo over that! About the only person who even likes Joey is Audrey. Though I'm beginning to think she likes him-likes him. In that way. And unfortunately for her, I know Joey doesn't feel the same. But for now, she's the only friend I've got that I can even mention Joey's name in front of without pissing off.

So today is Valentine's Day . . .

I was planning on spending it alone in my room watching yet another episode of—what else? "*Like sands through the hourglass . . . So are the Days of our Lives.*"

After months and months of planning, today's the big double wedding of Pete Jannings to Melissa Anderson and of Mickey Horton to his ex-wife, Maggie. But no sooner than I've crawled up into my bed and hit PLAY on my VCR remote, the phone rings.

"Ja-a-ckie!" my Mom calls from the other side of my flimsy accordion-fold door.

I don't know how many times I have to tell my friends . . . What's the first thing I do when I come home from school? I don't care who you are, you don't call between the hours of 3:30 and 4:30 PM.

"What's up?"

Unless your name happens to be Joey Palladino.

"Nothing," I totally lie. Suddenly, the goings-on in Salem, USA, seem insignificant. "What's up with you?"

"Just wanted to make sure we're still on for tonight."

I decided to take Joey up on his offer and started lifting weights with him in his Grandma's garage 3 times per week. I've gotta admit, after the first workout I thought I was totally gonna die. I was sooo sore the next day! But I'm actually starting to enjoy "feeling the burn," as Joey likes to say. Along with, "No pain, no gain."

"I can come over right now," I reply. It's not like I don't have *Days* on tape.

"I'll be out in the garage warming up," he says. "See you in fifteen."

"Make it ten." Normally I wouldn't haul my cookies through the snow for anybody. But like I've said, Joey's my Best Friend. Besides, I can't make excuses for not getting myself in shape, can I?

Once I'm over Joey's, I change out of my argyle sweater, blue jeans, and snow boots into the sweats I've brought along. I've gotta admit, I was a little self-conscious about changing in front of Joey when we first started lifting weights together. Not only does he have a much nicer body than me, but I have a hard time not staring at Joey in French class when he's got his clothes *on*. Imagine how hard it is for me to resist looking at him standing here in nothing but his BVDs.

"Oh, my God . . . It's freezing in here!"

"Somebody's got T-H-Os," Joey teases. Only I have no idea what T-H-Os are so I ask him to tell me. "Titty Hard-Ons," he replies. Then he totally tweaks my left nipple—hard! The dim light of the single bulb hanging down from the rafters casts a shadow over the muscles of Joey's smooth olive-skinned, Polo-scented torso. He totally reminds me of Pete Jannings from *Days of our Lives,* now that I think of it. Complete with the kinda chest that pushes together in the middle like cleavage.

"Bench presses?" Joey suggests, once we're both dressed and ready to go.

I watch as he fires off an easy set of 10 reps at 50 pounds. He doesn't even really need me to spot him. But for safety's sake, I stand at the end of the bench, poised and ready to take it should he want me to. By which I mean the weight bar.

"No fair," I tell him when he drops it on the rack with a thud. "You've had a lot more practice."

"Practice makes perfect," Joey tells me, flashing that shit-eating grin of his. Then I swear he gives me a wink. Again, if I didn't know better . . . Flirting!

I lie down on the bench, expecting Joey to remove two of

the gray 10 pound plastic weights. When he doesn't I say, "What're you doing?"

He looks down at me, his crotch no more than a foot from my face. "Time for you to step it up," he tells me. By which he means lift more weight. Then he adds, "I got your back."

I grab hold of the bar, take a deep breath, and give it my all. The last thing I want is to embarrass myself in front of Joey. And believe it or not, I manage to do a set of 6 good reps.

"See?" Joey says proudly. "You're not as big a wuss as everybody says."

Which makes me wonder what he's heard about me. While I can't expect the stupid things people have been saying about me since 7th grade to just stop because I've gotten to Hillbilly High, I guess I've been hoping they wouldn't get back to Joey.

"Did you like my VD card?" he asks out of the blue. By which he means the Valentine's Day card he presented me with at the end of French this afternoon.

"I did . . ."

One of the good things about being in French 1 is . . . it's like being back in elementary school when it comes to the holidays. For Thanksgiving we celebrated *Fête de Grâce.* At Christmas we made *Joyeux Noël* cards. Today it was *Le Jour de la St. Valentin.* Out of red, white, and pink construction paper, Joey made a heart and wrote *Joseph et Jacques . . . Meilleurs Amis Toujours* across the center of it. Which translates to "Joey and Jack . . . Best Friends Forever," in case you weren't sure.

"I know it's kinda dumb," he admits, blushing a little. "But since I didn't have anybody else to give a Valentine's Day card to, I figured I'd make one for my Best Friend." Then he smiles, radiant sunshine.

We stand there in the middle of Joey's Grandma's freezing cold garage, staring at each other, saying nothing . . . Till Joey licks his cherry lips.

"What would you do if I kissed you right now?" I say, looking into his chocolate brown eyes, scared to death.

"I don't know . . . Probably kiss you back."

And then it happens . . . Or should I say, nothing happens? I totally let the Moment of Opportunity slip by as Joey steps towards me and I break away.

"You wanna do some curls?" I ask out of nervousness.

To which he replies, "Do you?"

And I'm like, "Sure."

And he's like, "Okay." Then we continue lifting weights for another half an hour or so without saying a single word.

Why am I such a fool? What am I so afraid of? Isn't this what I've been wanting since the day Joey Palladino came back into my life? Here he is practically giving me *permission* . . . And what do I do?

Fuck!

That's What Friends Are For

"Keep smilin', keep shinin'
Knowin' you can always count on me, for sure . . ."

—Dionne Warwick & Friends

The only thing *worse* than being a Band Fag is . . . being a Drama Queer.

Don't ask me why, I don't make the rules. But everybody knows this. Which is why I can't even believe it when Brad tells me he's auditioning for the Spring Musical, *Oklahoma!* Or should I say, *Okla-homo!,* as it's becoming known around the hallowed halls of Hillbilly High?

Ever since Mrs. Malloy made us write a paper on "What I Want to Be When I Grow Up" during 1st hour English, Brad's got it in his head he's gonna be a Famous Actor someday. Or at least appear on *Days of our Lives.* The only thing is . . . Brad's never acted a day in his life.

"How hard can it be?" I remember him telling me the first time I questioned his career choice. "All you gotta do is memorize a bunch of lines . . . Then you just get up there and say them."

Personally, I've decided I'm gonna be a Professional Journalist. Or should I say, "Going to?" If I wanna—I mean, "want to" have any success as a writer, I should probably start using Proper Grammar, don't you think? Ever since I was a kid, I've always enjoyed writing. I think I'm pretty good at it, too. One time back at Longfellow, my 4th grade teacher, Mrs. Landers, assigned us a three-page Creative Writing assignment. I wrote like ten.

Okay, I'll let you in on a little secret . . . I spent most of last Summer writing a novel, believe it or not. Like a Total Nerd, I sat in my bedroom—day after day after day—slaving away over the electric typewriter I borrowed from my Aunt Sonia. I titled my work of genius *Portland Disaster,* after the fact that it's all about this group of people from the fictitious town of Portland, USA, whose plane crashes on a deserted island en route to a fashion show somewhere in the South Pacific.

I've got to admit, I pretty much stole the plot from the *Days of our Lives* Anna DiMera Designs plane crash storyline from the Fall of 1984. Though unlike Hope Williams-Brady, my heroine—Faith Winston-Bradford—is a blond. I mean, I'm not totally stupid. I don't want to get sued by NBC should I ever get it published!

Today after 2nd hour Sophomore Symphony, Brad sidles up to me . . .

"I need you to do me a favor," he says. We've been busting our butts getting ready for the big Spring Concert coming up. We're billing it as a Tribute to the Space Shuttle Challenger. I'm sure I don't need to explain why—unless you've been totally living on another planet since January 28th. "Tomorrow's my *Oklahomo!* audition . . ."

"You're really going through with that?" I ask, hoping he would've changed his mind by now.

Brad stops mid-step, halfway down the hallway between the

Band Room and the Choir Room. "I bet you don't realize how good it makes me to feel to have my Best Friend since 7th grade totally doubt my creative abilities."

"I'm sorry," I apologize. Even though I'm afraid Brad's going to make a fool of himself in front of all the Drama Queers, I realize I should probably start showing my support. So I say, "What do you need me to do?"

"Can I come over after school and show you my monologue?"

"Um . . ."

The thing is . . . Joey and I already made plans to go bike riding after school today. It's the first warm Spring day we've had and I want to take him on the route my Aunt Sonia and Uncle Mark used to take me on whenever we'd go bike riding back when I was a kid. Over by 10 Mile and Woodward near the Detroit Zoo. Which is technically located in Huntington Woods, don't ask me why!

Though I don't tell Brad any of this. Instead I say, "Since when do I know anything about Drama?"

"You watch TV all the time, don't you?" he points out. "All you gotta do is listen and tell me what you think."

"Bra-yad!"

From across the commons in front of the Auditorium comes the totally loud and totally obnoxious bellow of Luanne Kowalski. Out of the corner of my eye, I see her argyle print sweater fast approaching. But I don't dare turn around for fear of actually having to deal with her. Though Lou's been in a better mood ever since Alyssa and I broke up, I still don't trust her.

"Will you help me or not, Jack?" asks Brad again, also ignoring the call.

"Bra-yad!" Lou repeats, this time a little louder.

At which point, I cave. Even though I'd much rather spend my time riding bikes on a nice Spring day with Joey Palladino,

I've got to get away. "Meet me in the Band Room at 3 o'clock," I tell Brad. Then I'm gone!

Six hours later, here I am sitting on my bedroom floor . . .

Brad stands at the opposite end, preparing to perform his audition monologue. It's going to take all my effort not to laugh my head off the minute he opens his mouth, I just know it! Especially now that he's started rolling his head from side to side, around and around, faster and faster.

"What are you doing that for?" I ask, giving Brad a look.

"Dell says a good actor always warms up," he informs me. He's talking about the Hillbilly High Drama teacher, Mr. Dell'Olio. He also serves as Faculty Advisor for the school paper, *The Hazel Parker,* which I'm hoping to start writing for next year in preparation for my career as a Professional Journalist.

I listen as Brad begins running through a series of tongue twisters and nursery rhyme-type vocal exercises. "Red-leather-yellow-leather." "Rubber-baby-buggy-bumpers." "Peter-Piper-picked-a-peck-of . . ."

My eyelids grow heavy and my head begins bobbing on my neck. I'm thinking, *What have I gotten myself into?* For this I've given up spending the afternoon with Joey Palladino?

Brad says, "Okay . . . I'm ready."

"It's about time . . ." I open my eyes, wiping a bit of drool from the corner of my mouth. (Gross!)

"You were falling asleep!" Brad accuses.

"You're damn right I was," I reply. "Dah-dah, dah-dah."

"You're the one who said you'd help me."

"And you're the one who gave me no other choice," I remind him. "Now would you act, already?"

Brad takes a deep breath. He looks down at the floor for a good three seconds. Then slowly he raises his head, a slight smile upon his face. " 'The man of my dreams has almost faded now . . .' "

For the next minute and a half I listen in awe as Brad runs the gamut from elation to despair. I've got to admit, he's actually pretty good. Even the British accent he's adopted for the occasion sounds somewhat authentic. But what I'm wondering is . . . Why the Hell Brad's chosen this particular piece for his *Okla-homo!* audition monologue. Especially since it's one that I, myself, almost know by heart.

"So . . . What'd you think?" he asks, once he's finally finished and taken a bow.

Having no idea how to respond, I start with, "That's from *Somewhere in Time,* isn't it?" Just to make sure I'm not totally imagining things.

"Uh-huh . . . With Jane Seymour and Christopher Reeves," Brad replies.

To which I interject, "You mean, *Reeve* . . . No 's.' "

"That's what I said," he says. Even though he didn't. "It's my fav-rid movie." Which is how Brad likes to say "favorite" sometimes, don't ask me why!

I can't even believe we've never talked about this. I always thought I was The Only One. And here it is, the favorite movie of both of us. . . How could we not know this after all these years?

"I don't know, Jack . . . I guess maybe we don't know *everything* about each other," Brad surmises once I tell him this. Then he says, "Wanna know what part in *Somewhere in Time* I like best? When Jane Seymour first meets Christopher Reeves—"

"*Reeve.*"

"That's what I said," he insists.

"No, you didn't . . . You said 'Reeves' again." I hate to be all whatever. But I can't stand it when people don't get Christopher Reeve's name right!

"When she first meets Christopher *Reeve,*" Brad says, hitting the "v," smiling, "down by those trees near the lake and she says, 'Is it you?' " Which he *has* to say in his best Jane Seymour accent. Which I *have* to totally join him in perfect unison as he does.

"That's my favorite part, too!" I squeal. Like a Total Girl, I know.

"The monologue I'm doing," Brad continues, "is from the part when Jane Seymour's performing in that play at the hotel theater—"

"*Wisdom of the Heart*," I interject, unable to resist showing off my *Somewhere in Time* knowledge. "And she starts making up her lines as she goes along, instead of following the script."

"And Christopher Reeve—no 's'—is sitting in the audience," Brad adds. "And she's looking directly at him, saying the words."

"And the woman playing the maid starts freaking out," I throw in, " 'cause she doesn't know what the Hell Jane Seymour is doing."

"And of course, Jane Seymour is *brilliant*," Brad concludes. "And everybody thinks it's all part of the play and not just ab-libbing."

Okay . . . Even I know the word is "ad-libbing." Which is what I tell Brad.

To which he responds, "That's what I said." Even though he didn't. "Isn't it a great monologue?"

I hesitate a moment, not sure how to reply. I mean, yes, it's a totally great monologue. And I really think Brad's doing an excellent job with it. But it's all about "the *man* of my dreams." What's everybody going to think when Brad walks into the Auditorium tomorrow for his Drama audition and he starts performing it?

"Fuck them!" he exclaims when I express my concern. "Why should I care what other people think? We're supposed to pick something we like and this is from my favorite movie." Then to top it all off, he says, "What are you worrying about, Jack? It's not *your* problem."

Now I feel bad. I wasn't questioning Brad's choice of material just to be a jerk. But he's been my Best Friend since 7th grade and I know what Assholes the kids at Hillbilly High can be. Which is why I sincerely tell him, "I don't want people thinking things about you . . . That's all."

"You know I don't give a shit what people think," Brad replies. Which is true. In all the years I've known him, he's never cared if people like him or say mean things about him or not.

"I'm just saying—" I start to say. Till he cuts me off.

"What are people gonna think if I do the Jane Seymour monologue from *Somewhere in Time* for my audition?" Brad snaps. "That I'm a Total Fag or something?"

"That's not what I meant," I apologize. But it does me no good.

"Is that what *you* think?" Brad looks at me, all accusatory. He's totally got himself worked up. "Do you think I'm a Total Fag?"

"No . . ."

"Are you sure?" he asks, hands on hips.

"You're my Best Friend," I remind him. "I'd never think that about you."

At which point, he blurts out, "Maybe you should!"

Okay . . . I did *not* just hear Brad say what I thought he said, did I? Is he actually suggesting what I think he's suggesting?

"I'm sorry," he quickly apologizes. "I didn't mean to get so upset . . . I've got a lot on my mind, I guess." He crosses to my desk and begins futzing with my stapler.

I cringe as a bijillion tiny metal snowflakes fall to the floor with each click of the Swingline. My Mom will have a fit if she sees the mess! But I don't complain about it to Brad. Instead I say, "It's just a stupid audition . . . I wouldn't worry about it."

"It's not the audition I'm worried about," he admits.

"Then what is it?"

Brad puts the stapler down. "I've been thinking . . ." He turns back to me. "There's something I should probably tell you, Jack."

I reply, "Okay . . ." Even though I've got a feeling where this conversation is headed.

" 'member on New Year's Eve when we were at Luanne's house and you and Alyssa were off making out in the bedroom?"

I'm like, "Yeah . . ." Though for some reason I can't bring myself to look at him.

"So Lou and I were sitting in her kitchen, drinking that really cheap wine . . . And during the course of our conversation, a few things came up."

"About . . . ?" I sit on the edge of my brother's bed, waiting for Brad to Drop the Bomb on Me (Baby).

"About you and Alyssa," he answers quietly. "And me and Luanne . . . Stuff like that."

I barely recognize the tiny voice coming out of my Best Friend's body at this moment. In all the years I've known him, I don't think I've ever heard Brad sound so nervous . . . Or so serious.

Which is why I say, "Dah-dah, dah-dah." Hoping to lighten the mood a little.

But he doesn't take the bait. Instead, Brad soberly continues with his story. "So Lou and I were both pretty drunk by that point . . . And we pretty much decided we both feel the exact same way."

"About . . . ?"

"Well," he begins, "at first I just thought Luanne was rambling . . . But then finally she looked at me and said, 'You know what, Brad? I don't feel anything for men.' So I thought about it for a minute. Then I said, 'You know what, Lou? I don't feel anything for women.' "

After all Brad and I have been through—the JEH *Playgirl*, "If you were a girl . . . ?," plotting to seduce Mr. Grant—how could I not know this about him? Maybe he's just confused. I know how much Brad likes Luanne. Maybe by telling her he doesn't like girls, he thinks he'll gain her approval.

Or maybe *Lou* put him up to it?

Maybe she told him to tell me he's a Total Fag in hopes that I'll admit I'm a Total Fag, too. Then after Brad returns with the big news, Lou can use it against me. I wouldn't put it past her. Ever since I started hanging around with Alyssa back in the Fall, I've felt like Luanne Kowalski's totally had it in for me.

Which is why I ask, "How do you know for sure?" Just to be on the safe side.

"I don't know . . . I just do, I guess," he answers. "I think I've always known since I was like 7 or 8 years old."

I watch as Brad rifles through his memory in search of the perfect moment to describe exactly when he knew he was different. His face lights up as he finds it. Then he sits down beside me on the bottom bunk.

"This one time," he says, "my Dad took me and my sisters to see Santa Claus at the Oakland Mall. And all three of them asked for the exact same thing . . . A Giant Barbie Head." He looks at me a moment, waiting for confirmation. " 'member the Giant Barbie Head, Jack?"

How could I forget? It was only the best present my cousin Rachael got for Christmas 1978. In case you need reminding, the Giant Barbie Head was this bust—like a bust of a President. She had this long, white blond hair you could comb and style and fix. And on the bottom of the bust was a little tray of makeup you could put on her face . . . Believe me, it was all the rage.

"Well, I wanted a Giant Barbie Head too," Brad confesses. "But I knew I couldn't ask Santa Claus for one. Especially with my Dad standing right there listening to my every word." Then he adds, "I didn't know *why* I couldn't," sounding surprised. "I just knew it wasn't right."

Which is the exact same way I felt about my Aunt Mary knowing what I had written in my Dear Diary about Donny Osmond. Though I don't tell Brad this . . . I allow him to keep talking.

"Anyways," he goes on. "A few days later, I'm home helping my Mom in the kitchen, snapping green beans for dinner." His voice takes on an easy tone. Finally Brad's beginning to sound more like his usual self in telling me his Deep Dark Secret. "When out of the blue, she asks what I want Santa Claus to bring me for Christmas."

"What did you tell her?" I wonder. Though I think I can imagine his answer.

"For some reason—I don't know why," he admits, "I felt like I could tell her what I *really* wanted was a Giant Barbie Head . . . So I did."

I can totally picture Laura Victor-Dayton-Victor totally freaking out. Being the Good Christian Woman that she is. "What did your Mom do?"

"Nothing," Brad replies. "She just kinda smiled and said we'd have to wait till Christmas morning to see what Santa brought me . . . Then she said maybe she'd call up the North Pole and tell Santa what a good boy I'd been all year long, in case it might help."

I could totally see Laura Victor-Dayton-Victor doing something like that. Standing in her kitchen, singing her only son's praises to the dial tone.

"Later that night," Brad continues, "I'm lying in bed and I can hear my parents arguing in the next room. My Dad's shouting, 'I am not buying my son a goddamn Giant Barbie Head for Christmas and that's the end of it!' "

"Oh, no!" I gasp in response to Brad's spot-on impression of his father. All he needs now are the wire rims and the bald spot.

"Then when Christmas morning comes, lo and behold . . . There's *one* Giant Barbie Head waiting under the tree with all three of my sisters' names on it."

"But not yours?" I ask, sharing in Brad's heartbreak.

"Hell no!" He laughs softly to himself. "But wanna hear the best part of thc story, Jack? Later that morning when my Dad's taking a nap and my sisters are off playing with their Giant Barbie Head upstairs, my Mom leads me down into our basement." The stairs creak beneath his feet as he travels back in time. "With a finger to her lips," Brad says accompanied by a gesture, "she opens the closet door beneath the stairs . . . And guess what's waiting inside?"

"Your very own Giant Barbie Head?"

"All wrapped up with a big red ribbon and *my* name on it," he beams proudly. "Of course, my Mom swore me to secrecy . . . She said it was just between her and me and I shouldn't tell anybody else about it. And I could only play with my Giant Barbie Head in my bedroom when my Dad wasn't home and my sisters weren't around."

"Of course," I reply, nodding and smiling like a Total Dork.

"But still . . . I got *exactly* what I wanted for Christmas that year and I didn't care if I had to keep it a secret."

I honestly don't know what else to say. It took a lot of guts for Brad to tell me something as personal as that. And I'm so glad he did.

"You don't hate me now, do you?" he asks, becoming preoccupied with his lap.

"You're my Best Friend," I remind him. "I could never hate you."

Brad looks up, the biggest smile on his face I've ever seen. Then he sticks out his right pinky and says, "You have to promise."

So I do . . . I link my pinky with Brad's and I promise.

"Well," he says with a sigh. "Now that I've told you all this . . . Is there anything you wanna tell me?"

Where do I start?

Do I go all the way back to the Donny Osmond beginning? Or *Sooner or Later* Night with Rex Smith? Do I tell Brad the gory details about all the things I used to do in Private after reading *Now Let's Talk About Music* back in 9th grade? I'd hate for him to think I've been keeping secrets from him for too long . . . Even though I have.

So I start with, "You know Joey Palladino, don't you?"

"Oh, my God . . . The Total Babe from Clarkston?" Brad gushes. "What about him?"

"Well, 'member back on Valentine's Day when you and Max invited me to go to the movies with you guys?"

Brad nods. "Uh-huh . . ."

And then I proceed to share with him the entire story . . . How I think I might be *like that,* too, on account of I think I might be totally in love with Joey Palladino. How I can't stop thinking about him. Day and Night. Night and Day. How every time I'm alone with Joey, all I want to do is do *things* with him that I've never done with anybody else before.

"I'm your Best Friend, Jack . . . Why haven't you told me this before?" asks Brad when I've finished my rambling.

I answer, "I don't know . . ." Even though I do. Admitting it to myself was difficult enough. I never thought I'd be able to tell another soul that I'm not what I've been pretending to be all these years. How could I tell my Best Friend? But I'm relieved I finally have.

"You know what you need?" Brad says, ever the Machiavelli. "You need to get laid!"

Easy for him to say . . . Brad's the only other guy I know that's *like that.* And he's my Best Friend so that's not going to happen!

How will I *ever* find somebody to love?

The Edge Of Heaven

"It's too late to stop
Won't the heavens save me?"

—Wham!

I feel like a Total Ass!

Why I ever let Brad talk me into these things, I don't know. All I know is . . . There's no way I can go out in public dressed like this, that's for sure.

"Why not?" he asks me when I express my concern. "You look totally awesome." Peering over my shoulder into the mirror, he sizes me up. "Untuck your shirt." By which he means *his* shirt. Which he informed me I'd be wearing tonight. So I am.

"I don't know . . ." There's something about seeing myself in white rolled-up pants and a totally baggy green and white pin-striped shirt buttoned all the way up to the top and hanging all the way down to my knees that just isn't me. "I look like a Total Fag."

"You're supposed to," Brad tells me. "We're going to a Fag Bar, aren't we?" Then he reaches into his duffle bag and pulls out a small tub of greenish-blue gook. He picks up a plastic water-filled squirt bottle from on top of my dresser and begins wetting down my hair.

"Watch it!" I shiver at the shock, my shoulders tensing up.

Brad scoops out a dollop of Dippity Doo and begins working it into my hair, which desperately needs cutting. My head bobs back and forth under his complete control. After he finishes, I look just like the lead singer from The Cure.

"Tah-Dah!" Brad exclaims, looking pleased with himself. "*Now* you're ready . . ."

How he and Lou ever found out there's a bar down on 6 Mile and Woodward that would let them in, I have no idea. But they've been going practically every weekend since they both came out to each other back on New Year's Eve. And ever since I told Brad I think I might *like that* too, he's been on my case to join them. Now that I've agreed, I'm feeling a tad apprehensive.

"What if somebody we know sees us?" I worry. "On our way into the bar . . . Or when we're leaving." Even though I'm pretty much certain that I am indeed *like that,* I'm not too sure how I feel about being seen out in public just yet.

"If somebody we know sees us," Brad tells me, "then we'd be seeing *them,* too." Then he totally switches the subject. "What time is it?"

I look at my Swatch. "10:30 . . . When's Lou picking us up?"

"Soon as we're ready . . . You ready?"

My answer to that question would have to be "N-O." Still I say, "I guess . . ."

Brad picks up my phone, dials, waits a moment. I hear him say, "We're ready." Followed by, "We'll see you on the corner in ten."

We stand in front of the mirror, primping one final time.

Though there's not much more I can do considering the gel in my hair is starting to solidify. Which is why I decide I'd better not mess with it anymore. What's done is done.

After spraying me with a spurt of his Lagerfeld, Brad tells me, "I'm glad you're coming with." I watch as he scrunches up his new hairdo—long and curly on top/short on the sides, à la Simply Red. "We're gonna have a Total Blast . . . You know what I mean?"

Having never been to a bar in my life and having no concept of what goes on inside one, I can only ask, "What's so great about this place, anyways?"

"You mean the gay bar?" he asks. I can't help but notice how he says the G-word now with such ease.

"Do you really like going there?"

"Oh, my God . . . I totally do."

"Why?"

I sense that Brad senses I'm a bit anxious. So he does his best to alleviate my fears. "I like it," he says, "because I can be myself when I'm there . . . You know what I mean? I can wear the kinda clothes I like to wear."

Like the all black outfit he's got on right now.

"I don't have to worry about the way I walk," he goes on, "or the way my voice sounds when I talk."

Like that faggy-sounding guy, Clayton, on *Benson*.

"And it's the only place I can go and meet other people just like me . . . There's no wondering, 'Is he or isn't he?' Or, 'Is this person gonna think I'm weird if they know I like guys?' or 'Are they gonna hate me?'"

Which I can understand and totally relate to from past experience.

"And when I'm out on the dance floor," Brad continues, "in the dark with the fog and the lights, surrounded by all those guys—all those *gay* guys . . . I can see them looking at me. And for the first time in my life, I feel attractive." He pauses a moment, takes a breath, smiles. "I've never felt that way before, Jack . . . You know what I mean? Like somebody I'm looking at is looking back at me, too."

I know exactly how Brad feels . . . Whenever I'm out somewhere—shopping at the Mall or, say, at Cedar Point during the Summer—if I ever see a guy I think is cute, I can never tell if he's thinking the same thing about me. And it's not like I can just go up and start talking to him the way other guys do when they see a girl they're interested in.

Then Brad says, "Up till recently, I thought I was the only gay person in the entire world . . . It's nice to know there're other people out there who're *like that*, too."

Eight months ago when we started high school, if you would've told me that Brad Dayton and I would be sneaking out of my house and going to a G-A-Y bar, I would've never believed you . . . But that's what we do.

Why we have to climb out my bedroom window, I have no idea. Brad claims we can't risk my parents hearing us leave. Even though he knows perfectly well that it's a Saturday night and what that means with regard to my parents! It's a lucky thing I convinced them that an almost-16-year-old boy needs his privacy! Now my brother Billy sleeps in our sister's old bedroom, Jodi sleeps in front where my parents used to, and they sleep downstairs in our basement.

Twenty minutes later we're driving in Lou's car, heading south on I-75 . . .

"Have you talked to Alyssa?" Brad reaches over from where he sits in the front seat and turns down the radio. We're listening to "Smooth Operator" by some singer named Sade. Which is pronounced "Shar-Day," don't ask me why!

"She called yesterday," Lou replies. "We talked for like five minutes."

"How're they liking Daytona?" asks Brad.

"We didn't get into it."

"How come?"

"Duh!" Lou retorts. "Because Alyssa hates me now . . . What do you think?"

All this week we've been on Spring Break so Alyssa's been down in Florida with Cheri Sheffield and Erin Ahrens. And Kevin Ebersole. Not that I care, 'cause I totally don't. Though I can't say the same for Luanne. Not only were Brad and I right about her being a lesbian, it turns out she's totally in love with Alyssa and has been since she's known her. Which explains why Lou's been such a Bitch to me on account of I used to be her big competition. But now that I've pretty much joined "her team," she realizes I'm not a threat anymore and she's actually starting to be nice.

You can probably imagine how Alyssa felt finding out her Best Friend's a Total Dyke. At first she acted like she didn't mind. Like it was totally no big deal. Even though she's Miss Religious, Alyssa's not the type of person who'd turn her back on her Best Friend just because she's a lesbian. That is, till Lou confessed she also had feelings for her. That's when Alyssa started freaking out. Of course, she went and told Cheri. Who made the mistake of telling her Mom, who's even more religious than Cheri and Alyssa put together. So now Cheri's not supposed to have anything to do with Lou. Or Brad for that matter on account of he also made a confession to Alyssa. Who went and told Cheri. Who told her Mom.

And so on and so on and so on . . .

Which is part of the reason I feel like I'm making a huge mistake by going out with Brad and Luanne tonight. What if it gets back to Alyssa and she tells Cheri? And what if Cheri tells her Mom—or worse, her sister—and Betsy tells my entire Sophomore class? Then what am I going to do? It's not like it's something I can take back once I've admitted it. "Guess what? I really *do* like girls." Like Dolly Parton says in *9 to 5* after they discover Mr. Hart's still alive, "I musta made a mistake . . ." I don't think so!

What I really want to do right now is . . . jump out of the car at the first stoplight and walk all the way back to Hazeltucky. But from the looks of the area we've just driven into, that wouldn't be such a good idea.

"Are you sure this is safe?"

We've exited I-75 at McNichols, also known as 6 Mile. Nothing but burnt-out buildings surround us on either side of the road. Plus a few shady looking Party Stores you'd never catch me stepping foot in. Not even in broad daylight.

Which is probably why Brad tells me, "Lock 'em!"

Which is exactly what I do. I lock my door and make sure my window's rolled all the way up. "Why's the bar have to be down here in the ghetto?" I wonder aloud.

"You mean the gay-to!" Brad quips.

"Where else do you expect them to put it?" Lou muses. "Nobody wants a place like that out in the suburbs."

That's when I see it . . . My first G-A-Y bar.

"Welcome to Heaven," says Brad with a smile.

From the looks of the nondescript gray brick building, I would've never guessed it was "a place like that." I mean, yes, there's the 24 HOUR ADULT VIDEO next door, and the windows are totally blacked out so you can't see in. But other than that . . . it looks like a perfectly normal business establishment.

Dodging the pools and puddles of recently melted snow in the parking lot/back alley, we make our way to the entrance where a bunch of people—mostly guys—wait in line by a door where a beefy Bouncer Guy takes money from them after checking their IDs.

"How are we gonna get in?" I whisper to Brad as we file

into place behind Luanne. Being that we're both only 15-going-on-16 so neither of us drive yet, the only IDs we have are our Hillbilly High ones. And I never ever carry mine with me.

"Shut up and follow my lead," Brad mumbles without moving his lips.

Clearly nobody's going to be stupid enough to think either of us is 18 years old and let us into a bar. Though I have to remind myself that both Brad and Lou have been here before. So they must know what they're doing.

"Donald . . . How's it hanging?" Lou says to Bouncer Guy as she arrives at the front of the line.

With a black magic marker Bouncer Guy scrawls a large X on the top of Lou's hand. "That'll be five bones," he tells her.

Lou hands the guy her $5 bill and with that, she steps inside.

"Hi, Don." Brad offers his hand to be marked with an X. Then he pays his cover and says, "Thanks."

That's when I'm just about to do the same. Only Bouncer Guy doesn't mark my hand with an X when I offer it to him. Instead he sizes me up. "How old are you?"

To which I don't know how to reply. I mean, I could lie and say I'm 18. Which I know is the legal age to enter a bar. Though the way I look right now dressed in Brad's clothes, I barely pass for 12.

"He's with me," Brad chimes in, coming to my rescue.

At which point, Bouncer Guy marks my hand with an X and says, "No drinking." Then I swear he winks at us.

"Thanks," I tell him, forking over my own Abraham Lincoln.

And in we go . . .

Up a flight of rickety old steps we climb, the totally dark stairway leading to God only knows where. This must be why they call it "Heaven," on account of it's on the top floor of the building. But in spite of the name, the bar itself resembles nothing of what I'd expect the Home of Jesus to look like. No pearly gates. No angels. It's not even white. Instead, the place is kind of a dark gray/flat black with a nondescript bar on one end and a tiny pool table at the other. Not that I'm saying it's a dump or anything, 'cause it's totally not. But the place kind of smells. Like stale beer and cigarettes. And the music they're playing is like a Blast from the Past. Don't get me wrong, I totally loved Sister Sledge back in like 1979. But it's not what I expected to hear at a bar.

Brad and I find Lou bellied up to the bar. Behind it, a rather muscular shirtless guy with a look of stern seriousness on his face fills red plastic cups from a tap. His lower body's covered by army fatigues tucked into shiny black combat boots. I can't help but notice the six-inch dyed blue mohawk sprouting from the top of his otherwise shaved head.

"You wanna beer?" Lou takes out the black leather wallet she always carries in her back pocket. My Dad's got one just like it.

"We can't drink," I reply. "'member?"

Brad whispers, "Lou's got a Fake ID," again without moving his lips.

I start to remind him, "But the Bouncer Guy said—" Till Lou cuts me off.

"They don't give a shit what we do in this place," she informs me. "Just as long as we spend our money." Then she catches the shirtless muscular guy's eye. "Michael . . . How's it hanging?"

Bartender Guy reaches out a hand. I observe him and Lou as they perform this whole complex shake, ranging in moves from regular to soul brother to fingertips cupped together, culminating in thumb and middle finger raised to lips as they take a hit off an imaginary joint.

"What can I get you?"

"Three Labatt's," Lou orders.

"Sure thing," he replies with a smile. Followed by, "I just need to see some ID."

At which point, I figure we're totally busted. But Lou proudly forks over the Fake ID she got from God only knows where. Bartender Guy looks at it, nods. Then he reaches into a refrigerated cooler behind the bar and removes three green glass bottles.

"Works every time," Lou beams with manly pride.

I can't even believe Bartender Guy thinks for one second that the photo of the 35-year-old woman in Lou's Fake ID is really her. Though maybe it's more of a formality. That way if the bar gets busted for serving minors, they can at least say they checked ID and it was too dark to tell it was fraudulent.

"Bottoms up," Bartender Guy tells us after he's opened each bottle with his trusty opener. And for some reason, he looks right at me when he says it! Even though the thought of drinking a beer right now totally disgusts me, I graciously accept the Labatt's that Bartender Guy slides my way.

"Cheers!" Lou toasts and we clink our bottles together and drink.

"Thanks, Mike." Brad smiles timidly, leaving a couple dollars on the bar.

"What's that for?" I ask, having no idea.

"Duh! It's called a tip."

I'm about to say, *How was I supposed to know? I've never been to a bar*, when Bartender Guy addresses Brad.

"Well, if it isn't Chicken Little," he says, working his square jaw on a piece of what smells like cinnamon Dentyne. Then he says, "Who's this?" Totally looking at me again.

"This is my Best Friend," Brad announces. "Jack."

Bartender Guy cocks his head to one side. "Hello, Best Friend Jack," he says slyly. Like he's totally hitting on me! "This your first time?"

To which I simply nod and say, "Uh-huh."

There's something about Bartender Guy that reminds me of somebody. Not just from a movie or television. Somebody I've actually *seen* somewhere before. Though I can't imagine where I would've ever met a guy like him. By which I mean a totally hot one. And if I did, would I ever really forget?

I just about shit my pants when Bartender Guy says next, "I *thought* you were a Virgin." Till I realize he means Bar Virgin. Then he adds, "I'd never forget a cutie like you."

If I didn't know better I'd think Bartender Guy was flirting with me. But that can't possibly be the case. I mean, he's got to be at least 25 years old. And I'm just a 15-going-on-16-year-old *boy.*

"Is that guy really . . . *you know?*" I ask Brad after Lou ditches us to go talk to some chick she's totally hot for and Bartender Guy moves on to help somebody else.

"Who, Mike?" he answers. "Totally."

I can't even believe a guy who looks like that is *like that.* I thought all gay guys were totally effeminate and prissy. Maybe Brad's sister Janelle is right about the Village People after all.

We cross to the other side of the room near the pool table, a series of black-and-white framed photos hanging on the wall behind us. One of which shows this totally muscular guy, with his shirt off and holding a pair of steel-belted radials, called "Fred with Tires"; it was taken by some photographer I've never heard of, Herb Ritts.

Brad lights a cigarette and makes himself look available. "Mike's what I like to call SWB . . . Short with a Bod."

"He reminds me of somebody," I say, still obsessed with the fact that I can't figure out how I know Bartender Guy.

Which is when Brad replies, "He totally looks like that guy from *Risky Business* to me . . . Only with a mohawk."

Which is when it hits me. He *does* look like that guy from

Risky Business. Who also happened to play a football player in that movie *All the Right Moves.* Which leads me to conclude that the totally hot Bartender Guy is none other than . . . Audrey's ex-HPHS football player/brother from the photo, Mike Wojczek. Though I don't tell Brad any of this. I wonder if Audrey knows. I'd hate to be the one to inform her. And how would I explain how *I* know?

By the time Mike shouts out, "Last Call!" around 1:40 AM, I'm definitely more than a little tipsy. Luckily, Lou has no problem holding her liquor and she gets us home all in one piece.

Back at my house . . .

I change into my sweatpants and my blue Bruiser T-shirt while Brad busies himself in the bathroom. I pray to God he doesn't wake up my parents banging around in there—wasted! One thing I know for sure is . . . I'm too tired to climb the ladder up to my bed. So I plop down on the empty bottom bunk below waiting for Brad's return.

After a moment, I hear him struggling with the flimsy accordion-style door. Then I hear his voice in the dark say, "So . . . Did you have a nice time tonight?"

I barely have it in me to speak, I'm so sleepy. Still I manage to reply, "It was okay." Then I admit, "I felt kinda strange at first, being surrounded by all those guys."

Brad scoffs. "What are you talking about?" He plops down on the bed beside me. "That's the best part!"

"And that weird guy asking me to dance," I say, having a sudden flash of memory of the men-infested dance floor. Talk about being the furthest thing from a junior high Fun Night!

"You mean Bruce?" Brad laughs. "He told me he thinks you're kinda cute."

"Gross!" I say. Though it's a little fuzzy now, I seem to remember Bruce mentioning he's 30. Which is a year younger than my Mom. "He's totally old."

"Didn't you think Bruce was totally Mr. Klan when you first saw him?" asks Brad. He's referring to our Hillbilly High Band teacher. "I did."

"Oh, my God . . . You're right!" The entire time I kept thinking he reminded me of *somebody.* At first I thought it was John Ritter from *Three's Company,* only with glasses and a mustache.

"Wouldn't that be a scan-jul?" Brad says.

I wouldn't be surprised if we did run into Mr. Klan at the bar. Like I've said, a lot of people *do* think he's a fag on account of he's over 35 and he's never been married. He also likes to tell us to "Squeeze—the—marble" during Marching Band practice. Supposedly so we have better posture, but still . . . It's kind of a faggy thing to say, don't you think?

"You don't have to worry about Bruce," Brad assures me. "I told him you were my boyfriend." Which totally catches me off guard.

"What'd you do that for?" I ask, not appreciating his chivalry.

"I don't know . . . I could tell he was bugging you."

"I don't want people thinking I'm your boyfriend!" I blurt out.

To which Brad retaliates, "Why? I'm not good enough for you? Thanks a lot!" Then he totally steals the pillow out from under me and hits me with it. "This is my bed . . . Yours is up there."

"But I'm too sick to climb the ladder," I groan.

"You're not sick, Jack . . . You're wasted."

"I'm not wasted," I protest. So what if I slur my words a little?

"Whatever," Brad replies. Then he rolls over, elbowing me in the face.

"Watch it!" I elbow him back before reclaiming the pillow.

"Get your own," he says, tugging it away from me.

"Shut up!" I wail, yanking with all my might and hitting him in the face.

"Ouch!" He hits me back.

"Cut it out!" I hit him back.

Back and forth we continue beating on each other, like College Sorority Girls. Till I accidentally-on-purpose knock Brad onto the floor where he lands with a THUD.

"Are you okay?" I lean slightly off the bed, trying to see him. Which isn't easy considering my room is pitch dark. Which is when Brad grabs my arm and pulls me down—right on top of him.

I say nothing.

Neither does Brad.

I also don't move.

Neither does he.

It's got to be on account of we're both drunk. Otherwise, why are we still lying here like this, eyes closed, breathing as one? I keep thinking about what Brad just said a minute ago. About telling that guy Bruce I'm his boyfriend.

I mean, just because Brad's *like that* and all . . . That doesn't mean, if I should decide I definitely am *like that*, too . . . That doesn't mean we should be *boyfriends*, does it?

I think I'm going to be sick.

No One Is To Blame

"You can dip your foot in the pool but you can't have a swim
You can feel the punishment but you can't commit the sin . . ."

—Howard Jones

I can't even *believe* this shit!

It's bad enough I've got kids at school thinking I'm a Total Fag. Now check this out . . .

Dear Jackie,

Your probably wondering why I've been so upset for the past few days. Please understand this is a hard thing for me to talk about, so I'm writing a letter to you instead. I can't even believe this is really happening to us. I feel like we're living in a bad TV movie of the week. I keep hoping it's all a dream and I'll just wake up.

I know how you feel about Joey. Ever since

he started coming over here again, I noticed you been acting different. Then I found the Valentine's Day card he gave you in your room so I figured this had to be the case.

I know what your going through right now is one of the most difficult things that can happen to a person. But you have to realize there are other people who won't feel the same way, if they know. You don't know this but my Uncle Dick was gay. When I was little, he used to bring his boyfriends over our house all the time and I could see how uncomfortable it made your Grandpa Guff feel.

Maybe this is all my fault. I had you when I was so young. Maybe I babied you too much. But please believe me when I say I still love you and always will, no matter what.

Love, Mom.

PS—Please come to me if you want to talk.

Which is exactly what I'm about to do . . .

"Mom!" I burst out of my room to find her in the kitchen, hands in a bowl of raw meat, mixing up a meatloaf. "What is this?" I ask, practically waving the letter in her face.

She begins sniffling uncontrollably. Her nose turns red. Tears well in her eyes. Then she loses it. "I'm sorry," she apologizes, upset.

If there's one thing I can't stand more than disappointing a teacher, it's seeing my mother cry. But at this point, I don't give a damn. I'm totally pissed!

"You've obviously made a mistake," I tell her, " 'cause I don't know what you're talking about or why you would even think such a thing." I can't continue letting my Mom think there's something going on between me and Joey . . . Even though I might want there to be.

"Okay . . ." I watch as she scrapes pink hamburger from between her wedding ring and her fourth finger. "I just thought . . ." Then she trails off.

"Thought what?" I demand to know, not about to let her off the hook so easily.

"When you were little . . . The way you used to . . ."

"Used to what?" I ask. Now I wonder what exactly my Mom's driving at.

Maybe it's got something to do with my playing *Brady Bunch* and *Charlie's Angels* with my cousins Rachael and Rhonda when I was a kid. Or maybe my Aunt Mary told her about my Dear Diary Donny Osmond entry all those years ago. Or maybe she finds my recently revived interest in Rex Smith's *Sooner or Later* a bit reprehensible?

Nevertheless, she dismisses me. "I have to finish making dinner before Dad gets home." Then she goes back to what she was doing before I came waltzing in and interrupted her. "We can talk about this later." She plops the pale blob into the loaf pan and begins patting it into place.

"There's nothing else to talk about," I inform her. Then I storm out of the room.

How long has my own mother felt this way about me? All of my life? And if so, why hasn't she said anything up till now? Why did it take my hanging around with Joey Palladino these past two months to trigger this?

Unless . . .

A few nights ago, I was home in my bedroom working on my homework for Mrs. Malloy's 1st hour English when the phone rang. My parents have gotten to the point where they won't answer it anymore 'cause it's always somebody calling for me or my sister. At age 11, Jodi's starting to rival me for most calls in a single day. After the third ring, I set aside my copy of *The Fall of the House of Usher* and lifted the receiver from my wall.

Before I got the chance to say anything, I heard my Dad on the other end of the line. "I think Jack's in his room . . . Let me get him."

Then I heard, "Actually . . . Is Mrs. Paterno around?"

To which my Dad replied, "Hold on." Followed by, "Dianne, it's Alyssa."

Before my Mom had a chance to catch me eavesdropping, I hung up. Even though I felt a little whatever about Alyssa calling my house wanting to talk to her, it's not like we're going together anymore so it was probably none of my business.

I continued with my homework for another twenty mintues or so. Till I started getting hungry and decided to take a break. My Dad always keeps a stash of Fritos or Cheez Balls on top of our refrigerator in the kitchen. All of which are totally off-limits to me and my friends. But I usually sneak a few when I'm home studying by myself and he never seems to notice.

I was just about to head into the kitchen when I noticed my Dad and my sister and brother in our living room. "Your show's on," he told me when I poked my head in to see what they were watching on TV.

"Huh?" I said, having no idea what he was talking about.

"Mike Seaver," he replied. By whom he meant Kirk Cameron. Ever since I made the mistake of growing my hair out a little, that's all I hear. "You look just like that kid from *Growing Pains*." Which I've never even seen.

Which is why I changed the subject. "Where's Mom?" I figured maybe she was off shopping somewhere with my Aunt Mary or Aunt Sonia or something.

"She went out," my Dad answered, digging into his front T-shirt pocket, cellophane crinkling as he retrieved what had to be his twentieth Kool since he got home that day. With a SNAP from his silver Zippo, he lit the cigarette.

I held my breath. "Where'd she go?" I asked, trying not to breathe in any of the smoke my Dad had just exhaled into the room.

"I'm not sure," my Dad told me, totally vague. Then he added, "She'll be back." A cloud of smoke wafted about his head. Meanwhile, my poor little brother and sister sat there, their tiny little lungs being contaminated with Cancer.

Being the nonconfrontational son I am, I said nothing else. I simply grabbed myself some Pringles and returned to my Poe.

An hour or so later my Mom came home. But did she say anything to me about where she'd been? Hell no! In fact, she barely said anything to me at all before she went to bed—early. Which is something she never does till at least 11:00 PM. So I figured something had to be up. What the Hell could it be?

Now I know!

This afteroon around 3:30 PM, I arrived home from school. My parents recently rented one of those carpet cleaning machines from Farmer Jack's and my Dad's been a real stickler about us not tracking anything across the living room. So I entered through the back door.

"Mom . . . I'm home!" I called out. To which I got no response. Through the kitchen I went, into the hallway off the living room. I could hear the familiar voices of Springfield's Finest coming from the television where *Guiding Light* just resumed from a commercial break.

"Hello?" I said quietly, figuring my Mom was most likely napping on the couch. I poked my head in the doorway and sure enough, there she was asleep beneath the brown and gold afghan my Grandma Paterno crocheted a bijillion years ago.

The only thing is . . . she wasn't asleep. At least not for real. Because I saw her quickly close her eyes, *pretending* to be asleep.

Like I said, ever since she came home from going out with Alyssa the other night, she's been acting weird. And this time I mean, weird-weird. As in totally.

So I headed back to my room, closing my flimsy accordion-fold door behind me. And that's when I found my Mom's letter, lying on my pillow . . .

If she's going to think anybody's gay, it should be Brad Dayton—not Joey Palladino. He's the one who acts like a Total Fag all the time. Why has she never had any concern in all the years I've been friends with him?

Unless . . .

"Did you tell Alyssa I went to the Fag Bar with you over Spring Break?" I ask Brad, immediately getting him on the phone.

"No," he replies innocently. "Why would I?'

"Did Lou?"

"I don't know . . ."

"Which means she did."

I knew I should've never let Brad talk me into going out with him and Luanne that night. What's more, I should've known I couldn't trust a dyke. I'm sure the first thing Lou did after Alyssa got back from Spring Break was tell her I'm a Total Fag when all I ever said was I thought I might be.

"What's wrong, Jack?" asks Brad. "You sound totally pissed."

"That's because I totally am!"

I proceed to tell Brad all about what happened with my Mom finding Joey's VD card and her writing me the letter. Which I read to him, word for word.

"Quelle scan-jul!" he replies. "Have you told Joey about this?"

"Not yet . . . But I'm going to." As soon as I get off the phone.

"You know," Brad starts to say, "I always kinda thought Joey Palladino was a Total Fag . . . You know what I mean?"

"Well, he's not!" I exclaim with utmost conviction. Even though

I keep remembering Joey's response to my question *What would you do if I kissed you right now?* . . .

I don't know . . . Probably kiss you back.

Maybe Joey Palladino *is* a fag . . . Still, I don't like hearing Brad call him such names.

"Don't you think it's kinda weird for another guy to be giving you a Valentime's Day card?" Brad says now. Even though I know he knows the real word is "Valen-*tine*'s." Then he tells me, "I gave the one I made to my Mom."

"That was your choice, wasn't it?" I say with a huff. If I didn't know better, I'd think Brad was a little jealous of my friendship with Joey. Even though he has no reason to be. My feelings for Joey are totally different from the way I feel about him.

"You can tell me if there's something going on with you guys," Brad assures me. "You know I'm not gonna care."

To which I reply, "There's nothing going on . . . How many times do I have to tell you?"

"Are you sure?" he questions. Like he thinks I'm lying to him.

Which is why I suddenly shout, "Joey's my Best Friend for God's sake . . . That's it!"

To which Brad says quietly, "That's funny . . . I always thought *I* was your Best Friend."

Obviously he doesn't get what I'm trying to say . . . So I simply tell him, "Joey's a different kinda person than you are."

From the other end of the line, I hear him scoff. "You mean he's a Jock?"

"He's not a Jock," I affirm. "He just likes Sports."

"Yeah . . . He's a Jock."

"It's more complicated than that," I insist. How do I explain it? "Joey likes to do different things than you do, that's all."

"You mean he likes to go to football games and watch pro wrestling, right? Stupid Jock things like that."

Phone balanced in the crook of my neck against my shoulder, I cross over to my desk. Buried beneath a pile of papers, I see pink and white and red sticking out . . . Joey's Valentine's Day card.

Why did I leave it lying around like this? Did I unconsciously want my Mom to find it? Did I somehow think she'd understand?

I run my fingers across each letter of what has become to me the most beautiful word in the world . . . J-O-E-Y.

Then I hear Brad say, "It's probably 'cause you broke up with Alyssa right after Joey came back." I can't even believe he's continuing to speculate about what happened with my Mom.

"#1—" I say, "Alyssa broke up with me." I open the desk drawer and shove the card inside. "And #2—Joey moving back here has nothing to do with why it happened." Though I realize now in a way it did. It's not like I ever meant to hurt Alyssa. It's not that I didn't like her. I just didn't like her-like her. In that way. Which is really too bad 'cause she's totally a great girl. I wish I could be the one to give her what she deserves. But I can't.

"Well, how would you like it if you were 30 years old," Brad asks me, "and you found out your 15-year-old son was gay?" Totally taking my Mom's side.

Which is when I tell him, "I never said I was . . ." Even though I've been to a GAY bar where I've met some other GAY people, I still can't say the word GAY out loud. Especially not about myself. It's like, once I do—once I finally slap the label on my forehead—I'll never be able to peel it back off.

Brad says, "I thought you said—"

I say, "I said I thought I might be." Cutting him off.

"Same difference."

I've got this cowlick in the front of my hair, just above my left eyebrow. Whenever I'm stressed out, I frantically begin twirling it. Which I'm totally doing right now. I should've never told Brad anything about the way I've been feeling. I should've kept it a secret. Till I knew for sure.

Then Brad says, "You know, Jack . . . Maybe Joey feels the same way about you."

"Maybe you should just stay out of this," I politely inform him.

"Have you ever thought of that?" he asks, hopeful. "Maybe you should just come right out and ask him . . . Otherwise you're never gonna know."

Yes, I have thought of that. But I'm not going to come right out and ask Joey if he's a fag, let alone if he wants to get It on with me. Even if he does, we can never be together. We can never be "boyfriends." That'll never happen. Not in this Day and Age . . . Especially not now with my Mom thinking she knows what's up.

And what if I do ask Joey and he tells me he's *not* a fag. He'll be pissed at me for ever thinking such a thing about him. Or worse—what if he says he *is* but he has no interest in me whatsoever? Then what would I do? I'd just about die! Which is why I'd rather not know. I'd rather just keep things the exact same way as they were before today.

"Joey is not a fag," I inform Brad matter-of-factly. "And neither am I, okay?"

"But—"

"But what?" I challenge.

"What about what you said," he attempts to remind me, "after I told you about my Giant Barbie Head?"

Leave it to Brad to bring that up! Why can't he just forget I ever said anything? Why can't he accept that it's my life and I'm the one who gets to decide how I am . . . And I say I'm not *like that.*

"I've gotta go," I announce. Then I hang up, immediately

punching Joey's Grandma's number into the key pad with my thumb. Wait till he gets a load of this!

"What's up?" says Joey, ever cool.

"Oh, nothing," I reply. "Except my Mom thinks we're both Total Fags."

I proceed to recap the entire story for him, going back to the Alyssa phone call the other night when my Mom pulled a Benedict Arnold, up till the point where I told her she's totally FOS. As in "Full of Shit."

"What're we gonna do?" Joey asks. "Your Mom must hate me."

"I don't care," I say. "*I* like you and that's all that counts." I wait for Joey's response, listening to his silent breathing on the other end of the line. God, I wish he were here on Shevlin and not over on Carlisle, half a mile away!

Finally Joey says, "I'm sorry."

"For what?" I reply.

"If it wasn't for me," he insists, "you wouldn't be having this problem with your Mom."

"She's the one with the problem," I inform him. "It's got nothing to do with you."

Then Joey says the one thing I've been dreading . . . "Maybe we should stop hanging out together."

"No!" I practically yell, wanting to shake him by the shoulders. "That's the last thing I want right now."

"Just for a while," he adds. Though I get the feeling he doesn't mean it. I get the feeling this is *The End of Jack & Joey.* Like he's breaking up with me or something.

I choke back a sob. "Can't you see this is exactly what my Mom wants?" I'm so angry right now, I could spit! I pray Joey's not going to stop being friends with me all because my mother is totally overreacting.

"Well, I can't come over your house anymore," he points out.

"Yes, you can."

"How? Your Mom's gonna have her ear up to the door the entire time, making sure we're not fucking around." From the way Joey says this, I can't tell if he *really* thinks there's a reason for my Mom to be concerned. Even though we've still never done anything, we've gotten pretty close.

Just last weekend, Joey was over watching WWF wrestling—which, believe it or not, I'm seriously starting to like—and inevitably, we began rolling around on the floor together. You know, trying out some moves.

"Get off me, you Chump!" he grunted.

"Who you calling a Chump?" I groaned. In spite of having a good six inches on me, I managed to get Joey into a firm headlock. "How you like that?"

He pulled at my forearms, trying to pry himself free. "You think you're so tough, Paterno . . . Don't you?"

"I don't *think,* Palladino . . . I know!"

"Oh, yeah? I'll kick your ass . . ."

With one gigantic heave, Joey flipped me onto my back. Then he climbed on top of me, pinning my arms at my side beneath his knobby knees. "You give?"

"No fucking way!" I told him, struggling to break free.

At which point, Joey reached back behind him . . .

Sunshine smile.

Forcing my legs forward, knees folded against my chest . . .

Cherry lips.

With one hand, he held my arms above my head . . .

Chocolate eyes.

Breathing in the pine-scented wonderfulness that is Joey Palladino, I tilted my head back, spinning. With his face close to mine, Joey pressed his hips against my ass. Like he was about to . . . *You know.*

"Hello?" I hear Joey say, "You still there?" From the other end of the line.

I shake off the memory. "Not for long . . . I'm coming over."

To which he replies, "Um . . ."

"Um, what?"

Joey pauses a moment before saying, "I don't think you should." Which is pretty much the equivalent of plunging a dagger into my chest.

"You don't wanna see me?" I ask. A little melodramatic, I know.

"Would you shut up?" he teases. "I'll see you tomorrow at Lunch." Then Joey says, "Good-bye," and hangs up.

My heart goes dead.

Sweet Sixteen

"Well, memories will burn you
Memories grow older as people can . . ."

—Billy Idol

One down, two to go!

I can't even believe there are only three more weeks left of my first year of high school. I don't imagine being a Junior will feel any different from being a Sophomore. Except for the fact there's going to be a new breed of Hillbillies roaming the Hallowed Halls come September. It'll be nice not being on the bottom of the Social Totem Pole. Though it'll also be kind of strange no longer seeing Cheri Sheffield's or Alyssa Resnick's shining faces.

Fortunately, we're ending on good terms, me and Alyssa. We spent one final Lunch together in the cafeteria on Friday. Though we didn't exactly have a whole lot to talk about . . .

"Did you read *Arnold* this week?" she asked me over the non-twitching meatloaf.

"Nuh-uh," I replied. "I don't think I've read it since Tommy won the Biology Award for his anatomy project." At which point, Arnold presented him with a saliva gland. (Gross!)

"That was disgusting!" Alyssa laughed so hard she almost shot chocolate milk through her nose. Then we pretty much ran out of conversation . . . Till she came up with, "How's your Mom?"

"She's good," I replied. Thankfully she's been staying out of my business since the whole scan-jul with her and Joey and the letter. Which Alyssa didn't mention having anything to do with. And being my usual nonconfrontational self, I didn't bother bringing it up.

Two days later, I get the strangest phone call from Brad . . .

"Hey, Jack . . . What's up?"

"Nothing," I answer from my end of the line. Which isn't exactly true.

I'm lying on my bed about to browse through a magazine I found at my Aunt Sonia's yesterday when I went over for a cookout. Of course, I don't tell Brad it happens to be a copy of *Playgirl.*

I don't know what possessed me . . . considering after the whole incident with my Mom and Joey and the letter, I've pretty much concluded that I'm not *like that.* But when I discovered it lying facedown in the magazine rack in Aunt Sonia's bathroom, I decided maybe I should borrow it. Just to be certain. So I stuck it down my shorts and got the Hell out of there!

"Did I catch you at a bad time?" Brad asks.

"No . . ." Even though I was planning to thumb through *Playgirl* before taking a shower, it can wait. "What's up with you?" I hear what sounds like a radio blaring the "Hot Hits" of WHYT in the background.

"Just getting some sun," he tells me. Which is typical Brad. The minute the mercury hits the 70° mark, he's outside with his Speedo on. It doesn't matter if it's Mostly Sunny or Partly Cloudy, Brad will spend the entire Summer Vacation between the hours of 10:00 AM and 2:00 PM in pursuit of the Perfect Tan. What he doesn't seem to realize is . . . as a redhead, he doesn't tan—he burns. Unlike me with my Dad's olive complexion, I only have to be outside for twenty minutes and I'm totally dark. Not that I'm bragging or anything, 'cause I'm just stating a fact.

"How's your weekend?" I ask, not sure what else to say. It's been a while since Brad and I talked.

"Good," he replies. "How's yours?"

"Good." I turn *Playgirl* facedown on my bed. I can just imagine what Brad would say if he knew I was even contemplating looking at *Arnold "Commando" Schwarzenegger Unveiled.*

"Before I forget why I called," Brad begins after a brief silence, "I got some pretty exciting news . . ." Then he trails off.

I take this as my cue to say, "Oh, yeah . . . What?"

He pauses dramatically. "Have you ever heard of Stonewall?"

"As in 'General'?" I reply, wondering what the Hell the Civil War has got to do with anything.

"Not Stonewall Jackson, Jack," Brad groans. Like I'm a Total Idiot. "*The* Stonewall." Which he pronounces "thee." "It's this totally famous gay bar in New York City . . . I can't believe you've never heard of it."

"Why would I?" I ask. Though I can imagine why he thinks I should.

"Because you're Mr. Know-it-All, aren't you? Duh!"

Just because I've been a straight-A student for yet another year doesn't mean I know everything. Which is exactly what I tell Brad.

To which he tells me, "Whatever." Then he says, "I've been doing some research and guess what I found out?"

"I don't know . . . What?"

"Well, a long time ago in like 1969," he shares, "there was this *huge* riot . . . I think it had something to do with Judy Garland getting shot."

Even though I don't know how many times I've already told him . . . "Judy Garland died from a drug overdose, 'member? They found her dead on her toilet."

Brad scoffs. "Anyways . . . All these gay people were hanging out at The Stonewall," he continues. "You know, like that chick in Chekhov . . . They were in mourning for their lives." Again with the Dramatics! "Well, I guess they got carried away or something, 'cause the police raided the joint and everybody got arrested."

"So . . . ?" I reply, wondering what the Hell Dorothy from *The Wizard of Oz* has got to do with anything.

"So . . . Every June there's a big celebration to commemorate the anniversary of the Stonewall Riots," Brad announces. "And guess what the date is?"

I roll my eyes, shake my head, stating, "I have no idea . . ." Though I can imagine why he thinks I should.

"Go on!" Brad cries. "Take a *wild* guess."

The only date of significance in June I can think of is . . . "June 27th?" Only because it's my birthday and it's coming up in less than two weeks . . . *God, I'm getting old!*

"Isn't that an amazing coincidence?!" he squeals. Then soberly he adds, "It's too bad you're not gay after all."

To which I've got to ask, "Why?"

"You were born on the gayest day in History . . . How cool is that?"

I'm thinking, *Not very.* Though I don't tell Brad this.

"You know . . ." All of a sudden Brad is Mr. Eager Beaver. "Maybe you and I can go to New York at the end of the month . . . For your birthday."

"Why would I wanna do that?" I can't help but wonder.

"Because it'll be fun," he replies.

Yeah, right . . . I can just imagine spending my 16th birthday surrounded by a bunch of Total Fags and Drag Queens. No, thank you! So I tell Brad, "There is no way our parents are gonna let us go to New York City by *ourselves.*"

"Why not?" he asks in typical naïve Bradley Dayton fashion. "I'm thinking about moving there to pursue my acting career after I graduate . . . I'll just use it as an excuse."

"Oh, Brad!" I sigh. "#1—We're *only* 15 years old." Going on 16, but still . . . "#2—You should move to *L.A.* if you wanna pursue an acting career—especially if you wanna be on *Days of our Lives* 'cause that's where they tape it." At 3000 W. Alameda Avenue in Burbank, to be precise. "And #3—Why would I wanna go and celebrate the anniversary of the Stonewall Riots when you know I'm not *like that?*"

"Because I'm *like that,*" he reminds me, "and supposedly you're my Best Friend."

We sit in silence a moment, connected by a series of wires running between two small suburban cities, our friendship coming to an end. At least that's how it feels. I honestly wish I could be spontaneous and carefree the way Brad is. But I have to look out for my future. How will I ever be a Famous Writer someday if everybody thinks I'm a Total Fag?

Finally I say, "I'm sorry . . ." Truly meaning it.

"Don't be sorry," Brad replies. "Be happy you don't have to go running off to New York, Jack . . . Just so you can be yourself." Then he hangs up.

I don't see or talk to Brad again till June 27th when I decide to throw myself a Sweet Sixteen party . . .

Actually, I'm surprised he even shows up. Especially when I make him pinky-swear-promise he won't tell Luanne about it on account of she's *not* invited. The last thing I need is her coming around trying to make me all confused again. But all my other friends are on the Guest List. Audrey and Max. Betsy and

Cheri Sheffield apparently are both Up North at their cottage somewhere in a town called Beulah so they can't make it. Alyssa said she'll try to stop by. But I'm not counting on it.

Unfortunately Joey said, "Thanks, but no thanks," when I called with his invitation. After the whole thing happened with my Mom, he and I officially stopped seeing each other outside of school—which just about killed me. It doesn't help that "All at Once" by Whitney Houston is a favorite of Alan Almond, the DJ on WNIC's *Pillow Talk*. Which I've been crying myself to sleep with every night before going to bed.

At first, I was pissed . . . I told Joey not to let my Mom's overactive imagination destroy our friendship. But he said he wouldn't feel comfortable coming around anymore, knowing how it would make my Mom worry. In fact, Joey hasn't been over since the day I got the letter from her over two months ago. And now that school's out for the Summer, I'll probably never see him again.

I also invited Ava Reese and Carrie Johnson from Sophomore Symphony, along with Marie Sperling from my 3rd hour Geometry class. In case you don't remember, she's the girl I know from Webb who totally reminds me of Kristian Alfonso. Too bad Marie's *still* going with that Jock Jerk, Tom Fulton. Remember the so-called friend of Max's who used to say shit about Brad and I being Total Fags and probably still does? Of course, I couldn't say no to her when she called asking if she could bring Tom to the party. Marie's a Total Sweetheart. Tom Fulton does not deserve her!

Pretty much your typical Jack Paterno Boy/Girl party—more girls than boys—we end up sitting around my parents' basement listening to music, eating snacks, and drinking this concoction my Mom made out of Hawaiian Punch and Vernors. Too bad there's no alcohol in it! All of which eventually leads up to the traditional game of Spin-the-Bottle. Though it doesn't end up being nearly as much fun as the time we played it at my Halloween party last Fall. I don't know if it's because there isn't anybody I really want to kiss or what. All I know is . . . Marie Sperling is totally hilarious. Talk about putting the *I* in "naïve!"

"How do you play Spin-the-Bottle?" she asks when the idea first comes up. Totally serious.

To which Brad replies, "Um . . . First you take this bottle, Marie . . . Then you set it on the floor and *spin* it!" Then he laughs, as do we all.

Like I've said, Marie is a totally great girl. Pretty, smart, funny. But she's a little clueless about some things. Not that I'm saying she's dumb, 'cause she's totally not. She's just very innocent. You should see the look on Tom Fulton's face when Marie's spin of the bottle lands on me for the third time and we have to French kiss. Let's just say, he's not too pleased!

Leave it to Max . . . His gift to me is a copy of the August 1986 issue of *Playboy.* Which is exactly what I wanted—not! Though Playmate Ava Fabian, whose Turn-Ons include: *men in uniforms, whipped cream, massages, flowers, big fluffy pillows, ocean,* does look pretty good in her centerfold spread. But maybe that's because it's very tastefully done and she's not spreading her legs or anything disgusting like that. She's also got small areolas which, I believe I've already mentioned, don't gross me out.

The majority of the rest of my Summer I spend taking Driver's Education . . .

For six weeks, every Monday through Friday, I have to be bright-eyed and bushy-tailed at the Butt Crack of Dawn in the Choir Room of Hillbilly High. We're talking 6 o'clock in the freaking AM. Why I signed up for the first course of the day, I have no idea. You'll never guess who my instructor is. I'll give you a hint . . . He was one of my teachers at Webb. No, not Mr. Grant. Remember Algebra Man, aka Mr. Bond? Thank God he left the cape at home!

Other than the fact that I'll finally get my license at the end of it, the good part of the experience is . . . spending time with Betsy Sheffield who signed up for the exact same slot. In fact, I don't think I'd have *any* fun if it wasn't for her. Every day we sit side by side, cracking up at this woman in our class named Ella. I'm not even exaggerating when I say . . . Ella has got to be *at least* 60 years old.

Not only does she appear to be a little on the slow side . . . She's also dangerous! This became evident the day we all took to the back parking lot where they set up the driving course. Ella proceeded to wipe out half a dozen orange cones before steering her Renault Encore up onto the sidewalk where she almost plowed down some Sophomore riding a scooter! Which is why Betsy and I decided our official Driver's Ed. '86 theme song is "You Be Ella," sung to the tune of Run-D.M.C.'s "You Be Illin'." (Dog Food!)

When I finally do get my license in August, I drive Max, Betsy, and Audrey out to the Tombs in the new car that my Dad bought for me. Okay, it isn't exactly new. It's a 1979 Dodge Omni. It's also pea green. And it isn't exactly just for me—I have to share it with my Mom. After not being behind the wheel since the car itself first rolled off the assembly line, she decided she wants to start driving again, don't ask me why! But I get to drive it to school every day. And to work.

Oh, yeah. I forgot to mention . . . I got a job. My parents informed me that once my Sweet Ass turned Sweet Sixteen, my days as a Kept Child were over. So come tomorrow—August 26, 1986—I will join the Great American Workforce. For $3.05 per hour I'll be working as a Bagger at Farmer Jack's. Though not at Store #12 on 9 Mile and John R where my Dad is employed. Family members working together is strictly prohibited according to Union Rules. Which is why my Dad called up his former Boss and got him to hire me. Remember Lyle Waggoner? He's now the Manager of Store #142 on 12 Mile and Campbell in Madison Heights

Unfortunately when I met with him, I discovered the guy no longer looks *anything* like Major Steve Trevor. Fortunately, I don't think he remembered much from *Sooner or Later* Night—probably 'cause he was totally wasted by the time he left our house! At least he didn't mention it if he did.

The good new is . . . I'll only be working part-time. No more than 20 hours per week and on weekends. But never on Friday night on account of Marching Band playing at the Varsity Football games. Speaking of . . . Practice starts tomorrow, with the first Home Game against Warren Fitzgerald coming up on September 12th. But before that, we've got the Hamtramck Labor Day Parade on Monday the 1st. (Yippee!)

In case you can't tell, that was totally sarcasm. I really am over being a Band Fag. Especially since the '86–'87 HPHS Viking Marching Band Drum Major is none other than . . . Luanne Kowalski.

Talk about fun—not!

I can't say I've seen much of Brad since my Sweet Sixteen party. He got a job waiting tables at Big Boy's and when he's not working, he spends all his time with Luanne. Which might explain the following letter I found in my mailbox today . . .

August 25, 1986

Jack,

Hi, I have just returned home from a girl named Jane's house to wait for Max because he is picking me up after work to spend the night. Please forgive the lovely flowery paper, but in the Dayton household, bills don't get paid, so there isn't even hot water, let alone regular paper.

I had a rather uneventful week, working at Big Boy's, hanging out with Luanne. Stuff like that. Tonight we picked up Jane (met her at the bar 2 weeks ago, she works at Oakland Mall) and then we went to her house. She lives in this really cool upper-flat in Royal Oak with 2 skinheads that are really cool and we made some coffee and just sat around on the living room floor. All in all it was pretty boring. I really went because I needed to kill time before Max got here. I was gonna call you, but Lou said you were pissed at me, so I decided to drop you a letter.

Jack, I can't believe I've barely seen you this entire summer. How can you even think that we aren't Best Friends anymore? After all we've been through, all we've done? It really hurts me to think that someone who <u>I thought</u> was the closest person to me can't understand the position I'm in. You know I stood by you when all you talked about was Joey Palladino. Only a real friend, a really special friend would do that. Any other person would have said, "Jack, Fuck off." But I knew that you'd get over it—not that you have, but hey, things take time.

Not for once during that period of our friendship did I think that you weren't still my Best Friend. I just want you to know that I'll always be there for you, just like I hope you will always be there for me. I don't know if this letter has made any sense to you, but just remember that I love you Jack, and always will. <u>NO MATTER</u> what happens to us during the corse of this year.

I always thought we'd be friends forever, I know we will, but PLEASE remember what I said before, please?

Brad

Talk about feeling like a Jerk! As in Total. Leave it to Brad Dayton to lay a Guilt Trip on me for being such a Bad Friend.

Don't get me wrong, I appreciate him reaching out to me like this. And he's totally right. Why have we barely seen each other this entire Summer? In the past, we spent practically every single day together—riding bikes, swimming in Max's pool, hanging out at the Mall. I remember us dreaming of the day Max would be the first to get his driver's license and his own car. We had all these plans to go to the Drive-In and to Metro Beach and to Cruise Gratiot for Chicks . . . Now that day has come and what have the three of us done? Nothing!

Why did Brad have to ruin everything by letting Luanne brainwash him? According to her, everybody in the entire world is gay—or at least bisexual. They're just too afraid to admit it.

I suppose this *could* be the case with me. As much as I liked Joey, I know in my heart I still also like girls. I wouldn't have wasted so much time with Alyssa if I didn't. She just wasn't The One. But what Lou doesn't seem to understand is . . . I'm only 16. I'm not old enough to make a decision that's going to affect me for the rest of my life. Why can't she just accept that and leave me alone? And why the fuck is she telling Brad I'm pissed at him?! I haven't seen or talked to her in ages. Once again, this is her little plot to pit Brad against me, I just know it!

Well, I am *not* going to let that happen . . .

I head back to my room, closing the accordion-fold door behind me. Then I reach for my phone, sit down on my bed and dial.

"Dayton residence."

"Is Brad there?"

"Hi, Jack." It's his Mom. "How's your Summer been?"

"Good," I answer, realizing just how much I've missed her slight Southern drawl. I wonder if Laura's been clued in as to what's been going on between me and her son on account of Stanley—I mean, Luanne Kowalski. By which I mean the fact that Lou's been trying to ruin our friendship since Day One.

"He's in his room . . . I'll get him for you," she offers. Followed by, *"Br-a-a-dley . . . Telephone!"* It's been way too long since I've heard her say that.

An eternity of dead air passes. I imagine the phone facedown on the orange Formica while Brad in his bedroom refuses my request. Laura drags him into the kitchen by the scruff of his neck, keeping an eye on his every move.

After a moment I hear, "Hello?"

"Hi, Brad," I say.

"Who is this?"

"It's Jack."

"Jack who?"

"What do you mean, 'Jack who?' " I ask. "Paterno."

To which Brad replies, "Oh." Followed by, "What do *you* want?"

Good question. Why am I calling him now when we've barely spoken to each other this entire Summer? What am I even going to say?

And then it *pours* out of me . . . *How Sorry I am for Being Such a Jerk.* By John R. Paterno.

"Dah-dah, dah-dah," says Brad, interrupting me halfway through.

So I repeat, "Dah-dah, dah-dah." Then I quickly finish my apology.

"What time you picking me up for Marching Band in the

morning?" he asks, as if the last two months never even happened. Guess this means we're still Best Friends.

"6:45," I tell him, almost forgetting that tomorrow's the First Day of School and we've got practice on the football field at 7:00 AM sharp.

"Better make it 6:40," Brad decides. "Drum Major Lou will have a fit if we're late."

Here's to another year of being a Band Fag!

THE 1986 VIKING

Hazel Park High School
23400 Hughes
Hazel Park, MI 48030

Volume 51

. . . And such is LIFΣ

C'est la vie is a French phrase that's often used here in the United States. Translated into English it means . . . and such is life. It's often used whenever something goes wrong which can't be fixed. That's why the yearbook staff decided to use C'est la vie as our theme this year because you can't please everyone about everything . . . and such is life!

We Marched to Their Beat

Marching Band took part in their traditional performances this year. In November they welcomed Santa Claus and celebrated the annual tree lighting in front of City Hall. They also marched in three different parades, including the Hazel Park Memorial Day Parade, Western Frontier Parade in Charlotte, and the Hamtramck Parade where they won Best Band Award.

A Symphony of Music

This year Sophomore Symphony Band was happy to receive a rating of I in District Competition at Romeo High. Many students participated in sales to raise money for the band. Fundraisers included working at the flea market and baked-goods sales for night school students. Also, out of generous Christmas spirit, some band members played for the elderly at Hazel Crest Retirement Home.

. . . And LIFΣ goes on

Jack,

You're a real great guy I've known for a real long time. I'm glad we became Best Friends again, at least for a while. It's been an experience I'll never forget. I plan to see your book on a shelf one day and I better not be in it! (Just joking.)

Joey Palladino

Jack,

We've known each other for 4 years now & I've really had fun being your friend. Never forget all the fun we've had talking about DAYS. Don't worry about fitting in with the "In" Crowd. Don't ever change for anybody. Not even Kristian. I truly hope you get all the fame & fortune you want and one day you win a Pulit Surprise. (Remember that joke?) Don't ever forget me!

Love, Carrie Johnson

Jack,

I have no idea how we met and no idea when we met but hay here we are (and that's a fact). I'm looking forward to spending more time with you in French Club. We'll have a blast! Love ya,

Diane (Thompson) "89"

Cher Jack,

Tu es un très intelligent étudiant en français. Bon chance!

Mme Carey

'86

Jack,

To a real sweetheart I've known for a long time. Thanks for making me feel good all the time and for teaching me how to "Spin the Bottle" at your 16th birthday party. Well, next time you see me (Kristian) on TV, give me a call and I'll watch myself. Thanks, cutie!

Love always, Marie (Kristian) Sperling

JACK (JACQUES, as Mr. Borjes says!)

I hope you know how really GREAT I think you are. Thanks for being there when I needed to unload my problems.. You're the only person that I can talk to for hours. I hope we stay close friends and lunch buddies.

Love, Betsy ("Effie," the girl who broke your heart) Sheffield

Jack,

You're my best friend and we've been through a lot, haven't we? Please don't ever forget the awesome times we've had. You are the only person in this world that I can be my-self with, laugh with, etc. Thank you for being who you are. and please don't forget who you are. No matter how hard you try to be someone (or something) else, I'll know the REAL you. If you promise to be yourself I know that you'll become the star reporter/writer you want to be. When I'm basking in the neon lights on Broadway, I'll remember . . . Edna, BLFAC, EB's, Marching Band, Gaylord, Christmas vacation 1985, all the events and experiences our relationship have gone thru I'll cherish & remember forever. I hope you will.

love, Brad

PS—If I ever do get my driver's license, maybe we will make it to Florida in 1988.

Jack,

Life's too casual! I'm really glad we're friends again. We have to go out sometime soon, just the guys. We also gotta find a different place to hang out at besides the Tombs! I can't wait til we finally get a vacation and for the summer. Next time we go out, you're driving.

Max

"Daytona 88"

Jack,

There are so many things I need to say. When we met so long ago in kindergarten, I remember how cute I thought you were. Then I moved to Minnesota in first grade and then I went to St. Mary's when I came back. I used to think about you all the time. What you looked like, if you still lived in Hazel Park, if you would remember me. Then ninth grade came along and I couldn't believe it was really you. You didn't seem too excited to see me but finally we became friends again. For a while I liked you for more than a friend but I just couldn't tell you because I didn't want to ruin our friendship. So I decided to forget about you in that way. I really loved our late night movies together, just not "Sooner or Later." Ha ha.

We had some great times with Lu, (oops!) Lou, Brad, Max, and Aly. I'll never forget the first time I went to the Tombs and you asked me if I would bear your child if you died! We still haven't gotten to Mackinac Island to sit by the special trees from "Somewhere in Time." I hope this Spring Break we can go to someone's cabin Up North. We'll have a blast.

There are so many other things I want to say but I'll end with three little words, "I Love You."

Love, Audrey

—JUNIOR—

1986–1987

Take My Breath Away

"Watching, I keep waiting, still anticipating love
Never hesitating to become the fated ones . . ."

—Berlin

I cannot *stand* Pep Rallies!

Like rats in a Biology room cage, the Hazel Park Vikings are ushered into the Gym and forced onto the bleachers in their Designated Class Section. After listening to members of Chorale sing "The Star-Spangled Banner" in four-part harmony, they view the Vikettes kicking off the event with a high-energy dance number set to the stylin' tunes of Earth, Wind & Fire.

The entire squad of eighteen girls—including my First Love, Lynn Kelly, and the Kristian Alfonso look-alike, Marie Sperling—strut their stuff on the shellacked basketball court identically clad in white puffy blouses worn with maroon sequined vests, matching mini-skirts, and high-heeled leather boots.

Nobody's paying attention to any of this . . . Except for me. But I've always had a thing for synchronized choreography, be it ice skating, swimming or dancing.

That's when I first notice her, standing at the far end of the kick-line on account of she can't be more than 5' tall and they always arrange the girls according to height. Not that I find her particularly attractive, 'cause I don't. Though she is cute, with blondish-brown shoulder-length permed hair and an ear-to-ear grin. What drew my attention to her was . . . She totally reminds me of the actress who plays Gina Capwell's long-lost daughter, Lily, on *Santa Barbara.*

In case you're worried that I've given up on *Days of our Lives,* I haven't. But over the Summer I took to watching *SB* from 3:00 PM to 4:00 PM on account of there's this girl on the show I also kind of like named Robin Wright. She plays the youngest Capwell daughter, Kelly, and just like Kristian Alfonso, I predict someday she's going to be a Big Star!

Apparently I'm not the only one who notices the addition of incoming Sophomore Diane Thompson, to the HPHS Vikettes drill team . . .

"Bra-yad!"

The following Monday at Lunch, Brad and Max and I are all sitting together at an orange-topped table for four, when from across the cafeteria comes the totally loud and totally obnoxious bellow of You-Know-Who.

"Pretend you don't hear her," Max tells us. "Maybe she'll get the hint and go away."

But it's no use. There she appears, beside our table. Though I almost don't recognize Luanne Kowalski with her shoulder-length bob now cut up to just below her ear and slicked back on both sides. You should see the Marching Band photo we took last week outside in the cafeteria courtyard . . . I'm telling you, Lou looks more like Judd Nelson every day!

"So . . . What are we having?" she asks, before inviting herself to sit down with us. From the way she's become notorious for mooching food from the Undergrads, you'd think Lou didn't have a job working at Sam's Jams in Ferndale. Or maybe her Mom has stopped giving her lunch money. Regardless, she's becoming annoying with a Capital A.

"Wha's up, Lou?" Max groans, mouth full.

"Max," Lou replies all cool. "How's it hanging?" Then she picks up the apple sitting on Brad's tray and takes a bite. "So . . . I've got the scoop."

"You do?" Brad asks, the only one to oblige Lou as she babbles away. I'm too busy watching the way her jaw works from side to side as she chews, calling to mind the words "cow" and "cud."

"Her name's Diane Thompson," Lou continues. "She went to Beecher . . . Her locker's down the back hall near the Teachers' Lounge." Finally taking time to swallow, she adds, "She's in the French Club *and* she lives over by the Courts."

"Somebody's been doing their homework," I interject.

"Somebody's gonna have to teach me how to do a little *parlez-vous*-ing," Lou replies, knowing I've got Mrs. Carey again this semester for French II.

I should've known Luanne would get the dirt on the "totally cute Sophomore Chick." A bunch of us Band Fags decided to head out to the Tombs after the first Varsity Football game of the season last Friday night . . . The entire drive out Rochester Road, all Lou did was talk about Diane, informing us how she could tell just by *looking* at her that she's "a Bean"—code for "lesbian"—and how it would only be a matter of time before she had her way with the girl. (Gross!)

"Don't look now . . ." Max nods in the direction of the far end of the cafeteria where Diane Thompson and Hannah Danson just sat down with their lunch trays piled high from the Salad Bar.

Of course, Luanne totally looks, her face totally lighting up. "Watch how a real man does things," she gloats before making a beeline towards Diane's table.

"What a dyke!" Max sighs, shoveling in today's Mystery Meat with a side of Veggie Surprise.

Brad says nothing and neither do I. Though I'm tempted. But I'll admit the cool thing about Luanne is . . . She's made it perfectly clear to Max how she is. By which I mean sexuality-wise. But she hasn't said a word to him about Brad. As far as she's concerned, it's totally up to Brad to tell Max about himself when the time is right. Which leads me to believe that my secret's also safe with her. Though like I've already said, I'm not *like that* anymore. So I've got nothing to hide.

The following day finds Diane Thompson a Special Guest at our lunch table . . .

"You should join French Club," she tells me after I mention I've got Mrs. Carey for 4th hour. I've decided I might use *le français* as a backup in case the whole Journalist/Writer thing doesn't pan out. Though so far, so good. I talked to Mr. Dell'Olio at the end of Sophomore year about working on *The Hazel Parker* and he's allowed me to join the Staff.

"When do you guys meet?" I ask Diane, much to Lou's chagrin. I get the feeling she doesn't appreciate the fact that her *supposed* new girlfriend is taking a greater interest in me. "I just might stop by."

Which is exactly what I do. I join the French Club and the following wcck, I ask Dianc Thompson out on a datc . . .

"You know Lou's gonna be pissed, don't you?" Brad tells me as we cross the muddy football field after morning Marching Band practice. I've just told him I invited Diane to join us on our Friday night Triple Date. Which isn't exactly going to be a date-date as far as Brad's concerned. But last time we were out gallivanting around the Tombs, we ran into another group of kids from Clarkston High. One of whom just so happened to be Brad's date from the 9th grade Carnation Dance, Ginny-What's-Her-Name.

Of course, he'd totally lost track of her after *Operation Revenge of the Band Fags!* Something tells me the date that night didn't go so well. Considering Brad didn't even kiss Ginny goodbye when his Mom dropped her off out of fear Laura would see them locking lips and he'd end up Grounded for Life. Though we all know now the real reason why is . . . Brad wasn't interested 'cause Ginny's a girl!

Which is why I have no idea why he invited her and her Best Friend, Missy, out on a Triple Date with me and Diane and Max. Not that Max was complaining or anything, 'cause he wasn't. As far as I can remember, Max hasn't been on a real date with a girl in his life. In fact, I think the last girl he ever went with was Angela Andrews back in 7th grade. Which was totally a shock to everybody at the time, and looking back on it makes it even more so. Because Angela Andrews is a totally Popular and totally hot Vikette now!

This Friday night's football game is at Southfield so Brad and I don't have to march with Marching Band. Which is why he and Max and I end up taking Ginny, Missy, and Diane to see *Top Gun.* Even though I liked that Val Kilmer guy in *Real Genius,* I had no interest in seeing a movie about a bunch of guy Fighter Pilots. But all the girls wanted to, so . . . Needless to say, they were practically wetting themselves during the volleyball scene on the beach!

Afterwards, we have to drive Ginny and Missy back to BFC—Bum Fuck Clarkston. Though I should say *Max* has to drive them on account of we took his car on account of it being a LeMans and it fits in more people than my tiny pea green Dodge Omni.

One thing I think I failed to mention is . . . Max got his license back on May 27th when he turned Sweet Sixteen. But Brad—who celebrated his a mere fifteen days ago on September 4th—hasn't even gotten his learner's permit on account of he *failed* Driver's Education. But that's all I'll say on that subject being that it's a sore one with Mr. Dayton.

After cramming four in the backseat—me and Diane and Brad and Ginny—so Max could sit up front *alone* with Missy, we drop Ginny off first. Talk about fancy! She lives in one of those humongous two-level jobs with tan aluminum siding, brown shutters, and an actual two-car garage. You know what I'm talking about? The kind of neighborhood where the houses all look the same-but-different, none of the yards have fences around them, and the streets all end in a circle. Like the Courts in Hazeltucky, only much nicer—and bigger.

"Be right back," Brad tells us before walking Ginny to her door.

From where I sit with my arm around Diane, I can see him through the back window standing beneath the yellow light of Ginny's pillared front porch, looking totally awkward.

"Kiss her already!" Max says aloud, to nobody in particular.

To which I think, *Oh, Max!*

If he only knew his friend Bradley is a Total Fag. I mean, seriously, what would he say? After knowing Brad for how many years and defending his sexuality against Total Jerks like Tom Fulton, would Max really care if he found out Brad's gay and that—for a brief time—I thought *I* might be too?

And then he does it . . .

Brad leans over and kisses Ginny What's-Her-Name—right on the lips! I'm thinking, *What the Hell?* He's made it perfectly clear he "feels nothing" for girls. So why's he kissing one? Then I realize, he most likely did it for Max's benefit. Maybe Brad's not as comfortable with the whole being gay thing as he claims.

"Wha's up, Stud?" Max squeals, getting out of the car and pulling the front seat forward so Brad can climb in back. From the look on Max's face, I can tell our friend has done him proud.

"How was it?" I tease, giving Brad a look.

To which he just rolls his eyes. "Brrr!" he shivers. "It's fucking freezing out there!"

Next stop, Missy's house . . .

Which makes Ginny's look like Servants' Quarters. I'm not even joking when I say . . . There have to be at least five bedrooms in that place and an acre of land behind it. Talk about a fucking mansion! It's a wonder these girls want to have anything to do with us Hazeltucky Hillbillies.

Following Brad's example, Max walks Missy to her giant double-wide front doors.

"You think he's gonna kiss her?" asks Brad, climbing up front just as soon as Little Miss(y) Rich Girl is gone.

"If he doesn't," I reply, "he's never gonna hear the end of it."

Brad lets out a grunt. "Don't look now . . ."

Of course, Diane and I totally have to look. And what we see, we can't even believe our eyes . . .

"Oh, my God . . ."

"Did he just—?" I ask.

"He did," Diane confirms.

"What a fucking Pussy!" Brad sneers.

After a moment, Max gets back in the car, not saying a word. Then he puts it in gear and pulls away.

"Wha's up, Stud?" I mock.

"Oh no, you don't!" Brad chides. "I can not fucking believe you *shook* her fucking hand!"

Max cries, "I couldn't tell if she wanted me to kiss her or not," sounding totally frustrated. Knowing him, he probably had a Total Hard-on the minute he walked up to Missy's front door. Then BAM! Nothing . . .

"Turn this car around this instant!" Brad demands, sounding more like Max's Mom than one of his Best Friends. Though Annette Funicello would have added, "Young man!"

Max keeps driving down Sashabaw Road towards I-75. We're at least 30 miles from home and it's already after 11:00 PM. Diane needs to be home by Midnight. In the distance I see what must be the lights from the hill at Pine Knob. I haven't been skiing since the time Max conned me into going along with the Ski Club, back in 7th grade. Talk about a nightmare! I had the damnedest time getting up that stupid tow rope.

"I mean it, Maxwell Travis Wilson," Brad continues. "If you don't go back there and kiss that girl good night, you're gonna regret it for the rest of your life."

Max steps on the break. Then he makes a U-turn in the middle of the totally dark two-lane highway. I know for sure we're going to die. Or at least get hit by oncoming traffic. But we don't. Poor Diane does get banged around a bit in the backseat as Max beats a hasty retreat over to Heather Lake Road where he doesn't stop till he arrives at Missy Whatever-the-Hell-Her-Last-Name-Is' house.

"Go get her!" I call out after Max puts the car in park and practically flies out the door.

"Slip her the tongue!" Brad throws in for good measure.

Though I don't think Max hears him. He's too bound and determined to get the job done. From inside the car we watch as he knocks tentatively on Missy's double-wide front doors. Meanwhile, I take advantage of the additional room Diane and I have in the backseat by leaning against the side window, allowing her to slide in between my legs, curling up close to me.

"Are you tired?" I ask quietly.

Diane nods. She leans her head back against my chest, closes her eyes.

Wrapping my arms around her, I feel she's so small. Stroking her hair, I notice how soft and nice it smells. Clean. Like a Spring day after a gentle rain.

Suddenly, Brad squeals. Diane and I both jump out of our skin. "Oh, my God . . . He's gonna do it!"

We quickly sit up, pressing our faces against the cold glass . . . Just in time to see Max lay one on Missy the second she appears. Boy does she look surprised! A moment later, the driver's side door opens. Nobody says a word as Max crawls in, a smile upon his now acne-free and newly braces-less face. He pops a fresh piece of watermelon Bubblicious into his mouth, throws the car in drive, and drives away.

Half an hour later we arrive Home in Hazeltucky . . .

Ever the Gentleman, I walk Diane to her front door. "You don't have a date for the Homecoming Dance yet, do you?" I ask her, figuring it's Now or Never.

She looks up at me with a faint smile on her lip-glossy lips. "Not yet . . ."

"You don't wanna go with me, do you?"

"To the Dance," she says, "or 'go with you'-go with you?"

Good question . . . Here's my opportunity to have another girlfriend. I should probably take it. So I say, "Both, I guess."

To which Diane replies, "I thought you'd never ask."

And with that, I lean forward . . .

Her lips are soft and they taste like peaches. For a moment, I think of Alyssa. It feels funny to be kissing somebody and it isn't her. I wonder how she's doing off at Central being a College Girl.

Then I think of Joey . . .

What would you do if I kissed you right now? I can hear myself say, staring into his chocolate brown eyes.

I don't know . . . Probably kiss you back.

Many a night Joey and I spent side by side on the foldout couch down in my parents' basement. Ever since my Mom decided it was mean to kick my 8-year-old brother out of his own bed, that's where we'd sleep whenever he spent the night. Lying together, face to face in the dark—so close we could feel each other's breath—we'd talk about whatever for a while. Then ultimately we'd say good night.

Before rolling over, I'd always say it . . . "What would you do if I kissed you right now?"

But I never did.

I might let my hand fall softly on his shoulder. Firm and round, I'd give it a playful squeeze. Like a baseball. I might tickle his back ever so lightly, the way my Grandma Freeman used to tickle mine, back when she was still alive. Sometimes I might even write little words—letter by letter—between his shoulder blades. "Line down the Spine." Like the game me and my cousins Rachael and Rhonda would play when we were kids.

"Can you feel that?" I'd ask Joey, interrupting our silence.

In the dark I could see him nod.

"What is it?"

"I."

Then I'd write another.

"L."

Followed by another.

"O."

And another.

"V."

And—

"Good night," Joey would say. But there were never any Good Night Kisses.

Back on Diane Thompson's porch in the chilly Autumn air, that's when I notice it . . . I've got a you-know-what in my you-know-where. The question is . . . Is it for *real?* By which I mean, did it just happen of its own accord or on account of what I've just been thinking about? Which is when I decide . . . I need to pursue this thing with Diane Thompson further. Even though it means I'll have a girlfriend with the exact same name as my Mom—except with one N. It's the only way I'll ever know if I truly made a mistake by letting Joey Palladino get away.

When I return to Max's car, Brad climbs out, allowing me to climb in. Our eyes meet and I can tell he's not buying the Public Display of Affection he's just witnessed from afar. Much like I couldn't comprehend his locking lips with Ginny earlier in the evening, he's thinking the *exact* same thing about me . . .

But he says nothing.

Shell Shock

"No matter how I try and try
I hide the truth behind a lie . . ."

—New Order

My job sucks!

Okay, maybe it's not so bad most of the time, considering that during the week I work only Tuesdays and Thursdays from 7:00 to 11:00 PM. But every single weekend since August 26th, I've had to don these stupid navy blue corduroy *flares* my Mom insisted on ordering for me from the JC Penney catalog, along with one of my Dad's long-sleeved buttoned-down *pastel* work shirts—topped off with my official *orange* Farmer Jack's apron. All so I can spend my entire day bagging other people's groceries.

Finally after almost two months, I'm getting the lay of the land. Aisle 2—Baby Food and Home Center; Aisle 3—Canned Goods; Aisle 4—Prepared Foods; Aisle 5—Cookies, Cakes, and Candies; Aisle 6—Pet Food and Paper Products; Aisle 7—Breads and Cereals; Aisles 8 and 9—Frozen Foods. Of course, there's also an entire Produce department, Delicatessen, Hearth Oven Bakery, Meat and Dairy departments. around the store's periphery.

I'll admit, the world of "Paper or Plastic?" isn't exactly what I thought it would be back when my father first brought up the idea of my following in his footsteps. Let's just say . . . I never expected to be working alongside the kind of people who work in a supermarket. By whom I mean people with only a high school education who aspire to nothing more in life than working six days per week in order to feed their families and pay the bills. Not that I think I'm better than they are, 'cause I don't. Especially since my Dad happens to be One of Them. I just never realized what a simple job he's had all these years. And by "simple" I don't mean "easy."

But for the most part, the people are nice. Not that I'm there to socialize, but . . . considering I spend the majority of my time chained in back of the Cashiers while they fling various food items down the conveyor belt at me, it only seems fitting that I'd eventually get to know them. What I've seemed to notice is . . . Running a cash register in the world of Farmer Jack's is looked upon as Women's Work. In the entire two months I've been there, I've only seen one guy Cashier. Which for my sake I hope isn't a hard and fast rule. Because the last thing I want is to be a Bagger for the rest of my life!

My favorite Cashier is this woman, Colleen. Technically she's a Head Cashier. Which means she doesn't usually run a register. She works in the Office, managing the other Cashiers and telling us Baggers when to take our Breaks and Lunches. I heard one of the other Baggers say that she's 28. Though talking to her you'd never think she was that *old*. She's totally cool. And very pretty. You can totally tell she used to be New Wave, back in the day. She's got this great shaggy haircut—kind of long in back and spiky on top. Whenever she comes into the store on her nights off, she's always dressed in all black. She kind of reminds me of Pam Dawber from *Mork & Mindy*, another Michigander. The only negative thing about her is . . . She smokes. But for some reason when it comes to Colleen Kramer, it's not that big of a deal.

The other day she gave me a mix-tape with this band on it called Altered Images. You might recognize them from the "Happy Birthday" song in *Sixteen Candles*. But the main reason Colleen made it for me is because I told her I'm taking French in school and there's also this French band on it called Plastic Bertrand. They sing this song, "Ça Plane Pour Moi," which roughly translates to "That Works for Me." Though I can't tell what the Hell they're saying in the lyrics! I swear, there's something about a *l'anorak*. Which I'm pretty sure means "ski jacket." Or maybe it's *l'ananas*. Which means "pineapple." Either way, it's totally cool.

To be honest, I think I've got a little crush on Colleen. Not that it could ever amount to anything on account of she's 28 and I'm only 16. Besides, I've already got a girlfriend, Diane Thompson. Plus, I heard from one of the other Cashiers that Colleen's dating our Manager, Lyle Waggoner. In fact, once she found out Good Old Lyle's a friend of my Dad's, she started treating me differently from all the other Baggers, who for the most part are what I'd have to call Burn-Outs. A lot of them go to high school at Madison Heights, which, from what I've heard, makes HP look like a Prep School. And of course, they pretty much all smoke!

The other day Colleen and I got to talking and she started telling me all about *The Rocky Horror Picture Show* . . .

"Can't say I've seen it," I admitted, taking care not to mix food items in with the cleaning products I was bagging. Though I have seen the "Time Warp" video they sometimes show on *Night Flight*.

"Seriously?" Colleen asked me. She placed a ripe green pepper on the scale and hit 6-8-5 followed by the LOOK UP key on her register. Which is the one Produce Code I can remember as it's the same as my locker number at Webb Junior High. "Me and my girlfriends used to go all the time back in high school."

"Where'd you go?" I asked, smiling politely at the Little Old Lady waiting in anticipation for her total.

"$12.95," Colleen told her. Then to me she replied, "Dondero." Which is one of the two high schools in nearby Royal Oak. The other being Kimball.

"No . . . I meant, where'd you go to see *Rocky Horror?*"

"Oh." Colleen counted back the customer's change. "Have a nice night," she politely told Little Old Lady, who nodded and smiled as she scrutinized her receipt. Then to me Colleen said, "Prudential Town Center in Southfield . . . They used to show it every Saturday at Midnight."

Apparently, *The Rocky Horror Picture Show* has developed this Cult Following since it first came out in the '70s. Colleen said that a lot of people go see it all dressed up as their favorite character. They even stand up in the aisles and sing along with all the songs. Sounds like it could be a Total Blast. But to be perfectly honest, that guy from the movie totally freaks me out. You know which one I'm talking about? The one dressed up like a woman.

Now that I think about it . . . He kind of reminds me of my Dad. Not the way he looks now. But back in his Tony Orlando days.

I remember this one time, my parents had a Halloween party down in our basement and my Dad came dressed as a Girl. He didn't even bother wearing a wig, his hair was long enough. My Mom just put it up in hot rollers and styled it. Kind of like a bouffant. He wore this short little mini-skirt with black nylons and high heels and this supertight sweater under which he stuffed a bra with plastic L'eggs. It totally freaked me out seeing my Dad all dressed up like this. In fact, we've got this Home Movie taken on that night, and there I am in my Tweety Bird costume, looking scared to death the minute my Dad walks into the room. Though maybe it had something to do with the fact that he refused to shave off his Tony Orlando mustache just for one night. And how often do you see a Girl with facial hair?

But like I've said, I've had to spend *every* single weekend since August 26th working at Farmer Jerk's—I mean Jack's. Whenever anything comes up, I have to miss out on all the fun. Like yesterday, I got invited to a party at Ava Reese's house. But can I go? No!

"Why don't you just call in sick?" Carrie Johnson suggested as she and Ava and me and Brad were walking down the hallway after 1st hour Wind Ensemble. The party was actually her idea. But Ava's got the biggest house so Carrie suggested we have it over there. "We're watching *Pretty in Pink.*"

"Oh, my God . . . It's sooo good!" Brad gushed. "I love Molly Ringwald."

"You already saw it?" I asked, this being News to me.

"Sorry," he apologized. "I went with Luanne."

"Why didn't you guys invite me?" I asked, as if I didn't already know the answer.

To which Brad replied, "I don't know . . ." When what he meant to say was . . . *You were too busy hanging out with Joey Palladino.*

As she is often one to do, Ava applied the pressure. "So are you coming or what?"

As much as I hated it, I had to refuse her offer.

"Come on, Jack!" Brad whined. "You know it'll be fun."

"And you know my Mom's not gonna let me call in sick to work," I told him, "just so I can spend the day goofing off with the Band Fags."

"Hey!" Both Ava and Carrie cried out in unison, giving me a look. They're both so sensitive when it comes to our Social Circle being referred to in a less-than-positive way.

"Sorry," I apologized, "but my parents informed me if I want to drive a car, I've got to help pay for the gas and the insurance." Even if it means working every Saturday *and* Sunday whether I like it or not.

"So call in sick and don't tell Dianne you did it," Brad offered as a solution.

"Don't tell Dianne he did what?"

At that moment, Diane Thompson, aka "One-N-Diane," appeared at the end of the hallway near the Auditorium, just in time for me to walk her to 2nd hour Chemistry with Mr. Thomas.

"Two-N-Dianne," I replied, smacking her glossed lips against my own.

Right off, I noticed how cute Diane looked in her tan cardigan sweater and a brown mock turtleneck with matching socks, rolled up jeans, and brown leather Bass. I still can't figure out how she gets her laces all wrapped around and curly the way she does!

Ava gave her pink Izod collar a firm tug and smiled at my girlfriend. "Tell your boyfriend to stop being such a Wuss!"

"Stop being such a Wuss," Diane told me as ordered.

"I am not being a Wuss!" I objected.

"You are, too," Carrie stated with a smile. I noticed how nice her teeth look since she got her braces removed. Like a row of Chiclets all lined up next to each other. "Otherwise you'd blow off your stupid job and come hang out with us."

If there's one thing my mother taught me, it's not to give in to Peer Pressure. But Carrie was right. All we keep hearing is . . . "These are the Best Years of Your Lives . . . Enjoy them while they last." Why should I have to miss out, all because of a stupid job? Besides, I'll probably spend the next fifty years of my life working . . . God help me!

Which is why this afternoon at approximately 2:15 PM, I leave my house, get into my car, and *pretend* to drive to work. When in actuality, what I really do is . . . head directly over to Diane Thompson's house where she promptly places a call to the Almighty Farmer.

"This is Jack Paterno's Mom . . . I'm afraid he's not feeling well and won't be able to come into work today."

Standing in the doorway off the Thompson's Eat-In-Kitchen, I try getting Diane's attention. "Who is that?" I whisper.

But One-N-Diane simply smiles, doing the "Yakkity-Yak" thing with her hand, rolling her eyes. "Mmm hmm," she continues. "Sure thing . . . I'll tell him." Then she says, "Buh-bye," and hangs up the phone.

"Who was that?" I repeat after she happily informs me of our Mission Accomplished.

"Some woman named Colleen," Diane replies. "She says she hopes you feel better and she'll see you tomorrow."

Oh shit!

Why'd Colleen have to be the one working in the Office today? Now she's going to hate me for leaving her short a Bagger on a Saturday afternoon. Being the fourth weekend of the month, the store's always super busy on account of a lot of people get paid every other week. Which is something I never considered till I started my job . . . How about that?

"Would you chill?" Diane says smoothly. She wraps her hand around the back of my neck, giving my hair a firm tug. "My parents are gone . . . Wanna go in my room and make out?"

For the most part, things have been good with me and Diane. We've been going together for almost an entire month now. Mostly we just hang out together after school. We'll go to the movies or out to eat. Stuff like that. On one of our very first dates, I drove us downtown to Trapper's Alley. Which is basically this multi-leveled Mall in the middle of Greek Town. Not that we did any shopping or anything. Mostly we just rode the escalators and walked around holding hands. Like all the other couples. I'll admit, it feels nice to be seen out in Public with a cute girl on my arm . . . For once in my life, I actually feel Normal.

Though who knows how long it's going to last.

I keep waiting for Luanne to say something to Diane about me being you-know-what. Considering she got totally pissed when she invited Diane to hang out with her on the Saturday of Homecoming Weekend and was surprisingly informed that Diane had already made plans to go to the Dance. With me, of all people! And wouldn't you know? Lou showed up that night with Brad on her arm and proceeded to keep her eye on us the entire time. Talk about awkward!

For some reason, Lou couldn't seem to understand why everybody made fun of her . . . Maybe it had something to do with the fact that she came to the Hillbilly High Homecoming Dance wearing one of her Dad's old suits! Don't get me wrong, it was this totally cool iridescent blue sharkskin number from the '60s, but still . . .

"If Marcy Walker from *Santa Barbara* can wear a tux to the Emmy Awards," Lou reasoned, "why the fuck can't I wear a fucking suit to Homecoming?"

Speaking of awkward . . .

Making out with Diane in her room, I don't know what's up. Well, actually I do. By which I mean Down There. Based on the way things are going at this moment, I think I could totally do It with her. By which I mean have S-E-X. Though for some reason, every time we start and I think she wants to, Diane puts the brakes on. Like right now. Here I am, totally hot and bothered . . . And what does she do?

"We should probably head over to Ava's, don't you think?"

"What's the rush?" I ask, having just reached my hand up under her sweater.

"They're gonna start the movie without us," Diane worries as I continue going for the old bra clasp. "We're supposed to be there at 4 o'clock."

"It's a video," I remind her. "We can rent it sometime ourselves." And with that, I've worked my Magic and set the Puppies free. Let me tell you . . . Thank God Diane's got the kind of areolas that don't gross me out.

At that moment, she slaps my hand away. "Stop!" Then she rises from the bed, sounding totally annoyed. "Now look what you've done." She heads over to her dresser and begins fixing herself in the mirror on the wall above. Meanwhile, I adjust my steadily deflating goods.

"What's your problem?" I ask, speaking more to Diane's reflection than to her actual self.

"I already told you," she tells me, re-glossing her lips. "I'm not having sex with you."

Again, as much as I'm opposed to the Pressure that is Peer, doesn't Diane realize she could be my *one* chance at Salvation? In all the experiences I've had with a girl—and we know how few and far between they've been—Diane Thompson's the only one I've ever felt I could actually do It with. By which I mean *physically*. And here she is, totally rejecting me.

Diane snaps off the light, leaving me in the dark. "Are you coming or what?" Apparently I *won't* be anytime soon!

Nothing but bright sun and blue sky on this mid-October afternoon. A warm gentle breeze rustles the fallen leaves crunching beneath our feet. Their pungent aroma totally reminds me of being a kid. I remember me and my sister spending what seemed like hours raking our entire backyard, gathering each and every Oak, Maple, and Elm into one humongous pile right in the middle. After taking a flying leap, we'd cover ourselves from head to toe in Fall Foliage. Buried alive, we'd lie together enjoying the cool stillness. Not saying a word. Jodi and Jack. Not brother and sister who barely spend any time together anymore. But as Friends.

Arriving at Ava Reese's, we find the entire block of College between West End and Wanda lined with autos. Most are of the late '70s variety, a common denominator among the Band Fag Clique . . . Except for the brand spanking new black '86 Fiero parked in Ava's driveway.

"Isn't that Joey Palladino's car?" asks Diane of the Sweet Sixteen/Sorry-I-Divorced-Your-Mom gift Joey got from his Kmart's Executive father up in Clarkston.

"What the Hell's he doing here?" I wonder aloud. "This is supposed to be a Band Fags Only party."

"I'm not a Band Fag and I'm here," Diane reminds me. Which is totally different and beside the point.

Just when I thought any feelings I might have for Joey Palladino were long gone and forgotten, now I've got to walk through that door and face them all over again. In a matter of minutes, our paths will cross. Our worlds will collide, bringing us face to face for the first time in I don't know how long . . . *What am I going to do?*

"Come on in," Ava calls out after I've knocked twice and opened her front door.

The living room is wall-to-wall Band Fags. Like Sally from *Romper Room,* I see Ava and Carrie and Jenny and Joe and Michael and Barb and Erin and Mandi. Who I *don't* see is Brad and—thank God—Luanne . . . Or the aforementioned Joey Palladino.

"There's pop in the fridge," Ava announces. "Help yourselves . . . We're starting the movie in like ten minutes."

Before Diane and I begin navigating our way through the Sea of Band Fags, I ask, "Where's Mr. Dayton?"

"Out back *smoking,*" Carrie reports, shaking her head in disapproval.

"Is he by himself?" I ask, trying to sound oh-so casual.

"What do you think?" Ava replies. "He's with Herr Drum Major." Which is what Lou's decided all the Band Fags should call her from now on.

Strike One!

"And with Joey Palladino," Carrie throws in, sounding a little overly enthusiastic.

Strike Two!

Turning to Ava I ask, "Why'd you invite *him?*" As if it's any of my business.

"I didn't," she answers. "He showed up with Lou and Brad."

Strike Three . . . You're out!

I can totally imagine Luanne cozying up to Joey, trying to pump him for information she could use against me. Though I don't know why I'm so worried. Joey and I have been friends for how many years? It's not like he's going to stab me in the back or anything.

At that moment, the side door opens, accompanied by the sound of raucous laughter. I distinctly smell pine trees. Sure enough, Joey appears in the doorway with Brad and Luanne.

"Jack . . . What's up?"

The sound of my name falling from his lips stops me dead in my tracks.

Sunshine.

Cherries.

Chocolate.

In an instant, everything I've achieved these past six weeks—everything I've fought for—is completely undone . . .

I've fallen and I can't get up!

Rumors

"Look at all these rumors surrounding me every day
I just need some time, some time to get away . . ."

—Timex Social Club

I'm *totally* pissed!

Jamming the gold-colored key into the not-quite-frozen lock on the door of my 1979 pea green Dodge Omni, I give it a forceful turn, praying it doesn't break off. The black faux-leather seat sends a shiver up my spine the minute I climb in and sit myself down, causing me to jam the exact same gold-colored key into the silver ignition on the black molded-plastic steering column. Then I crank it.

The most disturbing SHRIEK erupts from the engine. Like metal scraping metal. The more-than-several warnings I've gotten from my Dad these past three months remind me that this is a bad thing. The "alternator," he calls it. What it's for or why it does this when I get impatient and do what I just did, I have no idea. But I can't help it right now, I'm so angry.

Guess I should probably tell you . . . After a mere six weeks of what I *thought* was Boyfriend/Girlfriend Bliss, Diane Thompson dropped me like a Hot Potato. All thanks to my Arch Nemesis, aka Luanne Kowalski.

I should've known something was up. I explicitly told Diane that 3:30 to 4:30 PM is my *Days of our Lives* time and never to disturb me unless it's an Emergency. Eve was right on the brink of revealing to Shane that she's really his daughter from his first wife, Emma, and not just some runaway. "Can I call you back?"

"It can't wait," she insisted.

"Twenty minutes," I promised. Maybe fifteen, what with fast-forwarding through the commercials.

"We need to talk, Jack . . . Now."

I paused the VCR. I knew full well what "We need to talk" meant. Especially in the world of High School Romance . . . *We're breaking up.*

I gave Diane my full attention, clinging to her every word, trying not to get too pissed. Her reasons were totally ridiculous. "Who you gonna believe?" I asked once she finished. "Me or Lou?"

"I don't know *who* to believe anymore," she admitted.

"I already told you . . . I'm not—"

"That's what you *say*," she said, "but Luanne says different." I found this hard to believe coming from the girl I'd been totally trying to have *sex* with just two days earlier right here on my bed. "She told me you went to the bar with her and Brad."

"So what? That doesn't make me a fag!" I knew I should've never let Brad talk me into going out that night with him and Lou. Now it had come back to bite me on the ass. Who the Hell does Luanne Kowalski think she is?!

To top it all off, today I found out she's been going around school telling anybody who'll listen that the *real* reason Diane broke up with me is because I'm gay. Though I'm sure she didn't bother to mention that the reason she *thinks* she knows this is because she herself is, too. It's one thing to let me and Brad and

Cheri and Alyssa in on her secret. But to share it with the entire Hillbilly High Student Body? Somehow I doubt she'd ever do that. After all, Lou doesn't want everybody hating *her,* now does she?

I blast the heat, allowing the engine to warm up just enough so it's drivable. God, I hate Winter! How can this be the place where Betsy Sheffield and I spent our days learning to operate a motor vehicle a mere four and a half months ago? No more hot yellow sun beating on warm blacktopped pavement. No more leafy green trees against bright blue sky backdrop. Now everything's gone gray—with a little white tossed in for good measure.

Speaking of Betsy Sheffield . . .

I get in line to exit the parking lot, pulling up behind the 1980 silver Chevy Vega she got for her Sweet Sixteen back on November 14th. Betsy waves and smiles at me in her rearview mirror. But being that I'm totally pissed at the moment, I pretend not to notice her. Instead, I focus my attention on the black rubber wrapped around my steering wheel. My Dad insisted he put the covering on the minute he gave me *la voiture.* Which is French for "car," in case it isn't obvious. I begin tapping a gloved hand in time to the beat of Jesse Johnson's "Get to Know Ya" off the *Pretty in Pink* soundtrack. I don't think I've listened to anything else since I picked it up at Harmony House a couple weeks ago . . . By the way, the movie was awesome!

Now if there's one thing I've learned, being ignored is something that does not bode well with Betsy Sheffield. Despite the frigid temperature outside, she rolls down her window, sticks her head out, and yells at me. Though I can't exactly hear what she's hollering over my booming back speakers. I have to lower the volume and roll down my window as well.

Betsy screams over her shoulder, "Jacques!" Which is what

she's taken to calling me on account of that's how our 3rd hour Advanced Algebra/Trig teacher, Mr. Borjes, pronounces my name. "What the Hell's your problem?"

I say, "What?" As in, *What are you talking about?* Because I have no trouble hearing her question. In fact, I bet they can hear Betsy all the way down the block and across the street over at the Blue Building. Which is what we Hazeltucky Folk call the Board of Education building on the corner of Hughes and Felker across from Hillbilly High, on account of why? It's a *building* and it's *blue*. I know, not very original. But we're a simple people, really.

The next thing I know, Betsy abandons her vehicle. I watch as she struggles to tie the belt of her long wool coat—or is it tweed?—tight around her waist, Treetorns slip-sliding away in the snow. "Too good to say hello?" she sternly demands, leaning into my window.

So much for INXS' "Do Wot You Do!" I turn my radio all the way down and mumble, "Sorry . . ."

"Why are you ignoring me?" Betsy barks.

Because I'm starting to get cold, what with the gusts of snow blowing into my car and all. I tell her, "Brad's waiting for me to pick him up in the Band Room and give him a ride to work." I can totally hear his voice in my head cursing, *Today!*

"Well, Brad Dayton is just gonna have to wait."

I'm at a loss for words. I have no idea why Betsy is in such a bad mood. She's not usually like this. Till all of a sudden, she cracks a huge smile and cries, "Psyche!" Which in Hazeltucky means, "Just joking." It's one of those slang-things, right up there with referring to having sex as "Getting some gravy." Or Shelly Findlay's "What's up, Fox?" Being that Shelly and Betsy are on Varsity Cheerleading together, Betsy probably picked it up from her.

"I'll call you later, okay?" I tell her.

"You better," she replies. Then she smirks and skulks away.

If I didn't know better, I'd think Betsy Sheffield was flirting with me. But that can't possibly be the case. She made it perfectly clear over the Summer that she wants us to be Just Friends . . . I wonder if maybe she's changed her mind?

I pull around to the opposite side of the school where Brad's been waiting since 3:15 PM. Thank God they came through with the snowplows already or he'd be late for his shift at Big Boy's for sure.

"Look," he informs me the minute he climbs in my car and I bring up the subject of Luanne Kowalski and what she's done. "I really don't wanna get stuck in the middle of this."

To which I inform him, "Too bad . . . You are."

Brad avoids my gaze, slipping into his seat belt, staring straight ahead. "I'm friends with you both," he reminds me, "so I'm kinda in a difficult position . . . You know what I mean?"

I play my Trump card. "But who have you known longer?" Then I drive away, past the snow-covered tennis courts. Beyond the frozen football field lies a vast wasteland. No Band Fags marching today.

"Careful, Jack!"

I almost overlook the red and white octagon on the corner of Tucker, halting rather abruptly across from Hoover School. "Sorry . . ."

The way Brad braces himself against the dashboard totally reminds me of my Mom. She'd do the exact same thing whenever we'd take Family Vacations together and my Dad's driving didn't comply with her standards. "I'd like to make it to work alive," he says all snarky.

I can tell he's trying to avoid the issue. So I say, "You *have* to take my side on this one." Then I burst out, "Come on!" Only

I'm directing my anger at some Kindergarten Babies crossing the street, all bundled up in their Arctic Snow gear, taking their Sweet Old Time. What would happen if I accidentally-on-purpose let my foot slip off the break at this moment? Hmmm . . . I wonder.

"You did kinda steal Diane away from Lou," Brad informs me, erasing the terrible thought from my mind.

"I did not!" I make the left turn, hand-over-hand turning the wheel. Then for added emphasis, I abruptly STOP at the next corner.

Brad braces himself against the dash, yet again. "Well, Lou saw her first," he says, trying to sound reasonable.

"Bullshit!" I exclaim, putting pedal to the metal, radials spinning. "We were all sitting at the exact same Pep Rally in the exact same Gym."

"Well," Brad stammers. "It was Lou's idea to go over and talk to Diane in the cafeteria."

I hit the brake at the corner of Vassar, two blocks away. The front end of the Omni starts skidding on the ice and we almost end up on the curb. "Damn it!"

"Would you get off this fucking side street?" my passenger begs me. "You're freaking me out *and* making me nauseous."

I take another left, follow Vassar down to 9 Mile where Brad's former place of employment looms, an ever-present thread in the fabric of Hazeltucky. How fitting is it that high atop the neon "Country Boy" sign, a Huck Finn look-alike spins round and round in straw hat and bandana neckerchief? Hillbilly High, indeed!

Looking out the window, Brad groans. "Get me the Hell away from this place."

I turn right on 9 Mile . . . But there's no way I'm letting Brad off the hook on this matter. "So what if Lou saw Diane first?" I say. "*I'm* the one who asked her out."

To which Brad says, "Lou says *she* thinks the only reason you asked Diane Thompson out in the first place is because you knew it would piss her off."

Which is kind of true . . .

Still, after a moment I reply, "It's not *my* fault Diane's not a dyke . . . And even if she was, there's no guarantee she'd even be interested in Luanne."

"Lou also says," Brad reiterates, "*she* thinks Diane is confused and you only made it worse by being a Total Closet Case yourself."

Which is sooo not true!

#1—Diane is *not* confused. She likes boys. #2—Lou can't stand the fact that just like Alyssa, the Object of Her Affection was more into *me* than her. And #3—I am not a Closet Case. Unlike Mr. Klan who Lou has started calling "KKK," as in Kloset Kase Klan.

"I asked Diane Thompson to go with me because I liked her," I tell Brad.

Which is true.

"Are you sure?" he questions, sounding more like the Voice of Lou than my so-called Best Friend. "I mean, it's not like you guys even had anything in common."

Outside my window, I notice Mauro's Dairy Queen and Mini-Golf all closed up for the Season. In a flash of memory, I see my maroon and white polyester-uniformed self, age 10. Along with the rest of my Kraft Services teammates, I gaze up at the menu board—*Dilly Bar or Jack 'n Jill sundae?*—after an exhausting Little League match against Hazel Park Bowl. Though honestly, how tired can one Benchwarmer possibly get?

Brad says, "You haven't been very nice to Luanne since she told you she's a lesbian . . ."

Up ahead on the corner sits the Hazel Park Memorial Library. I remember me and Joey Palladino spending many a Saturday afternoon there with the likes of *The Boxcar Children* and *Super Fudge*. Hard to believe a time ever existed when all we wanted was to turn 11 so we could finally venture upstairs into the Adult Fiction section. Now here I am, Sweet Sixteen already . . . How did I get to be so old?

"It seems like you really *don't* like Lou anymore," continues Brad, pulling me out of my reverie.

"Being a dyke has nothing to do with why I don't like Lou," I tell him. "I don't like her because she's a Total Bitch . . . And now that she's Drum Major, she thinks she's the boss of Marching Band."

Brad laughs. "She sorta is . . . You know what I mean?"

As we cross John R, I pull into the left turn lane and wait for the green arrow. Below us, a pre-Rush Hour river of orange-red winds its way north-south along I-75. I can't even believe this is the exact same spot—right by the Gas 'n Go—where just a little over a year ago Brad and I drove by with Luanne and Alyssa on our very first trip out to the Tombs. So much has happened since then. I feel like a totally different person. More grown up, somehow. I guess what's disappointing is . . . I always thought Lou would end up being a Good Friend. For a little while there, it seemed like she was. Not anymore.

"How can you stick up for her like this?" I demand, turning onto the southbound service drive. "Especially with the way she treats you." By which I mean the way Lou constantly calls out, *"Bra-yad!"* whenever she sees him in the hallways. Like she expects him to come running just because she's bellowed. "You aren't her little Slave Boy." And with that, I pull into the Elias Brothers' parking lot.

"I'm sorry you don't like Lou anymore," Brad tells me. "But she's the only friend I got who knows about me—besides you . . . And I need to stay on her good side so she doesn't start spreading rumors about me, too."

He's probably right . . . Best to look out for #1 . . . Guess I should have done the same.

Defeated I say, "I bet Luanne's happy Diane dumped me . . . Now she can chase after her all she wants."

"I guess you haven't heard the latest?" Brad replies. "Guess who's taking Diane Thompson to the Christmas Dance?"

"Not Luanne!" I gasp in horror. In all the time I spent with her, Diane made it perfectly clear she wasn't interested in Lou's advances.

"Hell no!" Brad declares.

"I was gonna say . . ."

"Do you even wanna know?" he asks me.

"I'm gonna find out eventually," I answer.

Brad lets out a deep breath. "None other than your boyfriend . . . Joey Palladino."

My jaw practically drops to my lap.

As I sit with Brad, my 1979 pea green Dodge Omni idling in the Big Boy's parking lot on this 27° Michigan—it's-technically-not-Winter-yet-but-it-might-as-well-fucking-be—day, I feel as if all the air in my body has been sucked out by an industrial strength vacuum. It takes just about all I've got in me not to let it show on my face how totally devastated I am at this very moment.

How could this be happening? Why would Diane Thompson even want to go to the Dance with Joey? Other than the fact that he's totally hot.

"For starters," I calmly explain to Brad, "Joey Palladino is *not* my boyfriend." My eyes start to burn. "He never was . . ." My breath grows shallow. "And he never will be." But I keep it together.

"Well, I still think he's gay," he responds.

I say, "He is not!" Though part of me still secretly hopes he is.

Brad rolls his eyes. "But he loves The Smiths!"

"So . . . ?" I question. "What's your point?"

"I think Joey Palladino is a Big Ol' Fag," he surmises, "and he's trying to hide it by taking *your* ex-girlfriend to the Christmas Dance."

Even if that were the case, Joey's been my friend for years. Why would he all of a sudden do something like this to me?

"Maybe he's getting back at you for not returning his affections," Brad replies when I ask him this. "I mean, that's what happened . . . Right?" he continues. "You *didn't* return Joey's affections . . . Did you?"

I give Brad a look. I've heard just about enough. "You're gonna be late for work," I remind him.

Getting the hint, he reaches for the door handle. Then he pauses. "What are you gonna do?" he asks, all concerned.

"What *can* I do?" I answer. "Deal with it, I guess." I can only imagine things are about to get worse.

"Hang in there," Brad tells me. Followed by, "Thanks for the ride . . . I'll call you later."

I watch as Brad makes his way up the snow-covered sidewalk leading to the restaurant's front entrance where the four-foot fiberglass statue of Big Boy himself stands all decked out in his red and white checked overalls. Holding a two-foot fiberglass hamburger high above his head, he's got this totally shit-eating grin upon his cherub-cheeked face . . . Which makes me want to slap him!

On my way home, I pass by Nick's Pizzeria—not to be confused with Randazzo's—which is next door to Harmony House. Sure enough, I catch a glimpse of Brad's sister, Janelle, working behind the counter . . . Boobs and all! I can't even believe this is all she's been doing with her life since she graduated from HPHS six months ago. Though last I heard she and her boyfriend, Ted, were saving up to get a place together. Much to Laura Victor-Dayton-Victor's disapproval.

I decide last minute to take a right near Joe's Drugs at the corner of 9 Mile. Then a quick left on Carlisle behind the Library, City Hall, and the 48030 Post Office. I figure I'll drive past Joey's Grandma's house—just to see if his car's parked out front. Chances are he's probably over Diane Thompson's house anyways, making out with her . . . The way I used to.

This is totally my fault. If I had never taken Diane Thompson to that *Pretty in Pink* party at Ava Reese's, she and Joey would've never started talking. They certainly wouldn't be going to the Christmas Dance together! The thought of seeing them in each other's arms makes my stomach churn.

My heart leaps into my throat. Why am I so nervous? It's not like I'm going to stop or anything. Though what if I happen to see Joey as I'm passing by? Then what'll I do? I can't just ignore him. Even if he is taking Diane Thompson—who just so happens to be *my* ex-girlfriend—to the upcoming Christmas Dance, it's not like I hate him or anything . . .

In fact, I think I still *love* him.

Return Post

"Writing the lines as they come to me
Scratching them out almost immediately . . ."

—The Bangles

Thank *God* for Betsy Sheffield!

If it weren't for her, I would've never been able to pick up the pieces of my shattered existence after Diane Thompson broke up with me. Every day since, we've had lunch together at school. Every night, we've talked on the phone. Of course, I haven't told her the *entire* circumstances pertaining to *The Demise of Jack & Diane.* I mean, I don't want Betsy thinking I'm a Total Fag, too. Though I'm surprised in all this time she hasn't heard anything from her sister, Cheri, about the similar circumstances pertaining to *The Demise of Jack & Alyssa.*

The thing is . . . Despite the whole fiasco with Miss Resnick and my feelings for Mr. Palladino, I really do like Betsy. As in like her-like her. In that way. How could I not? She's the kind of girl I've wanted to have as a girlfriend my entire life. I've already mentioned how cute she is. And super smart. Like me, she's been a straight-A student all her life. We have a ton in common. We're practically perfect for each other.

It's been no secret that I've been interested in Betsy since the day we met during Sophomore year in 1st hour with Mrs. Malloy. Talk about a crazy woman! Not that I don't love her, 'cause I totally do. But Mrs. Malloy is the epitome of an English Teacher. She wears these half-moon reading glasses on a chain around her neck. And whenever she gets the chance, she'll perch them on the end of her nose, reading aloud to the class—totally getting off on it. Especially when it comes to Edgar Allan Poe.

I'll never forget the day Mrs. Malloy shared his poem, *The Bells* . . .

Like Jesus addressing his Disciples, she stood at the podium. She took a deep breath, and closed her eyes before beginning. " 'Hear the sledges with the bells—' " She looked up, focusing her attention directly on Yours Truly as I was lucky enough to be sitting down front. " 'Silver bells!' " she burst out, startling me in my chair. Then to her left, " 'What a world of merriment their melody foretells!' " Then to her right, " 'How they tinkle, tinkle, tinkle,' " taking extra time to hit each and every T with the tip of her tongue. " 'In the icy air of night!' "

As if scanning the skies for satellites, she spoke softly now. " 'While the stars that oversprinkle/All the heavens, seem to twinkle/With a crystalline delight.' " Then faster and faster looking up at the fluorescents. " 'Keeping time, time, time,' " again with the rat-tat-tat Ts. " 'In a sort of Runic rhyme,' " now trilling the Rs. " 'To the tintinnabulation that so musically wells . . .' " At which point her eyes practically bulged out of her head. " 'From the bells, bells, bells, bells/Bells, bells, bells—' "

Reaching what can only be described as the Climax, Mrs. Malloy threw her head back in Total Ecstasy, panting. Then slow and steady she brought it Home. " 'From the jingling . . . and the tinkling . . . of the bells.' " I'm telling you, we all thought she totally wet herself, right then and there. That's how worked up she got . . . Clearly Betsy and I will ne'er forget that moment.

Actually, I've known Betsy Sheffield since long before 10th grade. Or at least *known of* her. Remember my 6th & 7th hour Enriched English & Social Studies teacher from 7th grade, Ms. Lemieux? The one whose first name happens to be Cinnamon?

Back when we were in 5th grade, Ms. Lemieux would come over to the different elementary schools once a week and teach a special class for Gifted Students. One time, I distinctly remember Cinnamon telling Joey Palladino and I about this "wonderful girl" over at United Oaks named Betsy Sheffield. Of course, I immediately became intrigued. Especially once I spotted a picture of her in the monthly Hazel Park Schools newsletter and saw how cute she was!

Finally during Freshman year at Webb, I had the distinct pleasure of meeting Betsy when we were both contestants in the annual Speech Competition held over at Beecher. I remember it being a typical Michigan Winter day so I borrowed this navy blue pea coat I found in Brad's locker. Once I arrived, there she was sitting in the front row of the Auditorium . . . The Girl of my Dreams.

"Cool pea coat," Betsy leaned over to whisper in my ear as I sat down beside her.

"Thanks," I whispered back, not bothering to admit it wasn't even mine.

Then she said with a metal-mouthed smile, "You're Jackie Paterno, aren't you?"

The rest—they say—is History . . .

I had actually thought about looking Betsy up in the phone book at the end of Freshman year and asking her to the Carnation Dance. Especially after Brad invited Ginny What's-Her-Name. But for some reason, I figured Betsy would never remember me so I didn't bother going through with it. Then when I met up with her at the beginning of Sophomore year, we got to talking and I made mention of my plan.

To which Betsy replied *sans* hesitation, "You should have asked me . . . I would've totally gone with you." Which resulted in my mentioning my fondness for Betsy to Audrey. At which point, Good Old Aud thought she'd do me a favor by mentioning my infatuation with Betsy—*to Betsy*. Unfortunately, the feeling wasn't mutual and Betsy started giving me the cold shoulder so I'd get the hint. Luckily, I managed to straighten things out with her and we were able to continue being friends.

In addition to 4th hour French II with Mrs. Carey, Betsy and I also have 3rd hour Advanced Alegbra/Trig together this semester. The running joke in class about our teacher, Mr. Borjes, is . . . his accent. For instance, he calls me "Jacques." Though he's not French; he's from Ecuador. Apparently, he also can't say the word "focus." Which in math is "a fixed point whose relationship with a directrix determines a conic section." I'm told if he attempted to, it would come out sounding more like "fuck-us." Even if you beg and plead for him to tell you what the thing represented by the letter F is called, Mr. Borjes will get angry and say, "No! I'm-a not-a gonna say it." In his cute little accent, a perpetual twinkle in his eye.

The thing about Mr. Borjes is . . . He might look like this tiny little bald man with a goatee and glasses who always wears a three-piece suit. But he can be a Total Powerhouse once you get him going. Believe me, I know!

The Friday before Christmas vacation starts, we're sitting in class waiting for Mr. Borjes to begin his lecture on sine (sin) and cosine (cos), tangent (tan) and cotangent (cot), secant (sec) and cosecant (csc). Of course, Betsy and I are the only ones *really* waiting, as per usual. The rest of our class is too busy goofing around.

"Okay . . . I'n-a gonna teach you now," Mr. Borjes calls out over the infernal racket. When that doesn't work, he walks right up to Kristian Alfonso look-alike Marie Sperling's boyfriend, and says, "Hey, Kid . . ."

Tom Fulton looks up from the last seat in the center row. "Yes, Mr. Borjes," he replies, a silver halo mysteriously appearing round his flippy-haired head.

"Shut up." And with that, Mr. Borjes returns to the board.

Of course, all Tom's Jock Jerk Friends start hooting and howling as he tries his best to remain unembarrassed. But the color of his face soon rivals the red Adidas sweatshirt worn by Junior Class Secretary, Varsity Cheerleader, and Staff Reporter on *The Hazel Parker*, Jamieleeann Mary Sue Good, aka Jamie for short. For once, it makes me happy to see Tom Fulton on the receiving end of such razzing. Can you believe, despite being a guest at my Sweet Sixteen party six months ago, that Asshole hasn't said a word to me all semester? Just wait till I'm a Famous Writer someday and he's still stuck working in Hazeltucky!

Never one to resist a pretty girl, Mr. Borjes can't help but pause a moment at Jamie's desk, where she sits in front of Shelly "What's up, Fox?" Findlay. Who this year—I should probably point out—has taken to spelling her name S-H-E-L-L-E-E, don't ask me why! Nodding and smiling, he greets them. "And-a how are-a you?"

To which Shellee replies sweetly, "I'm fine, Mr. Borjes . . . How are you?"

"Good, good," he answers, ear-to-ear grin. At which point, he looks down at Jamie's chest. Though not for the reason you might think. Mr. Borjes is far from being a Dirty Old Man. "What's-a that?" he asks, referring to the white logo printed across the front of her sweatshirt. Then he slowly spells out exactly what he sees . . . "A-D-I-D-A-S."

Jamie grins. "Adidas," she informs the South American mathematician. Surely Mr. Borjes has to be familiar with Adidas. He's got two teenaged sons—both rumored to be totally hot.

"Yes, I can-a read." His gray eyes crinkle at the corners as he smiles. "But what-a means this, Adidas?" he wonders innocently.

"It's a brand name," Shellee Findlay chimes in, coming to her Best Friend's rescue. "They make shoes, and clothes, and stuff."

From the back of the room, Tom Fulton's hand shoots up. "Ooh, Mr. Borjes . . . Ooh, ooh!" à la Horshack from *Welcome Back, Kotter.* "You know what Adidas stands for, Mr. Borjes?"

To which Mr. Borjes turns his attention to Tom for a moment, saying, "Kid . . . Shut up." And with that, he looks back to Jamie. "You-a gonna tell me or-a what?"

Perishing the thought of having to say it out loud, Jamie stands up to whisper in Mr. Borjes ear. Which immediately causes Mr. Borjes to lurch back, shrieking, "Don't you-a touch me!"

The whole class bursts into hysterics, while Jamie does her best to inform him, "I won't touch you, Mr. Borjes, I promise . . . I'm just gonna whisper in your ear."

Mr. Borjes gives her a look, eyebrows raised. "What-a for?"

Shellee Findlay answers, "It's a secret, Mr. Borjes," once more coming to her cohort's aid.

"Really?" he replies, beaming. "Why didn't you-a say so? I like-a secrets."

As we all watch in silence, Jamie puts her hand to her mouth. Then she leans in. "Pss Pss Pss Pss Pss-pss Pss."

If only you could see the reaction Mr. Borjes gives her . . . Brow furrowed, head tilted to one side, looking down his nose. "All Day You-a Dream About-a *What*?"

"Pss Pss Pss," Jamie whispers again, spelling it out letter by letter.

To which Mr. Borjes exclaims, "All Day You-a Dream About-a S-E-X?!" Spelling the word out. Like he's totally appalled. Though we can all see him suppressing a giggle, shaking his head as he returns to his post as Head of the Class.

Not more than five minutes after we've returned to the topic of Trigonometry, I feel a tap on my shoulder. Reaching up ever so discreetly, I take the folded up piece of yellow notebook paper from Carrie Johnson who sits behind me.

Jacques, what time are you picking me up tonight? Love, Betsy

Hunching over my desk, I promptly jot down my response.

What time do you wanna get to the dance?

Then I secretly pass the note back to Betsy via our go-between, Carrie. All the while, I can hear Mr. Borjes going on and on at the front of the room, his back to us, totally unaware.

What time does it start?

8 PM

But as I refold the slip of paper and get ready to make the drop, I feel a Presence at my side. It seems that Mr. Borjes has stopped teaching whatever it is he's been teaching and is now looming over my desk.

"Jacques," he says with a smile. "What do you-a think you're-a doing?"

"Uh-oh," I hear Tom Fulton drone from his perch. "Busted!" Followed by the snickers of his crony Jock Jerk Friends.

You can probably imagine the horror I experience getting caught doing something a straight-A student is not expected to be doing. But the next thing out of my mouth are the words, "I'm writing." Though I have no idea where the Hell they came from!

Maybe it's because I'm really a Bad Ass deep down inside. Or maybe it's because—after weeks and weeks of begging and pleading—I've finally convinced Betsy Sheffield to go to the Christmas Dance with me and I'm trying to impress her. Or maybe it's because I'm hoping to prove something to Tom Fulton and all his Jock Jerk Friends by showing them I'm really *not* such a Goody-Goody.

Judging from the blank look on Mr. Borjes face, this is not the response he had anticipated either. "And-a what are-a you-a writing?" he asks, growing stern. Meanwhile, the entire class has fallen silent, waiting to see what happens next to Mr. Straight-A Student.

The answer I come up with is simply, "Words."

At which point, Mr. Borjes has heard enough. "Words?!" he shrieks, all high-pitched. "That's what you're-a doing in-a my class? Writing *words?*"

Not used to being on the receiving end of such hostility, I don't know what else to say . . . So I say nothing.

"If you wanna write-a words," Mr. Borjes continues, "I'm-a not gonna stop-a you." Then he rips the yellow paper from my hand, tears it into pieces, and scatters it about his shiny little head like confetti. "Now get out!" And with that, he shows me the door.

It's not every day you see a potential Valedictorian being thrown out of Advanced Algebra/Trig. But not to worry . . . It's not like I'll get in any trouble. I mean, what's Mr. Borjes expecting me to do? March down to Principal Nowicki's Office and turn myself in?

There is no way I'm missing the Christmas Dance tonight by getting suspended. Besides, with vacation coming up, I know the whole thing will long be forgotten come January when we return from the break. Instead, I go down and sit in the cafeteria where I wait for Betsy to finish class and we go for lunch at Little Caesar's in the Universal Mall food court. Which has become our new favorite hideaway on account of all the Hillbilly High kids go to Taco Bell on 9 Mile or the Burger King on Dequindre in Warren.

As expected, Betsy and I have an excellent time at the Dance. You should see the look on all the Jock Jerks' faces when we walk into the cafeteria together. Betsy looks absolutely beautiful in a red and green plaid skirt worn with black leggings and a matching turtleneck sweater. I wear my black dress pants with the new Christmas sweater Betsy helped me pick out of the J. Crew catalogue.

"Very School Spirit," she remarks of the gray with maroon snowflakes.

Luckily, we manage to avoid Diane Thompson and Joey Palladino most of the night. There's one minor scare when we return from the bathrooms and see the Happy Couple sharing a kiss beneath the mistletoe tacked up over the doorway.

"I don't know what she sees in him," Betsy remarks. "You're just as cute."

"Thanks," I tell her. Then I add, "You're just saying that . . ."

"I am not," she insists. "Would I be here with you if I thought you were a Total Dog? You know how shallow and superficial I am." Which is kind of a running joke between us. Although it's true. Betsy once told me if she ever dated a guy and he was a crappy kisser, she'd have to break up with him. Lucky for me, I informed her what a good kisser Alyssa always said I was . . . To which she said she'd keep that in mind.

"God, I hate him!" I groan.

"Then quit staring and let's go dance." And with that, Betsy pulls me onto the dance floor where we "Walk Like an Egyptian."

But I can't help it. You should see Joey tonight. In his super-tight navy dress pants and super-tight white dress shirt, unbuttoned just enough to show off the little gold chain around his neck which I'm assuming Diane gave him as an early Christmas present. I can't remember when I've seen him look so handsome.

I'm still trying to figure out what's up with them. Of all the girls at Hillbilly High, why did Joey end up taking Diane Thompson to the Dance? I bet it's got something to do with Luanne. I can just imagine what she might have said to Joey before Diane and I showed up at Ava Reese's *Pretty in Pink* party. I bet Lou's the one who planted the seed in his mind in order to get back at me for stealing Diane away from her.

I'd love to talk to Joey and find out. But now that he and Diane are officially going together and I'm in love with Betsy Sheffield, what's the point?

Though two weeks later, I find the following letter stuck inside our mailbox . . .

12—31—86

Jack,

I thought that I better clear up a few things before we both get even more confused, especially me. As I write this letter, I'm lying in bed listening to the tape you gave me on my Walk Man. A song called "If She Knew What She Wants" just came on, and it made me think of you, so I decided to write. Here are some of the words. "He's crazy for this girl, but she don't know what she's looking for. I'd say her values are corrupt but she's all bent to change." That might not make any sense to you, but it means a lot to me.

Since we were sitting at E.B's tonight I've been thinking about a lot of different stuff. This whole thing is my fault and I'm so sorry.

I've been acting like a bitch, I know. This may sound dumb, that is if it even makes any sense. But to be honest, I think you're too good for me. You know exactly what you want and you're not afraid to be yourself. Me, I'm so confused, yet I know I don't deserve a guy like you.

I guess what I'm trying to say is that I think we should just be friends for now. I know what I said on Christmas was totally the opposite, but I also said that sometimes I feel that way and sometimes I don't. It's like I can turn my feelings on and off. That is certainly no way to have a relationship, not knowing when you want to be more than friends, and when you don't. I hope this letter hasn't been too stupid or confusing or boring for you. Please don't hate me, even though I've been acting like an asshole! Your friendship means a lot to me, you know?

Love, Betsy

P.S. Just think, a brand new year is hours away. Who knows what could happen in "87"?

How's that for a kick in the pants? Talk about a great way to start off yet another fun and exciting New Year! Why does my Love Life consistently suck?

First Lynn Kelly breaks my heart back in junior high. Then when I get to high school, I meet Alyssa and everything seems great. Till Joey Palladino walks back into my life and fucks it all up. When Diane Thompson comes along, Luanne convinces her I'm a Total Fag and she dumps me.

As you can see . . . It's never a dull moment in the Wonderful World of Jack Paterno and the Daytime Drama that is *Life in Hazeltucky.*

Kiss

*"Ain't no particular sign I'm more compatible with
I just want your extra time and your . . ."*

—Prince

The thing that sucks about Mid-Winter Break is . . . It's in the middle of *Winter.* Unlike Spring Break which takes place in the *Spring* when there's a slight chance the weather might be halfway decent. But Hazeltucky in February is a guaranteed Winter Wonderland. Which leaves nothing to do but stay home curled up under a blanket all day, watching *Days of our Lives.* That is, when I'm not working extra hours at The Farmer.

Speaking of *Days of our Lives* . . .

The other day, my Mom picked up the latest issue of *Soap Opera Digest* and guess who's on the cover? None other than Hope Williams-Brady, aka Kristian Alfonso. Normally, this would be an awesome sight to behold. Especially since she looks as gorgeous as ever. Skin, flawless. Hair piled on top of her head, rich and dark. Hazel eyes penetrating the camera's lens, a slight trace of a smile gracing her face.

But the headline is what kills me . . .

GOOD-BYE TO DAYS' BO & HOPE:
THE INSIDE STORY!

Even though I knew it was coming, I refused to believe it. I first got wind of the News back in January when I received my copy of the Winter 1987 edition of *Kristian's Korner.* On the pink cardstock cover I noticed a snapshot of Kristian, sitting at a table in what looks like a very fancy restaurant, cheek to cheek . . . with a man that is *not* her TV husband, Peter Reckell. Beneath the picture, a drawing of two hearts linked together with an arrow.

I immediately turned the page, only to find the following message, signed by Kristian Alfonso herself . . .

Thank you for sending the beautiful Christmas cards and lovely holiday gifts.

As you know, I will be leaving the show at the end of March. My departure will be a mixture of happy and sadness. I feel as if I am leaving a family who will always be an important part of my life.

You might also know about my engagement to Simon McCauley. We met in St. Martin at a very romantic restaurant. We plan to get married in the Summer in my hometown of Boston, MA, and I will divide my time between California and St. Martin.

Because I am leaving the show, I will reduce my Fan Club dues to $5.00/year to cover the cost of the continuing newsletters. For a while you can still write to me at the studio address after I leave. Once I have a new address for mail, I will be sure to let you know.

I hope you will continue to keep in touch.
Thank you for all your support!

The rest of the newsletter consists of more photos of Kristian and her fiancé, taken on New Year's Eve at the Golden Horn Restaurant in Aspen, CO. The last page features a cute picture of the Happy Couple out on the ski slopes with the caption "SNOW BUNNIES." Below, a photo of Kristian hugging "SIMON CLAUS." I'd be lying if I didn't admit that Simon's a good-looking guy. Short dark hair, a great smile, totally clean shaven. He couldn't be any more the opposite of Peter Reckell. But to see Hope Williams-Brady without Bo just doesn't seem right.

But getting back to the *Soap Opera Digest* . . .

On page 16, I read the "Tell All" story in which Kristian explains why she's leaving the show. How she's finally ready to move on after four years. How there are miniseries and films to audition for. And how her offscreen relationship with Peter Reckell was anything but amicable . . . Which comes as a Total Shock!

I can't even believe some of the other things she reveals in the interview . . . In all the years they worked together, Peter never wanted to appear on Talk Shows with her or make public appearances. Even though he's also leaving *Days,* it wasn't something they planned on doing together. It just happened to work out that way. Hearing all these things really burns me up! How could her TV True Love be so mean to her? Without Kristian Alfonso, Peter Reckell wouldn't even have a career. What a jerk!

Just wait till I tell Carrie Johnson . . .

Kristian also goes on to talk about her upcoming wedding. How she's getting married in Boston but no date has been set. How she'll be wearing Hope's wedding dress from the show. Which kind of bums me out on account of how much I hated the way she looked in that veil! I've been looking forward to seeing her in something new. I also can't help but think how déjà vu it's going to be for her. But she also makes a comment about how she's already performed an exorcism on the dress, taking Peter out and putting Simon in. Which is kind of funny, don't you think?

But what really pisses me off is . . . When I turn to page 105, I see an article titled "SPEAKING OUT: Peter Reckell At the Crossroads." In which he tells his side of the story. I can't even believe he has the audacity to say he's worried about Kristian and her future. He calls her a "young actor" and comments on how she hasn't done much. To which I say, what about *The Star Maker* with Rock Hudson in 1981? Peter makes it sound like Kristian won't ever do anything else. For her sake, I hope she goes out there and totally proves him wrong!

As angry as all this makes me, I've unfortunately got more important things to worry about . . .

Tonight a bunch of us are hanging out over Ava Reese's house—me, Brad, Max, Ava, Carrie, and Audrey. I don't know where Betsy is. Probably off somewhere with her sister, Cheri, who's home for the weekend from U of M. For some reason, Betsy's got this thing about hanging out with the Band Fags since she isn't one. Though I keep reminding her neither is Audrey nor Max. Secretly, I think she thinks all my friends don't like her on account of she's a Popular Cheerleader. Plus, all my friends went to Webb and Betsy went to Beecher so she tries to blame it on that.

Anyways . . .

Here we were, sitting around Ava's kitchen playing this totally fun drinking game called "Thumper" while making a firm dent in a case of Budweiser, which Max somehow managed to bring along.

"How'd you get beer?" I asked him when he arrived, red-white-and-blue cardboard suitcase in tow.

How Max knew I was quoting from one of my favorite *Facts*

of Life episodes when an underage Jo Polniaczek brings beer to a party at Eastland School for Girls, I have no idea. But he chimed right in with his best Nancy McKeon, "I got beer."

In case you've never played Thumper, basically what happens is . . . Before the game begins, everybody comes up with their own special hand gesture. Like rabbit ears behind the head. Or owl eyes. Or Max's favorite, sticking his tongue between his V-shaped fingers and flicking it. Which totally skeeves Audrey out every time he does it. (Gross!)

Then everybody sits around, drinks in front of them, *thumping* on the table with their index and middle fingers. Like voodoo savages around a campfire.

The Leader calls out, "What's the name of the game?"

To which everybody replies, "Thumper!" In unison, all the while continuing to thump.

"What's the object of the game?"

"To get fucked up!"

Then what happens is . . . The Leader has to perform his/her own hand gesture followed by somebody else's in the group. Then that person has to perform his/her own hand gesture followed by somebody else's, *and so on and so on and so on* . . . Till somebody skips a beat or doesn't respond quickly enough. At which point that person has to take a drink. Then play resumes with the person who just drank now acting as The Leader.

I know it might sound totally easy. But believe me, after a few rounds—and a few beers—it can get pretty complicated. And pretty hilarious!

I should probably set the record straight here . . . All my friends are firm believers in the policy that is *Don't Drink and Drive.* Whenever we go out and alcohol is involved, we always make sure we have our Designated Driver. Or on nights when we're hanging out at Ava's like this, I always stay over at Max's or Brad's house. Which are both within stumbling distance.

"Oh, my God . . . I suck at this!" Brad cries after forgetting his own Thumper hand gesture—yet again.

"Drink, drink, drink!" the other Thumpers chant till he takes a sip of his beer.

"That's not a drink," Max teases, chugging half a can of his own. "Now *that's* a drink!" Then he lets out a huge disgusting belch.

"Pig!" Carrie groans, making a face.

"I'll second that," adds Audrey. Then she starts to "oink."

Max just smiles, watermelon Bubblicious and Budweiser breath. "Thank you very much," he replies, in his best Elvis.

At which point the doorbell rings . . .

"I'll get it."

I sprint into the living room, my head dizzy with drink. I'm sure you can imagine my surprise when I discover none other than Joey Palladino standing beneath the moon's glow on Ava's front porch. Bundled up in that goddamn pea coat of his, he looks like the Old Spice Guy . . . Totally hot!

"Is this where the party is?" he asks with his shit-eating grin.

I reply, cold as ice, "I wouldn't call it a party."

"It is now." And with that, Joey invites himself in. The pine scent of Polo wafts over me as I follow him back to the kitchen.

"Jo-ey!" Max calls, reaching out for a High-Five as Joey enters. "Wha's up?"

"It's not a problem that I stopped by, is it?" Joey asks the group.

Of course, none of the girls mind basking in the Presence that is Palladino.

"Not at all," Ava tells him.

"Fine by me," Carrie adds.

"Take your coat off and stay a while," Audrey suggests with a sigh. Which Joey immediately does, revealing a skintight sweater clinging to his practically perfect pecs.

"There's a seat over here by me," Ava informs him, patting the available chair at the corner of the table. But for some reason, Joey chooses to pull the chair up beside me.

"You okay there, Big Guy?" he asks.

I notice his brown eyes look a little bleary and his breath smells of beer. He's obviously already had a few before showing up unannounced. "Where's Diane?" I ask. Then I pop open another can of Bud and take a big gulp. As much as I still can't stand the taste of beer, what I really need right now is to get good and wasted.

"She's in Florida with her parents," Joey tells us. "She's been gone all week."

"That sucks," says Ava, twirling a lock of her curly brown hair.

"Totally," adds Carrie, grinning.

Followed by Audrey's, "Big time."

From the tone in his voice, it doesn't seem like Joey even cares that his girlfriend hasn't been around for the entire Mid-Winter Break. I know if I had a girlfriend, I'd want us to spend each and every free moment we had together. Isn't that what being in a relationship is all about?

Max brings Joey up to speed on the evening's events. Leading up to the last round of Thumper where Brad had once again been thumped.

"Sounds like fun," Joey says enthusiastically. "Can I play?"

"Sure," answers Ava.

"Of course," adds Carrie.

"You bet," chimes in Audrey with a sigh.

At which point Brad lets out a groan. "I can't drink any more beer . . . I think I'm gonna puke!"

"Aim for the toilet," Ava advises him. "My parents will kill me if they come home and find barf all over the bathroom!"

"We don't have to play a drinking game," says Joey. "How about something a little more . . . interesting?"

"Like . . . ?" Ava, Carrie, and Audrey ask in perfect unison.

To which Joey replies, "How about Truth-or-Dare?"

This is the last thing I need right now! So I say, "Brad's not feeling good . . . Maybe I should take him home?"

"Don't worry about me," Brad answers. "I'll be fine." Then he laughs.

"Shall we move into the French Room?" Max suggests, leading the way.

We settle into our places, Ava on the brown and beige plaid overstuffed sofa between her Best Friends, Carrie and Audrey. "You sure you don't wanna sit over here?" she asks Joey.

"I'm good," he replies, opting for a place on the matching love seat beside Yours Truly.

"Am I squashing you?"

I inform him, "I'm good." How can I complain with Joey's thigh most definitely touching my thigh?

"I'll go first." Looking around the circle, Ava takes charge. Back and forth and back and forth, her eyes finally settle on Carrie. "Truth or Dare?"

Suppressing a giggle fit, Carrie covers her mouth with her hands and literally wipes the smile off her face. "Dare."

"I dare you," Ava says, slowly and with suspense, "I dare you to . . . kiss . . . Joey."

And so it begins . . .

Round after round, none of the girls have a problem with taking the Dare. It would be nice to come up with something a little more original than "I dare you to kiss so-and-so." Which is what Truth-or-Dare always ends up being whenever we play it. A bottle-less version of Spin-the-.

"Whose turn is it?" Joey asks a few rounds later, after returning from the kitchen with what must be his fifth or sixth can of Bud for the night.

"Dayton's," says Max, gearing up to go. Then he adds, "Yo . . . Wake up!"

Brad's eyes pop open and he wipes the drool from the corner of his mouth. "Me, again?" he whines. "Jesus!"

Joey stumbles a little as he takes his seat. "Sorry, Paterno," he apologizes, placing a hand on my shoulder to steady himself. Is it my imagination or does he give it a squeeze? Then to Brad he says, "Bring it on!"

All of a sudden, I can feel Brad's gaze burning a hole in me. "Ja-a-ack," he sings sweetly. "Truth or Dare?"

Because I don't like the look in his eye, I say, "I'll take Truth."

"Truth?" Joey scoffs. "Boring!"

"Don't be such a Pussy!" adds Max.

Followed by Audrey's "Yeah . . . Grow some balls for once in your life!"

"Fine!" I shout over the barrage of criticisms. "I'll take Dare."

"That's more like it," replies Brad, a glimmer in his eye. I can totally tell he's thinking up a good one. But what kind of Dare can he possibly give me that I'd be afraid to perform in front of all my friends? "I dare you," he begins. Then he blurts out, "I dare you to kiss Joey Palladino!" Followed by, "French."

All eyes focus on me. I can feel my face growing hot as the blood rushes to my cheeks. "Very funny," I reply, remaining calm. "Try again."

"It's my Dare," Brad tells me, "and *you* gotta do it."

"Kiss, kiss, kiss," the other Truth-or-Darers chant. Including Max, who I've got a feeling doesn't think I'll really do it.

I look into Joey's eyes, *warm and chocolaty.*

Radiant as sunshine, he smiles at me.

And with that, *his cherry lips* meet mine . . .

We become One . . . Time stands still . . . The World falls away around us.

Every overused cliché you can possibly think of—that's how I'd describe the next ten seconds. Better yet, like fireworks on the 4th of July. Or that time with Bobby Brady and Melissa Sue Anderson as Millicent.

But in all my 16-going-on-17 years, I've never experienced anything quite like it . . .

The Joey Kiss.

Point Of No Return

"The common road seems just like a dream
It's a mystery to me . . ."

—Exposé

What have I *done?*

Staring in the bathroom mirror, I'm totally disgusted with myself. Eyes puffy, nose red, I'm a Total Mess. I can't stand the way I look after I've been crying. But here I go again . . .

No!

I will not do this. No amount of tears or remorse or guilt is going to change anything. We can't go back in time. This isn't some sci-fi fantasy starring Christopher Reeve and Jane Seymour. This is Real Life. What's done is done . . . Though if we could, you can bet I'd do things differently.

I splash cold water on my face. Then I reach for the bar of Cashmere Bouquet lying askew in the pink Tupperware bowl my Mom uses as a soap dish. God, I hate the smell! But at 3 for 99¢, what can you expect? Roses, lavender, lilacs maybe? I don't know how to describe it. All I know is . . . There's nothing "cashmere" about the taste once I've stuck it in my mouth.

Back and forth I work my tongue, trying not to gag. Of course, I do, dry heaving the bar back into the pale blue basin. With my index finger, I scrub my mouth. Gums, top and bottom. Left side, right side. Lips. I reach down the back of my throat, coating my insides with glycerin . . . I think I'm going to retch.

Below the sink, I find the bottle of No-Brand mouthwash. Back in the day, we always used Scope or Signal, at least. Guess my Dad's gotten cheap in his Old Age. He'll be 35 next month, can you believe it? Unscrewing the childproof cap, I take a swig of minty green freshness. Swish, don't swallow. Faster and faster, burning the germs away . . . Then I spit them down the drain.

I stick out my tongue, pale and fuzzy. Then I scrape my teeth down its length, leaving emerald tracks. My reflection stares back, a Total Stranger. Who is this person I see before me? What happened to the little towheaded boy I once recognized? He used to read *Charlotte's Web,* go to Sunday school, and sing in the Church Choir. Young and innocent, all he wanted was to someday grow up . . . Now look what he's become.

One by one, I peel off my clothing. T-shirt, Levi's, Fruit of the Looms. White tube socks next. Sliding open the frosted glass shower doors, I reach for the H spigot, turn it on full blast. Then I step inside.

Chest, arms, back, butt.

I scrub and scrub my entire body.

Feet, toes, legs, crotch.

Anywhere and everywhere I can possibly reach.

Facing forward, I let my head drop, roll my neck. The water scalds my scalp. But it's not enough to wash away my sins.

I drop to my knees, the jets pelting my back like whips. Exposed in Total Nakedness, this is my sole chance for Redemption. Closing my eyes, I clasp my hands together, and—silly as it sounds—I begin to pray . . .

Dear Lord, please forgive me for I have sinned . . . I don't know what's happening to me.

I swallow hard, the floodgates of my eyelids holding back the tears, as I continue my silent confession.

I'm so sorry for what I've done . . . But I feel like I can't help it, sometimes . . . It's like the Devil gets a hold of me and he won't let go.

My chest heaves as I gasp for breath.

I know I promised myself—and You—that I'd stop. But I'm weak, Lord, and I'm scared . . . I'm scared You won't forgive me if I keep on living my life this way and doing these things.

But I know I'm not alone in this . . .

Please forgive Brad.

Raising my hands to my mouth, I kiss the feet of Jesus himself.

He's my Best Friend, Lord, and I do love him . . . But I know we shouldn't be doing these things together . . . Please, please, please, God . . . Help me to not *be this way anymore.*

I rock to and fro with each desperate plea.

I know that you'll love me no matter what . . . But I don't want to keep living this way. I don't want to be like this.

I know in my heart what I say is the Truth. But I've been saying it over and over again for I don't know how long. This time I need for things to work out differently . . . They've got to.

Please help me to be strong and have the will to overcome this.

I take a deep breath. Then for good measure, I cross myself. Even though my family's not the least bit Catholic!

In Jesus' name I pray, Amen.

How did this ever happen?

I should've never stayed over Brad's house that night after Ava Reese's Truth-or-Dare party during Mid-Winter Break. But there was no way I could drive myself home after all the beer I imbibed. And I certainly wasn't trusting Max—or God help me, Joey Palladino!—to get me there, either.

"So . . . How was it?"

Once we were back at *Dayton's Depot* getting ready for bed, Brad asked me this.

I replied, "How was what?" Even though I knew he could only be talking about *The Joey Kiss.*

"You know . . ."

"It was only a stupid game," I said dismissively. Then I changed into a pair of sweats I'd brought along to sleep in. "It's not like I was into it or anything." Even though maybe I secretly was.

"I still think Joey's hot for you," said Brad. "Even after all this time."

"You wish!" I told him. "That's *your* fantasy."

I noticed a patch of reddish brown fuzz sprouting from the center of Brad's chest as he began unbuttoning his shirt. "It's totally scan-ju-lous," he grinned. Then he stepped out of his pants and plopped facedown on his bed in nothing but a pair of white briefs.

The thing about Brad is . . . Ever since I've known him, he's had this thing about parading around half-naked. He's got a pretty decent body from swimming all those years. Nice legs, flat stomach, and a pretty decent butt. For a guy, I mean. I also can't help but notice the way he fills out his Fruit of the Looms. By which I mean Down There.

In all the years I've known him, I don't think I've ever seen Brad naked. Whenever we had to take showers after Gym or Swimming back in junior high, we'd always leave our bathing suits on. The only guys who had the guts to get fully undressed were the ones who had already started "developing." Like Rob Berger.

Remember the guy at Webb who thought Brad's Mom was his totally hot girlfriend the time he saw them at the Mall together? From Day One in 7th grade, Rob used to walk around the locker room totally naked. Needless to say, puberty had been kind to him. Me, I've always been *Leo the Late Bloomer.*

"I can't even believe I actually did that." I let out a groan, hitting the wall of harsh reality. "I'm sure it'll make for good gossip come Monday morning when we're back in school . . . People are *really* gonna think I'm a fag, now." I wrapped myself up in a scratchy wool blanket I found in Brad's closet, the room cold as ice.

Brad rolled over, propping an arm behind his head. "Can I ask you something?" he said quietly. "And don't think I'm being a jerk when I say this, okay?" A beam of light shined across the wall through the treatment-less window as a car drove down Wanda.

I looked down at Brad lying on his back in his underwear. "Okay . . ."

"When you kissed Joey Palladino tonight," he asked curiously, "did it gross you out? Or did you kinda like it?"

For a moment, I wondered if I should tell Brad the truth or not. I knew he was still friends with Luanne. What if he told her?

"It was kinda weird with everybody watching us," I reluctantly admitted. "But it was okay, I guess." Actually, more than okay. Which really got me worried. "Do you think this means I really might be . . . *like that?*"

Brad reached up and stretched. "You were drunk," he yawned, half-asleep. "Joey was drunk . . . We were *all* drunk." He assured me, "Just because you kiss a guy doesn't mean you're gay." Then he quickly added, "And even if you are, I've told you a million times I won't care."

I wanted to cry. "I thought I had everything figured out," I said, frustrated. "I thought I *finally* knew what I wanted. Who I wanted to be . . . And now I'm acting all stupid, kissing Joey Palladino and *liking* it!"

Brad chuckled. "I know how you feel." Then he said, "I felt the exact same way after I fooled around with Bobby Russell."

Okay . . . I did *not* just hear Brad say what I thought he said, did I? Is he actually suggesting what I think he's suggesting?

"After you did *what* with Bobby Russell?" I asked in shock.

Even though I got the impression he let it slip, Brad acted now as if he wanted to take back what he said. But it was too late and he knew it.

"Didn't I ever mention I fooled around with Bobby Russell before?" he asked.

To which I replied, "No! I think I would've remembered something like that."

"It's no big deal," he insisted. "It was back in 9th grade—"

"9th grade?! And you *never* told me?"

He gave me a look. "Well, what was I supposed to say?" he asked, exasperated. "You were sooo in love with Hope from *Days of our Lives*! I couldn't say, 'Hey, Jack . . . By the way, I'm a Big Fag *and* a slut 'cause I been giving Bobby Russell blowjobs on a regular basis for the last year.'"

After all this time, I finally knew the *real* reason why Brad had been such good friends with the Most Popular Boy at Webb Junior High. Of course, it took him over two years to share this juicy tidbit of information with me. Which was not part of our original agreement.

"You made me promise if *anything* sexual happened to either of us, we'd tell each other," I reminded him, laying on the guilt. "Who, where, when . . . What it felt like! And here you were, getting it on with Bobby Russell all through 9th grade and you never even told me?"

"I'm sorry," Brad apologized, holding himself like a 2-year-old. "But I *really* gotta pee."

This was not the end of it. "Sit down!" I ordered. "You can pee when you're finished with your story."

Realizing he wasn't going anywhere, Brad sat on the edge of his bed, defeated. "What do you wanna know?"

"Every detail." I sat down beside him.

"Well," he began. "It all started one time we were at Bobby's house . . . We were sitting around his basement smoking pot, and Bobby started playing with his dick through his underwear . . . Right in front of me."

Though I'd never been to Bobby Russell's house before, I could picture the entire scene clear as crystal. Brad and Bobby getting high, listening to Def Leppard or Quiet Riot or some other God awful Heavy Metal band.

"At first I didn't think anything of it," he continued, softly. "But then he pulled it out and . . ." If the room hadn't been so dark—and I hadn't been so busy trying to imagine Bobby Russell playing with himself—I'm sure I would've noticed how embarrassed Brad looked. "That first time, we just beat off together," he admitted. "But then the next time . . . I did it for him."

"You did?" I asked, in awe of his audacity.

"Uh-huh," Brad admitted. "And pretty soon after that . . ." Then he trailed off. "Well, you can imagine the rest."

I'm sure Brad was expecting me to start freaking out. Either that, or to launch into one of my famous lectures. Which I probably *should* have. But for some reason, all I said was, "You Little Slut . . . Good for you." Just because I hadn't gotten any action in the past, why shouldn't my Best Friend? Then I thought about what this Revelation meant . . .

"I can't even believe Bobby Russell's a Big Fag! I never would've thought that in a bijillion years."

"Me neither," Brad replied. I could tell he felt a sense of relief that I wasn't angry or upset. "But the amazing part is . . . He says he's *not*."

To which I scoffed. "He let you blow him, didn't he?"

"Yeah . . . But after we fooled around a couple times," Brad replied, "I was like, 'I can't believe you're a fag, too.' And Bobby was like, 'Just because I let a guy suck my dick, doesn't make me a fag.' "

Now I'd heard everything. "What an Asshole!" I cried. "He can get it up for a guy, but Bobby's not a fag himself?"

"I'm just telling you what he said, Jack."

I shook my head in utter disbelief. "Didn't Bobby ever do anything to you?"

"Never," Brad admitted. "It was totally one-sided . . . But I didn't care."

Even though I wasn't mad at Brad for keeping what he did with Bobby a secret, I felt kind of stupid for not suspecting it was going on at the time. Which is why I told him, "I had no idea you were *like that* or doing those kinda things back in 9th grade."

To which he groaned, "Please! All that talk about 'If you were a girl, would you think that guy's cute?' and propositioning Mr. Grant so you could get an A in Civics? It was pretty obvious I wasn't *totally* joking, don't you think?"

Not obvious enough. The entire time we were doing all those things, I just thought maybe Brad was trying to figure out if *I* was a Big Fag. I honestly never once thought he was trying to let me know that *he* was.

"I really didn't think you were being serious," I told him. "I thought you were just fucking around with me."

To which he laughed. "No . . . I was fucking around with Bobby Russell." Then he playfully hit me on the leg. "God, I was sooo serious! I was ready to stand by and guard the classroom door while you had your way with Mr. Grant."

Sitting beside Brad in the dark, I gave it some more thought. Why didn't Bobby Russell ever invite *me* over to his house? Why wasn't *I* the one he wanted to fool around with? And why didn't Brad ever invite me along to get in on the action?

After I confessed that I secretly thought Bobby was hot despite always saying how much I hated him, Brad replied, "I thought you weren't *like that.*"

"I don't know anymore," I groaned. "Maybe I am . . . Maybe everybody was right about me all along."

"They were right about me," said Brad. "And you're my Best Friend, so . . ."

All my life, I thought I was The Only One. What were the odds that one day I'd have a Best Friend who felt the exact same way? And yet, we had so much in common already. Why not this, too?

"How could we have both been so dumb?" I looked down at the floor, smiling to myself. "We were *both* such Big Fags!"

"How did everybody else know and we didn't?" Brad wondered. "I mean, I never even heard the word 'fag' before we got to junior high."

"Me neither!" I wailed.

Back at Longfellow, I was always the Most Popular Boy. Even though most of my friends were girls, nobody cared. It wasn't till I got to Webb that people started calling me names and I had no idea why. What was I doing all of a sudden that was any different than before?

"It's like, you turn 12 and boys aren't supposed to do certain things anymore," said Brad. "Who makes the stupid rules, anyways?"

I leaned my back against the wall. "I don't know. All I know is . . . Sometimes I do feel like I really am, you know . . . And then other times I don't." How else could I explain it? "Like, I really am in love with Hope from *Days of our Lives.* And I do wanna get married and have kids and live happily ever after and all that. Like in the movies and on TV. But then I see some totally hot Chippendales dancer on *Donahue,* or a picture of the Foxy Frenchmen in the *Free Press* and I get totally turned on."

Like the way I was right then and there, thinking about me

being the one fooling around with Bobby Russell, instead of Brad. Being the one forced into doing things with Bobby—*to Bobby*—against my will. Telling him I didn't want to . . . Even though I really did.

"I know exactly how you feel," Brad sympathized. "I've just learned to accept it, I guess . . . And so can you, if you really want to."

In all the years I'd known him, I never once thought of Brad in a sexual way. How could I? We'd been Best Friend since 7th grade. But I'll be honest . . . All this talk about Bobby Russell and giving blowjobs was totally making me horny. Wasn't I always complaining how I never took action in my life? How I'd always let the Moments of Opportunity slip by? Like with Joey Palladino.

Which is why I said, "So . . . What's it like to do that with a guy?"

Brad replied, "Do what?"

I said, "*You know* . . ." Then I gave his leg a gentle push.

"You mean, what's it like to give a guy a blowjob?" he whispered, not bothering to say anything about the fact that my hand was now lightly caressing his thigh.

At that moment I realized . . . I'd never touched another boy's leg before. It felt warm and meaty . . . and hairy! "Sometimes I'll have a dream I'm doing it," I admitted. "But I can never really tell what it *feels* like." Which has always been a thing with me. Even in my sleep, I'm sexually repressed.

"It feels good," Brad told me. "You really just have to do it to know what it's like." He closed his eyes, tilting his head back. "Oh, my God . . . I'm sooo drunk."

So was I . . . But not enough to stop myself from doing what I did next.

I stood up, took off my shirt, slipped out of my sweats. Tossing them aside, I positioned myself at the end of Brad's bed, where he lay stretched out. I looked down at him. All the while, he kept his eyes closed, saying nothing.

I'll admit I didn't know what exactly to do next. So I leaned over and kissed Brad's stomach. His skin tasted spicy. Like Lagerfeld. He flinched slightly, let out a soft moan. I could tell he liked what I was doing and didn't want me to stop. So I continued, working my way up the trail of reddish-brown leading to his chest. His body felt strange—yet exciting. With its pads of muscle, I couldn't help but notice how firm it was in places I'd only ever experienced softness.

"Careful," Brad whispered when my tongue traced his nipple. "Watch your teeth." Then he opened his eyes, looking into mine. For the first time, I noticed how blue they were. Like the sky over the football field on a cloudless day.

"You still gotta pee?" I asked.

Brad shook his head. "I can wait."

And with that, I got down on my knees . . .

Despite the dimness of the room, I could clearly see the effect my actions were having on him. By which I mean Down There. Beneath white cotton, Brad's body sprang to life.

I reached out and touched It—through the fabric. But it was a start. Sliding a finger beneath the elastic waistband, I gently pulled forward, setting him free . . .

So this was sex?

Friends & Lovers

"I don't know what we're afraid of
Nothing would change if we made love . . ."

—Gloria Loring & Carl Anderson

We slept together.

Okay, not slept together-slept together. But we did start fooling around on a regular basis over the course of the next couple months. Basically what would happen is . . . Saturday evenings I'd spend at Farmer Jack's. At 11:00 PM when I got off, I'd stop by Big Boy's, where I'd sit in Brad's section sipping my usual large Sprite with lemon. Around Midnight, he'd finish his shift. Then he'd sit down with me, smoking a cigarette, counting his tips.

We'd chat about our respective nights at work . . .

"Mine sucked."

"Mine, too."

What was up with which of our friends . . .

"Lou finally found a girlfriend . . . 'member Jane? She lives in Royal Oak."

"With the skinheads?"

Which assignment was due on Monday for what class . . .

"I've got a paper due for English Lit."

"You mean, English Shit."

After bidding farewell to the other waitresses, Brad would tell me, "All set." Then we'd walk out to the parking lot together.

"You want a ride?" I'd ask.

"I can walk," he'd reply.

To which I'd remind him, "It's late." Then we'd get in my car and I'd drive him home.

The entire way, we'd barely say a word. Instead, we'd listen to the radio, staring straight ahead, the hum of the Omni engine filling the void between us. We'd tell ourselves, *Nothing out of the ordinary is going on.* Even though we both knew well and good the scan-jul lying ahead.

Pulling up to a darkened *Dayton's Depot,* I'd ask, "You want me to come in for a while?"

"If you want to," he'd answer.

To which I'd reply, "I want to if *you* want me to."

The whole thing was ever so innocent. Best Friends hanging out together. The way we had on how many different Saturday nights over the past 4-going-on-5 years?

Tonight, it's pretty much Business as Usual . . .

"Be quiet," Brad warns as we climb the wooden steps to the deck of his back porch. I watch as he takes out his keys and unlocks the door. Ever the Gentleman, he motions for me to step inside first. Then he follows.

"Where's everybody?" I whisper.

"It's almost 1:00 AM . . . Probably in bed."

Entering Brad's house like this, I always feel the exact same way. Secretive. Aloof. Like we're up to no good. Which I suppose we are. But the feeling of finally being a full-fledged Sexually Active Adult, coupled with the fear of possibly getting caught . . . Talk about a Total Rush!

"Be right back," he tells me. "I'm gonna go freshen up."

"I'll wait in your room," I reply. Which is what I always do. Closing the door behind me, I sit down on Brad's bed in the dark, anticipating the Point of No Return.

"Can I get you anything?" he asks, eventually creeping into the room smelling of Lagerfeld.

I notice he's taken off the black work pants and coffee-stained white dress shirt he's been wearing all night. "No, thanks . . . I'm fine."

He steps in front of me. "You sure?"

I cast my gaze downward to the pair of gray Gym shorts Brad wears—with nothing else. "Positive." Then I place a hand on his meaty thigh.

Here we go again!

Once we finish—or should I say, Brad finishes?—he slips his underwear back on, along with an undershirt. Then he yawns and stretches. "Man, I'm tired . . ."

I take that as a Sign. Even though technically I'm not "done," I still enjoyed myself. "Yeah, it's late . . . Guess I better go." Then I'm on my Merry Way.

Brad walks me to the door. "Call me tomorrow," he whispers, releasing me into the Night.

"I will," I say from the other side of the threshold. Though for some reason, I can't bring myself to look at him.

The entire way home, thinking about what recently transpired, I'm totally racked with Guilt. Hence the washing of the mouth out with soap, the hot shower, and the Praying for Forgiveness once I finally arrive.

Sunday I work from 11:00 AM to 7:30 PM. Once or twice I pick up the pay phone in the vestibule when I'm on Break. But for some reason, the dimes never find their way into the coin slot.

"Call Brad," my Mom tells me the minute I walk through the door at a quarter to eight.

"I don't feel like talking to anybody right now," I reply. "I'm exhausted."

Come Monday morning, I find myself sneaking into the Band Room. I grab my trumpet case, and take my seat in the second row of risers just as Brad enters with Luanne—who gives me a look, saying nothing. Once again, she's cut her hair even shorter. At this point, she looks borderline Military Academy.

"What's up, Jack?" Brad asks, all smiles.

I quickly run through the B-flat Concert scale. C-D-E-F-G-A-B-C. "Nothing," I answer. Because there isn't. As far as I'm concerned, there's nothing out of the ordinary going on between us. It's not like we're *dating* or anything . . . Are we?

For an actual split second, I stop to ask myself if I'm in love with Bradley Dayton. Can you believe it? I mean, it's not like he's unattractive. I've already said what a nice body he has. He's also funny and nice and he's got an awesome personality—ask anybody who knows him. And let's face it . . . My choices of finding a boyfriend in the world that is Hillbilly High are pretty Slim Pickin's. It's not like there's an abundance of guys running up and down the halls screaming, "I'm gay!"

But if there's one thing my parents taught me . . . You don't have S-E-X with somebody you don't L-O-V-E. And I *do* love Brad. But in what way? At first I thought, *Wouldn't it be easy?* I mean, here's Brad. And here's me. If we're both *like that,* wouldn't it make sense for us to be a couple? But I'm finding out it doesn't exactly work that way. For some reason, I can't get past the fact that Brad's my Best Friend. He's like a brother to me. Despite any of the fooling around we've done together, when I look at him, I never quite feel the way I did when looking at Joey Palladino.

Which is why I have to keep in mind what Brad told me the first night . . . *There's nothing wrong with experimenting when you're young*. Which is exactly what we're doing. I know it doesn't mean *anything*. I've got nothing to worry about . . . As long as nobody else finds out.

Unfortunately, something happens that just might blow our cover . . .

After our most recent rendezvous, I wake up the next morning with a slight tingling sensation in the middle of my upper lip. At first I have no idea what to make of it. Till later in the day, when a nice little blister starts making an appearance.

"Looks like you've got a little cold sore," my Mom concludes when I finally get up the nerve to show it to her.

"A cold sore?!" I practically scream. How the Hell could I possibly have a cold sore? Then I flash back to the previous night's events . . . *Bra-a-d!*

Even though I remembered him coming to school on Thursday with a spot on his lip, in the heat of the moment—and the dark of Brad's bedroom—I guess I got a little carried away.

"I tried to warn you," he teases me when I immediately get him on the phone.

"What are we gonna do?" I ask desperately, standing in front of the floor-length mirror in my bedroom. The tiny little blisters forming their pustules on my mouth make me want to die! "What's everybody gonna think?"

"About . . . ?"

"I can't just walk into Wind Ensemble tomorrow morning with a cold sore after *you* just had one!" I turn away from my reflection. I feel like that girl in *The Scarlet Letter*. Everybody's going to know what a Total Slut Mr. Goody-Goody Jack Paterno really is, after all.

"If anybody says anything," says Brad, coming up with his

Master Plan, "we'll just tell them we shared a bottle of pop and that's how you caught it."

I roll my eyes. "Yeah, right! Like anybody's gonna believe that."

"Would you relax?" he advises. "I get these herpes all the time."

"Herpes?!" I exclaim, totally freaking out.

"Herpes Simplex 2," he informs me. "That's what it is, you know?"

"Great!" I throw up my arms and sigh. "So now I've got VD, all thanks to you."

To which Brad replies, "It's not my fault you're a Dirty Whore."

"Thanks a lot," I tell him.

"You're welcome," he answers. Then he laughs.

But it's not funny . . . This is serious . . . I need a remedy and I need it now!

"What do you do to get rid of them?" I demand to know.

"There's not much you *can* do, Jack . . . You just gotta wait a few days for it to go away by itself."

"A few days?!"

This is not the answer I want to hear . . . #1—This thing is in the exact same spot where I place the mouthpiece when I play my trumpet. #2—This week is the last week of April. Which means, #3—MSBOA State Band Festival is coming up *this* Saturday. Now what the Hell am I going to do?

In case you need reminding, MSBOA stands for the Michigan School Band and Orchestra Association. The entire Great Lakes State is divided up into Districts, ours being District 16, consisting of schools from Oakland, Macomb, and St. Clair counties. Each year, bands from all the member schools compete by preparing three musical selections—a march, a song from a list provided by MSBOA, and a choice made by the Band Director. A panel of three judges gives each band an overall rating based on their performance, with V being the lowest and I the highest. In addition, the bands must compete in Sight Reading. Which basically means you're sequestered in a room and given a piece of music you've never seen before. Then after an allotted amount of time—two minutes, I think—you're judged/scored on how well you play it.

Wind Ensemble already competed in the District 16 Band Festival back in March, at our very own Hillbilly High—of all places. Talk about a Band Fag's Wet Dream come true! Mr. Klan was in Seventh Heaven serving as Host School Director. He also managed to con a lot of us into serving as Band Reps for the day. Which consisted of making sure the Band Fags from the other schools knew where they had to be and when. Where the Coat Room and Sight Reading Rooms were . . . Stuff like that.

This year we played "Emblem of Unity March," "Incantation and Dance," and "Festivo," which is this totally awesome piece by a guy named Vaclav Nelhybel. We actually played it back in 8th grade with Jessica Clark Putnam and somehow all of us former Webb Warriors convinced Mr. Klan to allow us to play it again on account of we're much better musicians than we were way back when.

Of course, we totally kicked ass! Straight I's from the judges and a II in Sight Reading, giving us an overall I rating. Because of this fact, Wind Ensemble has been invited to participate in the Michigan State Band Festival held in Novi.

Which brings me back to the scan-jul of my cold sore . . .

You should see the look on Mr. Klan's face when I walk into the Band Room on Monday morning and inform him of my predicament.

"B-b-but," he stammers, biting his mustached upper lip. "Festival is *this* weekend."

"I know . . ." And how am I going to participate when I've been infested by herpes?

"You're my Star Trumpeter, Jack . . . You've gotta play."

Don't get me wrong, Mr. Klan is a totally nice guy. But the last thing I need is for him to start freaking out on me. The fact that I'm letting everybody down all because I can't control my own sexual urges only makes me feel worse.

"There's nothing I can do," I say, defeated.

To which he gives me a look. "Didn't Bradley Dayton have a cold sore just last week?" he remembers. "Why don't you ask him what he did for his?"

Hoping he isn't hinting around at anything, I tell Mr. Klan that I've already talked to Brad about the issue at hand. "I'm sorry."

"Isn't there *something* you can take?" he asks, hopeful. "Some kind of medicine you can put on it?"

"Not that I know of . . ." Like I've said, I've never had herpes before. This is an entirely new experience for me.

Thank God for Ava Reese's Mom! Being that she's the President of the HPHS Band Boosters, she's got a lot at stake in seeing us do well at State Festival. After being made aware of my predicament, Mrs. Reese suggests I put a little Desitin on it each night before I go to bed. Which, if you're not familiar, is Baby Butt-Rash ointment.

"My Mom swears it'll work," Ava assures me, first thing the following morning. "She even gave me an extra tube she had lying around from when she babysits my brother's kids."

Talk about disgusting! The thought of smearing the same greasy white goo used on an infant's ass all over my lip does not make me a Happy Camper. But later that night, I go home and before going to bed, do as Mrs. Reese advised . . . Two days later, I happily discover my herpes has completely vanished. Two days after that, I prepare to take MSBOA State Band Festival by storm—along with my fellow Band Fags!

Which we totally do . . .

Straight I's across the board. Even in Sight Reading. The 1986–87 Viking Wind Ensemble is clearly the Best Band Mr. Klan has ever had the pleasure of directing. Which is exactly what he tells us once we've piled into the official yellow School Bus en route to the Holidome in Fowlerville where we're staying overnight.

"I just want you to know how proud I am of all of you," Mr. Klan gushes. I swear, he looks like he's going to cry. That's how choked up he's getting. "I will never *ever* forget this group." Then he takes off his glasses and wipes his eyes.

"Mr. Klan rocks!" one of the guys shouts out over the hoots and hollers of the forty-three other rambunctious musicians. When I turn around, I realize it's not a guy . . . It's Luanne Kowalski.

"We love you, Mr. Klan!" Ava and Carrie add in unison.

At which Mr. Klan weeps like a baby. "I love you, too."

I can't even tell you how totally ashamed of myself I am at this moment. Despite what anybody like stupid Bobby Russell might say about him, Mr. Klan's never been anything but kind and supportive to me and Brad these past two years. So what if he's over 35, never been married, and probably is gay? It doesn't mean he's not a nice person.

As much as I complain that I hate being in Band, I really don't. At least not when I'm playing during a Concert. Especially at Festival. In case you're not a Band Fag yourself, how can I explain it? It's a lot like Sports. All these different players forming a team, coming together for the exact same purpose—to do their best and win. As the Section Leader, I'm like Captain of the Trumpets. There's an incredible amount of pressure that I don't think the other non-Band Fags can understand or appreciate . . . Especially the Jocks.

Why can't they understand how challenging what we do is, and how much Effort and Dedication and Team Work it takes?

Does Tom Fulton really think he could maintain a perfect 45° angle while pinwheeling around a corner *and* playing a Sousa march at the same time? Does he even realize how much work it is keeping your elbows out and your knees up? Maybe if he'd give it a try, he'd see what I'm talking about! Besides, without Band Fags at football games, can you imagine how boring Half-Time would be?

I don't know why I ever thought things would be different once I got to high school. It's pretty much been "same shit, different day" since Day One. If you're not a Jock, you're not Popular. And there's no way you can possibly *become* Popular without being a Jock! God forbid you should actually have some Artistic ability and want more out of Life than to graduate, get married, and squeeze out a couple of kids. Which is what I'd say 90 percent of the guys who go to Hillbilly High will eventually end up doing—mark my words!

But as they say . . . *If you can't beat 'em, join 'em!*

Ever since I can remember, I've had this image in my mind of what being in high school is *supposed* to be like. Making "Top 25." Spending Spring Break in Daytona Beach. Going to parties—other than my own.

Like in the movies and on TV.

Is it my fault if for once in my life, I want to be Popular? Don't I deserve it just as much as the others do? Lord knows, I'm better looking than most of the so-called Popular Guys. Why shouldn't they all want to be *my* friend?

Come this time next year, I *will* be Popular—no matter what. Which is why I've vowed to devote more time to making that happen . . . And less to being a Band Fag.

A few weeks later, I inform Brad of my plan . . .

"We've been in Band since 7th grade," he says when I Drop the Bomb. "Why would you wanna go and quit our Senior year?"

"I'm just kinda bored with it," I confide. Then I add, "You

know how much I hate playing at the football games *every* Friday night . . . And I'm sick of being called a Band Fag *all* the time."

To which Brad replies, "So am I . . . But you don't see me quitting." Then he says, changing tactics, "Luanne's graduating and going off to college in the Fall." "She won't be here to boss us around anymore."

"I know . . ." Still, I'm not changing my mind.

"Marching Band won't be the same without you . . . You know what I mean?"

Now I feel bad. So I tell him, "I'll think about it." Though as much as I don't want to abandon Brad and Ava and Carrie, my mind is pretty much made up.

Turning down the alley behind Taco Bell on our way for lunch, Brad says, "Please do . . . I don't wanna be a Band Fag anymore if you're not, Jack."

Stepping inside the faux-stucco building, it's all *Brady Bunch* kitchen orange and brown. We join the massively long line of Hillbilly High-Ons, bound and determined to cram down as many Taco Bell Grandes as they possibly can in twenty-two minutes.

"Maybe I can spend the night this weekend?" Brad says, looking up at the menu. "It's been a while . . ."

It's also been a while since he and I fooled around. I can't tell if this is Brad's way of hinting to me that he wants to again. Even though I'm usually the one who initiates things, I've been thinking maybe it's not such a good idea anymore.

Which is why I tell him, "Maybe . . . I'm not sure what I'm doing yet." Then I order my usual bean and cheese burrito, MexiMelt, and small pop.

"You're not mad at me, are you?" asks Brad, once we've carried our trays to an empty table in the corner.

I unwrap my burrito, apply some mild sauce. "Why would I be?"

Leaning in close, he whispers, "Ever since the whole herpes scan-jul, I just thought . . ." Then he trails off.

I tell him, "Don't worry about it," taking a bite of my Taco Bell Goodness.

"So we're still Best Friends?"

"Of course," I mumble, my mouth full of food.

Brad puts down his Enchirito, wipes off his hands with a brown paper napkin. Then he extends his right pinky finger. "You promise, Jack?"

At which point, I hesitate.

'87 VIKING

Hazel Park High School
23400 Hughes
Hazel Park, MI 48030

Volume 52

Jacques,

Well kid, it's been almost 3½ years that we've been friends. Who would have ever thought we'd become so close? I'll never forget back in 5th grade when Ms. Lemieux showed me the picture of "Jackie" Paterno from Longfellow. I thought you were so cute! Then when we finally met in 9th grade at the speech contest and you fell for me. Ha Ha. And now you're my Best Friend. Always remember the fun we had in Mme Carey's French class. Senior Year is gonna rule with NHS and the Banquet and Prom!! We've shared so many memories there isn't enough room to write them all down. You're a GREAT friend!!

Love, Betsy ("Effie")

"Jack-ster!!"

Jack—What can I tell ya? We've known each other since 7th grade and you always crack me up. You are a very unique individual and I want nothing but the best for your future. Look out New York Times Bestseller List—Here comes Jack Paterno! Remember how all the time you told me I looked like Nena? (99 Luftballoons!) We have a lot of memories but we have Senior year to make even more! Stay the same and maybe I'll read one of your novels someday!

Love ya lots!

Shellee Findlay☺

Jack,

To a great guy with a great mind. I've known you for years and we've had a lot of fun times. I'll never forget the parties. Maybe we'll see each other up at State? Good luck in everything you do.

Love always, Marie Sperling (Just call me Kristian—hee hee)

Jack,

I feel really terrible that we've drifted apart. But we're both to blame, I suppose. We still have time to make up for it during Senior Year, I guess. I hope you get all you want out of life. Even if you make it BIG and win a ton of awards and forget to thank me, I'll understand. I don't know what else to tell you except "I love ya" and you'll always be the little boy who never wanted to play House with me in Kindergarten!

Love, Audrey

Jack

I really don't know what to tell you. I've said it all before in other yearbooks. You've got great taste in "soaps." Even though Peter and

Kristian left DAYS. You've been a great friend since 7th grade. I wish you the best of luck and hope one day you find a girl that makes you happy.

Love always,
Carrie Johnson

Jack,

Between the Tombs and all the video parties, we've had a blast. I know we don't see each other much anymore and I really miss you. Have a great Senior year! Can this really be the end?

Love ya, Ava

The '87 Viking Presents . . .

The Year in Review...

AT THE MOVIES . . . WE SAW . . .

Aliens
Back to School
Beverly Hills Cop II
Ferris Bueller's Day Off
Friday the 13th: Part 6
Howard the Duck
Platoon
Police Academy IV: Citizens on Patrol
Stand By Me
Star Trek IV...The Voyage Home
The Secret of My Success
Three Amigos
Tin Men
Top Gun

WHAT WE SPENT OUR MONEY ON . . .

The Hazel Parker	$.15
Candy Bar	$.45
School Lunch	$1.10
Gallon of Gasoline	$.85
Record Album	$10.00
The Viking Yearbook	$14.00
Concert Ticket	$20.00
Pair of Levis 501 Jeans	$35.00
Pair of Filas	$50.00
Prom Tickets	$50.00

—SENIOR—

1987–1988

Break Out

*"The time has come to make or break
Move on, don't hesitate . . ."*

—Swing Out Sister

School is Boring, Sex is Great, We're the Class of '88!

As per tradition, the week leading up to the Homecoming Game is officially known as "Spirit Week," with the Big Dance taking place on Saturday night. Why it has to be held in the cafeteria, I don't know. All I know is . . . I tried convincing our Senior Class President, Jamie Good, aka Jamieleeann Mary Sue, that we should have it in the Gym for a change. Like they do in the movies and on TV. But nobody ever listens to a word I say.

The festivities kick off on Monday with College Day—dress in your favorite college paraphernalia. Tuesday, Sunglasses Day—sport your shades indoors. Wednesday, Unisex Day—which might as well be called "Opposite Sex Day" as all of the Jock Jerks like to use it to get in touch with their Feminine Side and come dressed in Drag. Thursday, Shoe Day—wear two different ones. And Friday, Maroon and Gray Day—which means Jocks in cool

Varsity jackets and Band Fags in pathetic Marching Band windbreakers . . . But not this year!

At least not for *me* as I am officially no longer a Band Fag . . . HOORAY!

Believe me, I thought long and hard about it. Coming to the conclusion that . . . What do I need Band for? It's not like I have hopes of pursuing a career as a Professional Musician. And with my newly appointed position as Editor-in-Chief of *The Hazel Parker,* I've got my hands full with plenty of activities of the Extra Curricular variety.

Of course, Mr. Klan wasn't too pleased when I Dropped the Bomb on him back at the beginning of June . . .

The Band Room seemed unusually dark and quiet after school that afternoon. I don't know if it was because all the Seniors like Luanne Kowalski and Erin Ahrens were off at Stony Creek on account of it being Senior Skip Day. All I know is . . . I dreaded walking into Mr. Klan's tiny corner office where I knew he'd be working on report cards.

"Mr. Paterno!" he exclaimed when I poked my head in. "To what do I owe the pleasure?" He closed his Grade Book, then offered me a seat opposite where he sat behind his gray metal desk.

"I can come back if you're busy," I told him.

"Don't be ridiculous! I'm never too busy for my Star Trumpeter."

In the two years he'd been my teacher, I don't think I'd set foot in Mr. Klan's office more than a handful of times. Unlike Jessica Clark Putnam's back at Webb, where Brad and I spent *almost* every single day after school. Behind his head I noticed the Michigan State diploma hanging on the wall, prompting my remembrance of the rivalry between Mr. Klan and Mrs. Putnam, who had gone to Michigan. Oh, yeah. I don't think I've mentioned . . . After we all graduated from junior high, JCP gave up her job as Webb Band Director to become a Principal at some other school somewhere. Of course, she kept the whole thing pretty hush-hush so none of us really knows where she ended up. Which is a darn shame, if you ask me. We all admired and respected her, and wish her well wherever she is.

But I guess it's keeping in line with the advice she gave me back in 7th grade . . .

"Friends hold you back."

Once I told Mr. Klan that I wouldn't be taking Band next year, he asked, "Does this have anything do with you and Brad?" Getting all serious on me. "Did you two have a fight or something?"

How the Hell did Mr. Klan know anything about me and Brad? Not that we were fighting or anything, 'cause we weren't. I just pretty much decided what was going on between us—physically—needed to stop. And the only way I could make sure it did was to start keeping my distance.

Mr. Klan said, "I was talking with Luanne the other day . . ." Then he trailed off.

I found myself staring at the wall of photos surrounding me, most being group shots of all the various Marching Bands Mr. Klan's directed over the years. But one in particular stood out from the rest . . . A college-age Mr. Klan stands beside a handsome young blond man, their faces sunburned from a day of parading on the Spartan football field. Arms around each other's shoulders, they grin for the camera. Even though there's *at least* a foot of space between them, you can't help but notice how close the two men are . . . connected.

"You might not think I remember what it's like being a Teenager," said Mr. Klan finally. "But believe me . . . Some things never change." He looked away, focusing on the far-off distant place adults call "Nostalgia." Then his voice grew soft. "When I was your age," he began, "I couldn't wait for the day I'd go off to college so I could start living my life . . . And you know what happened when I finally did?"

I looked down at my crossed ankles, noticing the black scuff mark grazing the left big-toe area of my penny loafers. I thought about the day Betsy Sheffield helped me pick them out last September. We rode the John R bus up to Oakland Mall, just the two of us. They were no longer my New School Shoes.

"I discovered that what happened in high school," Mr. Klan revealed, "didn't matter anymore . . . The friends I made at State, they were my *real* friends. Those so-called Popular Guys—the ones who made fun of me because I marched in the Band—I never saw them again." Then he added, with a sheepish smile, "Until my 10-year Class Reunion . . . By that point, they were all fat and bald!"

As much as I wanted to believe Mr. Klan, I didn't care. Maybe that's how *his* life worked out and he was happy with it. But this was *my* life we were talking about and I knew I had to do things *my* way.

Unfortunately, things aren't quite working out the way I had planned . . .

Okay, I realize I may not be the Most Popular Guy at Hillbilly High. I know I'm not in the A-crowd. But I'd say I'm definitely in the B. Maybe even B+. Despite what the Jock Jerks might say about me being a Total Fag, I'm friends with a lot of the Popular Girls. Like Betsy Sheffield and Marie Sperling. And Jamieleeann Mary Sue Good and Shellee Findlay. Now what I want to know is . . . If all of these Popular Girls like me, how come when they announced the 1987 Homecoming "Top 25" results, *my* name wasn't called?

I can't even tell you how humiliated I felt sitting there in the Auditorium that day shortly after Senior Year started. Out of all my friends, I expected *I'd* be the one to make The List . . . Guess I expected wrong!

Which explains why tonight is the night of my Senior Homecoming Dance and here I am at home, lying on my bed watching *Days of our Lives*—"Like sands through the hourglass" . . .

As much as I vowed I'd quit tuning in after Bo & Hope Brady sailed off into the sunset aboard the *Fancy Face* with their newborn son, Shawn Douglas, I got totally sucked into the whole storyline, "Who Killed Shane's Recently-Returned-from-the-Dead Wife, Emma?". Not to mention, Melissa and her new Russian dancer boyfriend, Lars. And the Frankie/Jennifer/Glenn love triangle. I also figured, I've invested so much time already, why should I abandon *Days of our Lives* just because Kristian Alfonso and Peter Reckell did?

"Knock knock."

I sit up and look over my shoulder as the flimsy accordion-style door to my bedroom slowly opens. Who do I see standing there, dressed in a fancy navy blue suit, complete with red tie to match his curly coiffed hairdo? None other than my so-called Best Friend since 7th grade, Bradley Dayton.

"Hey, Jack . . . I was in the neighborhood so I thought I'd stop by."

Being that I'm not in Band this year so we don't have any classes together, I've hardly seen Brad since school started a month ago. I've also been working a lot more at Farmer Jack's, so I haven't been doing much hanging out—with anybody. Including Ava and Carrie and Audrey and Max. Not even with Betsy Sheffield. By the way, you'll never guess who she's going with to the Homecoming Dance tonight . . . Would you believe, Tom Fulton? Don't even get me going on that!

I hit STOP on my VCR remote. At which point, I hear Alex Tribec say, "No, I'm sorry . . . The answer we're looking for is, 'What is *Das Boot*?' " Then I get up and turn off the TV. "Well, don't you look nice?" I coolly observe.

"Thanks," Brad replies, blushing. "I feel like a dork."

He kind of looks like one, too, what with the maroon and gray "Top 5" banner he's got draped across his chest. Still, I say, "Nice suit."

He brushes his hands over the lapels of the jacket. "I borrowed it from my sister Janelle's fiancé, Ted . . . It's a little big, huh?"

"No," I tell him. "You look good." Because, truth be told, he does. Like a Grown Up Man almost. No longer a Little Boy.

"I was wondering if you might wanna meet me after the Dance," Brad tells me. "I thought maybe we could go down to the bar together or something." By which he means the gay bar. Where I haven't been since the first time he and Luanne took me back in 10th grade.

"Won't your date get pissed?" I ask, kind of snottily.

"What date?"

I say, "I thought Shellee Findlay was your Homecoming partner? Aren't you taking her to the Dance?"

"Please!" he scoffs. "Shellee's got a boyfriend . . . I'm going Stag."

The last thing I really need right now is to be going out and getting drunk with Brad. Then ending up back at his house doing something we both will regret. "I don't think I'm up for the bar tonight," I decline.

Brad frowns, disappointed. "Okay . . . Maybe we can go out next weekend, instead?"

To which I decide, "I shouldn't be spending a lot of money."

"I can always treat you to a night out," he offers. "It's the least I can do for my Best Friend."

So I say, "Maybe . . . I don't know."

We stand in silence a moment, Best Friends since 7th grade, about to have it out for the very first time. Talk about tension filling the air! I don't even think a knife could cut it, that's how thick it is.

"You're not still pissed about the whole 'Top 25' thing, are you?" asks Brad, taking a seat on my bed. "Why are you letting it bother you so much, Jack?"

I can't even believe he has the nerve to ask me that. "All I ever wanted since we got to high school was to be on 'Top 25.' " I shouldn't have to repeat how much I think it's a crock of shit that the people who get nominated for Homecoming do *nothing* to support our school. For the first time in I don't know how long, we got a Foreign Exchange Student this year at Hillbilly High. Some guy from Sweden named Jens Andersson. For all of three weeks he's lived in Hazeltucky, and what happens? They make him an honorary Varsity Football player *and* he gets elected to "Top 25."

"There are plenty of people who've gone to school in this damn town their entire lives," I inform Brad, "and they never get *any* recognition."

"Meaning you?"

"God knows I deserve it *a lot* more than those other guys . . . But because they're all Popular, people vote for them."

He interrupts my rant. "Would you stop whining for a minute and listen to yourself? You know 'Top 25' doesn't mean *anything* . . . Nobody cares if you're on the list or not."

"Easy for you to say," I spit back. "You're the one wearing the sash."

Brad looks at me a moment. I can tell he's surprised by the spiteful tone in my voice. "You know I had nothing to do with the votes, Jack . . . I just about shit my pants when they called my name for 'Top 5!' "

To which I scoff, "You weren't the only one." I can't even tell you the shock I felt sitting in the Auditorium at the all-school assembly last week as Band Fag Bradley Dayton took his place alongside Homecoming King Tom Fulton, and the rest of the Jock Jerks' Homecoming Court.

Brad gets up and heads for the door. "My Mom's waiting for me in the car . . . I don't wanna be late." Then turning back he says, "I thought you'd be happy for me . . . But you don't even think I deserve to be on 'Top 5,' do you?"

What Brad doesn't realize is . . . People have been calling him names since 7th grade. Just because they've stopped saying it to his face doesn't mean they're not still thinking it. So I say, "Haven't you ever seen that movie *Carrie?*"

I can tell he's had enough. And to be honest, I just want Brad to get the Hell out of my house and leave me to my *Days of our Lives.* But he's far from departing without letting me have it.

"Just because people don't like *you*, Jack," he snarls, "doesn't mean they don't like me . . . We're not the same person."

Talk about a mean thing to say! So I come back with, "You think those Jock Jerks at school really like you? Wake up!" The only reason they're even nice to Brad at all is because his sister Janelle is totally hot and they all want to fuck her. Which is exactly what I tell him.

"Fuck you!" he replies, temper flaring. "It's one thing to insult me—I'm your Best Friend, I'll forgive you . . . But do *not* talk that way about my sister, okay?"

In all the years I've known Brad, I've never seen such an ugly expression in his eyes. I expect my Mom to burst through my door at any moment to find out what's going on, that's how totally fired up he's getting.

"I'm a good person and I'm nice to everybody," he continues. "That's the reason people like me." Then he adds, "Maybe you should try it, sometime. Instead of being so stuck-up and antisocial."

I toss my head back, insulted. "I am *not* stuck-up *or* antisocial," I insist. "How can you even say that?"

"All you ever do is complain that nobody likes you," Brad

says confronting me dead-on. "But whenever I invite you to a party or something, you won't even come with me."

"That's because *I'm* not the one who's been invited . . . *You* are!"

Brad wails, "It's a party, for chris'sakes . . . Anybody can go! There's no formal invitation."

I say, "I don't wanna go anywhere I'm not wanted." Because I don't. "I don't trust those Popular Guys like Tom Fulton and all his Jock Jerk Friends . . . I know they don't like me so why should I bother going to parties with them?"

Brad throws his arms up in defeat. "What reason could anybody have not to like you?"

"That's what *I* wanna know!" I answer. "What have I ever done to deserve being treated like this?" Then I say, "It's not like *I'm* the one going out to gay bars all the time." *Oops!* Open mouth, insert foot . . .

Brad shakes his head, hands on hips. "So that's what this is really about?" he asks. "The fact that I'm a Big Fag so I couldn't possibly deserve to have any friends or even be considered for Homecoming King?"

I tell him, "Your being the way you are has nothing to do with this." Trying to be as polite as I can.

"Yes, it does!" he snaps. "You're jealous because people like me . . . Even though I'm gay."

Which is about the dumbest thing I've ever heard. Why would I be jealous of Brad Dayton? I'm the kid who's got everything he's ever wanted . . . Aren't I? There's more to this argument, I'm afraid.

"Aren't you afraid people are gonna find out about you?" I ask, as calmly as I can. "Then what will you do?"

"Nobody's gonna find out anything," Brad insists. "Unless *you* tell them."

"I would never do that," I assure him. Because I wouldn't.

"Then quit your worrying."

But I can't. So I say, "You wanna be famous someday, don't you?" Everybody knows Famous People can't be Gay and Famous.

"It's not like I'm gonna go screaming from the bleachers at the Homecoming Game that I'm a Big Fag or something," he replies. "Besides . . . Look at Rock Hudson! He was famous *and* gay and everybody knew it."

"And look what happened to him."

I can tell Brad's thinking it over. Ever since we first started hearing about this whole AIDS thing, we've both been totally freaked out. It's getting to the point where nobody knows what is safe to do anymore. By which I mean sexually. Maybe being gay in this day and age isn't such a good idea, after all.

Of course, maybe I *am* jealous of Brad. For the life of me, I can't figure out how he gets away with making no attempt whatsoever to be somebody other than who he is. By which I mean gay. Not that he goes around *talking* about it, 'cause he doesn't. But he doesn't try to hide it, either. He's never even had a girlfriend. Unlike me, who's dated Alyssa and Diane and Betsy Sheffield—sort of—and been in love with Lynn Kelly and Kristian Alfonso. Here I've spent the last five years of my life busting my ass to convince people that I'm Normal, and yet they *still* don't think so . . . Why?!

"Normal?" Brad repeats when I mention this. "You think I'm not Normal?"

"That's not what I meant," I say, apologizing. "But it's your choice."

Obviously, my opinion doesn't bode well because Brad takes to his soapbox. "Being gay is not a 'choice' you can make," he states in his best Sally Jessy Raphael tone. "You either are or you aren't." Then he adds, "I'm not saying this to be mean . . . But I'm your Best Friend, Jack, and I really think you are."

I look away, chewing the inside of my cheek. But I refuse to cry. No matter how much I might want to. Why can't Brad just leave this alone? I don't *want* to be gay . . . Why can't he just accept that?

"I know you better than anybody else," he continues, softening a little. "But until you can admit the truth about who you really are—not just to me but to *yourself*—I don't think we can be Best Friends anymore."

And with that, Brad walks out the door.

Dude (Looks Like A Lady)

"So never judge a book by its cover
Or who you gonna love by your lover . . ."

—Aerosmith

At 25¢ per issue, *The Hazel Parker* is a Total Bargain.

Whether you're looking for the latest scoop on which Sports team won what competition against whom or you've got a problem and want to seek the advice of an expert, *Dear Blabby,* you'll find all that and more in the official school paper of Hazel Park High School.

One of the cool things about being Editor-in-Chief is . . . I receive a special Press Pass. Occasionally I'll get excused from class to venture about conducting interviews. Like the one I did last month with our new Principal, Mr. Messinger . . .

PUTTING THE "PAL" IN PRINCIPAL

by John R. "Jack" Paterno

It gives me great pleasure to introduce you to Mr. Jay Messinger, Hazel Park High's newest Principal. Mr. Messinger comes to HPHS after serving as Principal of Webb Junior High since 1980. He replaces Mr. Dick Nowicki who retired after serving as Principal of HPHS since 1962.

While there have been some negative comments about the new rules he's brought with him (especially his "No Skipping" policy), Mr. Messinger says he's not here to take over HPHS "like some Dictator."

A native of Kansas, Mr. Messinger has been married for 15 years. He and his wife, Stella, have a 12-year-old son, Jay Jr. Whenever he gets a chance, Mr. Messinger enjoys stepping outside of his office and mingling with the Student Body. "It makes me feel like I'm back in high school again."

Another one of my duties as Editor-in-Chief of *The Hazel Parker* is to help select the twenty-five pages of content that goes into each edition of the paper. Which is never an easy task with ten eager reporters all clamoring for a "byline."

Today being Monday, we've all gathered together around the table during 3rd hour for our weekly Staff meeting with our Faculty Advisor, Mr. Dell'Olio. One by one, everybody has been pitching their possible story ideas and we've been brainstorming new options for those having difficulty. I don't know why this happens more often than you'd think. All I know is . . . For a group of people who all claim they want to be Professional Journalists, I'd say 95 percent of *The Hazel Parker* Staff have no idea what they're going to write about each month!

"Marching Band's going to Florida," Ava Reese announces when it's her turn. Though she directs her attention towards Mr. Dell'Olio and not to me on account of she's pissed that I'm no longer a Band Fag. "I can write something about the trip, since I'm Drum Major and all."

"Gotcha," Dell replies, nodding vigorously. "When exactly is it?"

"Spring Break," Ava informs us all. Again not looking at me.

"And what are you guys doing while you're down there?" asks Dell, having no idea what exactly goes on in Marching Band Land, I'm sure.

"Marching in a parade in Cocoa Beach," answers Ava, "and playing at Disney World." Even though she doesn't look at me, I can tell that last part is meant as a dig.

It figures! The year I drop out, Mr. Klan decides to take the Band Fags on an out-of-state trip. Though the more I think about it . . . Who really wants to spend their Senior Spring Break with a bunch of Band Fags, marching around in the Florida heat? Not me! I'll be going with Max to Daytona Beach. Which is where all the Popular People go.

"Sounds like a good lead, Reese," Dell tells Ava. Like he's Perry White of *The Daily Planet* or something. "See about an interview with Klan after you get some more specifics, okay?" All he needs now is a big cigar or a felt PRESS hat.

Ava grins, twirling her hair. "Will I finally get a byline?"

To which Dell counters, "If you deserve one."

I can kind of understand why Ava and all the other reporters are so insistent on getting a byline. Think about how you'd feel if you spent all that time busting your butt working on a story or an article, only to find in the end you're not even credited. But according to Dell, in the Real World of Journalism not all stories are in-depth or personal enough to warrant a byline. As a reporter, you've got to earn it. That's the way it goes.

Dell turns his attention to the next Staff member in line. "Good?" he squawks. As in Jamieleeann Mary Sue. "You're up."

For whatever reason, Jamie Good is the only member of the Popular Crowd who writes for *The Hazel Parker.* Of course, being who she is, Jamie does just about anything one can do when it comes to Extra Curricular Activities. Not that *The Hazel Parker* is considered one. It's technically called "Advanced Journalism." But like I've said, Jamie's not only our Senior Class President, she's also Varsity Cheerleading Captain, Secretary of the National Honor Society, and she sings in Chorale. Which explains why she was recently elected Homecoming Queen 1987. Not to mention the fact that she's one of the prettiest girls in school. With shoulder-length chestnut brown hair and eyes to match, Jamie's the kind of girl who lights up a room the minute she walks in.

"I was thinking about covering Senior Breakfast," Jamie informs the group.

"Gotcha," Mr. Dell'Olio replies. "And when is that?"

"Last week Thursday," Jamie answers for all of us Seniors on Staff who are now shaking our heads and rolling our eyes.

"Well how was *I* supposed to know?" Dell asks, only slightly embarrassed. "I'm not a Senior."

I'm thinking, *Duh! You were there*. But instead I say, "Remember that *breakfast* you went to? At the Kingsley Inn . . . With all the *Seniors?*"

"Oh, yeah!" Dell recalls wide-eyed. "That thing in Bloomfield Hills . . . That was some good grub."

In the name of Tradition, every November the Seniors gather together for the first time as a Class over scrambled eggs and sausage with a side of hash browns and/or coffee and OJ. Throw in a few slices of French toast and some fresh Danish pastry and you've got what's officially known as "Senior Breakfast."

Not only were all of our morning classes cancelled, we got the chance to have a decent meal together and get all dressed up. I wore my navy blue dress pants, matching cardigan sweater, and gray turtleneck. Sitting at our assigned tables, we listened to various speakers talk about what lies ahead for our Senior year and beyond. Senior Class Secretary Stacy Gillespie gave the Invocation, welcoming us. Though I almost didn't recognize her all dressed up in a long black skirt worn with a charcoal-gray turtleneck and her usual Punk Rock hair now cut and styled into a neat short bob.

Max and I sat with Jamie Good, Shellee Findlay, Betsy Sheffield, and her official new boyfriend, Tom Fulton. Like I've said, when I found out she accepted his invitation to the Homecoming Dance last month, I was in Total Shock. Almost livid, really. How could Betsy do that? Especially when she's known what a jerk Tom's been to me all these years.

"Then why did you invite Tom to your 16th birthday party?" she reminded me.

"Because he was going with Marie Sperling at the time," I said in my defense. "And *she*'s my friend!" Secretly I'd been thrilled when I found out Marie had finally dumped Tom's ass. She always deserved a much better boyfriend . . . And so does Betsy!

But I've got to admit, over the course of the morning's festivities, Tom Fulton turned out to be a pretty cool guy. Certainly a lot nicer than I'd ever remembered him being in the past.

"Dude!" he said to me and Max over coffee. "Remember the time you guys hung out at my house?"

"When?" asked Max.

"Back in 7th grade," recalled Tom. "Remember we called the Party Line?"

The fact that he even remembered—let alone admitted it—totally took me by surprise. I'll never forget Tom's turn as Tammy. Or the things he said to turn those guys on! Too bad he totally blew me off once we got back to school . . .

"That was stupid, huh?" Acting all cool, Max rattled four packets of Domino sugar together before dumping them into his cup.

"No way, Dude!" Tom grinned. "I remember it being kinda fun."

"Dude! You gotta be joking." Max took a sip of java. "Calling those guys up and pretending we were chicks . . . How lame was that?"

Tom replied, "I don't know, Dude . . ." Then to me he said, "Dude! What do you think?"

I said, "I remember us having a good time." Because, looking back, I knew we did.

"Dude! Me, too," Tom confirms.

To which Jamie replied, "Dude! What's with the 'Dude'?"

"Yeah, Dude," Shellee Findlay echoed. "What's up, Fox?"

At which point, Betsy just rolled her eyes. "Don't ask . . ."

For some reason, beginning this school year, all the guys—and some girls—are running around the halls of Hillbilly High calling each other "Dude." I have no idea why or where it came from. But every time I turn around it's like, "Dude! You wanna go up to Taco Bell for lunch?" "No way, Dude! Taco Bell sucks . . . How about the BK in BFE?" "Dude! BK makes me puke."

I'm telling you . . . No matter how Popular I become, I've promised myself I will *not* start calling people "Dude."

"Dude! We should hang out again sometime." Tom said this later to both me and Max. Though he said it more to me. "A bunch of us Varsity guys are going to the game tomorrow night at Ferndale. To check out the competition . . . You should come."

"No can do," Max replied. "I gotta work at The Farmer." Back in the summer, Annette Funicello called up Lyle Waggoner and got Max a job working at store #142 with me. Only he's in Dairy. Which is part of the reason Max and I have started hanging out together again so much lately. Then Max said, "Jack's off on Friday . . . He can go."

To which Tom cried, "Dude! You said, 'Jack off'!"

Betsy rolled her eyes. Then to me she said, "You should go, Jack." Giving me a look that said, *Now's your big chance to make friends with the Popular Guys.*

Maybe Betsy's right. Maybe Tom isn't such a bad guy once you get to know him. Especially when he's not hanging out with his Jock Jerk Friends. He actually cleans up pretty nice. He's sitting next to me in a navy blue sports jacket, blue Polo dress shirt with button-down collar and yellow paisley-print tie, and I could see why Betsy's been secretly lusting after him for the past three years. He's probably one of—if not *the*—best looking guys in our school. With light brown hair that's kind of long and flippy in front, short around the sides, and wedged in back, he's got bright blue eyes, a totally perfect smile, square jaw—and dimples! No wonder he got elected Homecoming King. Though why Betsy never told me she liked him till recently, I don't know. All I know is . . . I hope Tom makes her happy and doesn't wind up being the Total Jerk I used to think he was.

The only drawback to the Senior Breakfast was . . . All my Band Fag Friends—Brad, Ava, Carrie, Audrey—sat together at a table directly across the room from me, right in my line of vision. And the entire time we were in the Kingsley Inn banquet room, not one of them said a single word to me!

"I like your dress." I tried complimenting Audrey as I passed by her in the lobby. She was waiting in line for the coat check with Rob Berger, who I heard she went with to the Homecoming Dance and was now officially dating.

"Did you hear something?" Audrey asked Rob, totally ignoring me. Then she grabbed her jacket and walked away in a huff.

I can't even believe all my Band Fag Friends are pissed off just because I dropped out of Band. I mean, what's the big deal? It's *one* class. So what if I'm not there marching with them at the Friday night football games? Who cares if I don't go to Disney World on Spring Break? It's not like we can't still be friends.

Of course, after what happened between me and Brad the night of the Homecoming Dance, he made it perfectly clear what it's going to take to get *him* to talk to me. And I don't care. I won't admit to something I know isn't true . . .

At least not 100 percent.

"Sounds good, Good."

Mr. Dell'Olio's enthusiastic approval of Jamie's Senior Breakfast story idea snaps me out of Daydream Mode. I do my best to focus my attention as he moves on. "Moody . . . What-cha got?"

Claire Moody leans forward, tucking her blue Papermate pen behind her ear. "How about something on the Preps versus the Burn-Outs?" she suggests.

Also a Senior, Claire serves as Co-Captain of Flag Corps and is responsible for talking Audrey into joining the squad this year. Which is part of the reason I'm on Audrey's Shit List. Claire claims the only reason Audrey ever joined the Flaggots was so she and I could spend more time together. But now that I'm no longer a Band Fag, I've pretty much screwed up The Plan.

"Moody, please . . ." Mr. Dell'Olio cringes at Claire's use of the B-O word. By which I mean referring to the kids at Hillbilly High who have nothing better to do with their free time than stand around smoking cigarettes as "Burn-Outs."

"Sorry, Dell," Claire replies. "But it's a Hot Button Topic right now . . . Ask your Editor-in-Chief." With that, she gives me a smirk.

All eyes focus on me. Except for Ava Reese's. She looks down at the table, doodling the Van Halen logo in her spiral notebook. Have I mentioned how devastated she was when David Lee Roth quit the group? Don't even bring it up!

Being that my main responsibility is handling the "Letters to the Editor" section, over the past six weeks I've received a handful of complaints from various students addressing a variety of issues pertaining to "school and community affairs." Which is the requirement for anybody wanting to write a Letter to the Editor.

Dear Editor,

Our school needs more Spirit. Whenever I go to a football game, the bleachers are empty. Or at a dance, hardly nobody is there. What's the point in putting on these kind of activities if nobody is going to show up for them? School would be a lot more fun if people would show some Spirit! Come on HPHS!

Signed,

Sally Spirited

Poor Sally's got a point . . . The bleachers at the football games *are* pretty much deserted. I never realized it before when I was busy with the Band Fags in Marching Band. But when Max and I went to watch Betsy, Jamie, and Shellee cheer at the first Varsity Home Game back in September, the stands were barely half-full. I remember being in 6th grade at Longfellow, Joey and I would come over to a football game on Friday night. Back then, you had a hard time finding a place to sit. Not anymore.

And the Dances . . . At Webb, I don't know anybody who missed a Fun Night. They were the highlight of each month. Of course, all the Jock Jerks sat around the periphery of the cafeteria waiting for the next slow song to come on before they would get off their asses. But here at Hillbilly High, nobody even bothers to attend. Last year, Betsy and I were the very first ones to buy tickets to the Sadie Hawkins Dance. Which eventually got canceled due to lack of interest. Though who am I to talk, considering I skipped out on this year's Homecoming Dance?

Dear Editor,

I really can't stand it that the 9th graders will be coming over to HPHS next year from Webb and Beecher. Why should they be allowed to start their Freshmen year in high school when we weren't? I happen to know a lot of Sophomores, Juniors, and Seniors who don't want the Freshmen here. And I'm one of them!

Signed,

Ticked Off Upper Classman

Remember how I said that back in the late '60s, the only junior high in Hazeltucky was Beecher, Home of the Beecher Burn-Outs—I mean, Spartans? And how once there got to be too many kids to fit into one building, they built another school and divided the Freshman class into two? Apparently after a mere twenty years, enrollment is down again in the "Friendly City." So the plan is to bring back the Freshmen, like the swallows to Capistrano. Of course, to the Class of '88 this is no big deal. Come June 16th we're out of here! But as you can probably imagine, the Juniors and Sophomores have all got their panties in a wad.

But as Claire said, the big concern among the Student Body this semester is . . . the Preppies versus the Burn-Outs. All because of a little area across the street from Hillbilly High that's officially become known as "Skid Row."

Dear Editor,

I've heard some rumors going around that the cops are going to start giving tickets to the Burn Outs who smoke over by Skid Row. Well, I say they should! I bet no other school around here has a place where kids hang out and smoke like Skid Row. No wonder kids from other

schools say we live in Hazeltucky and go to Hillbilly High.
Signed,
Choking to Death

"What do you think, Paterno?" Dell asks, directing his attention to his Right-Hand Man.

"Sounds like a good idea to me," I answer. Then to Claire I say, "Have you given any thought to your angle?"

"Um . . ." Miss Moody chews on her ink pen. "Let me get back to you."

I don't doubt that Claire would write a compelling story. She always did. In fact, out of the entire Staff at *The Hazel Parker*, she's the only one with her own regular column, "Fashion Faux Pas." Having also gone to Webb Junior High, Claire and I go way back to the days of 7th grade Enriched English & Social Studies with Cinnamon Lemieux.

I first got a taste of Claire's writing ability during 8th grade when she and Carrie Johnson and I collaborated on a short story together, "The Adventures of Angela," about a teenage girl named—what else?—Angela, who runs away from home and winds up living on the street as a Prostitute. Every day during Miss Shelton's 5th hour English, the three of us would take turns putting our two cents in. But it was Claire who came up with my favorite line of all time, as said by Angela's Pimp when she wouldn't put out for him . . .

"I'm a man with sexual needs, Babe."

While I consider her a friend, Claire's also my biggest competition when it comes to coverage. I always get the vibe that she resents my being made Editor-in-Chief. I guess I can't blame her. She's been writing for the paper since we started 10th grade—an entire year longer than I have. I don't know if it's got anything to do with my being the only guy on Staff. But when it came time to choose a new Editor-in-Chief, Mr. Dell'Olio went with Yours Truly. And I'm bound and determined to make Volume 60 of *The Hazel Parker* the best it's ever been . . . All I need now is a Killer Scoop.

The following week, I check my "Letters to the Editor" mailbox. And what do I find? Get a load of this . . .

Dear Editor,

As a member of Band, I've been called a "Band Fag" for years. It's always hurt my feelings but I've blown it off. Until I realized that for me the label really is true.

Because I'm GAY.

I also know for a fact there's <u>at least</u> one other (gay) kid in this school who's afraid to be himself all because of what the other more Popular kids will think. He even dropped out of band this year because he hated being called a "Band Fag." Which really makes me sad because he used to be my Best Friend and I miss having him around.

What the kids at HPHS don't seem to understand is that we didn't choose to be this way. We were born like this and there's nothing we can do about it. Why can't the people who make fun of other people think about how much damage their words can do? I'm sure if they were in our place, they'd hate it just as much as we do.

Signed,
A Real Life "Band Fag"

Dude! Who the Hell does Brad Dayton think he is?

He should know by now that after all these years, I can *totally* recognize his handwriting. Does he really think I'm going to print his letter? If Brad wants to go and be a fag, that's his business . . . Not mine.

How many times do I have to tell him . . . *I'm not gay and I* never *will be?!*

Venus

"Goddess on the mountain top
Burning like a silver flame . . ."

—Bananarama

Tonight, I've got a *date*. Not a date-date, but . . .

Remember my Uncle Roy? He's my Mom's brother with the *Penthouse* collection. Well, I don't think I've ever mentioned that he's a Stand-up Comic. He's been doing it for a while and he's getting to be kind of famous. At least in the Metro-Detroit area. While I've never seen his entire routine on account of it's loaded with Dirty Jokes, what I have heard is actually pretty funny.

Back when I was a kid, my Uncle Roy would try out his latest material at our family Holiday Parties. My cousins, Rachael and Rhonda, and I would stop playing *Charlie's Angels* or *The Brady Bunch* or whatever we happened to be pretending and hide around the corner, listening in.

"Yes, Virginia, there is a Roy Freeman," he'd begin. "And you, too, can check him out. That's right! Roy Freeman—Comedian Extraordinaire—has just booked himself on a coast-to-coast tour . . . For the entire month of May, I'll be playing the top clubs all the way from Lake Michigan to Lake Huron." This was obviously one of his Clean Jokes.

I remember another one about him getting high with his buddies and hitting the Late Nite Drive-Thru at White Castle's. He'd order a sack of Sliders, half a dozen fries, a couple large chocolate shakes . . . Then wash it all down with a Diet Coke. Maybe I haven't mentioned that Uncle Roy's kind of a big guy. Not that I'm saying he's fat, 'cause he's not. But as my new favorite comedienne, Judy Tenuta, would say . . . "He's big-boned!"

Speaking of the Giver-Goddess/Fashion Plate Saint . . .

Tonight, Uncle Roy's got a job at some comedy club in Ann Arbor and he's offered to take me along on account of he's opening up for none other than . . . Judy Tenuta. Like I've said, she's my new favorite comedienne and has been since last Summer when I first saw her on this HBO comedy special, *Women of the Night*. There she was . . . All decked out in this long flowing silvery goddess-like dress with a pink scarf-like thing wrapped around her shoulders and matching flower in her dark flowing hair—holding an accordion!

"Hi, Pigs!" Chewing her gum with Total Attitude, she addressed the audience. "You know my name is Judy . . . And I've got my own religion, Judy-ism."

During the course of her routine, she proceeded to talk about everything from her roommate, Mary Beth Easy—"She's like a landmass with a perm!"—to how she's dating the Pope. Though she's "just using him to get to God!" she declared with a sneer. Of course, I couldn't help but totally crack up. Especially when Judy spat her gum at some guy in the audience she called a "Stud Puppet" and demanded he "crawl for it!" I just about peed my pants when she started playing her "IUD"—her pet-name for her accordion—and singing a song about her Dad, who used to make Hot Dog Soup. "He'd boil the hot dogs . . . And we'd drink the juice!"

The next time *Women of the Night* aired, I made sure to set up the timer on my VCR so I could record it for posterity. The other three comediennes were pretty funny, too. First up was some woman I'd never heard of, Ellen DeGeneres. Apparently she won some "Funniest Person in America" contest on Showtime or something. Then came a lady named Rita Rudner. Followed by Judy. Then some Paula Poundstone woman, who kind of reminds me of Luanne Kowalski, if you know what I mean. Not that I'm saying she's a lesbian, 'cause I'm not. But the fact that she came out wearing what looked like a man's jacket from Oaktree, with a pair of jeans and cowboy boots, makes me suspicious.

Without a doubt, Judy was by far The Best. I can't even believe I'm going to see her Live and In Person. First Kristian Alfonso, now Judy Tenuta! I really wish Brad, Ava, Carrie, and Audrey weren't pissed at me because I'm sure they would get a kick out of coming along. With any luck, Uncle Roy says he can take us Backstage to meet her after the show. By us, I mean me and Tom Fulton.

Originally, I invited Max to come with. But once again, he's working at Farmer Jack's. Then I asked Betsy. But her Mom decided she couldn't go on account of the comedy club is in the basement of a bar. And how dare she allow her 17-year-old daughter to go anywhere they serve alcohol? Because as far as Mrs. Sheffield is concerned . . . Betsy's a Little Angel who's never had a drop to drink in her life. As one of her daughter's Best Friends, I know this isn't exactly true.

I don't know *where* she got it from, but Betsy happens to be in possession of a Fake ID that she uses to buy beer whenever she, me, and Tom Fulton hang out. Which has started becoming more frequent since the Friday after Senior Breakfast when I first accepted Tom's offer to go to the football game at Ferndale High with him and all his Jock Jerk Friends.

Talk about a strange night! There's me—a former Band Fag—hanging out with the 1987 Homecoming King and half of the Hillbilly High Varsity Football team; I could totally tell they weren't happy the minute Tom showed up with me in tow. But *none* of them said a single word. And I'm not even exaggerating when I say that. They acted like I didn't even exist. Maybe they were too busy hanging all over each other in the stands. Because that's what they did—literally. Call it Male Bonding, I don't know. All I know is . . . Arms were slung around shoulders, backs rubbed and massaged, and elbows found their home on the knee of the guy sitting on the bleacher behind them.

And they call me a fag!

"So what's the word, Jackie?"

On our way to Ann Arbor, we're not in Uncle Roy's car for more than ten minutes when he reaches into his front shirt pocket and pulls out a joint. He pops it into his mouth, lights it, inhales. Then he holds his breath till his face turns beet red.

I try acting like it's no big deal. So what if my almost-30-year-old Uncle is getting high in front of his 17-year-old nephew and his nephew's new Best Friend while driving down I-75 in a motor vehicle? I mean, the rule isn't *Don't Get High and Drive,* right? Though I can't even believe my own Uncle is a Burn-Out. The first time I found out he smoked pot, I didn't know what to think. All my life I've been taught to *Say No to Drugs* and here's a member of my own family, a Total Pothead.

"How'd you get this gig opening up for Judy?" I nonchalantly crack my window, trying to get over how embarrassed I am at this moment and hoping Mr. Homecoming King isn't judging me too harshly from the backseat.

"I know the manager of the club," Uncle Roy replies, taking another hit of Maui Wow-y or whatever-the-Hell kind of pot he's smoking.

The thing about Uncle Roy is . . . He graduated from Hillbilly High back in 1976. From what I've heard, he was always a Good Student. He appeared in all the Spring Musicals—*Li'l Abner, Guys and Dolls, West Side Story.* But he was also kind of a Jesus Freak, as my Mom would say. Long hair, wire-rimmed glasses, all "Peace and Love." Which explains why he still uses words like "gig" and every once in a while smokes a "doob," I guess.

"I'm opening up for Ellen DeGeneres in a couple of months," Uncle Roy brags, once he's had his fill and returned what's left of the extinguished joint to his shirt pocket. Then he informs us matter-of-factly, "She's a dyke, you know?"

To which I reply, "Oh, yeah?" I mean, what else am I supposed to say?

"Her and that Whitney Houston . . . Both of 'em, Lez-bos."

"I haven't heard that," I reply, making polite conversation with my mother's brother. I shoot a glance back at Tom, who's quietly listening to the conversation. He rolls his eyes and gives me a look that says, *Guess we should've driven ourselves!*

I've got to admit, I find it hard to believe that Whitney Houston is a lesbian. She's totally beautiful and all. Plus, isn't she dating Jermaine Jackson? Or maybe they just sang that song together on her album, I don't know. All I know is . . . Uncle Roy seems pretty confident in his assessment.

"Oh, yeah!" he confirms. "I read it in *The National Enquirer.*"

Around 8:30 PM, we pull into the parking garage of the Main Street Comedy Club in Ann Arbor. I get a little nervous when I see a line forming at the entrance and a very large, very mean looking man dressed in all black standing out front in the December cold checking IDs.

"What's up, Roy?" ID Checker Dude says to my uncle who bypasses the line and cuts straight to the door.

"Can't complain if I'm high," Uncle Roy answers with a snicker. "Which I am." Then he says, "These guys are with me," gesturing to me and Tom. "My nephew, Jack, and his buddy."

ID Checker Dude straps an orange plastic Over 21 bracelet around both our wrists. "Enjoy the show."

And we do . . .

I can't even believe that the minute we're seated—at a table *right* next to the stage, no less—the waiter comes over to take our drink order and Tom asks for a Labatt's.

"Can I see your bracelet?" Waiter Dude asks.

Tom flashes his wrist.

"And for you?" Waiter Dude turns to me without skipping a beat.

I had planned on ordering a Pepsi or Coke. But now I figure, might as well! So I tell him, "I'll take a Labatt's, too, please."

To which he replies, "Don't you have nice manners?"

If I didn't know better, I'd think Waiter Dude was flirting with me. Especially when he comes back with the two green glass bottles of Canada's Finest and says, "You look familiar . . . Did we meet at Nectarine?"

I take a closer look at him. He's got a nice face. Dark eyes and brows to match with an olive complexion. Perfect teeth. I guess you can say he's Tall, Dark, and Handsome. In a John Stamos—formerly Blackie on *General Hospital*, now on that new show, *Full House*—sort of way. Only with different hair. Kind of long and flippy in the front, short around the sides, and wedged in back. But being that I have no idea what Nectarine is, I reply, "I don't know . . . Maybe."

"It's a Fag Bar," Tom informs me after Waiter Dude sashays along on his fairy way. Apparently, his sister goes to Michigan and she's got a lot of Fag Friends . . . Who knew?!

Uncle Roy's routine isn't nearly as dirty as my Mom made it out to be. Sure, he drops the occasional F-bomb a couple times.

But for the most part he talks about how fat he is and how much he likes getting high, which leads him to getting the munchies which leads him to . . . White Castle. Guess he hasn't written much new material since 1980. Though it's pretty cool to see a room full of U of M college students cracking up at my very own uncle's jokes. How many nephews get to say they've witnessed that?

Even Tom leans over to me at one point and says, "Dude! Your uncle's ripping me up." Of course, maybe it's got something to do with the fact that Tom's totally ripped. As in drunk.

After Uncle Roy finishes his set, there's a fifteen minute intermission . . .

I say to Tom, "Dude! I gotta pee . . . Be right back." Then I toss in, "Want another beer?" Even though he's already had three—or is it four?

"You know it, Dude!" he replies, ear-to-ear grin and all glassy-eyed.

There's a bunch of guys waiting for the bathroom so I get in line. That's when I notice . . . about 90 percent of the dudes in this bar look like Waiter Dude. By which I mean they look gay. They've all got their hair cut the exact same style—long and flippy in the front, short around the sides, and wedged in back. And a lot of them are dressed in all black. Like this is the '60s or something and we're at a Coffee House for a poetry reading. Plus, the way they hold their cigarettes, all pointy-fingered and limp-wristed.

Though now that I think about it . . . Tom's practically got the exact same haircut as Waiter Dude and *he's* not gay. Maybe these guys aren't, either. But there's something about the way they all look at me. Like they're undressing me with their eyes. Which is why I decide the line's too long and I can hold it till the end of the show. Besides, I need to find Waiter Dude and get a couple more beers before Judy goes on.

Of course, the line at the bar is a mile long. And what if Waiter Dude isn't there and Bartender Dude won't serve me? I decide I better head back to the table and wait for him to come to us. That's when I hear Uncle Roy's voice booming over the microphone . . .

"Ladies and Gentlemen . . ."

The audience settles down as everybody takes their seats.

"I'd like to introduce you to a Petite Flower," Uncle Roy continues, obviously reading from a card. "Who's more Famous than anyone who's ever lived . . . Judy Tenuta."

And the crowd goes wild!

I slip back into my seat, just in time to see the Giver-Goddess appear before my very eyes. Accordion in hand, she's dressed in a similar outfit to the one she wore on HBO, only this time it's a gold pantsuit.

"Hi, Pigs!" the Earth Mother/Geisha Girl grunts, as if there's no other way to greet her Loyal Followers. "My name is Judy . . ."

From somewhere in the crowd we hear an echo of *"Ju-u-dy!"*

Judy reacts, hand to ear, hearing the distant call. "And I've got my own religion . . . Judy-ism!"

I've got to say, she looks even better than she does on TV. And thinner. Must be that damn camera adding an extra ten pounds again! For the most part, she puts on the exact same show as the one I've seen a bijillion times on video at this point. In fact, I've watched *Women of the Night* so much, I find myself reciting Judy's jokes along with her in my head. But it doesn't matter that I already know all the punch lines. She still totally cracks me up.

The highlight of my evening comes when Judy's just about to sing "The Pope Song . . ."

"It's a Country and Western love song," she informs the audience, "and you can dance to it."

But that isn't how the joke goes. At least not when she does it on HBO. She's *supposed* to say, "And you can dance to it . . . 'kay, Sponge?"

So I call out, "Sponge!"

Which causes Judy Tenuta to turn in my direction, literally stopping in her tracks. Our eyes meet. She looks at me—John R. Paterno of Hazeltucky—as if to say, "How dare you interrupt the Goddess? You Pig!" Then she bursts out laughing and we're off to the Rodeo!

After the show, Uncle Roy tells us we need to wait till the audience clears out. Then he'll take us Backstage to meet Judy, Live and In Person. It's a good thing Tom and I have both sobered up a little during her set. I'd hate to breathe on my new favorite comedienne with my nasty old Booze Breath!

"Come in, come in!" With a wave, the Goddess beckons for us to enter her tiny closet of a dressing room.

"Hi, Judy," Uncle Roy says. "This is my nephew, Jack, and his buddy." I don't know if it's just me, but . . . I can't help but notice how nervous Uncle Roy sounds.

"Hi, Judy," I say, surprised that I sound the same. I don't know what it is about meeting Famous People that totally freaks me out. They're *just* people, after all.

"Are you Nephew Jack or his buddy?" Judy asks me.

"I'm Jack . . . This is my friend, Tom."

Tom nods and smiles. "Hello." Even he sounds nervous!

Giving Tom the once over, Judy coos, "Hello to you, Stud Puppet . . ." Then she places her Petite Flower hand on his football player pecs.

"Would you mind if we took a picture with you?" I ask, taking out my camera.

To which Judy graciously obliges. "But of course."

Surprisingly, she's not nearly as crass, Live and In Person. In fact, she's kind of quiet and soft spoken. But when the camera turns on, so does she! She removes a couple flowers from the vase on her makeup table, sticks one behind each of our ears. Then she sandwiches herself between us, arms around my shoulders and Tom's, posing ever so seductively.

Not wanting to wear out our welcome, we only stay a few minutes. After we've thanked her for letting us worship at her feet, Judy reminds us, "You cannot possess me." Then she presents me with a tin of "Potted Meat Product" one of her Loyal Followers must have brought her—a parting gift to remember her by.

It's after 1:00 AM by the time we get back to my house in Hazeltucky . . .

"Dude! Let's play Super Mario Brothers," Tom says, getting all excited as I struggle to fit my key into the front door. Guess I'm still a little buzzed from all the Labatt's. Ever since he found out my brother has a Nintendo, we've pretty much taken it over. I don't think I even touched the game before I started hanging out with Tom. They make it way too complicated with all the A and B and X and Y buttons. Plus, it's left-handed! Whatever happened to the days of a single joystick and maybe a FIRE button or two?

"Dude! We can't," I tell him. "My brother's in bed."

"So what?"

"So it's his Nintendo and it's in *his* room."

Once inside, I turn off the living room lamp my Mom always leaves on whenever I'm out. Then we sneak through Billy's room where he's snoring away and into mine, closing the accordion-fold door behind us.

"Dude! You got any beer?" Tom asks, flopping down on to my bed.

"Like you need anymore," I answer, flopping down beside

him. The only problem with having my own bedroom is . . . No more bunk beds. Though I haven't had to worry about it too much since I haven't had anybody spend the night in practically over a year. "Dude!" I half-whisper. But Tom doesn't respond. Because when I look over at him, I see that he's totally passed out . . . Snoring away!

"Wake up," I insist. There's no way I'm sleeping on the floor just because Tom Fulton can't hold his liquor. When it comes to spending the night at Jack Paterno's house, that whole "Guest Rule" thing does not apply.

But it's no use . . .

As the song goes, it looks like we're "Sleeping Single in a Double Bed," only the other way around. Which is no big deal, I've done it before with Brad Dayton. The only thing is . . . Tom's a lot bigger of a guy. Not only does he play Varsity Football, he plays Varsity Basketball. So he's a good 6' tall, if not taller. And he's wider than Brad, if you know what I mean. Not that I'm saying he's fat, 'cause I'm not. But he takes up more space in a muscular-from-lifting-weights kind of way . . . Like Joey Palladino.

God! I haven't thought about Joey in forever. Which is probably for the best. Believe it or not, I'm finally over him. Every so often, I'll think back to the night of *The Joey Kiss* and smile. But the feelings that stir in me aren't nearly as strong as they once were. They've totally lost their power. Last I heard, he's still going with Diane Thompson.

Just as I'm about to doze off, Tom rolls over. He sticks his butt into my side, totally hogging the bed—*my* bed! I try rolling over, facing the opposite direction. But now Tom's butt is sticking into my back. I'm thinking, *Come on!* I'm 5'7" tall and weigh 125 pounds, I don't need much room.

This is never going to work. There's no way I'll get any sleep like this. The only solution I can think of is . . . I roll over again—the other way—facing Tom so our bodies fit together. Like two spoons.

All of a sudden, it's like I'm Up North in Grayling at Hartwick Pines.

Ah, yes . . . The familiar scent of Polo!

Shake Your Love

"I'm under a spell again
Boy I'm wondering why . . ."

—Debbie Gibson

Have you ever *driven* past somebody's house?

It's not like you plan to stop. You don't even actually have to see the person. But just passing by, knowing where they live and breathe and sleep is enough to make your heart skip a beat.

That's what happens whenever I take the long way home from a night's work at Farmer Jack's, exiting I-75 at 9 Mile instead of taking the usual I-696 ramp. Which leads me past Tubby's Subs and Gas 'n Go and Big Boy's, where I feel like I haven't been in forever. For a brief moment I think of Brad, wondering where he is and what he's been up to since I saw him last. But I quickly forget by the time I reach the corner two blocks down where my four new favorite letters reflect white on green . . . O-T-I-S.

To me, that one single word is as precious as the name of the person who resides there on that street. I'm talking about the new Love of my Life . . . Tom Fulton.

Not again!

How many times have I told myself, I'm not *like that,* and how many times have I found myself falling in love with another guy?! Of all people, why does it have to be him? Everybody knows you're not supposed to fall in love with a friend. Especially when you're a guy and *he's* a guy. A very Popular, very athletic, and very not *like that* in the least little bit kind of guy.

At least I think he's not . . .

Remember at Senior Breakfast when Tom pointed out how much fun he had the time him and Max and Brad and I all hung out together back in 7th grade calling the Party Line? Now I'm totally confused! Especially after that night he spent at my house a couple weeks ago. He made no qualms whatsoever about sleeping in my bed with me. Not even the next morning when we woke up—side by side—did he make any comments or jokes. In fact, the entire time I've been hanging around Tom Fulton, he hasn't said a single word about me being a fag or called me names or anything like I remember he used to.

Which leads me to believe that maybe Tom *is* . . . You know? *Like that.*

I wish there was some way to find out for sure. Believe me, I've tried. The other night we were looking for a last minute Christmas present for Tom to get Betsy out at Lakeside Mall—which is way far away from Hazeltucky out on Hall Road in Mt. Clemens and *way* cooler than Oakland and Universal put together. This fairly decent-looking older guy happened to pass us by. Tall, dark hair slightly graying at the temples. At which point, I pulled the old "If you were a girl, would you think that guy's hot?"

To which Tom replied, "Dude! Would *you?*" Then he gave me a look.

What makes matters worse is . . . Now that Brad wants nothing to do with me, Betsy's practically my Best Friend. She's definitely the person I spend the most time with, besides Max. During

Lunch, we go to my house for American cheese on white bread sandwiches. On the way over we always listen to our new favorite song, "I've Got My Mind Set on You" by George Harrison, which I picked up on cassette-single. Either that or the *La Bamba* soundtrack. Back in the Fall, Betsy and I went to see the movie four weekends in a row at The Berkley. She thinks the guy who played Ritchie Valens' brother is totally hot. So do I . . . But I haven't told her that!

She even spent the night at my house last Saturday when her parents went out of town and she didn't want to stay home all by herself. She slept in my brother's bed, of course, and he spent the night over his friend PJ's. We had a Total Blast staying up late, sitting on my floor watching TV, eating Tostino's frozen pizza, and talking. Which was when Betsy told me how much she really likes Tom.

"You guys haven't . . . You know?" I asked. By which I meant had S-E-X.

"No!" she insisted. Then she confided, "I think Tom wants to."

"He does?"

"He's a guy, isn't he? All guys wanna have sex."

To which I told her, "I'm a guy . . ."

"Yeah . . . But you're different." She gave me a smirk.

"What's that supposed to mean?" I asked, totally taking offense.

"Exactly what I said."

I bit into my slice. I love the tiny little pepperoni cubes, but I always scald the roof of my mouth on the steaming hot cheese. Which is exactly what I did just then. "Mother F—er!" I took a swig of Mountain Dew, the lime green sweetness temporarily soothing the pain. "So are you gonna?" I pried.

"Gonna what?" Betsy asked, all Little Miss Innocent.

"You *know* . . . Have S-E-X with T-O-M."

"I doubt it," she informed me. "I'm saving myself for my wedding night."

Which made me happy to know. I couldn't bear the thought of Betsy getting It on with Tom. Or the other way around, now that I think about it. I don't know what I'm going to do about this whole situation. All I know is . . . With tonight being New Year's Eve, the thought of being at Shellee Findlay's party and seeing Tom Fulton kiss Betsy Sheffield when the ball drops at Midnight . . . Makes me want to cry.

Did I mention I've been invited to my first Popular Party?

As you might remember . . . Jamie Good is on Staff of *The Hazel Parker*. And Jamie's Best Friend is Shellee Findlay. And being that Shellee and I go way back to the days of Webb Junior High when she used to remind me of "99 Luftballoons" Nena, Jamie told me of course I should come to Shellee's New Year's Eve Bash. Apparently *all* the Popular People are going to be there. Including the new Love of my Life, Tom Fulton. So you bet I'm going!

Right now it's 10:15 PM on December 31, 1987 . . .

I'm all dressed up in the new outfit I bought at Chess King in Lakeside—black pleated pants, charcoal gray sweater with zip up mock-turtleneck collar, and black dress shoes. Max just pulled up out front to give me a ride. I decided I didn't want to drive myself in case I drink too much. Besides, I figure I might as well be a Good Friend and lift Max along as I climb up the ladder of Popularity.

"Dude! I got beer," Max says the minute I slide into the front seat of the LeMans beside him.

"How'd you get beer?" I ask, picking up my cue.

To which he replies, "I got beer."

Shellee Findlay lives over in Ferndale on Harris, just a hop, skip, and a jump from our old Webb Junior High stomping grounds. I know her parents are out of town so I expect the party to be a little wild. But nothing prepares me for what we see once we get to her house . . . Cars everywhere! Up and down the street, in the driveway, even a few parked on the front lawn. Either that or they've been lifted and placed there by some drunk Jocks. Which, in Hazeltucky, is practically considered a Team Sport.

"What the Hell?!" Max grumbles, continuing to drive down the block. We end up around the corner on 10 Mile next to the humongous hole they've been digging for years to connect I-696 to I-96 out in Southfield. Supposedly it'll be finished by 1990, but I'm not holding my breath! Of course, I'm totally psyched when Max pulls up behind the '81 Impala belonging to You-Know-Who . . . Tom Fulton! This prompts me to promptly get out of the car and begin crunching my way through the snow, towards the blare of Salt-N-Pepa's "Push It."

Shellee's French Room is full to capacity with Jocks, Cheerleaders, and Vikettes—even a few Burn-Outs have made the cut. The minute Max enters the front door, twelve-pack of Bud tucked inconspicuously under the crook of his arm, we hear, "Wilson!"

The deep, masculine voice belongs to one Bobby Russell, who doesn't say a single word to me, of course. I'm a little surprised to see him here. Till I remember the "Dear Bobby" letter that Shellee wrote him back in 7th grade when she was still "Shelly with a Y" and they were going together . . . Guess they're friends again after all these years.

"Dude!" Max says to Bobby. He pops open a beer and takes a swig. "Wha's up?"

"Nothing, Dude," Bobby replies, his in-need-of-Visine eyes still not looking my way. "Can I grab one of those?" Then he helps himself to a Bud before asking, "Is Brad Dayton with you?"

For a minute I'm thinking, *I've got a secret, I've got a secret!* I'm almost tempted to ask Bobby if he's horny. But I would never say a word about what I know he once did with my former Best Friend. Instead, I snatch a beer from Max and make my way towards the kitchen in search of our Hostess. Or at least *somebody* I know. Betsy and Tom are supposed to be here . . . Where the Hell are they?

"Look you guys . . ."

Finally I hear a familiar voice. Unfortunately, the young girl standing in the corner by the mustard yellow refrigerator/freezer I know too well. I turn around just as she says to the group she's with, "It's my brother!"

Sure enough, my 13-year-old sister is here . . . I keep forgetting Jodi's a Parkerette and therefore knows a lot of the Vikette girls from various dance competitions and whatnot. Which explains why she's hanging out with Marie Sperling, Lynn Kelly, and Angela Andrews, all ear-to-ear grin and butt-wasted, her lips stained cherry red from what I'm guessing is the half-empty Seagram's wine cooler she's trying to conceal at her side.

"What are *you* doing here?" Jodi asks, surprised to see me.

Unlike her former Band Fag brother, my sister is pretty Popular in the social circles of Webb Junior High. And since she's starting as a Freshman at Hillbilly High next Fall, I take it she's getting an early jump on the Popular Party scene.

"What do you think?" I reply. Followed by, "What are *you* doing here?"

"What do *you* think?"

Suddenly our Brother/Sister Act is momentarily interrupted . . .

"Jacques!"

My heart drops to the proverbial pit of my stomach. Suddenly, I feel as shit-faced stupid as my sister. Only I'm drunk on L-O-V-E when I see Tom Fulton enter, looking ever so handsome in the navy blue and forest green plaid button-down I helped him pick out of the J. Crew catalogue, worn with the new pair of Tommy "Hilfinger" jeans he got last week from Santa Claus . . . He totally loves them on account of his name also being "Tommy." But I haven't got the heart to tell him it's Hil*figer.*

"Tommy!" I bellow, affecting my own Jock Jerk tone. Then I leave my sister to the Popular People after making her promise she won't drink too much.

"Dude!" Tommy says as I sidle up beside him. "You getting some action over there?" He takes a swig of his Magnum 40. I can't help but notice the way his Adam's apple bobs up and down when he swallows. Talk about sexy!

"Dude!" I make a face. "That's my sister."

Tom does a double take. "She's hot, Dude."

"She's in 8th grade," I inform him, so he doesn't get any ideas. Besides, he's got his own girlfriend. Who's nowhere to be seen at the moment. "Where's Betsy?"

"Fuck if I know." He drains the last of his beverage before letting rip the most disgusting belch. I'm guessing he had cabbage for dinner. "She got pissed at me and said she wasn't coming."

"It's New Year's Eve," I say, trying to sound concerned. "You want me to give her a call?"

"Fuck her!" Tom replies all cocky. Which secretly makes me jump for joy deep down inside. Not that I have anything against Betsy, 'cause I don't. But this way, I won't be the only one without Somebody Special to kiss at the stroke of Midnight.

Around 11:30 PM Tom says, "This party's lame . . . You wanna get out of here?" I watch as he spits into the empty beer bottle he holds. A bit of juice drips black and minty down his chin. I'm tempted to reach out and wipe it away . . . But I don't.

As much as I'm against smoking, I think there's something kind of sexy about seeing Tom's lower lip all fat and swollen with chew. By which I mean chewing tobacco. I also like the way the little round tin leaves a faded ring around the ass pocket on his jeans. Not to mention the sound it makes when he shakes it back and forth, thumping the lid with his thumb. I have no idea why he does this. All I know is . . . I love it! Most of the Jocks at Hillbilly High are all "Dippin' Dudes," as Tom calls them. Personally, I think they're all idiots for rotting their lips away . . . All except my Tommy Boy, that is.

"What else do you wanna do?" I ask, feeling the effects of my third beer—or is it my fourth?—trying not to slur my words like a Total Drunk.

"We can go back to your place and hang out," Tom suggests. "Bring some brewskis . . . Get fucked up." Then he adds, "I'm still spending the night, ain't I?"

"If you still wanna," I answer, trying not to sound too excited. I can't even believe this is happening. Am I really about to get my wish? I'm going to spend New Year's Eve with the new Love of my Life all by myself . . . All we have to do now is make it back to my house without getting into a car crash.

"Has anybody seen Max Wilson?" We pass through the room of Popular People on our way to the front door. Of course, nobody bothers to answer me one way or another. They're all too busy standing around like zombies, banging their heads up and down to some new band I can't stand in the least bit called Bon Jovi. I mean, maybe the lead singer is kind of hot. In that skinny, long-haired, and in-need-of-a-shower kind of way. But to me, it might as well be Heavy Metal. Have you heard that one song, "Livin' on a Prayer?" Me and Max like to sing different lyrics to it . . .

"Whooah, I'm halfway in
Whooah, cummin' on a friend
Take my dick and I'll shove it right in
Whooah, cummin' on a friend . . ." (Gross!)

When I finally find Max, he's standing in the corner of the French Room with Shellee Findlay—smoking a Capri cigarette. Talk about setting a Bad Example! Everybody knows Cheerleaders of all people aren't allowed to smoke. But I don't even care. Because I'm about to head back to my house with Tom Fulton, the Homecoming King of Hillbilly High. And with any luck, we'll be doing more than watching *Dick Clark* at the stroke of Midnight.

"Dude! You can't smoke that feminine thing," I tell Max, plainly and simplely, as he tries to hide the Capri from my sight.

At which point, he begins having one of his giggle fits. His face turns beet red and he doesn't actually make any sound. But his head starts bobbing on his neck and he begins to choke. I'm thinking, *That's what you get for smoking!*

I tell Max, "We're out of here."

He whines, "But it's not even Midnight, yet."

I say, "You can stay . . . I'm leaving with Tom." And with that, we make our exit. Somehow I don't think anybody will miss us.

It's a good thing Tom's a big guy and has a high tolerance for alcohol. The entire time we're walking down the street to his "Brown Boat," I'm practically tripping over myself. Which is why I decide to hop on Tom's back and let him carry me the rest of the way.

"Dude!" he cries out, soon as I knock him off balance. "What the fuck?" But he doesn't tell me to get off him either. So I continue holding on for dear life.

Oh, my God . . . I can't even tell you how delirious I am at this moment. And it's not just because I've had one too many beers. With my arms wrapped around his neck, I let my head rest against Tom's back. His massively giant back that ripples with muscles I can never imagine having. God, I want his body! By which I don't just mean, "I want a body like his . . ."

I *want* his body.

"Easy there, Big Guy . . ." Tom drops me to the ground beside his car. "We've got a long night of celebrating."

I tug at the door handle. "It's stuck," I groan.

"Dude! I gotta unlock it for ya, first." Then he does so, opening the door for me as I crawl inside. Like a Total Gentleman.

While we're driving down 10 Mile, I close my eyes, lean back in my seat. Cold vinyl cradles my swirling head as streetlights bathe me in comfort. At any moment, I'll be safe at home, in the confines of my own four walls, where the Outside World can't get in.

"Now what?"

Back at my house we break out the Buds that we pilfered from Shellee Findlay's fridge before we beat our retreat. I barely finish half a can when I'm ready to call it a night. I hear Tom say, "Dude! You're a lightweight." Then I pass out on my bed.

Next thing I see are the numerals 3-5-8 glowing red in the dark . . .

Fully clothed I wake up, the room pitch black. To my right, lying with his back to me, Tom Fulton snores away. "Dude," I whisper. "Move over . . . You're hogging all the room."

"Zzzz . . ."

"Dude!" I say, this time a little louder. "Scootch over, would ya?"

I give him a gentle push. At which point I realize he's got his shirt off.

Oh, my God . . .

I allow my hand to remain a moment. Firm and round, I give his bare shoulder a playful squeeze. Like a baseball. My fingers work their way across his traps, up to his neck. Then down his back, soft and smooth, I begin tickling ever so lightly. With my index finger, I begin writing little words—letter by letter—between his shoulder blades.

I.

Then I write another.

L.

Followed by another.

O.

And another.

V.

And—

"Dude!" From out of nowhere, Tom pipes up, "What the fuck are you doing?"

Slowly, my hand retreats. "You were snoring," I tell him. Then I roll over and attempt to go back to sleep. "Good night."

Tom says nothing.

Hopelessly Devoted To You

"But now there's nowhere to hide
Since you pushed my love aside . . ."

—Olivia Newton-John

Just my luck!

How am I supposed to know that Big Boy's on 9 Mile and I-75 serves as the Hillbilly High Drama Queers Post-Show Hang Out? Which might explain why several Cast and Crew members from the Spring Musical have just invaded the place. Of course, I pretend not to see Brad and Joey and Audrey and Ava as they're seated in the Smoking Section across the way from where Betsy Sheffield and I sit on opposite sides in our booth.

"What did you think of the play, tonight?" I ask, dumping a blue and white packet of sugar into my large Sprite, followed by a squeeze of lemon. Mount St. Helens erupts.

"It was good," Betsy replies, dipping a rather fat French fry into some ketchup. "I still like the movie better." She's talking about the 1978 Paramount Pictures blockbuster, *Grease.*

One of my all time favorites—right up there with *Sooner or*

Later and *Somewhere in Time*—my obsession began in the Summer of '78 with *Grease Day U.S.A.* In case you missed it, this was a televised broadcast of the official Premiere Party at Grauman's Chinese Theatre in Hollywood. The TV Special featured the entire Cast from the film as well as other famous '70s icons, including a pre-*National Lampoon's Vacation* Chevy Chase, my Aunt Sonia's look-alike, Penny Marshall, and Bee Gees Baby Brother, Andy.

Poor Andy Gibb . . . I'm still in shock over the report of his untimely death last week at the ripe old age of 30. Who knew he had such a problem with drugs and alcohol? While he was never one to compete with the likes of Rex Smith in my 8-year-old eyes, I'll admit to the flutter of butterflies in my stomach the first time I heard Andy Gibb sing "I Just Wanna Be Your Everything" on *American Bandstand* two years prior. I remember my cousins Rachael and Rhonda had his *Shadow Dancing* album. I'll never forget the cover with Mr. Gibb in that red shirt, open at the collar, chest hair popping out.

But back to *Grease* . . . Ten years later, as far as I'm concerned, it's still "The Word." Though I can't even believe it's really 1988, after all these years of waiting.

Back when I was in 3rd grade, my Mom hosted a T-shirt Party. Which is kind of like a Tupperware Party, only T-shirts with iron-on decals are sold instead of plastic food storage containers with airtight lids. I'll never forget the Royal blue *Grease* T-shirt I got this one particular time. A picture of Sandy and Danny, aka Olivia Newton-John and John Travolta, sporting their "You're the One that I Want" gear with the GREASE car logo above them adorned the front. On the back, my name, JACKIE, ironed on in black faux-velvet letters above a large number 88. I remember one of my non-straight-A classmates asking me the most stupid question the day I came proudly bounding into Mrs. Fox's class sporting my new T . . . "What's the 88 stand for?"

"It's the year we're gonna graduate," I informed him, trying not to sound too snotty. Though I would've preceded my reply with "Duh!" had people started using that expression way back then.

The entire Summer when *Grease* first came out, I begged my Mom to take me to see it. But for whatever reason, I guess she didn't find the content appropriate for her 8-year-old Jackie. It didn't matter that her husband had already taken him and his 4-year-old sister Jodi to see *Jaws 2* at the Galaxy Drive-In, and in that movie, people got eaten alive by a Great White shark! Instead, I had to spend my entire 3rd grade year at Longfellow School listening to my classmates talk about how they had all seen *Grease* and what a great movie it was, etc., etc.

I remember some boys in my class even had *Grease* trading cards. Kind of like baseball cards, only with pictures of Danny Zuko and Sandy Olsson instead of Reggie Jackson or Nolan Ryan. During Free Time, they'd gather together in the corner of Mrs. Fox's room, trading their cards, all the while saying the most disgustingly vulgar things about Poor Olivia Newton-John. By which I mean sexual. Don't ask me where they learned them from at their age!

That same year, I met Joey Palladino and we immediately bonded over the fact that we were both big *Grease* fans. Even though neither of us had yet to see the movie. Sometimes after school, Joey would come over my house and we'd put on my *Grease* 8-track. Then we'd sing and dance around my room, pretending we were John Travolta and Olivia Newton-John. Of course, Joey *always* got to be Danny. Even though both our last names are technically Italian, I never really looked it with my blond hair and blue eyes. Plus I had that over-the-ear longer hairstyle. On top of the fact that I sang soprano in Music. Unfortunately, in our production, Sandy never got to kiss Danny on the beach as the orchestra swelled to a climax during "Love is a Many Splendored Thing."

I'm happy to report that I eventually did get to see *Grease*. But not till it had been out for almost an entire year and it made its way to the Dollar Show on 9 Mile and John R, adjacent to Farmer Jack's. Somehow, Rachael and Rhonda and I conned our Moms into finally taking us. Looking back now, I can't even believe we ever pulled it off. The Northgate Cinema located next to the infamous Time Zone Arcade—next to Randazzo's Pizza—was a Total Pit. Though I'll never forget the feeling of excitement coupled with the fear of being mugged as I waited in line, my tiny red ticket in my hot little hand.

Of course, I'd already read my *Grease* FOTONOVEL™ about a bijillion times by this point so I knew the entire story. Though I didn't realize those thought bubbles in the pictures weren't actually part of the dialogue. But from the first animated frame, the vocal stylings of Frankie Valli sans The Four Seasons transported me to Heaven. I don't think I took my eyes off that dilapidated screen for a split second.

You can probably imagine my excitement when, on the first day back from Christmas Vacation this year, Mr. Dell'Olio announced to the entire student body: "The 1988 Spring Musical is going to be . . ." Insert drum roll here.

In case you're not aware . . . Before *Grease* ever found its way to the Silver Screen, it started as a play on Broadway back in like 1972, starring the guy who played Brad in *The Rocky Horror Picture Show* as Danny, and some woman I've never heard of, Carole Demas, as Sandy Dumbrowski. That's right! In the stage version, her name's not Sandy Olsson. What's more shocking is . . . She isn't even from Australia! She's a transfer student to Rydell High from some Catholic School somewhere.

Which isn't the only discrepancy . . .

The T-Birds aren't the "T-Birds," they're the "Burger Palace Boys." Putzie isn't "Putzie," he's "Roger." Miss McGee is called "Miss Lynch," and a bunch of the songs from the movie aren't in the play at all. Including "Hopelessly Devoted to You," "You're the One that I Want," and the title song, "Grease." Which was written by the late Andy Gibb's older brother, Barry, did you know? Back when I was a kid, I borrowed a copy of the Original Cast Recording from my Uncle Roy, only to discover how bad the original singers sounded. Though Adrienne Barbeau of TV's *Maude* did a halfway decent job as Rizzo with "There Are Worse Things I Could Do."

As much as I contemplated it, in no way was I going to try out for the Hillbilly High production. Like I've said, the only thing worse than being a Band Fag is . . . being a Drama Queer. Again, I don't make the rules. I just try to abide by them. Besides, I had a feeling that Brad was going to be in it for sure. Last I heard, he'd pretty much made up his mind about heading to New York City come September to pursue his acting career.

In fact, one day after school last semester, I was in the back room of *The Hazel Parker* office, copyediting the piece Claire Moody finally submitted, titled "PREPS WAGE WAR ON SKIDS," when I overheard Dell having a conversation with somebody . . .

"Would you mind writing me a letter of recommendation for my Juilliard application?" the familiar-sounding voice asked.

"You got it," Mr. Dell'Olio replied. "When's the audition?"

I peeked my head around the corner. Sure enough, there stood Brad Dayton, looking like a Poet decked out in all black, his red hair sticking out from beneath a black beret, wilder and curlier than ever.

"Sometime in January," he told Dell. "I gotta go to New York for it and everything."

"This is exciting," said Dell, looking over the application.

"Totally," Brad agreed. "Too bad I don't know how I'm gonna afford a plane ticket."

"I'm sure you'll work something out," Dell said with a wink and a smile. Knowing him, he'd pay for Brad's trip to NYC himself. That's just the kind of guy he is. On top of the fact that in all the years of Mr. Dell'Olio teaching Drama at Hillbilly High, nobody's ever shown the dedication and talent to the Art of Acting as Bradley Dayton . . . At least that's what Dell's been telling the entire Staff of *The Hazel Parker* on a daily basis since *Grease* rehearsals began in February.

"Wait till you guys see the show," Dell gushed just yesterday. "It's the best play I've directed since I was at Northern." By which he means Northern Michigan University in Marquette. In case you're not aware, NMU is all the way up in "da UP"—as in Upper Peninsula—where there's nothing but a bunch of Finnish immigrants and it's fuh-reezing cold nine months out of the year.

What I couldn't figure out was . . . If Brad Dayton is supposedly such a good actor, how come he wasn't playing the lead role of Danny Zuko?

Did I mention who is? None other than . . . Insert drum roll here.

Though you probably won't be surprised at the answer. But I'll admit, I was. My jaw practically dropped to the floor the day Mr. Dell'Olio posted the Cast List on the door outside the Auditorium.

GREASE

—CAST—

Danny Zuko .... Joey Palladino
Sandy Dumbrowski .... Liza Larson
Kenickie .... Will Isaacs

Doody..Brad Dayton
Roger...Keith Treva
Sonny..Allen Bryan
Rizzo...Jamie Good
Frenchy...Audrey Wojczek
Jan.......................................Tuesday Gunderson
Miss Lynch..Ava Reese
Eugene Florczyk........................Charlie Richardson
Patty Simcox................................Michelle Winters
Johnny Casino/Teen Angel.................Ron Reynolds
Vince Fontaine......................................Richie Tyler
Cha-Cha DiGregorio.....................Diane Thompson

Actually, what surprised me most was seeing Jamie Good's name on the list. Being that she's a Popular Cheerleader and has a million other things going on, I didn't think she'd lower herself to the level of Drama Queer.

"Duh!" Jamie replied, when I asked her why she auditioned. "It's *Grease*."

A lot of my former Band Fag friends are also in the show. Which made it a lot more difficult the day Mr. Dell'Olio informed me that as Editor-in-Chief of *The Hazel Parker*, I had been assigned to write a review.

"But Dell . . ." I did my best to protest. "I don't know the first thing about Drama." Even though I was dying to see the play, now that I knew who was going to be in it, how could I sit through the show?

"But me no buts, Paterno," I was told. "You've got two tickets for Opening Night . . . Be there."

And I was . . . I mean, we were. Me and Betsy Sheffield.

I'll admit the production was indeed good. Despite the differences from the movie, the basic story was still intact . . . "Boy

Gets Girl, Boy Loses Girl after Denying He Knows Who She Is, Prompting Girl to Change so She Can Win Him Back, Only to Find He's Changed Too." And as much as I hate to say it, Joey Palladino made a pretty much perfect Danny. Guess all that practicing he and I did together back in 3rd grade finally paid off.

Jamie Good did a "good" job as Rizzo—I'll be using that in my review—and Audrey was spot-on as Didi Conn, I mean Frenchy. You could totally tell she's seen the movie almost as much as I have. Though the colored spray she used on her hair during "Beauty School Drop Out" didn't look quite pink enough. And Brad surprised me with his rendition of "Magic Changes," which is only in the movie as a Sha Na Na song in the background at the Dance Off. I hadn't heard him sing since *Oklahomo!* back in 10th grade and his voice has really improved. Maybe he *does* have a shot at making it on Broadway someday.

But the real Star of the Show had to be Senior Liza Larson as Sandy Dumbrowski. Being a self-proclaimed Burn-Out, she normally wears her hair kind of curled and feathered-back on the sides or all ratted up. But when she made her entrance, all decked out in a pink poodle skirt with her bleached blond hair pulled back in a ponytail, Liza was a dead ringer for Olivia Newton-John. Without her signature spider eyebrow-penciled in the corner of her eye, I almost didn't recognize her. And when she sang "It's Raining on Prom Night," which is also only in the movie as a background song at The Frosty Palace, she totally brought the house down.

Once the final curtain closed and the lights came up, the crowd began gathering down by the stage in anticipation of the actors making their entrance. The last thing I needed was to be faced with the likes of Joey Palladino, Brad Dayton, Ava Reese, and Audrey Wojczek. Which is why I wanted to get the Hell out of there! Though I would've liked to have told Jamie Good what a "good" job I thought she did, it could wait till Monday.

"Where to now?"

It was Betsy's turn to drive so I slipped into the passenger seat of the silver Vega, taking note how low to the ground it felt compared to my pea green Omni. "You wanna stop at EB's and grab a bite on our way home?" I suggested.

Which brings us back to Square One. Jack and Betsy avoiding the Drama Queers over Slim Jims at Elias Brothers' Big Boy . . .

"You think he's a fag?" Betsy asks when the entire *Grease* gang passes by our table—without saying a word—en route to the Salad Bar.

"Who?" I wonder. She could be talking about either Brad, Joey, or even Little Richie Tyler who just joined them a minute ago. Remember the faggy little 7th grader from Webb who played flute in Prep Band and carried his books like a girl? I can't even believe Brad is hanging out with him after all these years . . . What's up with that?!

"Joey Palladino," Betsy replies, blatantly looking over at the Boy in Question.

"He's got a girlfriend," I remind her. As in my ex, Diane Thompson, who must have arrived with Richie and is clinging to Joey as we speak.

"So what?" Betsy replies, mouth full of ham and Swiss. "My Uncle Dave's a Detroit Cop . . . He busted a bunch of underage kids from Hazel Park down at some gay bar on Woodward and 6 Mile. He says one of them was named Joey and the other one Brad."

I'm thinking, *Interesting* . . . I wonder how come I haven't heard this? But I say, "So . . . Just because they were at a gay bar doesn't make them fags."

"Oh, come on!" Betsy scowls. "Why the Hell would they go to a gay bar if they're not?"

"I don't know . . ." Then for whatever reason, I decide to go for it. "I've been to that exact same bar before and *I'm* not . . ." Then I trail off.

Betsy looks at me a moment. She sips her Diet Coke, says nothing.

"What?" I ask, getting the feeling Something Wicked is This Way Coming.

"I never told you what Tom said, did I?" she says.

I'm thinking, *Oh, shit!* But I play innocent. "About . . . ?"

"About you."

What I've yet to mention is what else happened when Tom spent the night at my house back on New Year's Eve . . .

After he woke up in the middle of the night and found me fondling his bare back, what else could I say? Nothing. I couldn't even defend myself had I wanted to on account of I had a Total Breakdown. I started crying and carrying on and apologizing. Talk about embarrassing!

"Dude!" Tom said, a little aggravated. "What's wrong with you?"

"I don't know anymore," I cried. Literally. "I just feel . . ." Then I trailed off. All I wanted was for Tom to wrap his arms around me and hold me and tell me everything would be okay.

Instead he said, "What the fuck is your problem?" From the way he raised his voice, I could tell Tom was getting pissed. To be honest, I think he knew what I was trying to say—and I don't think he liked it. "Don't even tell me you're a fag . . . Are you?"

If I said "No," I'd be lying. If I said "Yes," and told Tom that not only did I think I *might* be gay, I also *might* be in love with him, he'd walk out the door never to return. Not to mention the fact that he'd tell all the guys at school what happened and they'd finally have the satisfaction of knowing what they'd been saying about me for years was 100 percent True.

So all I said was, "I'm sorry."

To which he informed me, "I gotta go." Though I couldn't help but notice he didn't look at me when he spoke.

"What about the game?" I mumbled. We'd made plans to hang out on New Year's Day and watch Michigan State in the Rose Bowl on TV.

I watched as Tom found his shirt where he left it wadded up in a ball on the floor. Slipping it on, he didn't even take time to button it . . . Nor did he say a word.

I suggested, "Maybe we can go to the movies tomorrow night." *Throw Momma from the Train* had just come out a few weeks before and we'd been talking about seeing it. Tom loves Billy Crystal. Then I added, "Call me?"

But he never did.

When I broke down and later called him myself, Tom's Dad informed me he wasn't home. The first two times. By the third, I heard his Mom in the background say, "You're being rude," forcing him to take my call.

And would you like to know what he said when I finally spoke to him?

"You know, all my friends told me not to hang out with you 'cause you're a fag . . . But I stood up for you. And you totally let me down."

And he was right . . . How could I have done such a thing?

Back at Big Boy's on *Grease* Opening Night . . .

"What exactly did Tom say about me?" I ask Betsy, who pretty much reiterates everything I've just mentioned. Which prompts me to wonder, "What did you say when he told you that?"

"I told him to shut the fuck up," she scoffs, all Bad Ass. "Then I broke up with him."

So that's the reason! I had no idea.

"Nobody makes up shit about my friend and gets away with it," Betsy Sheffield declares with conviction. "I don't care if he's the hottest guy at Hillbilly High or not." Then she adds, "He wasn't a very good kisser, anyways."

I'm thinking, *Too bad I'll never find out.*

Sign Your Name

"Time I'm sure will bring
Disappointments in so many things . . ."

—Terence Trent D'Arby

If I play my cards right, I might be having S-E-X . . . With a G-I-R-L.

Who would've believed it, right? Jack Paterno, ex-Band Fag—and probable Real Fag—is about to get laid for the first time in his 17-going-on-18-year-old life. Though isn't that what Max and I set out to do as we embarked on our Spring Break '88 Florida Adventure?

First stop Winter Haven . . .

We arrived five days ago on Good Friday, April 1st. My Grandpa Guff picked me and "Matt" up at the airport and brought us back to stay with him for the first few days. I didn't have the heart to tell him my friend's name is *Max.*

Not a whole lot was going on in terms of what you might call "action" at the old Hammondell Campground . . .

"Hey, listen to this . . ." Max tapped me on the shoulder. We were lying side by side by the deserted pool. Which was pretty nice for a trailer park. Though I can't imagine the Senior Citizens getting much use out of it. Nor did I want to see a bunch of Old People in bathing suits!

I opened my eyes, squinting. Max took off his headphones and held them out to me. From the two gray sponges connected by thin metal wire, I could hear the tinny sound of something melodic . . .

"She said: 'Eh, I know you, and you cannot sing'
I said: 'That's nothing . . . You should hear me play piano.'"

I can't say I recognized the voice. "Who is it?" I asked. More out of politeness than actual interest.

Max replied, "Dude! It's The Smiths." As if I should've known. "Don't you love the way Morrissey says, 'Pee-eh-noh?'"

I asked, "Who's Morrissey?" Then I rolled over onto my stomach.

Max and I agreed we wanted to look our best by the time we hit the beach later in the week, so we'd been working on our tans every day from 10:00 AM to 2:00 PM. "For the ladies," as Max so eloquently put it. Little does Poor Max know that I've recently had my heart broken—by a guy!

I only hope we don't run into Tom Fulton and all his Jock Jerk Friends while we're here in Daytona . . .

"You ready to par-tay?"

We arrived this morning after driving almost two hours in my Grandpa Guff's pickup truck—complete with cab on the back. Max and I met up with Jamie Good, Shellee Findlay, and Betsy Sheffield at their hotel and we spent the day with them hanging out at the beach. Talk about crazy! I've never seen so many half-naked and totally hot guys running around in one place. It's taken all I've got in me not to get too excited, if you know what I mean.

Around 8:00 PM, we showered, got dressed, and were just about to head out. God only knows where! I put on my red shorts and new white T-shirt with red SPEEDO across the chest that I got on sale at Hudson's in Lakeside Mall, so I figured it had to be cool.

"Cool shirt," Betsy confirmed when we met her downstairs in the hotel lobby. Sporting a navy blue and white horizontally striped, long baggy shirt over matching navy shorts, she looked as cute as could be. Especially with her hair pulled up in a ponytail.

We found Jamie and Shellee out front talking with some dudes I'd never seen before. "You guys are Cheerleaders?" I heard one of them ask, obviously clued in by Jamie's and Shellee's matching oversized *Cheerleader* T-Shirts. "Where you from?"

"Hazel Park," Shellee told him.

"Where's that?" You could tell just by the way this guy had his hair cut—short and buzzed on the sides—he's a Total Jock. He also had no neck.

"Near Detroit," answered Jamie.

No Neck's friend looked puzzled for a moment. "Dee-troit's in Ohio, right?"

"Yeah . . . Ohio," Shellee replied. Then she noticed me and Max standing with Betsy. "Oh, look . . . Our boyfriends are here. We gotta go."

And off we went!

I imagine Daytona Beach to be pretty much dead most of the year. But during Spring Break, a Sea of Teens floods the street, parading up and down and up and down Highway A1A. Better known as "The Strip."

"Where are we going?" I asked, trying not to sound too whiny. I'll admit, I felt a bit overwhelmed traveling from hotel to hotel looking for The Party.

"Following her," Max replied, tongue hanging out of his mouth as some Blond Bimbo in an itsy-bitsy pink and white polka-dot bikini passed us by. Like I've said, Max was bound and determined to lose It on this trip. By which I mean his Virginity. And in what better place than among hundreds of Horny Teenagers?

"Hey, you Guys . . . In here!"

We stopped off for a moment at some Cheap Motel. You know, the kind where the entrance to the room leads right out into the parking lot. Forget about there being any kind of lobby or even an ice machine. At Check Out, you walk up to some guy in a tiny little room behind a door marked OFFICE and pay your bill—most likely with cash.

Max and I found ourselves surrounded by a group of kids neither of us knew from anywhere. Most of them had slight Southern accents and I heard somebody say something about Tennessee—or was it Texas? Somewhere starting with T. To be honest, I'd already had two beers back at our hotel and was feeling a little tipsy.

"Dude!" Max said to the totally wasted looking guy who beckoned us in. "Wha's up?"

"Nada, Dude . . ." And with that, Wasted Guy handed us both a can of Bud and said, "Party on!" He kind of reminded me of the guy who played Johnny in *Karate Kid, Part II.* You know who I'm talking about? He was also in that movie *Just One of the Guys* as Greg Tolan. Kind of good-looking and muscle-bound, but like No Neck and Friend from before, not too bright . . . Why is it that all the hottest guys seem sooo stupid?

"Thanks," I replied, accepting Wasted Guy's offer. Then I popped open my beer, only to have it explode right in my face. Foam shot out across the room, drenching the girl standing next to me.

She let out a squeal. "You idiot!"

Wasted Guy started laughing his head off like it was the funniest thing he ever saw. Then he slinked away.

"Sorry," I said to the girl, looking for a napkin or something to assist her. Coming up empty-handed, I watched as she wiped at the wet spot on her extremely tight white tank top, barely concealing a pair of incredibly large breasts.

" 's all right," she replied in her slight trace of a Southern accent. "Not your fault, Sugar." Then she smiled, batting her Baby Blues.

If I didn't know better, I'd have thought this very pretty Southern Belle was flirting with me. But that couldn't possibly be the case. I mean this girl looked like a model. I'm talking 35-25-35. Long blond hair, nice legs . . . and thin! She kind of reminded me of Miss USA/Universe 1980, Shawn Weatherly. Remember her? She later went on to have a career as an actress in such hits as *Cannonball Run II* and *Police Academy 3: Back in Training*.

Max whispered in my ear, "Go for it, Dude . . ." And with that, he slinked away.

"So . . . What's your name?" The Shawn Weatherly look-alike asked me. Her breath smelled of alcohol and I got the impression she was probably already inebriated.

I told her, "Jack." Then I asked, "What's yours?"

To which she answered, "Gwendy." Though I could barely hear her over the roar of the crowd.

I said, "Wendy?"

She said, "No . . . Gwendy, with a G."

Turns out, Gwendy—short for Gwendolyn—was also 17, and a Senior from Austin, "Tayx-sis." A Cheerleader, she also played Girls Volleyball. She also made it perfectly clear she didn't have a boyfriend.

"What about you?" she asked.

"Do I have a boyfriend?" I replied, thinking, *She thinks I'm a fag!*

"No, Sugar . . . I meant, do you have a *girl*friend?" Gwendy reached out and tweaked my nose with her finger. "You're cute . . . You must be very Popular back where you come from."

I assured her, I did not have a girlfriend. Though I avoided her question pertaining to my level of Popularity in the World that is Hillbilly High. Then I decided, "I should probably go find my friend."

With that, Gwendy linked her arm in mine. "Wait for me." Then we slinked away.

It appeared that Max had also made himself a new friend. In the corner of the room, Gwendy and I found him surrounded by a circle of Gwendy's classmates—literally.

"Dude . . . Here's what you're gonna do." The practical joker known as Wasted Guy, aka Johnny from *Karate Kid, Part II,* stood in the center of the group. In one hand he held an extremely large funnel attached to a long plastic hose. "You're gonna get down on your knees . . ."

Max nodded, glassy-eyed. "Uh-huh."

"You're gonna put this hose up to your mouth . . ."

"Uh-huh."

"Then you're gonna tilt your head back . . . And suck."

"Gotcha."

Max followed Wasted Guy's instructions to the best of his drunken ability. He got down on his knees and took the end of the hose into his mouth. Meanwhile, Wasted Guy cracked open a can of PBR and poured it into the funnel. The crowd began to chant, "Suck, suck, suck!" Down the hose went the hops as Max inhaled for dear life. In a matter of seconds, he stood up, belched, the beer completely gone.

"Dude!" he exclaimed when he saw me standing nearby. "I did it . . . I bonged my first beer." Then he puked all over the orange shag carpet.

You'd think the stench of regurgitated pilsner mixed with Taco Bell would promptly clear the room. But nobody even noticed. They just passed the bong along to the Next Victim and continued to Party On!

Me, I played my part as Max's Sole Friend and led him outside. I figured the cool ocean breeze would do him some good and had no idea what happened to Jamie, Shellee, and Betsy after we found ourselves Deep in the Heart of Tayx-sis.

"Sit here," I said, indicating the yellow cement parking block at our feet.

Max followed my orders. Then he placed his head between his legs and let out a groan. "Sorry, Dude . . . I always puke whenever I smoke pot."

Even though I totally disapproved of Max's getting high, I told him, "Don't worry about it, Dude . . . I won't tell anybody you ralphed."

"We should get him somethin' to drink," Gwendy advised. "There's a 7-Eleven over on the corner."

For the entire walk across the street, Gwendy held my hand. Almost every single guy we passed did a double take. I could tell they were all thinking, *What the Hell is the Babe doing with the Fag?* Little did they realize, the Babe was totally wasted and once she sobered up, she'd be thinking the exact same thing.

One of the things I've noticed about Florida is . . . nobody here wears shoes. Not even when they go into a public place like 7-Eleven. Back in Michigan, that would never fly. Nobody would dare walk barefoot into Farmer Jack's, just because they didn't feel like stopping to put on their sandals! You know what I'm saying?

We found some Gatorade. I doubted Max would like it. He

only ever drinks Pepsi. But Gwendy assured me it would help. Standing at the register, I took some money out to pay for it.

"And a pack of Virginia Slim Ultra Light Menthols, Sugar," Gwendy said to the clerk behind the counter. Though I don't think he heard her at first on account of he was too busy staring at her tits.

Just my luck . . . Finally, a beautiful girl—albeit a wasted one—takes an interest in me and she's a smoker! It's all I can do not to gag the minute we stepped back into the night air and she lit one up. Again, she took my hand and led me across Highway A1A, back to what I discovered was the Thunderbird Beach Motel.

Where Max was nowhere to be found . . .

Luckily, when we asked some of Gwendy's friends if they'd seen him, they informed us that Max decided to head back to our hotel. I had no idea how he was going to get into Jamie and Shellee and Betsy's room. But that wasn't my problem.

Which leads me back to the point where I started . . . The part where I'm about to have sex with a girl.

"You wanna take a walk on the beach?" Gwendy asks me now. "It's a gorgeous night . . ."

I have to agree: 75°, a gentle breeze, the moon shining down upon us. Very romantic. Like something you'd see in a movie or on TV. "Sure," I say.

When I take Gwendy's hand, she pauses. "I could use another drink . . . Can we stop by my car first?"

I'm thinking, *Anything to keep her from sobering up and changing her mind.* Though I have no idea where this whole thing is really heading. And what happens if she really *does* wanna have sex with me? I mean, yes, there is a condom pressing a nice ring into the leather of my wallet. But in all honesty, I don't know the first thing about having sex. Especially with a girl!

I mean, I've seen movies and all. By which I mean porno.

Tom and I once borrowed a video from my Uncle Roy back when we first started hanging out together. He came over one Monday night to watch our new favorite TV show, *ALF*. Who also happens to be our Senior Class Mascot. Afterwards, we got to talking about porno. Next thing I know, we're watching some movie called *Teenage Games* with some totally tan, totally muscular blond guy named François Papillion, with a butterfly tattoo on his ass. Sure, I had no problem getting excited watching the video. That François guy was hot! But what if I can't get it up when it comes time to do It with Gwendy?

Inside her white Pontiac Grand Am, we sit passing a bottle of Baileys back and forth between us. "You like it, Sugar?" she asks.

I can't say I've ever had Irish Cream before. But it's good. Sweet and creamy, of course. I place the bottle to my lips, taking a sip. Just as I'm about to pass it back to Gwendy, I hear a tap on the window. Quickly, I stash the bottle down on the floor at my feet. Which is a good thing as there's a Man in Blue now standing beside the car.

He motions for me to roll down the window. To which I promptly comply. Minding my manners, I say, "Good evening, Officer . . ." Which almost comes out "Occifer." Partly because that's an old joke with me and my friends. And partly because I'm now occifially—I mean, officially—drunk. Who knew Irish Cream was so potent?!

"Step out of the car, would you?" Mr. Occifer asks, minding *his* manners.

At which point Gwendy and I do as we're told. She gets out on her side, me on mine. I feel like we should put our hands up. Though it's not like we're Armed and Dangerous. Unless you count a fifth of Baileys in the hands of a couple of 17-going-on-18-year-olds as an illegal weapon.

Now maybe it's because I'm down here in Daytona Beach

on Spring Break where nobody knows me. Or maybe it's because I'm trying to show off in front of Gwendy so I can get laid . . . But the next thing I know, I hear myself say in a voice reminiscent of *Leave it to Beaver*'s own Eddie Haskell, "What seems to be the trouble, Officer . . ." I pause a moment, focusing on the blurry name on his badge, DIAZ. He kind of reminds me of Erik Estrada, need I say more?

Officer Diaz replies, "All right, son . . . Hand over the beer."

Maybe it's because I've had a little too much to drink. Or maybe it's because I'm trying to show off in front of Gwendy so I can get laid . . . But the next thing I know, I turn into Billy Bad Ass!

"What beer?" I ask. "I don't have any beer." Which is true. Because I don't.

"Come on, son . . . Don't give me a hassle, all right?"

"I don't know *what* you're talking about," I say, all Mr. Innocent. Though I can tell Mr. Daytona Beach Beach Patrol is in no mood to be toyed with by the likes of this City Boy born and raised in South Detroit.

Don't ask what's gotten into me. Talk to any teacher I've ever had since 1975 and they'll vouch for me. I'm a Good Kid! But now, it's like I'm in one of those *Where the Boys Are '84* Spring Break movies with the likes of *Grease 2*'s Lorna Luft, and Lynn-Holly Johnson from *Ice Castles*—my fourth all time favorite movie.

The next few minutes are a blur . . . First I'm standing beside the open door of Gwendy's car. Officer Diaz reaches in past me. Then he finds the bottle of Irish Cream on the floor and literally goes, "Oh-ho-ho." Followed by, "Guess you *were* telling the truth . . . There's no beer here."

I'm tempted to say, *See . . . ?* But my buzz has now officially been killed.

Which is when Officer Diaz asks, "How old are you, son?"

Maybe it's because I've never been in this kind of trouble before . . . As in "With a Capital T and that rhymes with B and that stands for Busted!" Or maybe it's because I'm trying to show off in front of Gwendy so I can get laid . . . But we both know the answer to his question: seventeen.

But what do I say? "I'm 19."

"19?" he repeats, raising a brow. Because let's face it, I still look 12.

I nod.

"19?" Officer Diaz repeats again. "You sure about that?"

Again I nod, thinking that if I'm over 18, i.e., a Legal Adult, I won't get in nearly as much trouble for Possession of Alcohol.

At which point I'm informed, "You're under arrest, son."

Why is this happening to me? How am I going to get out of this? What are my parents going to think? Like Mario Andretti at the Indy 500, these thoughts race around the track that is my straight-A student mind. I'm sure you can imagine the panic I'm feeling at this moment.

I look around the parking lot . . . Suddenly, like Max before, Gwendy is nowhere to be found. Guess I *won't* be getting laid on my Spring Break '88 vacation after all.

"Looks like your girlfriend left you high and dry," Officer Diaz observes, as if I don't have two eyes of my own. "Now what're we gonna do?"

I have no idea what "we" are going to do . . . What *I'm* going to do is start kissing some Cop Ass to the best of my ability so I can get back to the hotel, find Max, and escape Daytona Beach without so much as a scuff on my Permanent Record.

"You got some ID there, Mr. 19-year-old?" Officer Diaz questions.

I hesitate. "Um . . ."

Now what?

"What's-a matter? You don't drive up there in Dee-troit?"

Reaching for my wallet, I'm about to pull out my license. Though I can't help but crack a smile.

"Something funny?"

I reply, "That would depend on your sense of humor." Then I hand over my Michigan Operator's License.

Officer Diaz takes one look at my DOB. Which we all know was just a mere seventeen years and ten months ago. "You sure are a lucky *boy*," he tells me. "Now get outta here."

And with that, I'm gone!

Friends

"But we'll keep you close as always
It won't even seem you've gone . . ."

—Michael W. Smith

There's been an accident.

Last night around 9:30 PM, I got a call from Betsy. I was sitting at my desk in my bedroom, editing Claire Moody's latest "Fashion Faux Pas." Being the end of April, the deadline for the final '87–'88 issue of *The Hazel Parker* is fast approaching and if Claire's final column doesn't make the cut, she'll never let me hear the end of it.

"My Uncle Dave called," reported Betsy. Remember her uncle, the Detroit Cop? He's the one who allegedly busted Joey and Brad down at the gay bar on Woodward and 6 Mile. "Some guy robbed a party store on 7 Mile and I-75."

"Did they catch him?" I wondered, not finding this to be earth-shattering news.

"Not till he ran a red light and crashed into another car over by St. Mary's."

Perhaps this explained the Doppler Effect filling my neighborhood earlier this evening.

"Was anybody hurt?"

"The guy walked away without a scratch," said Betsy. "But the other car was totaled. My Uncle Dave said three Senior girls from Hazel Park were riding in it and one of them was killed."

"Oh, my God . . . Any idea who it was?" The odds were pretty likely we'd know the person considering our class only has about two hundred students in it.

"Not yet," Betsy replied. "They haven't released any names."

At 11:00 PM, I turned on the Channel 7 News and waited for Diana Lewis' report . . . "A trip home from a high school Band concert ended in tragedy tonight for three teenaged girls from Hazel Park."

I sank to my knees, hands involuntarily covering my mouth. My heart dropped to the pit of my stomach at the reality of the situation. Something about hearing the Official News on TV made it all the more grave. I thought for sure I would throw up. Yet the Journalist in me paid close attention to detail. This could be the Killer Scoop I'd been waiting for. I imagined the story I'd write for my final issue as Editor-in-Chief of *The Hazel Parker* . . .

> A 25 year-old man robbed a Party Store on 7 Mile near I-75, holding the owner at gunpoint before escaping with less than $100. The suspect then headed north on John R at speeds of up to 70 MPH as police officers followed in hot pursuit. He was finally apprehended after running a red light at Woodward Heights where he struck a car driven by one of three girls from Hazel Park.

"All graduating Seniors," Diana Lewis continued informing her Metro-Detroit viewers, "the girls were on their way to an after-concert celebration at a nearby Big Boy restaurant. Two sustained minor injuries and were taken to Oakland General Hospital in Madison Heights, while the third girl died at the scene. Detroit Police Officer, Dave Sheffield, reported she was not wearing a seat belt. The girl's name is being withheld pending family notifi—"

I clicked OFF the remote. I couldn't listen anymore. Neither could I believe that somebody I probably knew personally had lost their life tonight. For a split second I thought about calling up Brad to see if he'd heard anything more about the incident. Chances are he was on his way up to Big Boy's after the concert, too, and would know who hadn't arrived safe and sound. Thank God *he* wasn't involved in the catastrophe. As much as our friendship has fallen apart, I couldn't bear the thought of anything happening to my Best Friend since 7th grade.

Driving to school this morning, I feared the worst . . .

Luckily, I've got Audrey in 1st hour World Literature with Miss Horchik. Being on Flag Corps, I assumed Audrey had been at the concert last night and would know something. And if not, she would've gotten word from her two Best Friends, Ava Reese and Carrie Johnson. It seemed lately, those three were inseparable. But for whatever reason, I found myself running late today. I don't know why I've been having such a hard time waking up. Back in 10th and 11th grade, I had to get up even earlier for Marching Band practice. I keep telling myself, *It's almost over.* Only six more weeks of school . . . Ever. Or at least till I start college at Michigan State in the Fall.

Did I mention that I finally applied and had been accepted? Not that I didn't think I would, 'cause I did. Based on my 4.0 GPA, my Guidance Counselor, Mr. Verlander, said I shouldn't have a problem. And he was right. Though I did feel kind of bad the day I received my acceptance letter in the mail. Ever since I've known her, all Audrey's talked about is how she wants to go to college at MSU. You should see her locker . . . Covered top to bottom in Green and White Spartan paraphernalia! Unfortunately for her, I recently heard that she hadn't been accepted. Of course, now that Audrey's no longer my friend, why am I even concerning myself with her? We're probably better off not being on the same college campus together.

The clock on the wall tells me it's 8:20 AM . . . Which means I'm officially Tardy. Which is no big deal, really. It's not like I'm usually late. Besides, Miss Horchik isn't going to care on account of she totally loves me.

March 30, 1988

Your son, Jack Paterno, is to be commended on his academic excellence as well as his polite, respectful attitude in class. He is an "A" student in every sense of the word. Thank you for your support.

V. Horchik

This is just one example of the appropriately named "Happy Notes" my World Literature teacher likes to send home for a job well done. In March alone, my parents received three of these. In the mail!

For whatever reason, not everybody likes Velma Horchik. Rumor has it she used to be a Nun, so I think a lot of people are afraid of her breaking out the ruler. But I don't know if I believe it. I mean, whenever anything the least bit sexual comes up in class, she seems very eager to discuss. I'll never forget when I wrote my paper on Tennessee Williams' *A Streetcar Named Desire,* Miss Horchik took a *great* interest in his description of the cats in heat out on the New Orleans fire escapes.

"Good morning, Jack," she says politely when I creep into

the room. With a short pageboy haircut, Miss Horchik always wears a simple plain dress, big shoes with buckles, and no makeup whatsoever. Which makes her dark brown eyes seem even more squinty than they naturally are. She kind of reminds me of what a Pilgrim might look like out of uniform.

"Sorry I'm late," I apologize, sensing Miss Horchik seems a bit subdued this morning. In fact, the mood among my classmates is nothing short of sober.

Nobody even looks at me or comments on the fact that I'm late. I thought for sure I'd never hear the end of it. Or at least everybody would be all, *Did you hear?* Talking up a storm about last night's accident. Especially with Audrey and her big mouth in the room. Let's just say she wasn't voted Class Clown at last month's Senior Banquet because she's a quiet girl. By the way, Prettiest Eyes went to Yours Truly. Apparently, my Class of '88 classmates think Tom Fulton is Most Likely to Succeed material. Even though I'm the one well on his way to giving the Valedictorian speech at Commencement . . . Whatever! I keep telling myself, *It's almost over.* Only six more weeks of school with these people . . . Ever. Period.

"No need to apologize," Miss Horchik assures me. "We're just happy to have you here, safe and sound."

I don't know why so many people have such a problem with her. I think Miss Horchik's a very sweet woman, despite her making us sit in alphabetical order. Like we're in Pre-School. Based on the way things fall, Audrey sits in the row right next to me. At times it's been awkward since we're still not speaking. In fact, I don't think we've said a word to each other since Senior Breakfast back in November. Almost six months ago!

But when I take my seat, I see Audrey's not in hers. She must be running later than I am. And that's when it hits me . . .

Audrey is dead.

Turns out, the car involved in the accident was driven by Ava

Reese. The passenger in the front seat, Carrie Johnson. Audrey sat alone in back. Which is the precise spot where the north-bound car hit them as they passed through the traffic light, heading westbound on Woodward Heights. Who would've guessed that Audrey would one day lose her life in front of the very church where she once attended Catholic School?

Listening to Miss Horchik explain the details of the accident, I can't even believe it. But for whatever reason, I don't cry. Not that I'm not devastated, 'cause I totally am. And numb.

This isn't the way things are supposed to go. As much as Audrey and I haven't seen eye-to-eye this year, I always expected we'd eventually make up. Especially with all the Graduation activities occurring next month. The Car Parade, Class Day, Commencement.

Now I'll never get a chance to tell Audrey how sorry I am that we drifted apart . . .

How could something like this happen?

I'll never get a chance to go to The Grand Hotel on Mackinac Island with her and sit by the trees from *Somewhere in Time* . . .

Why was I such an Asshole all year long?

I'll never get a chance to say good-bye.

Why did I waste so much time?

There's always the funeral . . .

Not since my Grandma Freeman's back in 1977 have I been to one. This is the last thing I expected or wanted to be doing at this point in my life. But two days later, here I am climbing the steps to the Shrine of the Little Flower on Woodward and 12 Mile in Royal Oak.

Even though her family belongs to St. Mary Magdalen's in Hazel Park, Audrey's Mom couldn't bear the thought of her funeral taking place right in front of the spot where she died. And I can't say I blame her. Whenever I pass by and see the makeshift Memorial of flowers and balloons and stuffed animals that have been placed before the tiny brick wall on the corner of John R and Woodward Heights, I can't help but imagine the Horror that occurred there.

All dressed up in my khaki pants and blue button-down Polo dress shirt, I'd much rather be going to a wedding when I enter this Church. I'm wondering now if I should've worn a tie.

In Loving Memory of AUDREY M. WOJCZEK.

I can't even believe it when I see her name printed on the back of the little prayer card I'm given at the entrance to the chapel. On the front is a picture of the Virgin Mary adorned in traditional blue and white.

> Audrey Melinda Wojczek, 17, of Hazel Park died on Wednesday, April 27, 1988. She was born May 24, 1970 in Duluth, MN. She is survived by her mother, Patricia of Hazel Park, and her brother Michael, of Royal Oak. Her father, Michael Sr., passed away in 1977. She was an honor student at Hazel Park High School where she performed in plays with the Drama Club and marched with the Flag Corps.

And that's it!

Is this what becomes of a Life? Reduced to a single column in the Obituary section of the Royal Oak *Daily Tribune*. Nobody's going to know anything about Audrey or what a great person she was after reading this crap. What about her favorite movie, *Somewhere in Time?* What about her "childbearing hips"? What about the way she turned her head slightly to one side, furrowed her brow, and pursed her lips when she gave you her "Don't Even" look?

I hate being in Church. Not because I don't believe in God or Jesus, 'cause I do. In fact, I pray almost every single night. But the way it always makes me feel . . . Like a Total Sinner. I'm surprised I don't burst into flames the minute I sit down in a pew near the back.

I take a look around, disgusted by what I see . . . Popular People everywhere! Tom Fulton and his entire Jock Jerk crew, all wearing shirts and ties, sit together three rows in front of me. Since when were *any* of them ever friends with Audrey? Did they even know her name? They're all just looking for an excuse to take a day off school. Which is Total Bullshit! If we weren't in a Place of Worship right now, I'd stand up and say something.

Then again, was I even friends with Audrey anymore? At least I *used* to be.

Poor Rob Berger . . . I can't even imagine burying the person I love at such a young age. He looks rather handsome all dressed up in a navy blue suit and matching tie, sitting down front with Audrey's Mom and now mohawk-less brother. I almost didn't recognize Mike with his head shaved and wearing a suit . . . He still looks hot.

I pray he doesn't recognize *me* from that time at the gay bar. Though it's been almost two years since I've seen him, so why am I worrying? As much as I should probably go over and give my condolences, I think I'll wait.

Over to my right, I see another familiar face . . .

Brad looks good, all tanned from his recent Band Fag trip to Florida on Spring Break. He sits at the end of his row beside Ava and Carrie. Thank God they both managed to escape the encounter with only minor scrapes and bruises. Though I've got a feeling the trauma will haunt them for the rest of their lives. All three have their heads bowed in prayer so I don't think they've spotted me. Which is probably for the best.

Uh-oh . . . Guess I spoke too soon!

Brad looks up and over in my direction. Our eyes meet, gazes hold a moment. There's so much I want to say . . .

I'm sorry.

Please forgive me.

Can we be Best Friends again?

But I can't . . . The funeral's about to start.

Feeling the sting of tears, I turn away. But I don't cry—at least not yet. I wait till after the service when I'm all alone in my car . . .

Then I lose it.

The next day, I stay home from school. I can't bear the thought of walking into Miss Horchik's class and seeing Audrey's empty desk right next to mine. I spend the entire day going through old letters and pictures. When I come across Audrey's photo from Junior year, I lose it again. It takes all I've got to remove the picture from the album, flip it over, and read the inscription . . .

Jack, my beloved friend

I'll never forget you. How could I? You're my "son!" I hope we keep in touch always. Not just when there's nobody else to love you, but forever.

Love, Audrey ("Mom")

I don't even remember how or when she got on the whole mother/son kick. Though something tells me it originated once Audrey came to the conclusion we would only ever be Just Friends. Nothing more. With her gone now, I worry I eventually *will* forget her. The way her voice sounded on the other end of the telephone. The way she laughed at all my Stupid Jokes. The way she *really* looked. Alive and In Person.

Thank God they had a closed casket at the funeral. I heard

part of the reason why they did this was because of what happened to her in the accident. Which I don't even want to think about. But even if that wasn't the case, I wouldn't want my last memory of Audrey to be seeing her lying in a box. I prefer to remember the Good Times . . .

Playing House in Kindergarten.

Dissecting frogs in Mr. Davidson's Freshman Biology.

Breaking into Fuck Face Fucker's locker at the end-of-the-year Carnation Dance.

Scaring the shit out of each other at the Tombs.

New Year's Eve at Luanne Kowalski's when Audrey singed her bangs on the stove.

And the list goes on!

I return the photo to its page. When I flip to the next one, I come across a bunch of pictures of Brad and I taken at Blue Lake Fine Arts Camp back in the Summer of '83.

I can't even believe how small we both look, dressed in our regulation blue BLFAC shirts complete with the BLFAC insignia, standing in front of Cabin Cabaret . . . Try saying *that* three times real fast!

Here's one of Brad holding his nose and pointing to the building marked RESTROOMS. Which was really just a glorified outhouse, if you ask me. For starters, there wasn't *any* hot water. Well, it was tepid at best. And get this . . . When you stood barefoot on the cold *cement* floor and touched the faucet, you'd get a shock. I'm not even kidding! You could actually feel a current of some sort running right through your body. *And* . . . There weren't *any* doors on *any* of the bathroom stalls. Which meant neither Brad nor I went poop for twelve days straight. All this for the affordable price of a mere $300!

But we did it . . . Together we somehow managed to survive . . . Because we were Best Friends.

I reach for the phone and dial . . . 3-9-8-5-8-3-6.

"Dayton Residence." It's his Mom.

"Is Brad there?"

"Who's calling, please?"

I can't even believe Laura doesn't recognize my voice. Obviously she's been clued in as to what's been going on between me and her son on account of once again I've been an Asshole all year. "It's Jack," I tell her. Then I add, "How have you been?"

"Fine," she curtly replies. "Let me see if he's available." Then I hear super loud, *"Br-a-a-dley . . . Telephone!"*

Why do I get feeling there'll be no dragging Brad by the scruff of his neck to the telephone this time? Guess I can't blame Laura for being mad at me. After all, he is her Only Son.

"Hello?"

"Hey," I say, surprised how quickly he picked up. "It's Jack."

To which Brad replies, "I know." Followed by, "What do *you* want?"

Good question. Why am I calling him now when I've barely spoken to him this entire school year? What am I even going to say?

And then it *pours* out of me . . . *How Sorry I am for Being Such a Jerk—Book II* by John R. Paterno.

"Dah-dah, dah-dah," says Brad, interrupting me halfway through.

So I repeat, "Dah-dah, dah-dah." Then I quickly finish my apology.

We say nothing about Audrey. Instead, we pretend the funeral yesterday never took place. Along with the last nine months of our lives. Hopefully, we can pick up where we left off and stop wasting time.

"So what's up?" he asks, nonchalantly.

"Nothing," I answer, employing the exact same tone. "Are you working tonight? Maybe I can drop by Big Boy's when you get off."

"Um . . ."

I quickly add, "We can go for a drive." The last thing I want happening is what happened between us before. Though I don't come right out and say so, I can tell Brad picks up on it.

"I'm not working at Big Boy's anymore," he informs me. "I got a job at the Gas Station."

Guess I can't expect to know everything. Still I'm a little surprised. So I say, "Gas 'n Go on 9 Mile and I-75?"

"Not the *real* gas station," says Brad. "It's a gay bar called the Gas Station." Then he laughs.

Dead air lies between us for a brief moment. The only thing I can think to say now is . . . "So who are you taking to Prom?"

"To be honest," he answers, "I don't think I'm gonna go."

With the big night only a few weeks away, I feel I need to remind him, "It's our Senior Prom . . . You can't miss it!"

"I'm not really up for it . . . You know what I mean?" Then Brad adds, "What about you? Have you asked anybody?"

"Well," I say, hesitant. "That's part of the reason I called." Then I casually mention, "Everybody knows we've been Best Friends since 7th grade, right?" Assuming after all that's happened, we still are. "So it's not like they'd *think* anything if—"

"If what?"

"If *we* went to Prom . . . Together, I mean."

For a moment, Brad says nothing. I figure he probably *does* hate me. He's got every right. I've been a Total Asshole this year. Our *Senior* year, and I've ruined it. "I don't think that'd be such a good idea," he finally replies.

I ask, "Why not?" Hoping I'm not totally right about him hating me.

"Think about it," Brad advises. "This is not a John Hughes film we're living in. I am not Molly Ringwald and you are most definitely not Andrew McCarthy."

"Thanks a lot!"

"Seriously," he sighs. "It's 1988 . . . We live in Hazeltucky, and we go to Hillbilly High . . . We'd either be the laughing stock of the school or else we'd get our asses kicked in the parking lot."

Brad's right. I can just see Tom Fulton and all his Jock Jerk Friends totally ganging up on us outside the Vintage House in Fraser. Why do we have to live in such a goddamn Hick Town?

"It's our fucking Senior Prom," I spit. "We should be able to go with whomever we want."

"Whomever?" Brad repeats, mocking me from all the way over on Wanda.

"Shut up!"

"You know just as well as I do," he says. "Two guys can't go walking into the Prom together—even if they are Best Friends since 7th grade."

Did you notice Brad just said "*are* Best Friends"—not "*were* Best Friends?" He must still like me . . . Even after everything I've done. Which is why I have to apologize, yet again.

"Would you shut up already?" he insists after I've done so.

But I can't . . . I have to get this out . . . I have to tell Brad how I truly feel, once and for all.

"Listen to me," I demand. "I'm trying to be honest with you." Which is something I haven't been very good about. It's also the main reason Brad and I ever drifted apart in the first place. "Instead of being grateful I had a Best Friend who would accept me for who I am," which I've known all along he would totally do, "I tried lying to myself, hoping it would all just go away."

Can you believe I honestly thought I'd wake up one day, look in the mirror, and be somebody else? Somebody other than who I really am . . . Somebody who's not *like that.*

Which is when Brad asks me, "And did it all just go away?"

What do *you* think?

Graduation Memories

This Book Belongs to John R. "Jack" Paterno

Homecoming King & Queen

Tom Fulton and Jamie Good

Valedictorian & Salutatorian

Jack Paterno and Betsy Sheffield

Lyrics

"Music for the Masses"
FAVORITE ALBUM

"Depeche Mode"
FAVORITE ROCK GROUP

Debbie Gibson
FAVORITE FEMALE VOCALIST

Rick Astley
FAVORITE MALE VOCALIST

"Naughty Girls Need Love"
FAVORITE HIT SINGLE

Tee Vee

"ALF"
FAVORITE HALF HOUR SHOW

"Days of our Lives"
FAVORITE HOUR SHOW

Miami Vice

WORST SHOW

Flicks

"La Bamba"

FAVORITE MOVIE

Lou Diamond Phillips

FAVORITE ACTOR

Kristian Alfonso

FAVORITE ACTRESS

Berkley Theatre

FAVORITE THEATER

"Grease"
"Dirty Dancing"
"Throw Momma from the Train"

MEMORABLE MOVIES

Sooner or Later

I predict

Betsy Sheffield becomes a wealthy engineer
Brad Dayton wins an Academy Award
Jamie Good hyphenates all her names!
I marry Kristian Alfonso

Autographs

Jack,

Maybe our friendship could have been more but we can't think about that now. I do know that you are one of my dearest friends ever. I hope we can become friends again. Best of luck at State and try not to forget the Wop back here in Hazeltucky.

Love,

Joey Palladino '88

Jack!

It's been great knowing you! You're a great writer and a special guy! To me and a lot of other people, I'm sure. I'll never forget the fun times, especially "The Hazel Parker" and Daytona. (Where's Max?) Hope you won't forget me when I'm away at EMU! Have fun at State and don't ever change because I love you the way you are!

Love always,

Jamie Good "Solange Putain" Rizzo (Betty)

Jack,

You will always be one of my best friends, even though you quit Marching Band the year I finally became Drum Major! (But I won't take it personally.) We had a lot of fun times hanging out at my house with "the Gang." Always remember "Thumper" and "Truth or Dare" (you know which time I'm talking about!)

I Love Ya Lots!

Ava Reese

Jackie—

Hi, Honey! You are a terrific person and I'm happy we met back in Ms. Lemieux's class at Webb. I'm happy that we got a chance to be close again. I can't wait to read your first novel. I hope you'll put a girl who reminds you of Kristian Alfonso in it! Well Stud, forget about Tom Fulton because you know I have! Best of luck at State. I'll have to come up for a visit sometime. Don't 4-get me!

Love always,

Marie Sperling

Jackie-

'S up? Thanks to the Almighty Farmer we'll still see each other over the Summer. Then you're off to MSU. (Thanks for abandoning me!) I still owe ya for saving my ass in Daytona. Glad you didn't get arrested.

Max "Willy" Wilson

Jack,

You are a most memorable English Student. May God bless and keep you in His care, V. Horchik

Jack,

There is nothing I can say that I haven't said before.

Brad

—FRESHMAN—

September 1988

The Promise

"You know in the end
I'll always be there . . ."

—When in Rome

God, I'm getting old!

I can't even believe I spent the past how many years of my life living in this room . . . What is it? At least a decade. Let's see . . .

My parents upgraded me from the front bedroom after my brother was born. March 1978–September 1988. So a little over ten years . . . How the Hell did I ever get to be 18?! Which is what I ask Brad as he sits here watching me pack.

"Tell me about it," he sighs. "I'm right behind you." By which he means this coming Sunday is *his* birthday. Not that I need reminding. How could I ever forget: September 4th?

"Sorry I won't be here to celebrate with you," I apologize. Then I cross over to my dresser, reaching into the top drawer. "Close your eyes," I order. "And hold out your hands."

"What for?" Brad asks, as if he can't possibly guess. Though he does exactly as I tell him.

I can't say it's the best birthday present. But the sentimental value alone I think makes it pretty special. "Okay," I say, slipping the so-called gift into his palm. "Open 'em."

Brad opens his eyes, smiling. "'They wanted to love . . . in a world that worshipped only pleasure,'" he reads. "Gordon Merrick. *Now Let's Talk About Music.*" About to burst, he squeals. "Where did you get this?!"

Years ago, back in 9th grade, I told Brad I got rid of this piece of trash. Believe it or not, I said I dropped it in the mailbox over by St. Mary's on my way to school one day. Truth be told, I had every intention. I lived in Total Fear that my Mom would by chance come across it, "cleaning my room." Then I'd be busted for sure! But when the time came to pull back the creaking blue louver door, I couldn't bear to let go. Besides, can you imagine the look on the mailman's face when he found a copy of *The Adventures of Ned & Gerry* in with everybody's bills and letters? So I stashed it in my red metal lock-box for safekeeping all these years.

"I want you to have it," I offer Brad. "It was yours to begin with."

"Thanks," he graciously accepts.

Then I add, "Don't let your Mom find it."

To which he replies, *"Oh, I won't!"*

You know how it is when you first meet somebody? You can't keep quiet. You have all this *stuff* you want to tell them. You have to get it out. But once you've known each other for a while, you don't have to talk so much anymore. You can just share the same space, breathe the same air, no words required. That's what Brad and I do now. We stand in silence, taking in the room, not saying anything . . .

Oh, the things these four walls have witnessed!

Finally he heaves a heavy sigh. "I still can't believe you're leaving for school tomorrow," he says, surveying the egg boxes upon egg boxes of crap I've collected and can't live without. "Are you excited?"

"I'm not excited about the school part," I admit. Four more years of studying and exams and pressure. "But I'm excited about getting away from here for a while."

Good old Hazeltucky! I'd be lying if I said I was going to miss you . . . Though I *will* miss the people—at least some of them.

I take down the last of my Kristian Alfonso *Soap Opera Digest* pictures. The knotty pine wall above what used to be my bed stares back at me, naked. Truth be told, *Days of our Lives* hasn't been the same since Bo & Hope sailed off in to the sunset. If the Producers were smart, they'd find a way to bring the Super Couple back to Salem . . . Maybe someday.

"I'm so jealous," Brad confesses. "You know how much I always wanted to go away to college."

"You will," I tell him.

It totally sucks that Brad didn't get into Juilliard. He really wanted it bad. And I can't blame him. Here I am, about to head off to the Home of the Spartans, where I'll finally be on my own. A Real Adult.

"I don't know, Jack . . . Sometimes I feel like I'll be stuck here forever."

"Two years isn't forever," I inform him. "And you don't have to stay at OCC if you hate it." By which I mean Oakland Community College in Royal Oak. "You can always reapply to Juilliard for next year."

"Why bother?" he replies, totally defeated. "I didn't get in this time, why would they want me next year?"

To which I say, "That's the Old Hazeltucky Spirit!"

Brad helps me pack up the things from my closet next. "Where should I put these?" he asks, holding an overstuffed black Hefty bag, a bunch of my long-sleeved shirts wrapped inside.

"Just throw them on the pile," I suggest, hoping my dorm room in Shaw Hall isn't too much of a shoebox.

Guess I should've known better than to tell Brad something like that. Because he *literally* throws the bag halfway across the room onto the growing heap in the middle of my floor. "I'm sorry," he apologizes.

"Forget it," I reply. "They're just clothes."

Brad scoffs. "Not about them . . . I'm sorry we didn't spend much time together this Summer."

I agree, "So am I." Though it's not like it's all *Brad's* fault. "It seems like all I've done since Graduation is work and work and work." In the two years I've been employed at Farmer Jack's, I don't think I put in as many hours as I did these past two months.

Did I mention, this past June 27th once I turned 18, I got a promotion to Cashier? You better believe it's sooo much better than being a Bagger. No more manning the Bottle Return or cleaning the Break Room or Fetching Buggies from the parking lot. Plus I got a raise to $5.25 per hour. Which is part of the whole reason I busted my butt working so many hours on account of I needed to save more money for college. Even though I got a Michigan Competitive Scholarship, it won't cover the entire cost of MSU. And my Dad said he'd only pay for my first year, so the rest is up to me.

"I still can't believe we graduated," Brad says now. "It doesn't seem real to me."

I know what he means. Even though I stood up there on the Hillbilly High football field at the podium in front of all my Class of '88 classmates, I can barely recall what I said in my Valedictorian Speech . . .

The End of Today is the Beginning of Tomorrow.

I'm sure I worked our official Class Motto in there somewhere. Betsy Sheffield came up with that one. Though I will take credit for suggesting our class song, "This is the Time," by Billy Joel. Just between you and me, it was *supposed* to be "Never Say Goodbye" by Bon Jovi. At least that's the song that got the most votes when the committee tallied the scores. But we all agreed that we couldn't imagine Chorale singing *"You lost more than that in my backseat, baby"* at Graduation. So the Piano Man it was!

" 'member back in 7th grade when we first met?" Brad asks, as if I could possibly forget. "You were sitting in the cafeteria with those girls . . ."

"Ava Reese, Carrie Johnson, and Katy Griffin." For a split second I wonder why Katy and I ever stopped being friends. Remember, she was the Tomboy trombone player I totally thought was a guy on account of her feathered-back hair and football throwing skills? I can't say I even saw Katy around much after we got to HPHS and she dropped out of Band. I did run into her at Jamie Good's Graduation party back in June. Believe it or not, she was there with Diane Thompson, of all people. What's up with that?!

You know, I always thought Katy might be *like that*. First Diane and Lou . . . Now Katy Griffin? I also heard she broke up with Joey Palladino. I don't know why. All I know is . . . I don't *want* to know.

" 'member, Ava had that Sign-In Book?" Brad recalls, growing giddy. "You guys were talking about which jeans you liked best: Calvin's or Jordache?" Already knowing right where the story is going, he begins giggling. Like a Total Girl.

"And you were like, 'Fuck those!'" I remind him, as if he could possibly forget. "'I like *Sergio Valente*'s better 'cause they make your ass look hot!'"

"And you were like, 'Oh, my God . . . I can't believe you just said that!'"

"I was not," I insist. Even though I totally was.

"You were all freaked out just because I said 'fuck' and 'ass,'" he remembers.

To which I tell him, "Shut up!" Then I pick up the pillow off what used to be my bed and whack him with it.

Brad collapses onto the bare box springs, his face beet red in hysterics. "You know, I only said it to get a rise out of you, Jack . . . You were the most Persnickety-Persnick I ever met!"

I think about hitting him again. Instead, I sit down beside him. "I was not."

"Oh, my God . . . You *totally* were!"

"Well, what did you expect?" I plead in my defense. "We were 12 years old . . . You know what a Total Goody-Two-Shoes I was back then."

Brad gives me a look, nostrils flared. "Back then?" Then he laughs.

Another tranquil moment passes. I have no idea what else to say . . . So I say nothing.

"I should probably take off," Brad decides, hoisting himself up. "You should finish packing."

He's right. As much as I hate to see him go, I've still got a bijillion things to take care of. My Aunt Sonia's coming by tomorrow—Bright and Early—to load all my shit into the back of her truck. The exact same one she taught Brad and I how to drive that Summer when he came Up North to my Grandpa Freeman's cottage in Gaylord. Remember, he wanted to climb inside the gigantic black rubber inner tube we found and roll down the steps into Otsego Lake—just like in the Mountain Dew commercial? I won't even mention him taking all those Correctol!

Brad says, "Walk me to the door, Jack?" So I do. The exact same accordion-fold one that's served as Keeper of so many Secrets these past six years. "Well . . . This is it."

Because I've never been one for Tearful Good-byes, I say,

"I'll see you soon." Besides, this isn't *The End of Jack & Brad*. I know for sure I'll be back mid-October for my Uncle Mark's 40th birthday party . . . Talk about somebody who's getting old! And I'm sure Max and Brad will drive up to MSU at some point for a football game or a Frat Party.

"Take care of yourself," he tells me.

"Stay out of trouble," I advise.

Brad smiles his old familiar smirk. "I'll try." Then he says, "You know my number, right?" How could I ever forget: 398-5836? "Call me anytime . . . If you get lonely and you need somebody to talk to."

"I will." With that, I unfold the accordion, setting him free.

But Brad doesn't budge. "And good luck with your writing," he stalls.

"Thanks."

Then he adds, "Maybe you'll write a story about us one day?"

To which I think, *I don't know if anybody would believe it.* Still I say, "Maybe . . ."

"But make sure you change the names to protect The Guilty," Brad orders.

To which I concur, *"Oh, I will!"*

He breathes a sigh of relief. "Good . . . 'cause I don't want everybody knowing all my Deep Dark Secrets . . . You know what I mean?"

I couldn't agree more. "Yours and mine, both!"

He laughs.

I laugh.

Then Brad gets all serious. "I love you, Jack."

Even though I never liked him—not in that way—I say, "I love you, too." Because I do. We embrace, wet each other's shoulders, clinging to The Past yet knowing full well we can't stop The Future . . . *Why does growing up suck so bad?!*

Finally pulling away, Brad says, "If you ever do write that story . . ." He dries his eyes, a twinkle shining bright, a hint of Blair Warner in his voice.

"Uh-huh," I say, waiting to hear his latest Brilliant Idea.

"Maybe you can call it *If You Were a Girl, Would You Think That Guy's Cute?*" Obviously, he thinks this is the Greatest Idea Ever, he's beaming with pride.

Not wanting to disappoint him, I take it into consideration. "I'll think about it."

"Please do," he begs. "I bet it'll be a Best Seller." Then he adds all serious, "But no matter what happens . . . No matter how successful you get, I'll always be your Best Friend, won't I?"

"You know you will," I guarantee him. I've never been more certain of anything in my life.

At which point, Brad sticks out his pinky. "You promise?"

Here we go again!

"You have to promise, Jack."

So I do . . . I link my pinky with Brad's and I promise.

Standing here before him, alone amidst my belongings, I can't help but remember what our junior high Band teacher, Jessica Clark Putman, once told me . . . "Friends hold you back."

Well, you know what? I don't believe her.

A READING GROUP GUIDE

BAND FAGS!

Frank Anthony Polito

ABOUT THIS GUIDE

The suggested questions are included to enchance your group's reading of Frank Anthony Polito's *Band Fags!*

DISCUSSION QUESTIONS

1. Were you a Band Fag? If so, what instrument did you play? What was it like being a Band Fag at your school?

2. Who was your Best Friend growing up? Where is he now? Do you still keep in touch? What were some of the crazy things you did together as kids?

3. Jack denies being gay at several points during the story. He even goes so far as to say he doesn't *want* to be gay. Did you find his attitude to be one of self-loathing or could you sympathize with his desire to be "normal"?

4. Jack confides in us that he had his first crush on Donny Osmond at 6 years old. At what age were you first aware of your sexuality and who was your first crush?

5. If you happen to be gay, at what age did you first realize you might be "like that"? Who was the first person you told and what was the reaction?

6. If you suspected your child was gay, would you have confronted him or her like Jack's Mom did? Even though Jack's

Mom totally sympathized, he continued to lie about his sexuality after the fact. Why do you think this is?

7. Jack's high school Band teacher, Mr. Klan, is most likely gay. What responsibility do you think gay adults, especially teachers, have in helping teens they suspect to be gay realize it's okay to be so?

8. *Band Fags!* is told only from Jack's point of view. Would you have preferred to hear more of Brad's side of the story? If so, what moments from Brad's life might you have liked to have seen?

9. The author consciously chose to use repeated phrases and bits of dialogue throughout *Band Fags!* Were you aware of this device, and did it enhance your experience of the story? What were some of the more memorable moments of repetition?

10. What do you imagine happens next for Jack and Brad? Do you think they'll really be Best Friends Forever?